BENEATH the BLOODY AURORA

First published in the United States of America July 2022 by Lake Country Press & Reviews

Cataloging-in-Publication Data is on file with the Library of Congress.

Author website: https://www.bekawestrup.com

Publisher website: https://www.lakecountrypress.com

Editing: Samantha Costanilla

Cover: Mars Lauderbaugh

Formatting: Dawn Lucous of Yours Truly Book Services

A Note From the Author

Dear Reader,

Beneath the Bloody Aurora is a representation of the religious trauma and other abuse I experienced in my formative years. As such, there are themes explored in the story that may be sensitive to some readers. I have listed them below (**spoiler warning**). My hope is that this story makes those who have gone through similar experiences feel seen and understood, but please... don't hesitate to put your mental health first.

Much love,

Beka

CW (**contains spoilers**):

- Explicit Sexual Content
- Religious and Physical Abuse
- Violence
- Alcohol Use
- Blood
- Mention of Suicide
- Death
- Animal Death (polar bears)
- Assault

To the girls who search for light in the darkest places and forget to look within.

Playlist for Beneath the Bloody Aurora

Panic Room by Au/Ra
God Must Hate Me by Catie Turner
Iris by The Goo Goo Dolls
Hurricane by Fleurie
In My Veins by Andrew Belle
Dancing in the Dark by Svrcina
Never Be the Same by Camila Cabello
Ruin My Life by Zara Larsson
The Archer by Taylor Swift
Only Us by Kygo & Haux
Foolish by Forest Blakk
Something to Lose by june
Afterlife by Hailee Steinfeld
Lose You Now by Lindsey Stirling & Mako
Dangerous Woman by Ariana Grande
Clean by Hey Violet
NO ONE'S IN THE ROOM by Jessie Reyez

1

Nikolai Trousseau was running out of demon blood.

He sank back into the silky cushions of his armchair and grimaced, cradling his jaw in one hand. Between the two flickering candelabras on his desk, a charmed decanter taunted him, the crystal blackened from the inside. That damned cloudiness kept him from discerning his depleted reserve until moments ago.

The curtains of his office were drawn behind him, though the sky wouldn't lighten beyond a lavender twilight for more than a month yet. Endless night shrouded the Arctic and that translated to safety, at least for a little while longer.

But shadows danced on the walls around him, laughing soundlessly. Dust particles swirled. Each snow-kissed acre the estate sat on, from where polar bears lumbered across tundra miles away to the chatter of guests lingering in the lobby nearby, hummed like static in his ears.

Two doses of blood remained, and then he'd have to hunt.

There was no one to blame for this oversight but himself. He usually kept a closer eye on his supply, but he'd been understandably distracted. A new plague had swept through the human world, and it was his job to accommodate his patrons, the nervous guests and irritated brides. To reassure them that his manor, tucked away in the heart of the Arctic, remained untouched.

The past five weeks wore on his patience, but if he were honest, he couldn't pinpoint a time when it wasn't at least a little grated. This century was the same as the last. Every century, every *human*, lived the same story. Sickness and death; longing and fear. Unless the earth managed to ensnare them as it had him. And Nikolai did not wish that on anyone.

The manor's mid-season holiday began tomorrow, for both his staff and himself, so at least the timing of his supply running out was lucky.

Lucky...

A harsh chuckle rumbled in his chest and the blood rumbled back—all the blood, everywhere. He could count individual arteries, tried not to.

He uncorked the decanter, filled a glass dropper with its black sludge, and deposited the dose beneath his tongue. From the instant it bypassed to his bloodstream, the rising in his body settled. His temperature spiked a few degrees, the incessant ache in his teeth eased, and his senses dulled. He reveled in it— that taming of *the beast*.

Nikolai was not so desensitized that he didn't sense footsteps barreling down the hall. He concealed the container in his desk and grinned, preparing for the woman that knocked once and promptly barged through the door to his office.

Mrs. Itzli was a mother first, a characteristic that too many humans claimed in title but not identity. She was a brazen old biddy, often postulating her own opinions or muttering complaints under her breath when she felt exceptionally fresh. And in some fine manner of paradox, he never knew what brilliant idea she would pitch to him next, whether it be for the menu or renovations to the property.

Her nurturing nature toward the manor's young brides spared him heaps of unwelcome conversation. So Nikolai heartily forgave her temperament and dreaded the day he would have to send her away.

She set a glare on him and braced her hands on her hips. "Mr. Trousseau, shame on you for hiding in here. What will the guests think?"

Nikolai rose, blowing out the candles on his desk. He collected the hard-cover booklet from the drawer and slipped it inside his blazer. "Guests don't concern themselves with my comings and goings." He herded Mrs. Itzli into the dazzling light of the chandelier-lined corridor—and he was thankful not to cringe beneath it, as he had that morning.

She shook her head, the silver-threaded black mane that cascaded down her back glinting with the movement. The woman crossed her arms as they walked toward the lobby but left one hand out to wag a finger at him. "So you think, but don't be surprised when the reviews come in for this season. You've been especially reclusive."

A fist of apprehension clenched his gut. The dreaded annual travel ranking. Lately, it only served to remind him of how stagnant business had become. *How the mighty have fallen.*

Plastering a smirk on his face, he said, "That's why we pay a small fortune for publicity. Besides, an unhappy guest would be more likely to gripe about you, I think."

She gasped, ready to quarrel.

He continued, "Even heaven couldn't help the poor bastard that sends his plate back to your kitchen."

"Oh, manners," she chided, her thick brows stitching together. "You'll chase the sweetest girl away with that mouth."

The slight struck him, and something close to pain lanced through his dead heart.

Most women carried a sweet, delicate flavor—like ripe berries on his tongue. Even Mrs. Itzli gave off the scent of grapes... perhaps ones that were fermenting into wine, but sweet all the same. He couldn't understand what was in her words that made his gut twist, so he said teasingly, "You are already more woman than I know what to do with."

"Och, you." The bronze skin of her nose crinkled like folds in a wool blanket. Mrs. Itzli's husband passed away over a decade ago. With her children grown and working on families of their own, she hadn't known what to do with herself. No one jumped to hire the little loud lady with sharp edges.

But Nikolai had sensed her great joy in taking care of others when he met her. He wished more humans had the ability to provoke his spirit, or whatever scrap of humanity it was he still possessed, the way she could.

Her head tilted to one side as she asked, "Is that dark, handsome fellow keeping you company during the holiday again?"

Nikolai's lips twitched.

Mrs. Itzli met Reuben two years ago, when he appeared on the mansion's doorstep and stayed for most of the winter season. She must have developed certain suspicions about the relationship, but it was more complicated than friendship or romance. The truth was that Nikolai owed Reuben his salvaged existence—a debt he felt he could never repay.

"No, Reuben is occupied with a trade deal in the East Andes."

Nikolai left him high and dry in the midst of it, when the latest winter season started. He didn't dare call Reuben up, not until he was sure his old mate wouldn't grab him by the proverbial balls and squeeze. On the other hand, Reuben really should have known. This property was Nikolai's anchor, one constant in millennia of uncertainties.

The annual auroral lights always called him home.

"I see." She frowned. "Well, I prepared a few casseroles for you and stored them in the fridge, so you won't waste away."

"You're a gem," he said.

She flushed, a proud grin cracking her face in two. He tried not to think of how many times she hand-delivered meals to his office, and how he scraped them into the trash the moment she turned her back. "Is there anything else I can do for you before I head home?"

"Actually, would you bake up a batch of your cinnamon cookies? I have a showing in a few hours for a bride. She might fill the slot for the wedding that canceled on us this year."

Mrs. Itzli whistled. "Ambitious lady. That only leaves a couple weeks to coordinate everything."

"I'd expect nothing less from the daughter of Clarissa Farren."

Her eyes grew wide. "The supermodel? Are you serious?"

"Dead," he said, and repressed the urge to cackle. "If all goes well, her event should help place our manor back in the public eye."

Mrs. Itzli nodded, her face slacking. She'd interpreted the gravity of his words, why he'd even bother to share so much. Free media exposure like that was invaluable, especially when the manor's permanence depended on it. "I'll get to baking once my luggage is squared away."

"Thank you."

They passed under a peaked archway into the lobby.

Marble swept the floor into a white sea, interrupted by seating arrangements upholstered in green velvet and gold. Picture windows lined the face of the mansion, looking out over the dark blue expanse and pristinely plowed drive. Stone alcoves framed the entrance, which let in gusts of blistering wind with each new departure.

The recent concierge hire, a spry blonde from the nearest college town, waved from behind the front desk. Her white teeth flashed beneath the antique chandelier in the center of the room and Nikolai had to remind himself why he didn't sleep with the staff—the same reason he didn't sleep with guests: it was nasty business.

Nikolai smiled politely and the girl flushed. He made a mental note to hire a man next time, obese and balding.

Mrs. Itzli followed his gaze. "Are you sure you don't want me to stay this year? These breaks weigh on me when I know we leave you alone. I think it makes you more... *melancholy*."

He set a feather-light hand on her shoulder, her warmth seeping up into his fingers. She didn't flinch much anymore. "You mistake my tranquility for sadness. I enforce these holidays so I can enjoy some solitude." It wasn't a lie. Nikolai never tired of how the icy earth settled without human interference, the way the charged atmosphere built to a radiant climax just for him.

The thought of missing it this year in exchange for a hunt threatened to fracture his composure, and he knew he would not convince Mrs. Itzli of anything if that happened. He said by way of distraction, "I'm happy to hear you're taking full advantage of the language classes I gifted to you."

Her eyes brightened. "I'm enjoying them, Mr. Trousseau. My youngest son visited me over the summer, and I carried on with his wife into the wee hours of the evening. She hails from the North, like you, and has no desire to learn our mother tongue. I'll never understand Northern prejudice. Our country's language is far easier to understand." She paused, as if catching her own antagonism for once, and added, "No offense."

"None taken." Nikolai hid his amusement. "I think your mother tongue is lovely, Mrs. Itzli. *Me'yete.*"

She blinked at the familiar dialect and his perfect, throaty accent.

In the five years she had worked for him, Nikolai never let it slip before—the fact that he knew every word she spoke under her breath. He figured he would not have many more opportunities to do so. Not if the Manor went under, and certainly not in a few more years when she grew suspicious of his timeless appearance.

She grasped his face and planted a tender kiss on either cheek. "Farewell to you, too, sir."

If Nikolai possessed the ability to blush, he would have. And as Mrs. Itzli flitted back to her seasonal quarters, he mused that the woman wielded a charm of her own, evident only to those who were patient enough to discover it.

2

"I've been waiting for your call for over an hour." The frustration in Duncan's voice was poorly concealed.

A chill ran up Clio's spine as her bodyguard, Enzo, opened the airport door for her and they stepped into the Arctic climate. The late afternoon could easily pass for midnight, it was so dark. "I know, I know. I'm sorry. Our connecting flight got stuck on the tarmac before liftoff."

Her shivering threatened the phone's perch between her shoulder and ear. He was upset. She hated when he was upset. One of her bags caught on the doorframe.

"Fuck," she swore as it nearly wrenched her arm out of socket.

Enzo reached for the handle, nodding to the town car parked at the curb. Casting a thankful glance in his direction, she surrendered the bag, even though he was already pushing the cart with the rest of her luggage.

Her face burned as she heard Duncan say across the line, "What was that?"

"Nothing, sweetie," she said quickly.

"Don't *lie* to me."

She sighed, quietly enough that he wouldn't hear it. "I'm sorry. Forgive me."

"You should really guard your tongue, Clio. Those words are too foul for you." With every word he scolded her, she felt her spine grind a little more.

My innocent little dove, he liked to call her. She tried to live up to it. "You're right," she said—only half-believing it. "I'll do better."

"I know you will."

She bit the inside of her cheek and asked, "How are the islands? Is the congregation doing well?"

Duncan was laying the foundation for a Church of Divine Light in the Southern isles. The islands that broke off of Africa during the Third World War. A secluded community, so many thousands of miles away.

When he replied, she sensed a smile in his voice, and it eased some of the tension in her neck. "Very well. Thriving, in fact. I can't wait for you to meet them."

"Me, too."

The car's tailgate flashed as she approached, the trunk popping open. She shifted her phone into her open hand and heaved her carry-on into the back hatch, ignoring Enzo's withering stare as he parked the cart behind her. Her hired companion always fussed too much—even now, seven years later, when her girlishness was forgotten under the mantle of *Woman*.

By the time she slid the first case in, Enzo had hefted the two largest bags into his arms and started arranging them in the trunk, twisting them to fit like pieces in a puzzle. She waited for his soft grunt of approval before leaning in to shove a duffel bag into the space above the hard luggage. As she withdrew, her head smacked against the lid of the hatch. She ducked and stumbled back with a hiss, pressing a hand to the back of her skull. It came away bloody.

"Are you alright?" Enzo reached for her, but she waved him off.

"Clio, what happened?" Duncan demanded.

She rubbed at the wound. The cut was small. It would stop bleeding soon. "I just hit my head on the trunk. Don't worry, I'll be fine."

Tucking herself into the front seat of the car, she managed to avoid another *look* from Enzo. She couldn't avoid Duncan though. "You should be letting your chauffeur take care of the luggage—that's his job. I'd prefer not to come home to a broken bride."

"I don't break that easily," she muttered. "Speaking of coming home—"

"We've been over this. Please don't make me repeat myself. I'm already shirking my responsibilities to accommodate this new venue. It's another day of travel that should be spent here." Dedication. It's one of the things that initially attracted her to Duncan. Recently, though, it felt more like a wall.

"I understand," she said, even though she didn't. "Thank you for making that sacrifice for me."

His tone softened, that rare sweetness she craved reappearing. "I was happy to, dove. Nothing gives me more pleasure. Look, I'm sorry if I'm coming off harsh about the timeline. I only want what's best for us."

"I know." The trunk slammed shut, shaking the seat beneath her. "I think I should let you get back to work. We're about to start driving and I might lose service."

"As will I. The islands need me to pastor in the hills for a few days, so you may not hear from me."

She frowned. *The hills again?* Enzo slipped into the driver's seat as she said quietly, "Alright. Well, I love you."

"You, too," he shot back. The phone clicked as his only means of goodbye.

Depositing her phone in her purse, she pulled out her wool hat. A good preparation on her part, especially since she wouldn't be able to rinse the blood out of her hair before the meeting at the manor. Enzo's hand appeared to her left, holding a handkerchief. She accepted it, braving a glance at his face as he pulled onto the road. He was too focused on the icy roads to scold her.

"Thank you," she whispered, dabbing at the back of her head, trying her best not to wince. He grunted as they left the airport behind.

Once she absorbed as much blood from her hair as possible, she stowed the stained cloth in her bag and pulled the beanie down over her ears. For the forty-five-minute drive, the car remained quiet, serene. Her thumb found the back of her engagement ring, tracing the thin gold band around and around as the tundra blurred past outside. It slid over her skin easily, the sizing not quite right. She hadn't worked up the courage to ask Duncan to fix it yet.

The sky darkened further, the light of the dashboard illuminating her face just enough to produce a reflection in the passenger window.

Clio had an "odd" look—at least, that's how her mother so indelicately put it.

That vile word ping-ponged around in her head as she stretched her sweater sleeves over her fists. She tried not to glimpse her imperfection as Enzo finally pulled onto the mansion's private drive.

Clio carried a defect: a mutation that starved her eyes of melanin. To anyone looking at her, it would appear as if a flashlight shone from within, rimming her pupils in stark white before spidering into the chocolate brown of her outer irises.

Odd, she thought again. *But not in a beautiful way.* Not like her mother, Clarissa Farren.

She'd inherited two things from that woman—thick chestnut hair and spidery-long legs. Well, okay, three things if she counted her temper, but she didn't want to, because she was working on that. Hand raised to The Divine Light, she was.

Clio fisted her hand, the small solitaire setting biting into her palm. A callus was already building there, where the ring dug into her skin. She almost couldn't feel the pain of it anymore.

As if sensing her arrival, green and blue lanterns sprung to life along the driveway. They permeated the banks of snow on either side of the road and glanced off the salted pavement ahead. She rolled down her window, ignoring the biting breeze and Enzo's gasp as she leaned out. She wanted nothing to hinder her view.

There, coming into focus at the end of the lane, was the venue she'd obsessed over for months. *Raðljóst Manor.* She'd read enough to understand it was an Icelandic term. The meaning of the word had stuck with her, spinning like a broken record in her head.

Raðljóst—enough light to find your way by.

Violet flood lights lit the staircase leading to the entrance. It reminded her, not so subtly, of the red-carpet affairs her mother often attended. Warmth swelled in Clio's chest, knowing that this was a treasure all her own.

The town car swung around the turnabout at the end of the lane, and she popped the door open before the car even came to a full stop. She looked back at her middle-aged companion long enough to ask, "Can you handle the bags on your own, Enzo?"

Her escort smiled indulgently and reached over to unclip the seatbelt she'd forgotten to release. "Yes, Ms. Clio." She twisted to step out of the car, but a warm hand grabbed her lightly around the wrist. Enzo was studying her, his sun-freckled face twisting.

Her heart stuttered. "What is it?"

"Are you sure," he asked, "that this is what you want?"

She rolled her eyes. "Not you, too."

"I don't mean this place," he said quietly, avoiding her gaze.

The cold hit her all of a sudden, seeping under every layer. She pulled her hand out of Enzo's. Not harshly, not after all the years between them, but firmly.

Clio told herself it was his instinct to protect her that made him ask. That it was his way of saying goodbye. That, after the wedding, she wouldn't need him anymore and he would miss her. She *hoped* he would miss her.

"I'm doing the right thing—doing exactly what I should," she told him. "And that's all I will ever want." All she *should* want.

Something crumbled in his hazel eyes, but he nodded his acceptance. She clutched her coat tight around her and leapt out of the car quickly, hoping it hid her shaky legs.

As she ascended the staircase, she marveled at the sturdy, romantic architecture. Above the windows lining the first level —an obvious modern renovation—the ivory stone of the building twisted into ornamental columns. Several sunken oval windows punctuated the edifice, marking individual rooms. Her wonder imploded as she passed through the golden-gilded entrance and took in the lobby. *It is better than the pictures.*

The extravagance kept her frozen to the doorstep until a man appeared, entering the foyer from a corridor to her right. He greeted her with a friendly smile, but the expression struck her rather hollow.

As he approached, she noticed a stiffness in his tall posture, a glaze in his blue eyes. The angles of his face were sharp and dramatically square, and his lips dripped with wicked promise. More handsome than she expected the hotel owner to be. In fact, a fleeting notion crossed her mind that he might be the most attractive man she'd ever laid eyes on.

She'd met plenty of above-average looking men thanks to her mother—models and industry executives alike. Enough to know that looks were of little consequence when it came to integrity.

Clio extended a hand. The man embraced her palm with his own and purred, "Hello, Ms. Farren. Welcome to Raðljóst Manor. I'm Nikolai Trousseau. It's nice to finally meet with you face-to-face."

The name of the manor slipped off his tongue like a rush of water, tinged with an accent so faint she couldn't be sure whether it was feigned or authentic. She'd definitely been saying it improperly.

It sounded the way she imagined a Frenchman might say the word croissant, but without the c. Clio tried to imitate the pronunciation in her head, in case she ever needed to repeat it, but quickly decided to save herself the embarrassment and avoid it by any means necessary.

"Likewise," she replied, quickly dropping his hand. His fingers were cold and long enough that they had pressed against her wrist. Her heart pounded so hard that for a moment she felt sick. Maybe she was panicking after all.

"I was expecting you in the afternoon." He glanced at the blackened sky behind her, his white smile splintering. *Oh yes, he's irritated all right.*

"They delayed my plane. I landed a little under an hour ago."

His face smoothed some, but his eyes looked through her as if he were distracted by another task entirely. "I see. No worries. Let me take you on a tour and if you're satisfied, we can look over some paperwork."

Clio nodded. "If you think that's what we should do."

Nikolai led her through the mansion at a leisurely pace, through the multiple ballrooms and covered terraces, barraging her with questions about the wedding she knew he didn't really care about. When he glanced in her direction during the scattered conversation, he did so with distant eyes. She replied only when she had to, crushing her fingers together at the small of her back.

The halls were lovely, but wrong. Too flashy. Too cavernous. Too *bright*. They made her eyes hurt.

As they exited the final event hall, one with golden columns and a mirrored ceiling, Nikolai halted their stroll. "Ms. Farren, be frank with me. Has my manor disappointed you?"

Clio suddenly recognized the scowl on her face, her wrinkled nose, and promptly composed herself. "Oh, not at all." She shifted on her feet. "It's everything I expected."

"Well, you haven't said a word about the halls I've shown you. And I hope you'll pardon my saying so, but you look positively sick. Do none of my rooms suit your needs?"

She tried to swallow, but her tongue stuck to the roof of her mouth. "If I'm being honest, Mr. Trousseau, I came here with only one room in mind. I'm sorry I let you trouble yourself with a full tour."

"That's no trouble at all. I like a guest that knows what they want—it makes my work all the easier," he drawled, threading his fingers in front of his stomach. She tried not to stare at the length of them, the pale slenderness. "Which room would you like, then?"

Rolling her shoulders, she said, "The observatory, please."

He blinked, his elegant brows pulling together as the torpid glaze in his eyes faded. "You want to get married in my observatory?"

"I'd like to see it first—but yes, that was the plan."

His eyes tracked every inch of her face. "How did you even know about it? We don't advertise that room on our website."

She smiled politely. "You didn't need to. I came across a blog that mentioned you gave a guest access to your library, and that they found the observatory attached. The way they described it, it sounds breathtaking."

After reading that blog, she'd requested every blueprint filed with the county. She was fully aware of when they passed by the library during the tour. She had also memorized the exact square footage of the crystal dome within: nine hundred and twenty feet.

Nikolai's lips were a hard line. "I've rewarded the occasional devoted lodger with access to my private collection, but I don't make that public knowledge for a reason."

"You like your privacy," she guessed.

"Yes."

She swallowed dryly. "Or maybe you're just selfish with it."

Nikolai went gravely still.

Clio dug her fingernails into her palms and fixed her gaze on a spot above his head. She wasn't sure he was breathing anymore, but she couldn't back down. Not after she'd come so far. She hoped the shame she felt wasn't transparent on her face, though it seemed he still wasn't looking close enough to detect something like that. "Well," she pressed.

His eyes narrowed, those brilliant blue irises frothing like a river rapid. "Well?"

"Can I see it?"

Nikolai glanced at the hall's ivory molded ceiling, his shoulders relaxing fraction by fraction as he deliberated. Abruptly, he folded his hands behind his back and marched down the corridor. Clio leapt to catch up.

When they reached the door to the library, he grasped the gold knocker in the center of the door and slid it to the side. A little bronze key sat in the nook beneath. He took the key and opened the door, standing flat against it as she entered. Nikolai returned the key to its cubby and then the door swung shut behind them.

Darkness fell, warm and soft and delicious. She made out a faint viridescent glow coming from the other side of the room, drifting in through a curved archway.

The lights flicked on and Clio squeezed her eyes shut against the shock to her vision. She'd always been too sensitive to light—developing migraines when she spent too much time in the sun, unable to sleep if the city lights found a crevice in her curtains. It was just another way this manor lured her in.

Polar night. What a wonderful promise.

The library was a quaint, square room, with all four walls covered in bookshelves. Dust and ink and parchment invaded her senses. The stacks overflowed with worn fabric and leather spines. *Collection—more like obsession.*

In the middle of the room stood a simple wooden table with a chessboard, frozen mid-game, and a clawed-foot sitting chair upholstered in red velvet.

Clio felt Nikolai's intense stare on her as she passed through the room, walking under the archway and up the dim, narrow staircase. If he followed her, she didn't hear him. She allowed her hands to brush the walls on either side of her as she ascended, her fingertips tracing a crack in the beige wallpaper.

With every step she took up the stairs, that green gleam wrapped tighter around her. It called to her; moth to flame, mortal to holy. She thought, for sure, she was about to be scorched.

Cresting the staircase, Clio watched the dome stretch out before her. *Nine hundred and twenty feet. Pure crystal.* She wandered in, face turned to heaven. The globe provided a full view of utter blackness, the flickering stars, and... the aurora polaris.

The purple and electric-green rifts hung like fissures in the sky. They vibrated, fluctuating like a heartbeat, like the lifeblood of earth itself. She didn't imagine they would look so alive.

A gentle knock sounded behind her, demanding her attention, and she shoved away the sudden urge to cry. Clio wrapped her arms around herself and faced Nikolai. "This is perfect."

Nikolai watched her with dark eyes. He remained on the threshold to the dome, as if unwilling to enter. His shoulder was braced against the door frame, as if the mere sight of it made him weak.

A smirk tugged at her mouth as she added, "My mother will have to cut the guest list in half to accommodate." Clarissa was going to give her hell once she found out, but at least now Clio had an excuse to mediate the enmity. How could anyone look at this sky and not want to celebrate love beneath it?

Her 'friends' can simply send a check, she thought sourly. *Like celebrities usually do for charity.*

Nikolai continued to stare as a small, arrogant smile surfaced. "I'll require an additional deposit for the collection's sake. Most of it is impossible to replace." She knew it was greed that warmed his voice, but it didn't matter.

"Just name your price and tell me where to sign."

His smile grew. "We'll hammer out the details in my office. Come."

Nikolai retreated down the stairs, leaving Clio to pass through the chill that swirled in his wake—a chill that smelled of soot and copper. Strange, but not unpleasant. It reminded her of old, well-loved homes and the allure of gasoline. And just as she knew to resist huffing toxic fumes, she resisted leaning into the lingering essence of him.

Clio followed him back through the library, flicking off the light and reaching out to catch the door slowly closing between them, but she hesitated.

A tickle brushed against her mind and she turned to the table in the center of the room. The board taunted her, the transparent chess pieces glimmering under the glow sifting down through the stairwell. She reached out and made the final move for the game, exposing one side's queen. Everything had to come to an end at some point. It seemed wrong to her, *infuriating* even, to walk by without freeing it from the stalemate.

A smile tugged at her lips as she tore herself from the soft radiance of the room.

As she was swallowed once more by the manor, Clio wondered why a man would keep such a spectacular view locked away... especially when he did not seem to appreciate it himself.

3

The office was warm enough that Clio surrendered her fur-lined coat to Nikolai when he reached for it. He held the collar, his cool fingers briefly brushing her neck while she shimmied her arms free. She stamped out the prickle in her spine and studied her Mary-Jane heels as he hung the coat on a tall brass rack next to the door.

He walked to the modest, mahogany desk in the center of the room. Two candelabras burned on either end of the desk, white wax dripping down the brass and sealing each base to the surface. Wooden filing cabinets spread out behind him, interrupted by a foot of lavish burgundy curtain aligned to the center of the wall.

Before Nikolai sat down, he unbuttoned his blazer and withdrew a thin book from his jacket. As he stowed it in the top drawer of the desk, Clio noticed the fit of his black button-up and leather belt. She fixed her eyes on his chin to keep from looking any lower, but it only made her realize he wore his shirt unbuttoned below the hollow of his neck. No tie.

Her host eased himself onto his chair and motioned for Clio to join him.

"Unsupervised candles are a fire hazard, you know." She slipped into one of the two chairs arranged before the desk.

Nikolai smiled tightly, glancing by her as he replied, "We have excellent insurance should anything go awry." His head lowered to tend to the paperwork lying on the desk. He produced a red pen and set about striking out and rewriting various sections of text.

The room turned quiet, palpably tense, so she asked, "Was that a journal?"

His brow furrowed. "Of a sort."

She waited for him to turn the page before she said half-jokingly, "For your dreams? Eloquent sonnets?"

"More like ideas. And reminders."

"Are you very forgetful?"

His fingers froze over the paper. "Not usually." But the way he said it made her think he had been of late.

"That's understandable. This year was trying for all of us. How has business been?"

"Booming, now that you've come along." Nikolai slid the contract across the table to her. He plucked a black pen from his desk and set it upon the papers. "If you would do the honors, Ms. Farren."

"Always happy to do my part in reviving the economy," she muttered, and scanned the revisions before initialing away.

She was on the last signature when she heard Enzo shouting from the lobby, "Ms. Clio, I've left your luggage next to the doors."

"Luggage?" Nikolai repeated.

Clio sprung from her seat. She slipped into the hallway and called Enzo over. "All sorted?" He asked as he made it to the corridor.

21

"Just about. Does your flight board soon?"

"Yes, in a little less than two hours."

"Oh, you'd better go." She threw her arms around him and patted his back. "Give your new granddaughter a big kiss and squeeze for me. I'll see you at the rehearsal party."

Nikolai's chair scraped against the floor in an abrupt screech, drawing her attention back to the room. His fists braced the surface of his desk. "I'm afraid there's been some sort of misunderstanding. My manor is closed through the Solstice."

She gave him a flat look. "I *need* to be here. I have vendors to oversee, a color scheme and decor plan to reinvent. Did you really think I would fly a thousand miles just to sign paperwork and leave?"

"Boarding you is not a possibility." His voice was professional, detached. *Real fucking annoying.* "There are no maids to clean your room or kitchen staff to feed you. If you stay, the Earth will snow you in for weeks. We're entering the peak of an Arctic freeze."

"That doesn't bother me. I can clean up after myself and I'll eat whatever you had planned." Nikolai frowned, so Clio added, "Unless you're selfish with your food, too."

Enzo glanced between Clio and the hotel owner. "I don't know, Ms. Clio. This doesn't sound like such a good idea."

"Food is not the issue," Nikolai growled.

His tone turned her stomach. "You're absolutely right. The issue is time. And I'll have you know that if I don't get the time I need to properly prepare, then I have no intention of getting married here."

"Then I'll have you know that the deposit is non-refundable, and you've already signed it away." He scowled.

She faced him fully, crossing her arms. "Do I look like someone who gives a shit about deposits? I'm not losing anything of significance." His face fell, spine straightening until he stared down at her from several feet away. He seemed liable to snap like a pencil under the burden of her. *Nothing new there.*

"But if it's money you're amenable toward," Clio stomped to her purse and withdrew three large reams of cash, placing them ceremoniously on the desk, "Trust me, I have every intention of making the inconvenience worth your while."

Nikolai's gaze locked on the stack. Then, his eyes flicked past it to her gaping purse, as if expecting another ream to spit out like a money gun at the end of a gameshow. His nose flared. He screwed his eyes shut and took a small step back. "*Surely*, you would prefer to be with your loved ones over the next couple weeks. Your bridal party, your family, your groom?"

Clio steeled her nerves. *Here goes.* "My fiancé is an apostolate whose service is keeping him in the Southern Hemisphere until our rehearsal dinner. My mother sold her condo last week and flew to an island to celebrate, spouting some bullshit about perfecting her tan for the wedding photos." She had to make a genuine effort not to scoff. "And as for the bridal party, there isn't one. The only friend I would want to stand with me at the altar died a year ago."

Nikolai's throat bobbed and Clio got a whiff of victory. These dirty tricks left her queasy, more akin to her mother than she ever wished to be—but she had to get her way, had to persevere here somehow. Even if it wasn't by being herself.

She composed the perfect disguise: an expression of disgust and entitlement. She knew the mask well. "Every other lodge in this area is crawling with rats or cockroaches so I certainly won't stay at any of them, and if I fly home, I return to a condo that has grown so horribly familiar that I've started admiring the passionless art hanging in it. You are asking me to coordinate a wedding without being able to see or touch it until the day before the ceremony, and I am saying *no*, Mr. Trousseau. I would prefer to stay here."

From the corner of her eye, Clio saw Enzo's head dip. Not in disappointment or shock, as she might have expected. He had been the sole witness of the loneliness, of the tears she rarely shed. She found the car was as good a place as any to let it out. Other than handing her his handkerchief, the incidents went unacknowledged, but she saw that he remembered as well as she did.

Nikolai saw, too. He studied Enzo, then her, his fingers rubbing together.

"Please," Clio murmured, allowing the steel in her tone to melt and mold to her design. His head tilted slightly, as if she finally piqued his interest. It wasn't a favorable interest, judging by the muscle in his jaw.

Nikolai reached across the desk and dragged the stack of cash to his side. "Okay, Ms. Farren. Let's work something out."

Clio lingered in the foyer as the town car vanished on the horizon.

One moment she was alone and the next Nikolai said from beside her, "Second thoughts already?"

She turned to find her host frowning at the road. "Not in the slightest. I was only thinking of how much I'll miss him."

He inclined his head. "Yes, two weeks must feel like a long time to go without a driver." The statement was diplomatic, but she recognized a mocking tone when she heard it. Her core kindled, wishing to retaliate, to draw out his judgement and bleed it dry. But no... she needed to control herself.

She only said, "I'll miss his companionship."

Nikolai glanced at her from the corner of his eye, too briefly to assume he'd meant to. "I can show you to your suite now."

Channeling a vein wholly her mother, Clio had requested the honeymoon suite for the duration of her stay, knowing it was the nicest room in the manor. If she had to play a role, she would play it well. And since Duncan had every intention of departing from this continent directly after the reception, it might as well get a little use.

"All right."

He led her to the elevator, steering the bell cart of her luggage to sit between them.

As soon as the doors closed, the small space closed in on her. She gasped, the air resting on her tongue like a coin—bitter and metallic. An aria drifted from the speakers on the ceiling, the orchestra building to a crescendo. She shrunk into the corner behind her, desperate for any extra room to breathe, to think.

Is this what claustrophobia feels like? The possibility seemed foreign and ridiculous. She'd never been afraid of small spaces in her life. Perhaps it was more about the company with her than the actual space. Closed in with a stranger. *Deep breaths, Clio, everything will be fine.*

Beneath the metal filling her senses, she suddenly detected an undercurrent of wood. *Cedarwood*—like a forest on the brink of dusk. Clio hadn't spent much time outside of the city, but there were a handful of times. It smelled like the cabin she used to visit with her father... before he left. She inhaled deeply and it granted her a measure of comfort. Though, she still wasn't sure why. *Those aren't pleasant memories anymore.*

Clio made every effort to stare straight ahead, leaning away from the blue eyes that peered at her through the bell cart and that strange toxic allure that beckoned to her.

Closer, it seemed to say.

When the matte gold doors of the elevator slid open, Clio burst into the hallway ahead of her host. Striding across the embossed vermilion carpet to the end of the hall, she waited at the threshold of the final door. It was only when she looked up at Nikolai's wary expression that she realized she shouldn't have known where the honeymoon suite was.

No normal guest would have.

He parked the cart next to suite 405 and handed her a bronze key. A red satin ribbon hung from the end. "I hope you enjoy your stay, Ms. Farren."

"Thank you, Nikolai."

His brow furrowed again, a feature she bet camouflaged a spectrum of emotion. Before she could determine what emotion that might be in this moment, he retreated. He nodded stiffly as the elevator doors slid closed between them.

She remained there, gazing at the same spot long after he was gone, consumed by a bitterness divorced from the taste of the air.

Clio unearthed one more thing in her research: a record that was expertly expunged from all public forums. She hadn't brought up the dead body found on Nikolai's property two years ago—the carcass drained of blood, throat ripped open, and chest cavity ravaged by wild animals.

Nor how her best friend, who had indeed died the previous year, was discovered down a city alley in similar condition. What Clio *did* plan to do with all she knew and suspected had not yet been determined.

But she just bought herself time to decide.

4

Nikolai stalked back to the library and passed through the hidden door to his residential quarters. He didn't bother with lights as he crossed his bedroom to the basement door and hurtled into the depths of the earth. He followed the musty, stone corridor to a second hall lined with rickety arched doors. Most hung ajar as he drifted by, a burial ground of masterpieces from dead and forgotten artists. He had admired them once, but could no longer remember why.

The last door led to the bedroom he used during the spring, whenever he lingered long enough to need a place to sleep through sunlight hours, but the room before that held his greatest treasure... and best kept secret. He flung himself toward it, into the rich red luster of the nursery.

Not the sort of nursery for a baby—no, never children.

This room was barren, save for a small square table crowded with tools and a two-foot-wide plant sitting in the corner. Several red and blue bulbs bathed the bush in a violet glow. The plant emitted a gleam of its own, a soft golden hue. It sang in his presence—calling to that piece inside him that answered without words, from like to like and death to death.

Nikolai took a deep breath, scrubbing his face. *What am I going to do about that woman?*

Approaching the table, he began his daily routine of testing the light levels on the plant, the pH balance of the soil. He shook one of the spindly, scaled branches and listened to the rustle of the leaves. They were small tasks, but crucial—crucial because they anchored him with a sense of purpose and provided him clarity of mind, if only for a minute or two.

He had the satisfaction of looking at the plant and knowing that he'd helped it thrive rather than die. Though he supposed he should have let it go a long time ago.

Nestled among the bright yellow foliage, a flower bud was starting to unfurl. The plant produced only one or two blooms a year. He could almost see the red core hidden behind its large, opalescent petals—the lethal womb prepared to burst open.

Finding the pH balance too alkaline, he turned to his table and grabbed the tin of coffee beans. He shook some into the stone mortar and set about grinding it into a powder. Amidst the remedial task, he considered his options.

The first, and simplest, solution would be to put Ms. Farren out of his mind entirely. If he were careful, he could keep their paths from crossing too often in the manor. If he were strategic, he could make the last dose of blood stretch to cover the next two weeks. He might get a bit peckish but not to an extent he couldn't manage. And if he grew desperate, he could always hunt those white bears out in the tundra. It would all be fine.

He'd made the right decision letting her stay. His till was warm with stacks of cash and surely his hospitality would leave a lasting impression on the young bride. Once his staff returned from their hiatus, he could leave the property and the event in Mrs. Itzli's capable hands. Ms. Farren seemed in desperate need of some nurturing anyway.

Yes, but—

Nikolai's thoughts clung to his new guest like thorns in a ball of cotton. He could not detangle himself from her fibers.

It was something in the way she spoke, the inflection and lilting cadence, as if she were reciting poetry. The way she walked down the hallway to the honeymoon suite. The way she looked up through the crystal ceiling of the observatory. He did not understand.

And the scent of her.

It had hit him in a wave when she opened her purse. He tasted the hint of copper in the air, though the details were dulled by his recent feeding. Her blood was different, he just didn't know how, and he hadn't allowed himself to draw close enough to analyze it.

Nikolai didn't try to fool himself—he knew this curiosity played a part in letting her stay. Curiosity and perhaps a bit of shock. She surprised him the way humans rarely could.

The rustle of leaves drew Nikolai's attention to the herb in the corner, where a fluffy white cat batted a branch and stretched her neck to nip at the foliage.

"No, Poppet. That's a naughty girl." He stamped his foot, but the cat was unaffected. She glanced at him with a meow and batted the branch again, her teeth coming within millimeters of a leaf. "*Dammit.*"

Nikolai charged across the room. The cat didn't even flinch. As he scooped Poppet into his arms, he snarled, "You'd think you would learn your lesson after the first thousand times. If you eat that, you'll be yacking for hours, and I don't feel like cleaning up after you."

Poppet writhed. He took two steps toward the door before

the cat extended its claws and dug them into his neck. He swore, prying her paws away, and Poppet flung herself out of his embrace. The cat landed on her feet and darted out of the room with a low growl.

He knew that tone. Poppet wanted food.

Rubbing at the scratches on his neck, Nikolai followed the cat to her bowl in the bedroom next door. Poppet paced back and forth, her yellow gaze locked on the plastic tube protruding from the wall. Nikolai pressed the button above the siphon and a muted screech echoed from beyond the concrete wall. A trickle of blood, clumped with whiskers and hair, quickly filled the porcelain dish.

Poppet lapped her dinner as quickly as it pooled and Nikolai grimaced at the crimson stain spreading over her snout.

"Hateful little bloodsucker," he mumbled. Like with most things lately, he wasn't sure why he bothered—but the cat had been with him so long, he could barely recall a day before her. She was just another anchor. *An irritating one, but still.*

He often wondered if it was rodent blood that made Poppet so feral and talented at finding her way into places he didn't want her, like a lab rat traversing a maze. Rodents were easy to source, though, which kept Poppet from contriving a way into the rest of the manor to feed on his guests. He could live with her quirks.

As Nikolai returned to the plant room, he heard shuffling. Footsteps coming from the kitchen of the manor, directly above him. He held his breath and tilted his ear toward the ceiling. Maybe it crossed a line to listen in, one he rarely felt the desire to cross, but his guest had pushed her boundaries today, too.

After the stunt she'd pulled, Nikolai couldn't help himself.

A faint, distorted voice filled his ears first, layered over static, and he knew he was eavesdropping on a phone call. "Oh,

Clio," the crackly, female voice said, "you really try my patience sometimes. We've already sent out save the dates to all those people. What am I supposed to say to them?"

He closed his eyes and strained to catch every small detail. The demon blood from that morning had limited his range of hearing, but he managed... just barely.

Clio walked in ambling lines, her heart beating rapidly. A small sigh escaped her that Nikolai was sure the other woman couldn't hear. "Just tell them we decided to keep the wedding intimate. You know, only family."

Nikolai could almost imagine it. His guest, wearing that darling brown sweater and leather leggings. She paused in the middle of the kitchen, where the granite island stood, and started chewing something very slowly.

Mrs. Itzli's cinnamon cookies, he suddenly recalled, sat there.

"I can't believe you're doing this to me. You're my only baby. I wanted to show you off in your lovely wedding gown and marital bliss," the woman whined. "This was my last chance to really spoil you before you flit away to Mount Serry or whatever you call it."

Clio swallowed and said, "Montserrat, Mom."

"Yes, yes, that's right. Oh, honey, you know I'm happy for you. You found such a nice young man. I wish I had possessed your sense of men when I was your age. Instead, I settled for your father, and just look how *that* played out."

"Uh huh."

"Are you sure you want to switch venues? The chapel we reserved in the city is so beautiful, and it fits everyone."

"I'm sure. Once you see this place, you'll understand. The observatory is incredible." Clio walked to the fridge and opened it. Nikolai heard her breath hitch as she shifted her balance from one foot to the other. "And the lights—the lights are spectacular. They're so vibrant, like green and purple lightning bolts frozen in the sky."

Nikolai started. Humans couldn't see the full spectrum of the aurora. Not like that. He'd heard many the disappointed traveler gripe about the utter "grayness" of the lights, perhaps with the rare report of a faint green hue, but he'd never met a human that could see them like he did. Not without the help of a camera, at least.

He heard the fridge slam shut, and then the clatter of Clio rummaging through drawers.

"What about the staff," Clio's mother asked, her tone bland. "Are they attentive? Are they pleasant? I won't deal with mediocre service."

Clio took a deep breath as another drawer opened and he detected the sound of silverware scraping together. "The staff is great. I think you're in for a shock when you meet the owner."

"And why is that?"

The soft pop of a paper lid sounded. Clio sighed. "Well... he's very handsome."

Nikolai smirked and grabbed his mortar. He kept listening as he knelt beside the plant, sprinkling coffee grounds over the soil.

"Honey, I really doubt that." Clio's mother chuckled. "Men rarely impress me."

"This one will."

Her mother hesitated. "On level with ex-husband two? Or three?"

Clio's heart thundered in the silence. He heard a clinking, and it took him a moment to pinpoint it as the sound of her teeth biting on the silverware. "Better."

There was a sharp, gravelly intake of breath. "Maybe your venue change won't be such a deprivation after all."

Clio almost choked on something as she sputtered, "Oh, for heaven's sake, Mom. I didn't mean you should seduce him. He's far too young for you."

"If only she knew," Nikolai muttered to the plant, working the layers of topsoil with his fingers.

Her mother huffed, "Are you eating right now, at this time of night? Sweetie, you really should be more mindful of weight gain this close to the big day." Clio stopped breathing.

Nikolai hadn't seen a single thing wrong with her body, in his expert opinion, but he sensed an enormous tension in her silence.

"Clio, honey? Did you hear me?"

She replied curtly, "Yeah, Mom. I've got to go."

"Oh, all right. Remember to practice walking around in your heels. Divine Light forbid you trip while walking down the aisle."

"Mhm," Clio tapped her foot. "Love you. Goodnight."

"Love you, too. Ciao, sweetie."

The kitchen fell silent, and Nikolai only realized he was holding his breath when a loud clanging occurred. She must have hurled her silverware into the kitchen sink. Clio returned what he guessed was an ice cream carton back to the freezer and rushed out of the kitchen.

Nikolai stared at his hands, covered in soil, black beneath the nails. A pit opened in his stomach, detached from the primal hunger that usually gathered there. He hadn't believed Clio's speech in the office. He thought her manipulative and vain, like most wealthy young ladies he'd had the displeasure of meeting. As long as they were doling out the cash, it didn't really matter to him what they were like or why they were that way. But this time, his shredded humanity called out to him, whispering like a babbling brook, urging him to understand.

It's not my place, he reminded himself. *She's not my bride.*

He would simply ignore Ms. Farren, avoid her, and the Freeze would be over before they knew it. Outside, as if mocking his resolution, the storm surged with a predatory howl.

5

The gown wasn't how Clio remembered it. *It's worse.*

She stood in front of the suite's bathroom mirror, steadying herself on the counter as she adjusted to heels. Glittery, blindingly-white fabric swathed her body, the bodice pulling tight around her chest and wispy waist. She debated calling her mother to say, *I haven't gained so much as an inch, thank you very much,* but it was too early for that.

Mommy dearest would sleep off her signature mojitos until early afternoon.

Clio didn't mind the corset. She even fancied the sheer sleeves—the way they hung off her shoulders and fluttered with every movement. The skirt, however, made her feel like a festival balloon.

She'd wanted a different sort of dress. A cut that draped down her shape like the rivulets of a stream and swept the ground like a wave kissing the shore. Something blush, to bring out the warmth in her eyes and counteract the mutation.

When she'd explained that vision to Duncan, her dreams

were crushed. He had a certain idea of what a bride should look like. Pure. Bright. Modest.

Wanting to please him, Clio conceded the dress design to her mother's tastes. She figured if she couldn't get exactly what she wanted, why bother getting hung up on details at all? Clarissa had a well of experience when it came to designers anyway.

But as Clio stared at the bride in the mirror, all she felt was tremendous disappointment. The creamy skin of her face seemed paler, her hair drab beneath the gauzy veil. And her mutation—the twin spheres of alabaster now highlighted by the gown—pierced her through.

Sterile. Sharp. *Odd.*

She hated the dress. Hated it with every smoldering ember in her gut. No matter how many times Clio doused her temper, those few sparks held fast. They goaded her to rip the dress off and bury it in the snow. They reminded her of all the reasons she should call the wedding off entirely.

Reasons that made her back tingle.

For an instant, her discontent dissolved into a frenzy that might liquefy bone if she let it loose. As she turned that intrusive thought over and examined it, giving it more than the brief acknowledgment she usually did, her eyes began to burn. Her vision blurred.

The sting brought her up short. When her eyes cleared and she saw her expression whetted with passion, she shook the thought away. *No.* She made a commitment and she could learn to be obedient. She could learn to be better.

Happiness on earth was fleeting, impossible to maintain. It always ended. She needed a guaranteed happy ending, and Duncan promised that.

After making sure her legs weren't going to buckle, Clio let go of the counter, looking anywhere but at the mirror in front of her. As she stepped back, something crunched under her heels. Lifting her skirt, she saw the problem. Coarse, ivory particles were scattered on the floor beneath her.

She frowned, backing up another step. Bath salts, probably, judging from the crystalline look of them. The maid must have missed them. She hadn't noticed them herself until now and they were so small, like tiny, cloudy diamonds barely catching the light.

Whatever. She wasn't cleaning it up.

Clio ripped her veil off and threw it on the counter, suddenly realizing that bath salts littered the white granite there, too. She shook her head. The walls of her suite threatened to suffocate her. She needed to move, to get away from the mirrors hanging on every wall. Clio grabbed her phone and left the room.

The gravitational pull of the elevator engaged her core, the operatic music lulling her nerves as she puttered between floors. That claustrophobic sensation she felt in Nikolai's presence yesterday was gone. Now that she was alone in the golden box, it felt a lot like the passenger seat of a car. Compact. Comforting. As good a place as any.

She made all the necessary phone calls to her vendors, informing them of the venue change and scheduling deliveries for the tail end of the Freeze. She called Duncan twice but they, of course, forwarded to voicemail. At least he would know she tried.

As the elevator made its last descent toward the lobby, she dialed a familiar but unsaved number. The phone rang, each trill stretching longer than the one before. Her heartbeat filled her head and a lump creeped into her throat.

When the elevator arrived at the main floor, a voice boomed in her ear, "Hey there, you've reached Marc—" She terminated the call and emerged into the lobby.

Beyond the face of the manor, snow fell in thick drifts across the staircase. A sparkly carpet caked the road, climbing up the lantern posts, and Clio was forced to acknowledge how quickly she would be snowed in.

She knew it should worry her, but this didn't seem like much of a prison. The earth gleamed periwinkle as the sun loitered just past the horizon. The tempest that pummeled the outside of her suite last night had been replaced by a lilting whistle this morning—now, she thought it resembled the notes of a flute.

Meandering through the lobby, Clio allowed her fingertips to trail the backs of the velvet furniture. She counted the brass buttons in the upholstery as she passed, diverting herself from the throb of her feet. Clio suddenly found herself wondering what Nikolai did to occupy his days. She wondered if the hotel owner ever felt lonely, or if he were one of those terrifying individuals that preferred to be alone. One of those people who didn't need or want anyone.

Clio bit her lip and glanced up at the painting behind the front desk. The piece displayed a group of naked wood nymphs frolicking through the forest. She couldn't help it when her gaze caught on their breasts, their bodies stretched out in wild abandon. Two were spinning in a circle at the forefront of the painting, heads thrown back and hands gripping tightly to each other. The air seemed to swirl in a vortex around their legs. Another nymph sprawled stomach-first on a boulder to the left, her dark hair spilling over the side and knees buckled as if pinioned by some invisible force. The last nymph was plumper, a female with a round, haughty face and red hair cascading down her curves. This one leaned against a tree and beckoned to someone off-canvas.

At the edge of the painting, Clio saw the boot of a man entering the pastel grove. The forest itself around them cast long shadows, as if dusk bloomed all around them.

Clio's gaze dropped to the desk. A large leather book was split open on the counter, so she drew close to inspect it. The volume bore a list of signatures, presumably of guests who checked in this season. She appraised the half-empty page and the golden pen resting in its ink reservoir to the side. It was an outdated method of tracking guests.

Considering the sleek computer peeking up behind the counter, this record book was more for novelty's sake than anything else. Every room in this manor intertwined history with the present and it made her want to smile. If only she could.

She picked up the pen, dipped it in the jet liquid, and signed her name on the next empty line. As she crowned the i in her name with a tiny arrow pointing north, the memory surfaced.

The PI was a condescending asshole, but at least he was good at his job.

Clio learned quickly that investigators had that luxury—of being rude—as long as they were resourceful enough. It was a rare occasion when she felt thankful for her mutation, and that day was one of them. The PI couldn't look her in the eye, so he stared at some point on her forehead as he gave his final report.

His voice was thick, Russian, and incredibly grating to her short nerves. But when he finally shared the information he'd found at the city's airport, Clio perked up in her seat on the couch across from him. He said, "She bought tickets for three separate flights that week, two bound for the Southern Continent and one for the Arctic Ring."

Why would she do that? Wasn't the Arctic an icy waste-land? "Do you think she planned on using any of them?"

"Her body was discovered less than an hour after the final gate call of the second flight. If you ask me, I think it suggests misdirection."

"That's proof, then—that she was being harassed. We need to take this to the police."

He rolled his eyes. "They won't take this information at face value, Ms. Farren." When Clio's brow furrowed, the PI sighed and withdrew a carton of cigarettes from his jacket. "Do you mind?"

She did mind. A lot, actually. But she nodded in permission. She didn't want to piss him off today. Not when he'd finally found something of interest.

As the man lit his cigarette, he began a muffled explanation. "I had to dig through several levels of witnesses before I came across this clerk." He pulled a deep breath of smoke and slowly released it. The smoke billowed over the coffee table and assaulted her senses, reminding her of the only other man she'd seen have the gall to do this indoors. Her father.

The PI shrugged. "She admitted to seeing someone by Nyah's description purchase the tickets with cash and, presumably, a fake ID. There's no telling how often your friend did this, or even if it was truly her in the first place. The clerk spoke to me under the condition that it be anonymous and that she wouldn't be subjected to police scrutiny. She's afraid of losing her job."

"Fuck her and her job."

His lips twitched. "As much as I'm tempted to agree with that sentiment, I keep confidence with my sources. And honestly, Ms. Farren, the circumstances of your friend's death troubles me. Our city is a dangerous place." He stood, his leather clothing squeaking. "This wouldn't be the first time a young woman was caught in the wrong place at the wrong time. It *wouldn't be the first time a youth got caught up in the gang community that rules our streets, either. Maybe she believed someone was stalking her—but that doesn't automatically mean it's true."*

She heard the vile meaning behind his words: that maybe someone stalked Nyah, but, if they did, she probably deserved it. Clio bit back her urge to scream at the PI, and asked instead, "Where was the second flight bound to?"

"The Arctic."

Clio blinked a few times, coming back to reality in the manor's lobby. One statement echoed in her head—*there's no telling how often your friend did this.*

She glanced over her shoulder. Finding the lobby empty and silent, she flipped through the pages of the book until she reached last season's signatures. Her eyes devoured the names, scanning carefully. There was no logical reason for her hands to clam up, or for a hot flush to envelop her cheeks.

She tried to master her heartbeat as the air thinned—as it honed into a blade to slash her throat and the darkness pressed in on the manor's windows to watch. The wind outside died, singing in her ears like a phantom tone.

Clio didn't realize she'd burned through the season's signatures until she turned to an empty page and the stark, blank parchment wrenched her from the inky railroad. She sucked in a breath and peeked behind her. Nothing. Beneath the segment she'd leafed through, Clio's hand trembled as it held the page away from her wet signature.

Of course there's nothing out there, she frowned at the records. *There's nothing here, either.*

But before she could put the book back in order, she glimpsed the impression of a name on the backside of that blank page. And her heart stopped dead in her chest.

Turning to it, she wasn't sure whether to be horrified or

relieved to find proof she hadn't lost her mind. There wasn't much of it these days—proof. On the last page of records from two years ago, one name flared like a beacon. *Nyah Gazini.*

She reached out to touch it, as if hoping it might bridge the gap between them. Though, she knew the separation was permanent.

She'd suspected, but didn't believe until now, that her best friend stayed here—not the year she died, as Clio originally suspected, but the year the other corpse cropped up on this property. It all fit together: the way Nyah rarely visited the city in the months preceding her death, her jumpy nerves, and the agitated drivel Clio couldn't make sense of. This manor, the condition of the remains, were the only leads Clio found to hold onto since city authorities let Nyah's case run cold. There must be a connection, a monster who checked in and set its sights on her.

Clio's eyes drifted to the computer. Every date and room number, every activity and charge would be specified there. She could find out why Nyah came here and who she might have met. A creak echoed from one of the corridors and Clio jumped, flipping the book back to the present page.

She watched the archways, but nothing appeared to have caused it. A settling pipe, then. *Or a ghost.*

Clio laughed brusquely, shying from the desk. She would continue her investigation later, when she was sure Nikolai retired to his quarters. Right now, she needed to get lost in a good book and find someplace comfortable to peel off these shoes.

6

Nikolai had finished some bookkeeping in his office and was headed back to his room when he heard the giggle. A silky, bubbling trill. He barged into the library and blinked rapidly at the scene awaiting him.

Clio sat in his reading chair, drowning in a gaudy wedding dress. On her lap lay an open book and... Poppet.

The cat stood on her hind feet, kneading her front paws against Clio's chest. Poppet licked and licked at his guest's face, the glistening fangs bared but brushing harmlessly over the woman's flawless skin.

His back tensed, prepared to jump between them—but Clio wrapped the cat in a gentle hug and kissed her snout. Poppet nestled into the crease of her elbow, sniffing for a vein. Nikolai knew it would only take one nip for disaster to ensue.

Nikolai lurched forward. "Poppet," he growled.

Both Clio and the cat jumped about a foot.

Clio gasped, reaching for the claws stabbing through her corset. Before she could get scratched by Poppet's steely nails, Nikolai gathered the hissing creature in his arms.

The ability to think returned to him. "I'm sorry my cat is pestering you. Let me put her away." Nikolai glanced at the cracked passage to his room, trying to remember how he'd left it open.

Clio leapt up and reached over his arms to take the cat back. Her fingers warmed his skin. Gentle but firm. "Oh, that's alright, I like her. Poppet, right?"

Nikolai leaned away, stepping back. Clio followed him. He held his breath. "Yes, but she's liable to lash out without warning. She can get downright vicious, actually. So if you would just hand her over—"

"Vicious?" Clio gaped, eyes flashing. The glare she turned on him made his knees weak. He hadn't noticed before, her eyes. *So peculiar.* She reclaimed the small monster and turned her back on him. "This sweet little thing?"

Nikolai searched for words, any words at all, but came up empty.

Clio settled into the chair and nuzzled Poppet's neck, muttering, "You wouldn't hurt a fly, would you? You're a perfect little angel."

To Nikolai's eternal shock and amusement, Poppet began to purr and turned flaccid in Clio's arms. Clio giggled again, kissing the cat between her eyes.

Poppet's tail flicked contentedly, her icy gaze daring Nikolai to attempt another separation. *Nasty, conniving little brat.*

A different approach, then. Nikolai crossed his arms and snarled, "What are you doing in here?"

"Reading," she said flatly. "Is that not apparent from the book?"

He bit back a chuckle. "Is it not apparent that you don't have permission to do so?"

"Permission to read?" She countered.

"Permission to loiter in my library."

Her brows furrowed, creating a lovely little v above her nose. Poppet slipped into a light sleep, body idling like an engine. *The woman is a tiny beast whisperer, clearly.*

She said, "I'm paying you an exorbitant amount of money, you know."

"Yes, and I'm renting you a room for your nuptials that I normally don't. You've also interrupted my holiday, which I'm not charging you extra for even though I should. Access to this vicinity and my collection apart from your event was not included in the contract."

She scoffed, and he waited for that word to slip off her tongue again. *Selfish.* His ribs tightened around his useless organs. But she only said, "Will you deprive me the pleasure of reading when you clearly understand the comfort in it? Tell me you'd rather the stories collect dust. Two weeks is a long time, especially if you plan on leaving me to my own devices."

"You should have thought that through before intruding on my home."

Clio flinched. His gums twinged, but he ground his teeth to bridle the reflex.

Averting her gaze, she whispered, "Don't throw me out." It wasn't a vulnerable request, not with her voice resounding through the room like pure steel like that and her body coiling like a snake about to spring. If Nikolai didn't know any better, he might think *she* was the true predator in this room. And damn it if she wasn't sticking again, like stringy cotton in his brain.

He sighed and retrieved a chair from his bedroom, hesitating as he planted it on the other side of the table.

She noticed his gaze locked on the chair beneath her and smiled, the curve as feline and cruel as Poppet. "I'm sorry, did you want *this* chair in particular?"

He shook his head and sat in the one he'd retrieved from his room. "It's fine."

Nikolai scanned the chess game he'd started a week ago and decided to reset the board. He would give her what she wanted, but wouldn't let her out of his sight. Not until she released Poppet.

Clio went back to her reading and the room fell quiet. Belatedly, he realized that the board wasn't as he'd left it. He picked up the dark knight, rolling the crystal between his fingers. This one had been guarding the queen. Or, at least, that was what he remembered.

Icy panic seized his spine. Was he wrong? Could his mind have slipped? His hand rose to graze the hard outline of the journal against his breast. Was it simply another thing he needed to record in ink?

Clio had been so shrewd, so perceptive, in his office yesterday. She'd sniffed out his greatest weakness in mere minutes of conversation, and he worried that meant it was becoming so severe that he could no longer hide it.

The chasms in his head were growing darker, larger. And lately, he feared the day they would swallow him whole—it was inevitable, wasn't it? The more he searched for answers, the blinder he felt.

For whatever reason, he was losing hope that there were any answers to be found. Any relief. Except the woman across from him.

She was the first thing to stick in his head, the first sense of permanence, in ages.

Now, much like the previous evening, Nikolai pondered why that might be. He studied her in brief, flitting glances. There was obvious beauty there, shocking in its intensity the more he looked, as well as a certain darkness beneath her eyes that made her more fascinating than the average human. *What keeps her awake at night?*

He wondered if she was really reading, or if she was as distracted as he felt considering she didn't turn a page in all the time he watched.

After a few minutes, Clio's legs stretched out beneath the table, ankles crossing. She wiggled her toes. He clenched his teeth so hard that venom welled in his cheeks, reining in the instinct he harbored from an era when women concealed everything below the collar. Her wedding dress was just as voluminous as the ones he'd ripped apart back then. It made him want to find out if modern gown design had strengthened their seams.

Nikolai shook his head sharply. *Yep. I'm a light-damned idiot.*

Clio cleared her throat and he looked up to find her staring at him. It took an enormous effort to meet the intensity of her gaze. He couldn't work out what color they were yet, but he knew they were like nothing he'd ever seen. They weren't brown exactly—not *only* brown.

She murmured, "I'm sorry for angering you."

"I wasn't angry," he said carefully. "I was flustered."

"Okay." She smiled slightly. "I'm sorry for flustering you, then. Thank you for being generous with me."

"You're welcome," Nikolai replied quietly.

A faint softness swirled in the air about her, like a potent fragrance hiding the scent of poison. He blurted, "But I get the feeling you're just going to do it again."

Her smile faltered. "Yes, well, I do tend to have a frustrating effect on people."

Nikolai blinked. He wanted to dig into that particular sentiment, decided not to. "Why exactly are you lounging around in your wedding dress? Isn't that bad luck or an omen of some kind?"

She frowned at herself. "I suppose I'm trying to get comfortable in it."

"Is it wise to buy a wedding dress you aren't comfortable in?"

"My mother bought it and my groom will like it, so it doesn't really matter what I'm comfortable in." Nikolai glanced up at the bitterness in her voice. Her face was motionless, hard. She stared intently at the book in her hands and added, "Besides, if my mother's history is any indication of the future, I have at least two more wedding dresses to look forward to. I can be comfortable in one of those."

He thought he could detect a twitch in her lips, but he didn't dare laugh—even though the joke *was* funny. "You're very pessimistic for a bride. Especially one your age."

She nailed him with a withering look. "I'm realistic. Marriages rarely last, even for couples who serve The Divine Light."

He pressed his lips together and cocked his head. "I really shouldn't say this as the host for your venue, but if that's how you feel, why get married at all?"

After a moment, she shrugged and said, "Call me a hopeless, cynical romantic."

"That doesn't make any sense."

"Neither does love."

He blinked, speechless for a second time. She paid no mind to his reaction, lifting the book in her hands to stand between them. Silence rippled over them, and Nikolai slowly gathered his good sense up off the floor.

Clio turned a dozen pages before lowering the partition. "Is that your bedroom," she asked, nodding at the passage, "Is that why you keep this room locked up?"

"Do you plan to encroach on that, too?" he teased. "What would dear fiancé number one think?"

She scowled. "Don't be absurd."

"Just covering my bases."

"Well, you won't need to cover those. I have no intention of setting foot in your bedroom."

"Good," he said, and moved his first pawn on the fresh board.

She shut the book in her hands and stated, "I don't recognize most of the authors in your collection."

"That's because they're dead and no one cares about them."

She chewed her lower lip. *"You* do."

"I'm the rare exception. I like undistinguished writers," he replied. "They have a wealth of vision and nothing to lose."

"How did you discover them all? There must be hundreds here."

Nikolai pressed his lips together. "I have my sources." *Never mind that the sources tend to be the authors themselves.*

"Do you have a favorite?"

"Author?" He shrugs. "Not really."

She studied the chess board for a moment, eyes flitting up to meet his and around the room. "What about a favorite book?" *Chatty, isn't she?*

He thought for a moment, then admitted, "I find the best stories are ones never written down. Folk tales, for example."

The v above her nose reappeared. "I'm not familiar with any of those."

"None at all?"

Clio shook her head.

He considered the repository of stories he held within and the woman before him who seemed to be searching for one. It had been a long time since he last perused that moonlit lane in his head. Dusty and arid. Untouched.

On either side of the street, monsoons vibrated in their crystal containers, begging to be let free. But if he opened even one... He could remember how they twisted around him, how they had the ability to sweep him away.

Fuck it.

"I could remedy that," he offered. "Tell you a tale, if you'd like."

Her eyes brightened. "Now?"

"If you have the time." He smiled.

She beamed back, teeth glinting as she cuddled Poppet closer and sank into the cushions of the chair. "I'd like that very much."

So, Nikolai dug up ancient history and told it.

7

"The story begins with a boy, many centuries ago." As many nightmares often do.

Clio smiled, her body at ease across from him. It warmed a piece of Nikolai deep inside to see it. Her smile encouraged him to speak freely about things he'd rarely deigned to think about before today, before this moment. The memories were dusty, foggy, but in her presence, he thought they could finally come to life. And maybe she wouldn't hate the story.

"He belonged to a nomadic people that roamed the mountainous and forested regions of Northernmost Europe. In the winter, the days were short, and the snow was brutal. They were sometimes faced with several weeks of night, the world illuminated only by the colored lights hanging above through the starkest hours." Nikolai waited for the words to hurt, but they didn't. This woman was his temporary buoy, keeping him afloat in the torrent of the past. He kept talking, because it was such a relief to be able to do so, because he wasn't sure how long this precarious safety would last. "They were a small but strong people, who sustained themselves on the land and made their livelihoods from herding reindeer."

Clio's eyebrows shot up. "They kept them as pets?"

Nikolai blinked. "No. The nomads considered them to be life-giving spirits. Reindeer provided warmth and food, precious tools, and toys for their children."

"Oh." Clio pressed her lips together, her expression darkening. "You mean, they ate them?"

He chuckled. "Of course. But that has nothing to do with the story—you're distracting me."

She bared her teeth in a grimace. "Sorry. Go on."

Nikolai could tell she was still thinking about the reindeer. Frowning about them, actually—her sensitivity was rather sweet—but he said, "In the summer, when the snow melted and the world was warm, the nomads traveled more frequently, chasing the sun that so often hid from them in the winter.

"The children wandered further from their villages, emboldened by the sun and the lack of monsters they believed might drag them into an icy grave. One summer night, as twilight fell, a boy playing in a dandelion field discovered that monsters knew no season."

"Hold on." Clio's eyes widened. She sat up. "Are you going to kill him?"

"What?"

She shifted in her seat. "The little boy."

"There are worse tragedies than death, Ms. Farren." Nikolai scanned her dress again, the way the fabric almost swallowed her whole. She was so delicate, so *human*. And the glimpse of distaste in her expression—it came too close to the hate he feared, expected. He shook his head. "Perhaps I shouldn't be telling you this story."

Her lips parted, a thread of hurt weaving through her eyes. "Why not?"

"I don't want to make you uncomfortable."

Clio's eyes hardened, and she scoffed. "Unbelievable. I'm not uncomfortable, I'm just—" She chewed her lip. "I just wanted a warning if that's how the story ends, to prepare myself."

Nikolai studied her face, determined she was telling the truth, and muttered, "No, he doesn't die."

"Okay." She leaned back, a silent encouragement for him to continue.

Nikolai cleared his throat and said, "From the forest, a voice started singing. It lured the boy—"

"Wait."

He blew out a sharp sigh, raising his brow at her. At this rate, he'd probably never get through the story anyway—she was like a child with a fear of wandering, never quite able to let go. "What have you taken issue with now, Ms. Farren?"

"His name."

Nikolai blinked, repeating those words in his head, trying to make sense of it. He didn't think he'd slipped up.

"You keep saying 'the boy'," she clarified. "But what was his name?"

Ah. "It's just an old folktale. He doesn't need one." Clio tilted her head in annoyance, glaring at Nikolai until he sighed. "Fine. For now, we'll call him...Dmitri. Happy?"

She shrugged, but the smug smile teasing her lips told him she was.

"*Dmitri,*" he said with a roll of his eyes, "was lured from the field in which he played, and into the trees. Once under the dark canopy, he was taken."

Clio opened her mouth, but Nikolai clicked his tongue in reprimand.

"Patience, Ms. Farren. You'll never find out anything if you keep interrupting me." His tone was meant to taunt Clio... test her. The words came out more frustrated than he intended them to. She squinted, her cupid's bow whitening as she pressed her lips together in a vow of silence. He doubted it would last long.

"Dmitri was taken by a woman," he continued, "or what *looked* like a woman, at least—at first. 'Beautiful' was what he thought when she first emerged from the shadows. She wore a dress weaved of blue satin and silk. Her skin was so pale it seemed to glow like the moon. Her hair twisted into perfect, dark ringlets. He'd never seen someone who looked like that before, who dressed like that, so he forgot to scream as she scooped him into her arms.

"When Dmitri started fighting, he realized something was off about her. No matter how hard he kicked, how deeply he scratched her arms, how many times he bit her, she wouldn't let him go. She held him against her chest without flinching, walked without faltering. Any harm he dealt, any blood he drew, healed within minutes. She continued to hum her song as she carried him, for miles and miles. And after he stopped shouting, she whispered to him. One word, over and over."

Nikolai's voice dropped, the truth churning in his head, too violent to be spoken above a murmur. "By the time she carried Dmitri into a cave near dawn, he realized the word she whispered was a name. *Julian*." He dared a glance up from the thread he'd been picking at on the arm of his chair.

Clio watched from beneath her dark, thick lashes. Her fingers sifted through Poppet's fur, gentle and doting. Listening, enraptured. Her attention did strange things to his stomach. Maybe it was thirst. Maybe it was something else entirely.

She smiled slightly, and it was enough to urge him on.

"He didn't understand much else of what she said as they camped out in that dark cave for the day. Nothing but that name, spoken directed at him so often that he started to suspect she'd mistaken him for another child. But when he tried to tell her his real name, she turned away and spoke to shadows dancing on the walls."

Clio frowned. "She was sick, wasn't she?"

Nikolai raised a brow. "More than that, I'm afraid. The shadows—I'm not speaking metaphorically. They were real. They fluxed over the walls, stretching toward the woman like long fingers reaching. The shadows curled around her, weaving through the ringlets of her hair, and hovering above her head like black and violet storm clouds. Like the winter nightlights that rattled his sky back home. Dmitri couldn't hear anything beyond his captor's cries echoing through the cave, but he guessed from the way she spoke that the shadows were talking back to her."

Clio stared at him, her eyes wide, her mouth parted as if she might ask another question. Nikolai waited, but the question didn't come. After a minute, she seemed to return to herself and clamped her mouth shut. Blinked expectantly.

Nikolai shrugged one shoulder and said, "This pattern continued for several days, walking through the night, camping under cover during the day. She kept a vice grip on his wrist or close enough to grab him should he run off, night and day. They stopped several times along a nearby river to keep him hydrated. The woman foraged berries from the forest for him, but Dmitri's stomach still began to ache. He was starving and he only assumed the woman was, too. She never ate, not a single thing for all the days they spent traveling."

"I'm not feeling confident in their survival right about now," Clio grumbled, pursing her lips as if to call him a liar.

He rested a hand over his silent heart. "Have a little faith, Ms. Farren, please."

Clio laughed, just a tiny little huff. "Get to the point then."

Nikolai smiled, but that grin faded as he said, "On the tenth night, instead of waking Dmitri to continue their journey, the woman snuck out of the cave without him. When he woke alone, to a dwindling fire and the woman's cloak laid over him, he ran.

"He didn't know the area. It was farther south than his family had ever traveled, but he didn't stop, didn't look back, didn't pause. The night was alive around him, animals watching his escape, growling as he passed them by. The forest absorbed his panic and returned it to him as he flew between the trees.

"Then, a darkness closed in. A heaviness. Those living shadows found him.

"The canopy rustled above him, and a dark mass fell from the trees. It took a moment for the boy to realize that it was the woman who had taken him. He'd ran right into her. And in her arms, she held a snarling mountain cat. She sank her teeth into its neck and tore it open. Blood surged from the animal's arteries and the woman angled herself to keep it from marking her clothes. With all the grace of an animal herself, she closed her mouth over the wound and drank."

Clio paled. "She drank the blood?"

He nodded. "The woman was so preoccupied with her meal that she didn't seem to see Dmitri, so he ducked through the trees again, running as fast as his small human body could carry him. He made it to a dirt road. And it was pure chance that a carriage rumbled by in that moment. Pure chance that the occupants of the cab were awake and had taken that moment to look out the window to see him stumbling over the dusty thoroughfare."

Clio slumped in her seat, a look of relief softening her features.

Nikolai's ribs tightened. The story wasn't anywhere close to finished. Everything within him demanded that he continue —that he speak the truth that so desperately wanted to be known. For her sake, he squashed it, even as it writhed in his chest like a pinned, bleeding creature.

It would be so much easier to just leave the story there, with the hope of a rescue.

Nikolai had offered his origin before he could stop himself and now he wanted to reel it back in. He wanted to retreat to his room, but didn't—*couldn't*—because Clio was still cradling Poppet.

This young woman was seeing parts of him no one had ever asked for before. And even if she never knew the truth, maybe it was enough, that she listened for a minute or two. He racked his brain for a way to guide her away from the story and out of his library.

"Well?"

Nikolai met her eager gaze. "Well, what?"

"What happened?" Clio cocked her head, her lips trembling as if she sensed the bitterness on the other side of that question. "Did he find his way back home?"

Home. What was home, really? "I'm not sure you want to know what happened next, Ms. Farren."

"Don't tell me what I want," she snapped. "I want to hear everything."

Nikolai considered the uncompromising will on her face, the same that he witnessed yesterday in his office. It was a look he imagined might terrify mortal men. Hell, it unsettled *him*.

He rapped his fingers on the armrest.

A low rumble sounded across the table—her gut growling. He pounced on the escape. "I'll finish the story if you follow me to the kitchen and let me feed you. I can hear your stomach from here."

She blinked, but he only rose from his seat and gestured to the hallway with a smile. Clio stood, licking her lips, and laid the slumbering monster on his reading chair.

8

Nikolai nodded to the breakfast bar as they entered the kitchen. "Sit down and make yourself comfortable." *As much as you can in that fluff.*

Clio arranged herself on one of the stools. She'd brought the book from the library, setting it on the counter but leaving a hand on it, as if the feel of the leather under her hand was a comfort she couldn't be without. He understood that feeling better than most.

The more he watched her move in that dress, the more glaring her disapproval became.

It *did* overwhelm her natural beauty. He wondered how she might dazzle in a curve-hugging slip of a dress, how her dark hair might stand out against a rich color like green or red.

Turning away, he banished the thoughts. He shouldn't be imagining such things of a guest—of a bride. He told her, "The manor's chef and manager, Mrs. Itzli, prepared a few casseroles that should be sufficient for your stay. I'm happy to see you've already been enjoying the cookies. Anything you find in here, you can have."

As he opened the massive stainless steel fridge, the scent of animal meat smacked into him, and he suppressed a gag. Holding his breath, he leaned in and inspected Mrs. Itzli's casseroles. He peeked at the first, sniffed shallowly, and asked over his shoulder, "Pork?"

Her nose wrinkled.

Chuckling, Nikolai moved on. "I'll take that as a no." He smelled the next dish and bit his lip against the threatening heave. "Chicken?"

When he looked over his shoulder this time, a soft smile pulled at her lips, and she nodded. He pulled the blue glass dish out of the fridge and set it on the counter between them, letting the appliance slam shut at his back. As he turned to the cupboards, he filled his lungs with familiar, clean air and held it.

Nikolai felt Clio stare a hole through his back as he flipped through the cabinets, hunting for a plate. He finally found the right shelf after half a dozen tries and when he pivoted back to the counter, the woman leaned forward on her elbows, hiding a smile behind her fingers.

With confusion pulling at his brow, he returned the faint grin and peeled back the beeswax foil. It was at that moment he realized he needed something to scoop the creamy portion out and he dove into another investigation of the drawers.

Clio's smile grew, fingers curling under her chin as he found the jangling drawer of silverware and withdrew a spoon and fork, unsure of which was proper for a dish like this.

He scooped a generous amount onto the ceramic plate, cleaned the dirtied spoon off in the sink, and returned the dish to its place in the fridge.

Her grin split, revealing sleek, straight teeth as she rested her head on a softly curled hand. Her amusement radiated into the air, bristling at his edges.

"What is it?" he asked.

Lips pursing, she raised her free hand in surrender and shook her head unconvincingly. "Nothing."

Nikolai carried her plate to the small square appliance set into the wall beside the ovens, knowing its general use. He'd seen staff warm food up in it before, but never watched closely enough to determine how. *What use does my beast have for a quick heat?*

Warm blood only satisfied directly from the tap.

He pressed the largest button and the door swung open. After placing the plate inside the white, glassy miracle oven, he scanned the black board on the right. The dozens of buttons imposed on his brain, taunting him with strange symbols.

Clio's haughty voice made him jump. "Haven't you ever seen a microwave before?"

"Of course I have. I just—"

She giggled. "What sort of privilege prevented you from using a microwave?"

Privilege? He frowned at her. She had no clue. None at all. And so he couldn't be upset.

Clio pressed her lips together, stifling the laughter, and nodded at the appliance. "Just press the button that says, 'Quick Start' a couple times."

He did and the machine roared to life. Nikolai watched apprehensively as the glass plate revolved. Clio chuckled again, into her fingers, and he dutifully ignored her.

After the appliance beeped, he gave the food to his guest, arranging the plate neatly with the fork and spoon beside it.

She leaned in to smell the plate, eyes fluttering.

"Wait." He reached across the counter and plucked a green satin napkin from the folded stack in the middle of the bar.

Snapping it open, he stepped close, tucking the edges into her collar. The instinct surprised him, the urge so immediate and undeniable that his body acted before his head could interfere, but what surprised him more was the way she didn't recoil from his approach or flinch as his fingertips brushed her skin. Her soft, warm, flawless skin.

She only gasped, eyes flicking up and down and all around as her cheeks filled with color. This close, he could see blue veins beneath the translucence of her skin and silently praised himself for holding his breath. He bet she would smell sweeter than most.

Best not to tempt fate. He let his hands fall back to his sides and backed away.

"Would hate for you to stain your *uncomfortable* dress," he explained.

"Thank you," she murmured, staring intently at her lunch as she picked up her fork—*not a spoon, then.* He snatched the utensil up and, after cleaning it a second time, returned it to the proper drawer.

"Aren't you going to eat?" she asked, swirling a speared piece of chicken in the white-gray sauce.

Smiling warmly, he said, "I already have." Her eyes flicked to the fridge behind him, as if weighing his lie. As if she were counting the chances.

"Well," he sighed, stuffing his hands in his slacks. "I'll let you eat in peace."

She set her fork down, metal clinking against ceramic, and glared at him. "You promised to tell me the rest of the story."

"It doesn't have a pleasant ending, I'm afraid. Maybe it's best we stop."

"Do you usually break your promises?" She gripped the edge of the counter like she might climb up on it.

A rock lodged in his throat. Her eyes burned his skin. And for some reason, he couldn't answer. He wanted to say he always kept his word, but the unhinged, beastly part of him laughed mockingly.

"Fine," he breathed. "But please suppress the frustration on your face. At least until I'm finished. You look like you've been drinking curdled milk."

She gaped at him, her lips twitching at the corners. Words formed on the tip of her tongue, but she caught herself, shut her mouth, and raised her brows in expectation.

"And eat," he demanded. She popped the chicken in her mouth and chewed. As her tongue registered the flavors, she moaned.

The sound made every hair on Nikolai's neck stand on end. Those glass containers in his mind roared. One cracked at last, spewing a torrent toward him like a snake wrapping around his ankles.

Nikolai leaned against the counter, steepling his hands in front of his mouth. The torrent of waves flooded the moonlit lane in his head. A shattered crystalline box floated in shards. Glimmering memories lapped at his neck, but he could still breathe. For now.

He took a deep breath and said, "The carriage stopped and the man who had shouted the order to halt them stepped out of the cab, beckoning to Dmitri. *He was strong*, the boy thought. Strong and kind and visibly alarmed about a child being left alone in the middle of nowhere. Dmitri had every confidence that this carriage was sent by the gods themselves, stirred into action by the family that must be praying and searching for him.

"It didn't matter much that these strangers couldn't understand him when he spoke, when he tried to explain what had happened. Not as he was led into the carriage, where two women waited. And it didn't matter much that he couldn't interpret their many questions either. Not as they fed him treats and fussed over his haggard appearance. The carriage rolled onward, and for the first time in several days, Dmitri felt safe."

Clio set her fork down, the silver clinking again. She glared at her food as she muttered, "Why do I get the feeling I'm going to hate you here in a moment?"

"Because you have a healthy dose of cynicism running through your veins, as you've already admitted. What good story could end before the villain dies?"

Her brow stitched and she glanced up out the corner of her eye. "That's a very sad thing to say."

Nikolai chuckled. "Let me guess: you're a firm believer in redemption?"

"Well," she glanced around the room, thrumming her fingers on the edge of the counter, "yes, I guess I am."

"Not everyone deserves redemption."

She met his gaze. A look of true confusion contorted her face.

"Not every heart can afford it," Nikolai clarified. "The change that requires." And sometimes change meant nothing at all. It didn't erase the bad. Sometimes change only served to make someone feel prettier on the outside, while the heart within rotted away.

Clio continued to blink at him, as if wrestling with the meaning of what he said.

There was one sure way to help her understand. Her stomach gurgled and Nikolai nodded at her plate. "Please keep eating, Ms. Farren." She rolled her eyes but picked up the fork.

When she'd stuffed her mouth, he continued the story. "The carriage jerked, as if it had hit a pothole. But then the wood was groaning, the wheels weren't turning, the driver was screaming. The horses at the front danced, crying out from the sudden stop. When the man in the cab steadied himself from the jolt, he opened the door and looked out into the night. So quick there was no tracking it, something wrenched the man up and out. Above them, there was a screech and blood fell around the cab like rain. It streaked the windows and dribbled down into the cab through the cracked entrance.

"They shied back from that open door, but then the other side of the cab ripped open. One of the women was snatched out before Dmitri had time to blink. It was at that moment, he realized he was the furthest thing from safe."

Clio had stopped eating again, but he couldn't bring himself to scold her. This was enough to make anyone lose their appetite—even a beast like himself. His every muscle was tight, so tight he had to make a conscious effort not to leave a dent in the counter under his fingers.

Mrs. Itzli would kill him if he damaged her kitchen—well, she'd try.

He just had to finish the story, had to get through this so he could pack up the boxes and drain the lane in his head. *Pretend it isn't real.*

Nikolai swallowed the venom welling under his tongue and said, "A fresh storm of blood cascaded over the cab. Shadows seeped in from either entrance, swirling over the ceiling. The last woman in the carriage with Dmitri didn't seem to notice the shadows. Dmitri shrunk to the floor as the door on the right was torn from its hinges.

"His captor—that beautiful woman in blue silk—stepped up into the confines of the cab. Her clothes were drenched in crimson death. The ringlets of her dark hair were plastered down and dripping. Her teeth were bared, lined with red as she hissed, the sound rumbling through the night like a low roll of thunder. The last victim surged for the other door, but it snapped shut as if the shadows were holding it in place. Dmitri's captor grabbed the last woman and snapped her neck, and his only hope for rescue slumped to the floor. He peered up at the monster before him, but it did not attack.

"The woman who had sung him into captivity only stared at him. And he suddenly realized that blood streamed down her face, not from her mouth but from her eyes. She was crying. The stain around her mouth was dark, half-dried. She hadn't fed on the bodies that now painted the carriage, and as she glanced down at the woman at her feet, she wept harder. The shadows closed in to swirl around her head."

Nikolai shuddered.

The memory of her shouldn't have the power to affect him like this anymore. She was gone. Out of his life. He was free...

And yet.

"Dmitri didn't need to speak her language to interpret what he saw on her face—the regret and loss and anger. So much anger it seemed to roll off her like storm clouds. She blamed him for what happened that night, blamed him for running off. And the boy came to blame himself, too. It was his fault the carriage stopped, that it took him in, that it tried to protect him when there was no protection great enough to save him."

"He didn't know," Clio interjected softly.

Nikolai grimaced. "Four people died that night because of his actions."

"He was a child," she argued.

Nikolai paused, gripping the edge of the counter to ground himself. "Yes, he was."

She knows it's not real, he assured himself. *It's just a scary fable to her.*

Her head bobbed as if she had gone dizzy... and he saw it. The white surrounding her pupils so completely—that light in her eyes that bordered metallic silver. *Lovely.*

She hadn't looked away, not once as he finished the story. And Nikolai wondered what she found in his eyes that made her stay. Whatever it was, he knew it didn't hold a candle to the silver ice he found in hers.

Clio finally broke eye contact, groaning softly as her eyes landed on the plate in front of her. "I can't stand the thought of food anymore."

Me neither.

She swallowed in a way that deafened him. "Is that how it ends?"

"Yes and no," Nikolai said quietly. "One end weaves into other beginnings. The story goes on and on, if you wish to hear what comes next."

She rose from her seat. "Thank you for indulging my curiosity, but I think I've heard enough for one day."

He figured she was being delicate about it, that she'd actually heard enough for a lifetime. And perhaps it was a foolish, broken hope to wish someone would listen to the entire story—to wish someone would want to.

"You can take it," he said before she disappeared into the hall.

She paused. "Take what?"

He gestured toward the book on the counter. "Any book you'd like, as long as you return it."

Clio's throat bobbed as she slid the novel into her grasp. She muttered a thank you and turned away. He watched carefully as she walked to the hallway—but then she tripped over her skirt.

Nikolai was there in an instant, crouching in front of her, gripping her arms to suspend the nosedive. He'd moved without thought, without gravity. Knowing only that he had to keep her safe.

Clio huffed a curse, her heart thudding loudly. He chuckled at the foul word as her breath caressed his face, and his laugh cut off as he finally scented her.

She wasn't sweet. Not like the ordinary honeyed veins he'd tapped before. The artery in her neck radiated dense floral notes, a blooming rosebush, hinted with pillars of ancient sea salt.

His beast took notice from the confines of its chamber.

Nikolai leaned into it. He lost himself in her eyes. The silver winked at him, and he could only pluck one word from the chaos of his mind to respond. "*Fascinating,*" he murmured.

Everything about her hardened as she ripped out of his hold. She pushed past him, and his flared nose followed every step. Her bare feet slapped against the floor as she exited the room and continued in a steady march all the way to the lobby.

He no longer knew what the next two weeks had in store for him, or what life would be left by the time this freeze thawed.

9

Clio read until the sky outside her window faded to onyx. The snowstorm resumed a menacing beat against the manor as she devoured chapter after chapter without so much as a pause to breathe, battling waves of drowsiness as she stretched across the king-sized bed.

The clock on her nightstand was creeping towards two by the time she peeled herself off the duvet and reached for her robe. Although toasty, dry air blasted through the vents every hour on the nose, the floor bit at her toes.

There must be some sort of fault in the windowsill of the bedroom.

Last night she'd needed to layer a sweatshirt over her nightgown before she could get to sleep. Not that she had much luck sleeping in recent months anyway, but an initial hour or two before the dreams started was better than nothing.

Midnight. That was the threshold at which they appeared, drawn to her like crowds to a church bell. Or flies to a corpse.

Clio glanced at the oval window seat, ignoring her shadowed, hazy reflection. She couldn't see an inch into the flurry beyond, nor could she hear herself think without first acknowledging the hum of the storm.

It was as good a concealment as she would ever get.

The hall smothered the wind to a dull roar as she tiptoed to the French doors adjacent to the elevator. Slipping into the stairwell, she swallowed back a hiss as her bare feet met the marble of the landing. *Socks would have been a good idea*—but she pressed on without turning back, welcoming the chill.

Her mind sharpened, bursting from the harbor of that afternoon's distractions.

Clio had softened when Nikolai led her to the kitchen and fed her. When he floundered to navigate the cabinets and operate a basic appliance. He was charming, in a strange way. Maybe even kind.

It had been years and years since someone tried to care for her like that.

Fascinating, he'd said.

It was better than odd but not by much. Sore memories swelled to greet her. Everything about Nikolai's story reminded her of Nyah, and of all the questions she had no answer to.

As she rounded the second landing, Clio lost grip of the thoughts that longed to wander. She fell back to the day she met Nyah. The tall, dark beauty approached Clio's desk at their all-girls private school and initiated a friendly conversation.

At first, she anticipated cruelty. But when Nyah did comment on Clio's eyes, it wasn't the way their peers did. She used words like *badass*. Words that didn't make Clio feel ashamed for existing.

Nikolai's use of *fascinating* made her feel the same way. The problem was that she couldn't be sure what that actually meant—whether he was freaked by it or surprised or intrigued in the way that an artifact collector would be about a bone found in excavation.

And then, there was his story. The shadows.

Nyah was just as odd as Clio, in her own way. She'd admitted to approaching Clio because of *"meddling visitants"* that encouraged a friendship between them.

Clio always assumed Nyah revered those guides like a god. She never thought Nyah could have seriously *heard them*—those voices. Seen them.

Not until that damn voicemail.

Not until Nikolai.

What are the chances, she thought dizzily, *that everything is only coincidence?*

Clio halted on the last landing, in front of the lobby doors. The wind howled just beyond, screaming against the glass at the front of the manor. She bit her lip to stifle her labored breathing and squeezed through the doorway.

The darkness swallowed her, but her vision quickly adjusted, bringing the room into a dim, foggy focus. Night was always such a gentle companion to her—never hurting to look through, never demanding her time. She preferred the world that way, even if it was a little ill-defined.

Clio made her way to the front desk, weaving through the decorative columns and skirting the belly of the room where she knew most obstacles were.

Her feet had gone entirely numb by the time she ducked beneath the red velvet rope and golden sign that read *Staff Only*. As she straightened, she scanned the desk. It was tidy, occupied by only the computer screen and a thin binder.

The wood gleamed as she approached the desktop, no settling of dust to be found—or disturbed. She fingered the edges of the monitor until she found a button on the back. She shielded her eyes as she pressed it, bracing herself for the blinding blue light.

What she didn't anticipate was the robotic chime that blared through the speakers, echoing out into the rest of the room.

Her heart skipped a beat, every muscle in her body freezing. Only her eyes moved as she tracked the shadows and marked the archway to the library. To Nikolai's room. She stood there for what felt like an eternity, listening for movement in the hall, finger at the ready to switch the monitor back off. But she only heard the storm and the immediate stillness all around.

Though her heart continued to pound in her ears, she turned her attention to the screen. She tugged the keyboard drawer open and double-clicked on the only account available. The screen shifted.

A password. She needed a password to get in.

Glancing through the rest of the drawers, she only found office supplies and various feminine items, including a ridiculous number of fruity lip balms. As she rolled her eyes, her gaze caught on the binder at the edge of the desk.

She took the flimsy folder in her hand, trying and failing to ignore the sticky note on the face addressed to Nikolai. The receptionist wished him a "very nice hiatus."

Clio could guess what else the girl wished for.

She flipped the binder open and could barely contain her triumph. There, on the very first page, was a list of the passwords for everything from the computer to the website to the security system that she hadn't caught a whiff of since arriving. There really wasn't much use for one out here, in the middle of... well, nowhere.

With a few taps of the keyboard, she'd been granted access to the account and then the reservation software. She pulled up

Nyah's name and scanned every line of information. Nyah stayed for three days in a suite on the second floor, but there weren't any other charges. No meals? And the reason listed for her stay: Earth Conservation.

Clio's eyebrows stitched together. Nyah hadn't given a shit about things like that, *had she*? How much did Nyah withhold from her during their friendship? Too much was left unspoken, she *knew* that. But what if this was all her fault? What if it was this ignorance that killed her best friend?

On Clio's second scan of the page, she realized: the dates for Nyah's stay were during the first week in January, the last freeze, when the manor should have been closed.

Like it is now.

The voice came quiet as a trickling fountain but edged in cruelty. "What are you doing?"

10

Clio jolted and her eyes met Nikolai's across the counter.

Darkness danced across his face, lingering on his furrowed brow and the taunting slant of his mouth. His hair was tousled, damp and curling at the ends. Fresh from a shower.

"I—I, uhm," She battled back the swelling of her throat as he coasted around the corner of the desk. She gathered her wits enough to tap a few keys on the board, effectively killing the software before Nikolai could glimpse the screen.

He frowned as he unclasped the rope barrier and slipped behind the desk. Then, he reinstated the barrier behind him—a silent, pointed threat.

"Well? Anything to say for yourself?"

Clio dug her nails into the skin of her palms and twisted to face Nikolai, mustering a contrite look. Her voice betrayed her, trembling as she said, "My mother asked me to make a reservation for her."

"Is that so?" Nikolai took a step forward and Clio echoed

the movement by pressing back against the desk, and the drawer to the keyboard slammed shut.

Her composure unraveled against her will. She grappled at the fraying ends. "Yes."

Dark sweatpants hung from his hips and his button-up was replaced by a tight tee that exposed his chiseled arms. He trapped her in the crook of the desk with one calculated, idle stride.

The glow of the monitor crept past her shoulder to illuminate his face. She could smell his soap—woodsy and warm. His mask, the glaze that made him seem like fine china, refined and hospitable, was gone. He had transmuted into something closer to the marble beneath her toes. Immoveable... unrelenting.

Nikolai's teeth flashed as he towered over her, "In the middle of the night?"

Her heels lifted off the ground as his hands gripped the desk behind her. The hard, wooden ledge dug into her lower back. She endeavored to regain some space, some air that was not steeped with his presence, but it was a useless effort.

His woodsy presence filled her senses—not just the smell this time, but the actual sensation of being enveloped by dense forest. Her heart raced to the beat of the wild animals prowling amid those trees, the creatures that came to life in his darkness.

Clio shuddered. He was so close, and she wondered why she couldn't feel the heat of his body. She wondered if he were just as cold as she was.

"I couldn't sleep." She cleared her throat. "I decided to walk off the extra energy."

"But avoided the elevator?" His head tilted to the side, his eyes prodding for a weakness.

She shrugged. "I wanted to take the stairs."

"Says the woman who spent half the morning floating between levels."

Her stomach hollowed out.

Nikolai grinned, but she saw nothing comforting in it. His left hand whipped out, a blur of moonbeam skin, and Clio couldn't stop the gasp that issued from her mouth. She couldn't contain the wince in time to realize that Nikolai was reaching for the monitor behind her.

Her reaction registered with him instantly, and he went still. Shadows crowded his face as the screen went dark behind her. She saw the question in his eyes though, even without light, and acid pumped through her veins.

Clio planted her heels back on the floor and spat, "I didn't think my daily activities were any of your concern."

Behind her back, she heard the sound of the power cord being ripped from the monitor, then from the wall. His eyes hardened. "It is when you're invading my privacy and lying about it." he hissed. Nikolai looped the cord around his hand and slipped it into his sweatpants.

Well, that opportunity for mining answers is officially gone.

"I have no idea what you're talking about." Clio side-stepped, but Nikolai's arm blocked her path. Her head snapped up, tongue poised with rebuke, when their eyes met for a second time—and something changed.

She couldn't decide whether it was a trick of the sudden darkness or the flaw in her vision, but his pupils seemed to dilate to the point of consuming her. The black orbs eclipsed every trace of the pretty blue that had been there a moment ago.

Clio couldn't breathe. She found herself paralyzed in all places but her heart as he huffed a laugh, and the warmth of his lungs caressed her cheek.

Nikolai's expression softened, opening like the gates to a fortress—as if he'd been guarded against her until this instant. As if he had been holding back but wasn't anymore. He crooned, "You don't want to run away, do you? We haven't finished talking."

Her skin prickled. *No, of course not.* Why would she run from him when he was being so gentle, when he looked at her like... like *that?*

Her body responded in contradiction to her instincts. She leaned toward him, so close that her breasts might brush against his chest if either of them breathed too deeply. The tension in her brow smoothed, her jaw slackening and lips parting. Her eyes surrendered to a dream-like wilt.

Clio couldn't think clearly, but she felt the mutiny of her innermost being, begging her to walk away. She willed herself to turn her head, trusting the gut she too often ignored at great personal cost—but Nikolai caught her chin. His thumb pressed down enough that her lips parted further. He might as well have shackled her wrists... might as well have bound her body in chains and gagged her for all she was able to fight against him.

He clicked his tongue, eyes glittering with amusement. "Now, that's not very polite." His voice was so melodic, she found herself hoping Heaven sounded even half as beautiful. She could listen to the low tenor for eternity. *But this isn't heaven. And he is no god.*

Clio tried once more to pull away—a weak, lethargic tug. His fingers tightened.

"Stubborn," he muttered, bending close enough to share breath. He smelled absolutely delicious. "Would you like to tell me what you're doing down here, or do I need to coax it out of you?"

And she nearly told him. About Nyah and everything else that led her to the manor. The thoughts sprung up easily, forming in her throat like a knot she wished to be rid of. He exhaled, a sweet breath that invaded her senses. Her mouth watered for a taste, to devour in a way she wasn't familiar with.

NO.

Clio's mind rebounded, the world returning to a crisp focus. She smacked Nikolai's hand off of her face and said, "*I told you I was taking a walk.*"

Nikolai recoiled, eyes and nostrils flaring. His pupils contracted and a sliver of blue reappeared. It was enough for Clio to expel the scent of him from her lungs, enough for her to start trembling in frustration.

He didn't acknowledge the murderous scowl she aimed at him. He only whispered, "What are you?"

"Right now?" Her tone corroded. "Agitated mostly, and uncomfortable."

His gaze lowered, scrutinizing her body inch-by-inch. Clio didn't need to look down to know what it was his eyes snagged on. She crossed her arms over her chest.

"I would ask if you're getting cold feet about the wedding, but I think that's a given considering you're barefoot. Nothing you're wearing is suited to a midnight stroll. You've gone a bit... stiff." He smirked.

She squinted at him. "I can't say my room is any better— I'm freezing everywhere. You need to invest in better insulation."

"Oh, I wouldn't dare carve into this old girl's walls," he said, as if there were skeletons hidden in them. "But I'm more than willing to adjust the thermostat for you."

Clio replied through gritted teeth, "If it wouldn't be too much of an inconvenience."

Anger flashed in his eyes, the color returned to brilliant blue, and he leaned in. "We're past pleasantries now, don't you think? You've been nothing but an inconvenience to me. Seeing as how you've displayed little respect for boundaries and my personal property, you might as well cut the bullshit and speak your mind."

Her upper lip curled. "I want for you to back *the fuck* off of me."

Nikolai smirked as he pushed away from the desk and gestured to the red rope, inviting her to leave. As she ducked under it, he said, "Sleep well, Ms. Farren."

And she pretended not to hear him.

Yet the words followed her into the elevator, up through the floors, and across the hallway to the honeymoon suite. She clutched at her robe, wishing the thin material could warm the icy spear of dread in her spine. She wished she could stop looking over her shoulder, wished she could stop imagining Nikolai emerging from the stairwell or one of the other suites as she walked by. She wished she could forget those unfathomable black eyes.

Her hands shook as they unlocked her suite. Her whole body trembled as she slipped inside and collapsed against the door.

She knew if Nikolai wanted to, he could follow her. He could get into her room. He could do anything and no one would be around to stop it. Her phone was in the bedroom, but who could she call? What could she say? No one would believe her... they never did.

Clio had told Duncan she didn't break, that she was stronger than he assumed, but that wasn't true. She only existed. As dust, or something else equally as worthless. If life swept her away, the world wouldn't even notice. Maybe it would even shine a little easier without her.

Her legs buckled and she slid to the floor, tucking her knees to her chest. She watched for shadows in the crack beneath the door and didn't move until morning.

11

"Fuck," Nikolai peddled backwards, slamming the door to the library shut with enough force that he heard a few books on the other side fly from the shelf.

He had just opened his passageway for the first time in three days, intent on stealing away to his office, when a cloud of her scent struck him. Her salty essence burned up his nostrils like an ocean breeze. Thick, visceral, immediate.

She was close by, perhaps still in the dome where she'd laid out beneath the lights last night. He expected her to return to her room, but instead of listening for her retreat, he fell into a willful hibernation instead.

The scent of her had been creeping into his quarters through the vents, past the seal of his bedroom door, beckoning to him with tantalizing tendrils. He could only barely shove down the instinct to follow their lead.

Against his will, the beast rose.

It began when he caught Clio behind the front desk, when he drew so close he could feel her breath on his skin. When she resisted his enthrallment. *That* had been a goddamn shock, and the other inside him didn't like it. His beast should not have risen so quickly, not mere days after a dosage. But here it was, scratching from the inside, filling his mouth with so much venom he wanted to spit.

Clio didn't leave her suite the day after the incident. She shut herself away, not even braving the main level for meals, which concerned him more than he was willing to admit at the time. He blew out a heavy sigh of relief when he heard the elevator rolling the second morning and she shuffled around the kitchen for breakfast. She called her mother as she ate, and made two other calls that led to voicemail.

He had hoped she would call someone to pick her up, but she didn't.

The worst of the urges started that afternoon, when Clio paced the hall to his library and eventually slipped inside. Her second library visit was brief—he only heard the whisper of leather against wood as she returned the book she'd borrowed and picked out a new one, then her hurried footsteps back to her room. Her scent seeped in afterward, a belated effect, and he'd dug his nails into the surface of his desk as he wrestled with himself.

He relocated to the basement, resting in the musky bedroom and meandering through the corridors like a ghost— but her scent still found him through the layers of stone, turning the basement into a prison of his own making.

Nikolai hadn't been able to hide from the bits of her that drifted down to him last night, especially as she sat in the dome. So, he chugged enough vintage moonshine to drown a lesser deceased man. His brain shut down entirely to repair and he slept in blissful ignorance until this morning.

Maybe that had been a mistake—maybe he had compromised the demon blood's longevity by injuring himself—

because the torture of the last two days were nothing compared to *this*. This profuse, metaphysical wrench in his core when she filled his senses without barrier.

Find her. Draw her in. All will be well.

He shook his head.

No, it wouldn't. He knew it wouldn't if he submitted to that voice. The voice was his own, but detached from humanity, detached from everything he wished to hold onto.

He returned to the basement to wait out Clio's slumber, even while the thoughts kept coming. They followed him into the corridor, sticking to him like her scent in his nostrils, like her thorns in his brain. Nikolai could imagine what it might be like to wait for her to descend the stairs in the library, what her cries might sound like when he grabbed her—what she would taste like.

He shivered.

Nikolai wanted to hold her down and see exactly how long she could resist his enthrallment if he hovered above her. If he dragged his teeth across her skin and let the venom sink in. He drew in a shaky breath and paused at the end of the first hall, focusing on the hair-line crack that spidered down from the top of the wall.

He needed to anchor himself.

The likelihood that she would still resist, that he would have no power over her, that there would be no way to quiet her screams or keep her from exposing him when he was finished with her, was too great a risk. If he submitted to that beastly voice, what he did to Ms. Farren would not be gentle or sensual like what he did with women in his bed. Feeding on her would be purely predatory and the outcome unpredictable.

But he knew, if she could resist his influence, it could only end in death.

So what if it does, the beast growled. *Let her die.* He

couldn't leave for a hunt—not when the woman stepped over boundaries and threatened everything he built for himself here. His manor. His home.

And that last dose, he would need it soon—too soon. What would happen when that dosage ran out on him in another three days' time? Was he only delaying the inevitable? The scene flashed in his mind again, of Clio stretched out beneath him, her hands gripping his arms as he pressed down, as he licked and nipped—

Nikolai punched the wall. Once, twice, needing the pain and the scent of his own blood to cleanse his senses. He needed to feel breakable. Human.

It's her fault. She had it coming from the moment she forced her way into your manor.

Nikolai landed another blow against the wall, this one hard enough to leave a streak of his blood behind. He'd let her in. He hadn't fought it very hard. It was his own damn fault for—for not wanting to be alone.

Mrs. Itzli was right, she'd always been right.

But she's digging into your personal affairs. She's forcing your hand.

He threw a wallop that had the basement shaking.

You've heard the way her mother speaks to her, the others that won't return her calls. No one would miss her, not really.

Again.

Again. His bones fractured and snapped back together all at once. He welcomed the sting.

Come on, when was the last time you had a spirited hunt? The demons are all the same. Her blood is different.

NO. He didn't hunt like that anymore. The concrete shuddered beneath his fist, fissuring at last, and the thundering crack seemed to breach something in him—sequestering the beast away.

Nikolai braced his palms on either side of the rift and hung his head. He squeezed his eyes shut as his breathing calmed.

He heard the shuffling then, of Clio waking above him. She descended the stairs slowly and Nikolai dug his fingers into the wall, crumbling concrete to keep himself contained. Clio made it to the library and paused. She walked across the room to his passageway.

A gentle knock sounded, followed by her voice saying, "Nikolai, I think we've just had an earthquake. Should I be worried?"

He ground his teeth.

Clio waited a moment, weight shifting to and fro, but seemed to pick up on the pointed silence because her feet padded back across the library. *Barefoot.*

His mouth flooded.

To his left, a mewl echoed through the hallway. Poppet stared daggers at him, her tail flicking like a whip. Her tongue licked at her whiskers, taunting him.

"Mind your own business, cat," he snarled, and aimed for the musky bed to hibernate again.

12

Clio's phone finally lost reception. She'd tried every public area of the manor, even bundled up and took a few steps into the blustering storm outside. The snow hadn't stopped since yesterday morning when she woke up in the dome to the ground vibrating beneath her.

A quake, she guessed, though she'd never experienced one in the city. She knew the weather was building to a blizzard, to the peak of the Freeze. The research she'd done suggested the possibility of a storm like this interfering with cell service.

Now, the true isolation would begin.

She drifted toward the edge of the lobby, behind the columns where the tarnished brass vents were located.

Clio let the warm air billow up her pants and melt her hands as she decided what to do next. She'd read enough in the last four days to make her brain hurt, had loitered in the kitchen enough to bring her mother's voice to the forefront of her mind.

And Nikolai did as she asked—he'd left her alone.

The development of an amicable relationship with her host

was the only logical next step. His office, where the physical records for the manor were filed away, was sure to remain inaccessible. Not to mention that he likely watched her too closely now to get away with much.

With all the time alone she'd been given, she ruminated on Nikolai's story.

If she could use it as a means of establishing conversation—if she could get him *talking*—then she might be able to coax information out about Nyah's stay. Maybe she'd learn something worthwhile about those voices, too.

She could play a new role. A friendlier one... even if those black eyes haunted her from the dim corners of every nightmare.

Clio stripped her coat off and walked to the library, folding the thick material in front of her stomach as if it would keep her gut from spilling all over the marble.

She'd felt this way once before. The sense of standing on the ledge of a cliff with the world spread beneath her. She was lost again—in that morning when she'd raced to Nyah's home and her father answered the door. When she shoved past him into their glamorous house and found Nyah's bedroom emptied out. The cops arrived while Nyah's father, Greg, tried to extract an explanation from her, but she couldn't think right, couldn't speak right. The officials asked to come inside. They ushered her out of the house.

Only family, they'd said.

She had been left to crumble by herself on her best friend's porch, as ice-cold reality set in. Alone in the open air, millions of thoughts ran through her and dispersed outward like a panicked hive. Only one stuck, burrowing its stinger into the honeycomb, depositing failure and betrayal into her heart.

Clio had missed the opportunity to stop whatever happened to her friend the night before. She would have done anything, no matter the cost—no matter the threat. But instead, she woke that morning to a haunting, shitty goodbye. She wanted to hate Nyah for it.

Clio most definitely hated herself for hearing her phone ring in a sleepy haze. For not turning to answer it.

She entered the library, releasing the memory.

Laying her coat over one of the sitting chairs, she faced the door to his quarters. She knocked. The air beyond didn't stir, not until she heard scratching at the base of the door. Then, meowing. Her gaze caught on the small latch on the inner wall of the shelf and she reached for it.

The door popped open and Poppet slipped through the crack, winding between her legs.

"Oops," Clio murmured, crouching to pet the cat's back. "I'm not the one who let you out of the bag, got it?"

Poppet curled into her touch, licking her fingers. The door remained ajar, the room inside stale and dark.

"He's not in there, is he?"

The cat brushed her shins, staring at the door to the hall with large, yellow eyes. Clio chuckled and scratched her fluffy, white neck. "You stay here. I'll be back in a minute."

The hallway to Nikolai's office was pitch black, as if the breaker for the entire corridor had been flipped. It rose the hairs on Clio's neck, but she pushed against the instinct. She was done letting her imagination get the best of her.

Even so, she paused in front of the office. Before she could turn back, she rapped on the wood. "Nikolai?"

The lock clicked free, and she watched the door creak open a sliver.

Nikolai's blue eyes were bloodshot, the angles of his cheek-bone sharp, the fuzz across his jaw neglected for a day too long. The dark crescents beneath his eyes were almost startling. He looked... *sick.*

Nikolai didn't waste time with pleasantries. "What do you want?"

"Oh, I'm sorry," she blurted, clutching at her torso.

"Sorry?" The word hissed through his clenched teeth.

"Yes, for bothering you. I just—"

Nikolai's gaze dropped a fraction, below her chin, seeming to narrow in on her twitching pulse. She hesitated, biting her lip. His gaze narrowed in on that, too. "Just what?"

"Will you continue the story we started the other day?"

Her question snapped every thread of tension.

Nikolai gripped the edge of the door, letting it creak open another inch. Wide enough to see his whole face but not the rest of the room. *What is he hiding?*

The door shook slightly, as if Nikolai were trembling and trying with all his might to hide it. "You want to hear more?"

She nodded and stepped forward. "As much as you're willing to share."

"Okay," he said tersely, leaning back. "I'll meet you in the library once I'm done here."

She reached out to stop the swing of the door. Her fingers brushed his and Nikolai's eyes bulged, his body seizing up as he studied the point of contact. "Are you feeling alright?"

He frowned, ripping his hand back. "I'll be there shortly," he said, and shut the door.

Clio swallowed her thundering heartbeat as she blinked at the door, as she heard the lock flip to keep her out.

The cat was sweet. Starving for attention maybe, but Clio didn't mind that. She walked around the library with Poppet held in one arm. Her other hand slid along the spines of books as she paced the room, her lungs filling up on the scent of aged paper.

Poppet drifted to sleep, her little white paws twitching as if still kneading them in a dream.

Clio had always wanted a pet, but her mother was allergic to the hair and had little patience for beings that took more from her than they could return. Clarissa dealt with life like she would a series of investments and Clio frequently wondered if her mother viewed her in the same manner. An inconvenience that offered little profit.

It would explain why Clarissa worked so much, why Clio's childhood memories all belonged to someone else. Someone who didn't exist anymore and who might as well have never existed at all. *Dad.*

Clio puttered to a stop in front of one of the bookshelves. Her gaze caught on an item sitting on the shelf above her head. An item distinctly not-book-like.

Reaching up, her hand closed around the smooth, dark cylinder and pulled it down. Her brows shot up as she studied the pipe.

She scanned the shelves lining the rest of the room. This was the only odd item resting alongside the books.

Nikolai entered the library.

Clio's breath caught when she saw him. The dark circles around his eyes had lightened. Even the wrinkles in his brow had smoothed. She quickly set the pipe down on the shelf in front of her and turned toward him.

His mouth pursed in that sensual curve as he spotted Poppet. He glanced at the cracked passage. "And how did *she* get out?"

Clio bit her cheek and said, "I don't know, the door was open when I got here. Maybe you need to get the tumbler checked out."

"Mhm," he smirked, eyes glittering. *Wow, what a shift.* He slowly ambled towards her. "Faulty doors and shitty insulation. Perhaps I should tear the whole damn manor down and start fresh."

The joke felt hollow, even as he said it. Clio had a suspicion that he would protect this manor until it was a dilapidated pile of rubble, even if he had to haunt it like a phantom.

Clio pointed out the pipe. "I didn't expect you to have a random bong laying around."

Nikolai laughed. "That's not a bong. It's an old tobacco pipe."

"Oh." She blinked at it, suddenly noting the strange depth of the bowl. Dust coated the black interior. "Why is it sitting on a bookshelf? Do you smoke in here?"

He frowned, shaking his head. "I don't smoke."

"Then why do you have it?"

"Why not? It's an antique, as irreplaceable as any of these novels."

Clio turned his words over in her head. Eventually, she muttered, "I didn't realize you were a collector of more than books."

He pursed his lips, stuffed his hands into his trouser pockets, and shrugged.

She picked up the pipe, bringing it close to her chest to admire the glazed clay, the wooden mouthpiece, the subtle etchings on the underside of the bowl. It was beautiful. And when Clio turned the pipe in her fingers, holding it properly, the clay seemed to welcome her fingertips, seemed to mold to them.

It felt so right, she couldn't help but slot the piece between her lips and wiggle her eyebrows at Nikolai. "What do you think?" She garbled around the mouthpiece, bracing her hand on her hip. The pipe was heavy, but she held it up between her teeth. "Do I look posh?"

Nikolai scanned her face, a small smile ghosting over his face. "I think the pipe fits you just right." He hesitated, then said, "Do you want it?"

Her lips parted and she nearly lost the pipe but caught it in her hand. "Wait—you would give this to me?"

"Sure." His smile was real now, creasing his cheeks. She almost detected a dimple there. Maybe two.

"But... why?"

His head cocked to one side. "You seem to like it better than I ever have."

Clio gazed at the pipe. Everything in her body seemed to scream *yes*. But what use could she have for it? How could it belong with her more than it belonged with the thousands of old stories in this room?

It didn't.

She grimaced and replaced it to the shelf above her.

"Thank you, but I shouldn't. I don't smoke either, and if Duncan saw me with it—" Clio caught her thought midsentence, then said in a rush, "He'd make me throw it away. The Light doesn't approve of bad habits like that."

She glanced up and found Nikolai's smile evaporating. His demeanor subtly shifted, and he was back to the distant stranger Clio met so many days ago.

"I'm sorry about the other night," he said flatly. "For spooking you."

"You didn't spook me," she lied.

His eyes seemed to say, *yeah, sure*. And then he smiled in a synthetic manner that made her want to explode. "Well, I still apologize for my behavior. For touching you. It was inappropriate. I hope you can overlook my faux pas when reviewing your stay."

Faux pas. Who said shit like that?

"Thank you for the apology," Clio murmured, but her nose scrunched anyway.

Nikolai rubbed his jaw. "What *were* you doing the other night?"

"I told you. I was checking on reservations."

He hummed, nodding, but his eyes told her he didn't believe that at all.

"You look different all of a sudden," she blurted.

"Do I? More or less handsome?"

Clio rolled her eyes. "More smug."

"Well, isn't that to be expected? I have to get into character for the story, don't I?"

"How often do you do that?" She felt brave, far braver than she should. That consistently seemed to happen around him. *Go figure.* "Pretend to be someone you're not?"

His head tilted in scrutiny. "As often as you, I think."

Clio's face pinched. "I don—"

"You put on quite the performances for your mother."

Her jaw dropped. "Are you eavesdropping on my phone calls, now?"

"For the record," he continued, ignoring the outrage in her voice. "I like the girl that stood up for herself the other night, even if you were sticking your nose somewhere it didn't belong." His smile gave her pause.

She swallowed the argument. This wasn't a battle she wanted to fight. "I'm sorry for that."

He shook his head. "You don't need to apologize. Not to me."

"Why?"

"Because you don't owe me anything. It was my own fault for hiring a receptionist that leaves private information sitting out like that."

Yes, not the brightest bulb in this gilded manor. Clio suddenly wondered why he did hire her—if the decision was based solely on looks. *That's what most men do, isn't it?* Perhaps she could work that to her advantage, to *Nyah's* advantage. Maybe she could work him up a little. She fluttered her lashes. "And the story?"

"Is a peace offering," he replied, smirking. "If you can agree to be polite from here on out."

Clio nodded, keeping a friendly smile plastered to her face.

Nikolai pressed in, and she was suddenly acutely aware of how much space was between them. How much space he was eating up with every step toward her. The air thickened in her throat, and she held her breath as he reached out and—

His arms slid under Poppet and removed her from Clio's embrace. The movement was so swift that by the time Clio understood what was happening, Nikolai had already set Poppet on the chair and turned back.

He held out his hand. "Then I have a better place in mind to do this."

Nikolai's eyes anchored in hers, so wide and blue and unhindered that Clio slipped her hand into his without a thought. She didn't even flinch at the chill of his fingers.

13

Clio revolved in the center of Nikolai's favorite ballroom—at least, she assumed this was his favorite from the way his face lit up as they walked in. She could see why. The oblong walls with robin-egg blue detailing shimmered under the chandeliers. Light danced along the pale paint and disappeared into the cushioned nooks arranged around the circumference of the room.

She imagined Nikolai sitting in one of them, curled into the narrow alcove with an old book, his dark curls drooping over his forehead.

Clio bit her lip as the real Nikolai guided her to the deepest recess of the room. He smiled broadly, and it was too difficult to resist returning that smile, especially now that his dimples were appearing.

Nikolai led her to a nook of gossamer blue ruffles and dark brown velvet. "Stay here, facing the alcove," he instructed before pivoting on his heel.

She heard the squeak of his patent leather shoes against the marble, retreating to some spot on the other side of the room.

"Good morning, Ms. Farren."

She jumped as his voice resounded through the alcove. Her head whipped up first, marking the metal lattice embedded in the domed ceiling of the cubby, then behind her at Nikolai, who smiled over his shoulder in front of an alcove of his own.

She faced forward again, leaning into the small space.

"Hi," she breathed, wondering if he would hear such a small sound.

His chuckle rattled down in answer. "Isn't it magnificent?" he enthused. "They don't make halls like this anymore—ones with little treasures and secrets. Couldn't you imagine? A bustling party, deafening music, all while you whisper sweet nothings to your lover from across the room."

She smiled at the alcove, at his voice. "It's very nice."

His voice lowered a few octaves. "Nice? Ms. Farren, you're breaking my heart here."

"I mean it," she giggled. "Nice is a compliment, isn't it?"

"It sounds like a scapegoat to me."

"Don't worry." She fought another giggle. "I'm not 'goat'ing you."

Nikolai groaned and the sound traveled down her spine the way it traveled through the vents—echoey and lingering. "That was awful, Ms. Farren. Very cheesy. But, you know, two can play games."

What does that mean?

His next words came in a whisper, fluttering down to rest on her shoulders. "You look exquisite today."

She stifled a gasp, knowing it would travel back to him, and glanced down at her outfit. The pink blouse cinched tight around her waist and flared softly around the top of her hips, the hem ending along the edge of what Nyah used to call her "nice ass" jeans.

If she lifted her arms, a sliver of pale skin would appear.

That part of her hadn't seen the sun since three summers ago, when Nyah had stuffed her into a bikini and dragged her to a lake house.

"What *exactly* is your game?" she asked.

"To make you blush as hard as you made me cringe. Did I succeed?"

Clio rolled her eyes and Nikolai laughed as if he could see it. She bristled, rubbing away the goose pimples on her arms. "All right. Moving on. Tell me more, story man."

"More what?" His tone remained teasing. "Things I find exceptionally darling about you this morning?"

Her head spun around, the motion fast enough to dizzy her. She found Nikolai raking a gaze down the length of her body, his eyes catching south. When her mouth dropped open, his eyes flicked back to her face. He grinned and had the decency to look a little shy.

Clio folded her hands behind her back, covering her asset.

He was flirting with her, or messing with her for entertainment's sake. A small part of her was relieved someone still appreciated the jeans, but frustration weaved like threads through her head, knowing it should have been Duncan. It *needed* to be Duncan.

"I meant the story, Nikolai," she said sharply.

"Ah, yes." Nikolai sighed, the playfulness seeping out of his voice. "I suppose I could do that." The rustle of fabric sounded through the vent. "You may want to sit. We might be here for a while."

Another glance back confirmed Nikolai had nestled into the nook, looking exactly the way Clio thought he would. Cradled tight, those long legs bent nearly to his chest, but he melted against the wall—completely at ease. His legs parted, the space between his thighs perfectly-sized for cuddling.

Clio shook her head. *Where did that come from?* She

slipped her shoes off and settled into the cushions, tugging a satin pillow to her chest.

Nikolai gazed straight ahead, at the curve of the arch sealing him into the cushioned seat. He ran a hand through his hair. "Now, where were we? Oh, yes, the carriage."

"The woman threw the bodies to the side of the road and drove the carriage hard, until a city appeared on the horizon. Abandoning the carriage just beyond city limits, they snuck through back alleys to a manor sitting above the boroughs."

"Wait, wasn't she covered in blood?" Clio asked.

Nikolai's chest expanded, a grim smirk tugging at the half of his face she could see. "Her dress was, yes. But she'd discarded her cloak before descending on the carriage, so most of the aftermath lingering on her was covered as they entered the city. The woman knew this place—she knew which alleys would be bare enough to slip by undetected."

She frowned. "And Dmitri just let her drag him along? All he needed to do was scream, bring attention to her long enough for someone to notice and try to help."

"Help how?" Nikolai's eyes met hers from across the room. "The boy had been baptized by death that night. He couldn't see a way to save himself without hurting another person. He was a child, but not so young that he couldn't feel the pain of those around him. The pain he'd had a hand in dealing out."

Clio didn't have anything to say to that.

"If he called out, anyone who heard him would die. So, he kept his mouth shut and followed his captor into the mansion." He turned his face back to the pale, cracking paint of the arch. "They walked into a lavish receiving hall, then into a room off to the right. Dmitri was hit first by the glamour of the room— the paintings and sheer curtains. Then, he looked at what was within it. They'd walked into a dimly lit soirée.

"The room was packed with people lounging on chairs and

cushions, and a few stretched out on the marble floor, wearing little to nothing. The room swirled with an iron taint—the taint that had clung to Dmitri that entire night. It was blood.

"Partygoers bled from their necks, their arms, their thighs. Across the room, he spotted a red-headed woman bowing her head over a male's lap and drinking blood from his leg. It wasn't at all like what he saw in the forest, when his captor ripped open and fed from a spurting artery. The look on this new woman's face was gentle, her movements careful. And where Dmitri expected to find terror in the man's face leaning over her, there was only a gasp and a ripple of bliss that passed over his features.

"The room enveloped him in a sea of laughter and dancing, carrying them straight toward that redhead. She lifted her face from the tap she'd started, pressing against the seeping wound with her fingers as her eyes scanned the room. It was as though she could sense the presence, the disruption, before she saw the two of them. When her eyes landed on Dmitri, she stood from her seat on the chaise.

"Redhead was tall, her substantial curves visible through the panels of her sheer nightdress. And as she sauntered toward them, he saw the dagger peek out from where it was strapped to her thigh. She walked fluidly, with an elegance more stunning than his captor had when he first met her. Only the blood on her chin and fingers served to remind him of what she was, only the fact that she quickly licked her hand clean before she met them in the center of the room. He stood in a monster's house."

"And the other people in the room didn't run?" Clio interrupted. "Even though they were being fed on?"

"They were there because they *wanted to be fed on*." Nikolai's eyes glittered with a new playfulness that made her breath catch. "Every person in that room was intoxicated, but not by alcohol or any substance made by man. The bites gave them an ecstasy that had no parallel in all the world, and so those who found that house lingered there as long as they could, and returned as often as possible without being drained to the point of death."

Clio scoffed. "And no one thought that was suspicious? No one expressed concern over the bites showing up on their loved ones' bodies?"

Nikolai shrugged. "Perhaps there were a few, but the bites were not the only thing about those women that could intoxicate. That entire city was under a spell, whether through the venom of their teeth or the charm humans found themselves submitting to once they looked in their eyes."

"Weren't they human, too?"

"At one point, yes, they were mortal. But they weren't human anymore."

"What changed? *How?*"

Nikolai smiled, but his dimples were nowhere to be found. "You're getting ahead of the story, Ms. Farren. Do you want to spoil the whole thing?" His tone was teasing, but a tension vibrated underneath it.

She sighed, allowing her head to fall back against the wall. "Alright. Keep your secrets."

Secrets. Nyah. Those nights of forbidden pleasures. Popcorn and soda and long snuggles. All the moments she'd never get back, and all the ones stolen from her future. Clio had never felt so cold, so bereft, as she pushed those memories away.

Listening to Nikolai's low, silky voice helped.

"From the look of alarm on the redhead's face and the growl in her throat as she spoke to his captor, Dmitri could tell she wasn't pleased with their arrival. In a matter of minutes, the redhead had the mansion emptied out. All that remained was the three of them and two blonde women that wore blood on their lips and moved with the same unsettling poise. He was surrounded, cowering on the chaise that the redhead used as a dinner table. His captor was holding his wrist so tightly that he couldn't quite feel the tips of his fingers anymore. He thought this was the end of his story, to die in this place he had been dragged so far from home to find, at the hands of the most beautiful women he had ever seen. But then one of the blonde women stepped forward and knelt before him."

A shiver speared through Clio's spine at the shift in his voice. The shift from ice to a simmering warmth, so minuscule, like the dissolving of frost on a spring morning. And maybe, if Clio hadn't closed her eyes and been listening to every consonant that fell through the vent like gold sifted from river rock, she wouldn't have caught it. But she did.

So she looked.

Nikolai had closed his eyes as well, and a gentle smile rested on his lips—a smile she'd never seen before. She prized the different facets of Nikolai's mouth. The hard line and sweet curves. The wicked smirks. Everything, really.

It was a nice mouth.

Clio jerked her head, shaking the thought away. The *very inappropriate* thought. Maybe deciding to spend more time with Nikolai was a mistake. *He* was working *her* up, and he hadn't even done anything. Except talk.

She frowned. That was it.

Nikolai *talked* to her, with her. Included her in the conversation, didn't talk over her, let her ask questions even when they annoyed him. And maybe it was just his excellent manners kicking in, or the fact that she'd gotten so used to being talked down to, but Clio couldn't remember the last time she'd felt so heard.

That was why she kept having *thoughts* about him, obviously.

What was he talking about, again? Oh, right. The blonde.

"...the tray she offered him was filled with the plumpest berries he'd ever seen and fresh bread. He didn't bother to think about self-preservation as he devoured the tray. All he felt was his hunger, his need to remember what it felt like to be full and happy and safe, even if there was an icy hand shackling his wrist. And as he ate, the blonde woman spoke to him. Like with the others over the last couple weeks, he didn't understand her... until suddenly he did."

"When she spoke to him in a broken language similar to his own, close enough that he made out her question of if the tray was enough food for him, Dmitri almost choked on the grape in his mouth. He began to weep, and the blonde moved in, perching on the chaise next to him. The blonde wrapped her arm around Dmitri's shaking body and he fought again, his hope reviving, against the woman who brought him here. He turned into the blonde woman who smelled foreign, of lilacs and iron and ash, but who held him the way his older sisters did back home.

"There was a commotion that he could not decipher over his own crying, and suddenly the hand around his wrist fell away. He clung to the blonde tightly, braving a glance to where his captor had been sitting. She was gone, arguing on the other side of the room with the redhead, shadows swirling around her like a mounting storm. No one seemed to notice the shadows, especially not the woman holding him, who took that moment to introduce herself in a broken accent.

"He caught that her name was Marie. That she wasn't going to hurt him. She introduced the woman standing beside her—the other blonde, Alice. When he didn't respond, Marie nodded at the two women raising their voices in the corner.

And he was finally given a name for the monster that took him. *Genevieve.*" Nikolai said the name like a curse, and it was filled with so much contempt that Clio flinched. His body, which had been relaxed moments before, seemed ready to crack apart into a million brittle pieces. It was the sort of tension she'd grown too familiar with, most often felt whenever she came within spitting distance of her mother.

Nyah had been the one to ease it, the reprieve Clio needed while a prisoner in her mother's house. She found herself wanting to extend that comfort to Nikolai. To reach out and touch him somehow.

But this is just a story, she reminded herself. *He's just pretending.*

"What little attention Dmitri could spare to listen to Marie evaporated in that instant, because those vibrating shadows hovering around Genevieve exploded. The room swam with streams of darkness, offering only glimpses of what happened beyond. The glint of a dagger. Red and black ringlets mingling over the marble floor. Snarls and the snapping of bone. Marie's firm body disappeared from his arms, and then it was over.

"The darkness parted. Genevieve was pinned under the red-headed woman. Marie was beside them, pushing the redhead back, off of Dmitri's captor. The dagger that had gleamed through the darkness was discarded at Genevieve's side. As Marie helped Genevieve up, Dmitri's eyes slid over the marble floor to the body lying nearby. To Alice, whose neck had been snapped and now looked up at the ceiling with lifeless eyes. Whatever Genevieve had done in her shadows, it was as fast and brutal as what she did to those riding in the carriage earlier that night.

"The redhead watched from the corner of the room, clutching a mangled hand to her stomach, as Genevieve returned to Dmitri and took his wrist for a second time. All he could do was surrender, *shake* with fear as that dark-haired woman led him toward the exit. He would have screamed if she hadn't halted at the threshold, hadn't turned back to wait.

"Marie knelt beside Alice and pressed a gentle kiss to the dead woman's lips. Then, she stood and joined Genevieve and Dmitri at the door. As they left, Dmitri's last glance of the room etched permanently into his mind. The vision of a splintered piano, billowing sheer curtains, and the woman in the corner, crying tears as bloody red as her hair."

Nikolai paused, breathing in a slow, measured rhythm. Too slow. Too measured. Too—

"What happened next?" Clio urged.

"Nothing good," he rasped, picking at an invisible seam on his trousers.

"But something dramatic and story-worthy, I bet."

Nikolai snorted. Actually *snorted* as he glanced across the room. Even from yards away, she saw the faint light playing in his eyes and relief flooded her chest. "You'd win that bet," he admitted.

Nikolai spun towards the alcove, turning his back to Clio, and before she could ask why, he dove back in.

"The boy learned to live with monsters, in a bunker, deep enough underground to secure their sleeping chambers and keep them warm in the winter. The women treated him kindly, especially Marie, who hardly left his side for more than the occasional hunt. After a few years, he saw them as family and gave up any hope for his previous one. By eighteen, his real name and every memory of that life faded. He was only *Julien*.

"Genevieve was away more than present, bringing home books to Julien from her travels. Her moments of peace, of motherly affection, were brief. They happened just before dawn, when the creak of his bedroom door would signal her return from whatever journey she'd been on. He would hear the rustle of cloak as she slipped in—smell the earth and manure on her clothes. Most of the time, he pretended to sleep. But on days when he particularly longed for love and affection, Julien watched her glide across the room and perch on the edge of his bed.

"She ran her fingers through his hair, twirling the curls whether he opened his eyes or not, and if he dared to watch, she spoiled him with adoring smiles and the hum of a lullaby. In those moments, he truly believed she loved him. He let himself love her back. The moments didn't last, of course. The shadows hiding in her cloak always creeped up to whisper in her ear and she would war with them until she cried or bolted from his room.

"In the winter of Julien's twentieth year, things changed. Marie began slipping out into the night during Genevieve's absences. The oddity was enough to rouse him from his bed and follow her. He watched, night after night, as she embraced a figure that emerged from the night. The allure and promise of love led Julian to sneak into the woods, watching, hidden away, as Genevieve and the woman greeted and kissed each other. He allowed himself one minute of absorbing the love he'd only ever read about before, until they slipped away into the woods, and he returned to the bunker.

"One night, however, he risked drawing a foot too close to the reunion. The blonde, the one whose features he memorized but could not name, pinned him in the snow. Marie intervened and re-introduced Julien to her wife, Alice, the woman who had her neck snapped so many years ago. He asked why she'd never been brought around the bunker, why they'd remained separated for so long when Alice had survived that terrible night. They only said their reasons were best kept until he was older."

Nikolai's back curved. He looked like he might crumble from the inside out.

Clio bit her lip. Her ribs squeezed, leaving imprints on her organs, on her ballooning heart. She wanted him to turn around. She wanted to see his face.

"He wanted to say he was old enough already. Old enough to experience the world in its entirety. He wanted to know what it might be like to have someone that would search for him, someone to embrace him in the woods and darkness."

Clio slid to the edge of the alcove, letting her tiptoes rest on icy marble. She squeezed the soft cushion in her hands to keep from standing, to keep from crossing the ballroom and wrapping an arm around Nikolai's shoulders.

"But instead of asking, he took all those words, all the desires seeping out of their rightful places, and locked them away in a tidy little box. He knew no one cared a lick for what he thought about the world, about what was right or wrong, or even whether he was happy. Julien headed back to the bunker... but he did not know what evil was waiting there for him."

Silence stretched, long and heavy and incomplete, between them. Nikolai's curls reappeared as he threw his head back, staring at the vent.

Clio took a deep breath. "Nik?"

His shoulders tightened at the sound of her voice, confirming that her proximity was the last thing he wanted right now. So she remained where she was.

"The door to the bunker had been cleaved down the middle. As he descended the stairs, muffled screams rose to greet him. In the dirt-walled kitchen, he found Genevieve standing beside the rickety dining table, her face glowing despite the dried slashes of blood on her face and neck. Her clothes hung in tatters.

"Movement in his peripheral drew his attention to the man bound and gagged in the corner. He writhed like a worm, attempting to break free from scraps of his mother's bloody cloak.

"Genevieve loosened a tall burlap sack on the table, revealing a half-wilted shrub. She plucked a bloom from the plant and turned to the hearth, humming as she prepared the kettle for a pot of tea.

"It wasn't like Genevieve to do things like this. Marie could barely suffer through her lectures about human preservation and Julien usually found the arguments between them a fine source of entertainment. Until that night, sitting at that table, listening to the muffled screams of a man he knew would be dead soon."

Clio dug her fingers deeper into the cushion, cheeks chilled from silent tears. Because she was crying now. She didn't know why she was crying.

"She pulled the kettle out of the hearth and with a bit of coaxing, Julien choked through the better half of the tea. When he finally pushed it aside, Genevieve wrapped her arms around him and pressed his ear against her chest.

"Resting on her bosom, he heard nothing. Not a heartbeat, not a breath. Nothing to suggest she had once been human or that she remembered what it meant to be afraid, and he let himself rest in that precious, fleeting moment. She held him through his turning, but he was only barely aware of her presence, of her arms tightening like a vice, as if she might take the pain away if only she could. If only she hadn't been the one to cause it.

"After Julien woke in a sea of blood and vomit, he drained the man in the corner. And he knew then that there was nothing amusing about death. He learned through the blood-thirst that he may very well hate himself. There was more, so much more, to despise now. He stared at his first kill until his eyes burned—until they dried out in the absence of the most basic human instincts.

"Genevieve drew close to him and asked if he remembered. But remembered what? He didn't know. He couldn't muster words. And in his silence, Genevieve panicked. She said he should have remembered. The moment of hope in her eyes, that precious love and affection, ended the way they always did.

"The spirits swirled around her temples. She fled the bunker, and he wasn't sure how long he remained there, stuck in that spot—but it was long enough for the eyes of the man in front of him to deflate, long enough to listen to his mother wail at the moon and to catalogue her subsequent departure into the woods.

"As morning drew closer, the beast rebelled in his chest. Paralysis left him. Shaking off the maze of his mind, Julien lifted himself from the floor and searched for Genevieve. He needed to find her before Marie discovered the state of their bunker. Julien tracked the footprints to a steep cliffside."

There, sitting on the edge of her seat, with twilight creeping across the white marble floor, Clio closed her eyes and traveled to that place with him. She imagined—imagined she could.

It flickered to life behind her eyes—*the blue hued snow under her feet, the parsing of trees on either side of the crag, the faint glow of dawn growing brighter with every second. She saw everything. As if she'd heard the story a thousand times before.*

"The sky brightened to a deep purple as he dragged himself up over the ledge and Genevieve's silhouette came into view, facing the horizon. His skin crawled, ordering him back down the cliff."

Clio glided through the snow, toward those two figures standing at a precipice. Wind battered the woman's slim frame, billowing her shredded clothes in such a way that exposed her malnourishment—her ribs a xylophone of milky skin and shadows. A male figure stood beside her, creamy limbs reaching. She skirted the silhouettes until she stood between them and the horizon. They stood as soft clay figurines, their faces blurry and featureless like a dream, living at the story's mercy.

"He grabbed his mother by the arm and tugged, telling her it was time to go home. Wrenching her elbow away, she replied that she was, but didn't budge from her place. She watched the gleam alter with every passing second, expression caked in blood and tranquility. But strangest of all—her shadows were missing.

"She said, 'I've missed the sunlight. In mortality, morning always chased away my darkness. I have hope it will do so again.'"

Clio watched as Genevieve's figurine gained a little clarity, black curls whipping against her temple and leaving flawless pores behind. A long, thin nose appeared in the center of the clay figure's face.

"Battling the flood of venom and spear of dread in his gut, Julien asked her what would happen once the sun rose. She didn't respond. Her eyes glazed over, seeing but not present, hardly registering his second attempt to guide her away from the plateau.

"She replied, 'The spirits are not all the same. Some are so loud and they talk so much that it's hard to doubt them. They're not like the ones that followed me in mortality. In death, I heard more. I heard too much.'"

With every word Nikolai spoke, the figure's face stretched and molded—becoming as real as anything Clio might have seen with her eyes open. A heart-shaped face came into focus, with high cheekbones and thick arched brows.

"The sky fluxed and triggered an itch under Julien's skin. Instinct had him shying from the horizon, slipping behind Genevieve's body like a frightened child. He never expected to find solace in her shadow—but he did that day."

Bright, red-rimmed blue eyes surfaced, deepening like a cloudless summer sky. The figure looked so substantial, Clio almost reached out to touch her, but—

"Smoke curled around him, and he realized that Genevieve's bare skin was puffing, reddening. She twisted suddenly to face him and produced a booklet from her waistband, shoving it in his hands. She told him to go, promising that there was a better life out there for him, a better *way*, and that her time for atonement had come.

"At that moment, Marie pulled herself up from the crag, eyes wild with fear. She screamed at them to retreat, to get home."

Clio looked over Genevieve's shoulder at the third faceless figure: pure golden waves of hair twirling in the wind, navy satin and lace hanging off pink shoulders.

"Marie surged forward, while the sun crested the mountain range. He knew he only had a moment before she gripped his collar and dragged him away. He knew she would save him over Genevieve, without question.

"He demanded to know what was about to happen to her, demanded to know where she was going. But Genevieve twisted toward the sun near-bursting on the horizon as he staggered back into Marie's open arms."

A wave of dawn singed Genevieve's face, bubbling black and red, and though Clio couldn't see Julien's features, she witnessed the loss—the frantic pain affecting the figure as though someone twisted the clay in his face.

"Marie flung both of them toward the tree cover on the plateau. And Julien heard Genevieve whisper in wonder, 'I don't know.'

"Then, the day broke and fire filled the air."

14

"Marie pulled them into cover, but it was too late for Genevieve.

"Her body burst into flames, the purple-hued heat licking away the snow and reaching into the sky like hands stretching to heaven. Genevieve screamed as skin melted from bone."

Clio didn't know how it was possible, but she saw it.

The world exploded in lavender flames. She blinked at the smile on Genevieve's face, her blue eyes reflecting the dawn. Unable to stomach the sight of her boiling skin, Clio looked up at the flames—the effervescence worshipping in the sky.

"The sun spilled through gaps in the canopy, searing welts into Julien's skin. But his hands flew out, grasping the trunks around them for an anchor. Anything to stop Marie from tearing him from the woman burning on the plateau."

The clay figures struggled with each other between the trees, a flurry of pale limbs and vibrating tension.

"That fire sank through muscle and cloth until only

Genevieve's bones remained, standing upright like a living skeleton. They created a funnel of light around her and the bones blackened. That circle of thawed earth shuttered, reality blurring as a second figure appeared amidst the whirlwind."

Clio watched the air behind Genevieve's bones slash open, creating a black slit in the atmosphere. Bronze skin slipped through. A naked chest and broad shoulders. A dark, wicked smile.

"The male blinked in and out of existence. Shadows and fire spun around each other as the being stretched its arms out and tilted its face towards the sun. Two rotting, infected caverns were burrowed into its back, over each shoulder blade. It beckoned to the flames and they relented their dance, hurtling for the open embrace."

Clio saw the being's face then—square and beautiful, every edge sharp enough to cut her open. As the flames absorbed into his chest, the figure's dark eyes fell upon her. They narrowed, almost cognizant, and she stumbled back.

Her feet staggered off the ledge and, unable to catch herself, Clio plummeted through the frigid winter air.

She landed back in her body with a violent jolt, sitting on the cushion in Nikolai's ballroom. Scanning the room, she anchored herself in the lavender gleam and golden chandelier light.

Her heart thundered so hard, she thought it might burst through bone and sinew to dance across the icy floor. She wondered if it would dance over to Nikolai, who had evacuated his nook and instead stood before it—his back still turned to her.

"The being consumed his mother's lingering essence, it's bronze body solidifying with each spark that seeped into its chest. At that moment, Julien wasn't sure what to believe in, whether it be himself, or a god, or some other darker power. But he knew deep down that this shadow had fed on his mother longer than that day.

"Perhaps this creature drove her mad itself. Maybe, in another world, Genevieve would have been good, would have been the mother he so desperately wanted and needed. He screamed for her, demanding to be heard just once.

"The purple flames heard his screams and halted. Turned toward him." Nikolai's hand lifted to the side of his head. His fingers curled and twisted, as if to show exactly how the fire moved. But then they fell back to his side, lifeless.

"The magic tore away from the shadow-being and chased Julien through the trees. It slammed into his chest, spreading through his heart and spine, down into the very tips of his toes. The impact broke his hold on the plateau. For a moment, the wave of knee-buckling power threatened to consume him. It crashed over his head, reminding him of where the ripples had started. Of who had been lost in its gravity.

"Marie launched them over the edge of the crag and his last glimpse of the plateau revealed the result of his plea to the universe. Genevieve's bones collapsed, clattering in a song that would follow him for a lifetime. The shadow-being's figure faded to nothing above the bones, snuffing out like a dying star.

"That shadow may have preyed on Genevieve, but Julien stole the magic out from under it. And that would have to be justice enough. Julien surrendered to the drop, and let the darkness of his new life swallow him whole."

Clio waited a moment before forcing herself to breathe.

Nikolai remained across the room. His snark and confidence and stars, all gone. Usually, a story rooted itself in truth—touched deeply because a reader saw themselves between the inky lines. What was it about the story that sprung from his heart?

Did his mother die?

She shouldn't hold him. He wasn't hers to hold. She knew it would cross a boundary somehow, but—

Clio stood and walked toward him. Nikolai heard her. He shied back, lifting a hand without looking at her, and she went still. "Please. Don't."

Her heart skipped. "Don't what?"

"Get close to me."

He left the room before the words sank in, before she had a chance to respond. Dejection rushed through her veins, wiping away all the warmth that had sparked for him—leaving her ice cold and bereft once more. *Don't get close to me.*

Only one person had ever wanted her to get close like that, and now she was gone. Clio should be used to the hole Nyah left in her heart, but it had been nice to imagine for a moment.

I was stupid.

Clio headed for the door, intent on returning to the snuggly cat in the library, but stopped short when her gaze caught on dark spots dotting the marble where Nikolai had stood. Crouching where Nikolai stood moments before, she discovered vermillion droplets splattered against the sleek white stone.

Four marks of blood.

Nikolai emerged from his quarters in a fresh button-up, smiling politely when he saw Clio sitting at the chess table, kitten-in-lap. He approached slowly, ambling toward his chair as he folded the cuffs on his shirt.

"Are you okay?" Clio asked.

Nikolai's brow remained impressively still, but the corner of his mouth tightened. "Of course I am."

"You were bleeding."

He lowered himself into his chair, displeasure rising in his eyes. "Was I?"

"Yes. Was it a nosebleed or—"

"A nosebleed," he repeated, offering an even *less* convincing smile. "Yes, I get them sometimes. Nothing to worry about."

Nikolai turned his attention to the chessboard. Resetting it. Again.

Clio scrutinized the scattered pieces. He hadn't finished the match from the other day and so the board froze in a stalemate, the way it had been the first day she entered the library.

She suddenly found herself guessing Nikolai hadn't surprised himself in an awfully long time. The constant stalemates. The quiet, empty manor. The worn books all around them, drenched in the oils from his fingertips.

"Are you going to finish the story?" Clio ventured.

"I did."

"No," she argued. "You didn't. Did Julien and Marie survive the sunrise?"

He rhythmically tapped the top of each pawn. "They endured. That was the last night they ever spent in that bunker. Marie returned to the city with her wife."

"And Julien? Did he join them?"

Nikolai's brows drew together, but he replied, "Eventually. After he made the mistake of ditching Marie to search for his human family."

"What happened?"

"There were marks burned into the reindeer hide he wore the night Genevieve took him, unique brands specific to a nomadic clan in the North and beyond that to his actual family lineage—each had their own. He traced it all back to his home."

Nikolai looked up, looking through her as he did the day they met. "And promptly slaughtered them. Got too close when he didn't understand how to control his urges well enough. To creatures like him, love and thirst feel all too similar."

"That's terrible," she muttered.

Something in Nikolai's eyes quivered. "Yes, it is. In his grief, he went on to massacre hundreds that crossed paths with him on country roads or dark alleys."

Clio bit her lip. "These stories," she said. "They seem so real."

"To some," he considered, "they're very real. To most, they're only fairy tales. That's something you have to determine on your own."

"And the thing in the fire, with Genevieve's bones. What was *that*?"

Nikolai cocked his head, pursing his pretty mouth. "Theoretically?"

"Sure."

"An angel."

"Right." She chuckled.

Nikolai raised a brow. "Truly."

An angel? A real, light-damned angel? Clio's breathing shallowed. "But—how?"

He shrugged. "I'm aware of what the New Church preaches: that angels were the Divine Light's first hope for life on Earth, before they fell short of expectations. Though they had wings and beauty, they lacked soul, so the Light annihilated them. But do you really think, if they existed the way your church says they did, that an entire population of scorned beings would disappear?" He smirked. "Don't you think it more likely that The Divine would leave them to their own devices?"

"So... what? Angels live in the shadows?"

"Perhaps they live wherever they can and feed off of whatever life they can find, searching for light in a world that left them Lightless. I've heard them called other things—demons, in those countries the New Church has yet to influence."

Clio didn't entertain beliefs like that. Her *mother* didn't entertain those beliefs. The idea was fascinating, but heretical. *All lore and pretend*, she assured herself. She didn't let herself dwell on it. "You never explained what Julien became, though. If he wasn't human after his 'turn', then what was he?"

Nikolai frowned at the board between them. "Simply stated—a beast. That's what legend says, anyway. The oldest records, written by those who are said to have seen too much and lived to tell the tale, use the term Nosophorus. *Plague carrier*. The plague—that beast—is assumed when digesting the scourged plant."

"And Genevieve was more than that."

"Yes." His face pinched.

"What, exactly?"

"I—" His throat bobbed and he shifted in his seat, leaning back to glance at the ceiling. "Lore never says for sure."

Clio traced the edge of her chair's upholstery. "Did Julien find happiness in the end? The better life Genevieve mentioned?"

"It's like you've said before." Nikolai sighed. "Happy endings aren't realistic, especially for a monster."

"But he wasn't a monster," she retorted. "Neither was Genevieve, really. I think they were just sad and lonely."

"Not many would agree with you," he pointed out, eyes drilling into her so profoundly that Clio glanced around the room.

"I don't care. People see what they want to see."

"Oh?" Nikolai raised a brow. "And what does that mean for you, Ms. Farren? What do you see?"

Their eyes met, even as Clio's focus turned inward, like a

beacon of light illuminating her darkest corners. No one had ever asked her that so simply before and she realized she'd never even asked herself. The answer was there, a small gem embedded in the tissues, catching the brilliance and refracting it all around inside her.

And because he had the nerve to ask, she voiced it. "Hope."

Nikolai's amusement slipped.

Clio swallowed. "I choose to believe the best because I would want someone to do the same for me." His eyes softened, simmering as she shrugged. "We're all capable of terrible things, Nikolai. Some of us simply forget that we're capable of just as much good."

After a stretch of silence, he leaned over the table as if to divulge a secret. She moved in to listen, afraid she might miss it, and he whispered, "You're less cynical and more romantic than you give yourself credit for."

She blinked a few times, her brow furrowing as he averted his gaze to the game between them. Like he hadn't just ripped the air out of her lungs. *Yes. Perhaps.* Though she didn't know how that part of her lived on... how it had survived the grief.

Clio indulged a smile as Nikolai finished resetting the board. "Can I play?"

His hand stilled, holding the crown of the white, clouded queen piece between two fingers. He looked up at her through his lashes and said, "If you're not a sore loser."

Her smile deepened as she shuffled to the edge of her seat. She interlaced her fingers and cracked them with a fluid stretch. "No promises."

Nikolai mashed his lips to hide a smile. A cocky one. Every hour they spent together, Clio read him a little easier. He was like a book, a story that fed her clues if she looked in the right places. And Nikolai... he was looking right back at her. Peering through the locks to her inner chamber the way Nyah used to.

Clio wondered, as some pang in her chest sharpened to a point, exactly how much they saw there.

15

Her feet slapped against the wet, black cobblestone. They echoed off the stone buildings on either side of her, the alley narrow enough that she could touch both walls if she tried. But she didn't dare—not when one trip meant ruin. She gasped for air, cursing her body's frailty as she turned another corner in the maze of dimly lit streets.

A flame flickered in a window. A torch snuffed out on the corner. It wasn't much light, but it was enough. At least for her. She glanced over her shoulder and saw him. The silhouette pursuing her around every turn, across every mud-sheeted stone.

Just a shadow, but it would become so much more if she let him catch up.

Hitching her petticoats, she stopped caring about the larger puddles. She bounded through them, murky water splashing and staining her undergarments. Her slippers were ruined, the seams fraying from the force she put into the balls of her feet. She may need to go barefoot and risk whatever illnesses lay beneath her.

Down another alley, slipping through a crevice to the parallel street, she ran. Smoke curled in, drifting from the epicenter of the city. People were bleeding out there, dying in the civil revolution. *Why didn't the monster go after one of them? One of those already bleeding?*

She turned corner after corner, so many that she lost count. So many that she nearly lost her way. The predator remained a cold kiss at the nape of her neck. She prayed for an escape.

The next turn barreled her into a wrought iron fence.

She whimpered as she seized and wrenched at it. The rough metal tore at her palms, ripping her open for the world to feast on. Her knees wobbled. Ice encroached on the dead end, fondling her hair, stroking her back, whispering empty promises. She stilled, frozen at last.

No light would save her. Not tonight.

Hands gripped her shoulder and spun her. Blue-black eyes glowered, rendering her breathless. A cloak of night hung from his collar, pushed far enough back to reveal disheveled golden hair. *Duncan.*

His lips curled in a snarl and three sets of razor-sharp canines glinted in the partial moonlight. She couldn't find the strength to scream before he hauled her into his arms and sank his teeth into her carotid.

Clio found her voice as she woke. Her cry echoed off the bulbous dome, the auroral lights pulsing over her, pinker than yesterday but fading as the morning twilight loomed beyond the horizon. She coughed, feeling those teeth at her neck. Feeling the blood flood her throat.

Peace, the lights whispered. No one was attacking her, no one was touching her. But she wasn't alone.

As she sat upright, she acknowledged Nikolai's presence in the doorway to the stairs. He watched her with large eyes, hands braced against the threshold as if he held himself there. "What was that about? Are you hurt?"

She wrapped her arms around her knees. The auroral lights stabilized her thoughts enough to say, "I'm fine."

"So the scream was for fun?" Nikolai pressed, agitation coating his voice.

"I'm sorry I bothered you."

"That's not—I—" He huffed a sigh and shook his head, clamping his mouth shut. His hands fell from the doorway. "What are you doing up here so late anyway?"

"I fell asleep while sketching for the wedding." She glanced at the sketchbook laying open beside her, the page she'd worked on torn and crinkled, the pencil dispersed a few feet beyond that.

She crawled to collect them. When she finally stood, he asked, "Can I see what you have planned?"

He leaned across the threshold, his entire body weight hinging on one broad shoulder. She glanced at the book in her arm. It *was* his dome. Clio nodded, flipping to her most recent sketch before handing the pad over. He accepted it with both hands, drawing it close to his chest.

As his eyes devoured the design—the arrangement of chairs and drapery that would serve as her guide for the actual decoration, she crossed her arms over the tenderness in her chest. She could count on one hand how many people had looked at her sketches.

A smile spread across Nikolai's face. So quick she could hardly track it, he thumbed through her previous work, page after page, eyes vibrating as he scoured them in a matter of seconds. His smile grew.

"Hey," she protested, reaching out to confiscate the book.

He chuckled and lifted it above his head, neck craning as he continued to flip through the pages. "Don't get bashful on me now."

Her gaze flicked between the booklet and his boyish amusement. "Bashful? I think I have a right to be. Those sketches are personal."

He nailed her with a *look*. "At least I had the decency to ask beforehand." The reminder struck her. What right did she have to lecture him about privacy, especially when she had violated his?

Nikolai lowered the book to his ribcage, one long finger tracing the asymmetrical design of a chapel she'd dreamt up. "You've got real talent," he said, turning to a page filled with twisted columns and a mosaic ceiling. "Have you considered work as an architect?"

She scoffed. "No way."

"Why not?"

"They're just silly drawings."

His eyes narrowed. "They're incredible. The lines are clean —the dimensions exact."

"How would you know that?"

"I just do. And I'm assuming it's all freehand?"

"So what?"

Nikolai laughed roughly. "You could be a damn brain surgeon if you wanted to."

She grabbed the book. He let her take it this time. "No guts or gaping wounds for me, thank you very much."

"I mean it." He waited for her to tuck the sketch book under her arm and return his gaze before he said, "I would hire you for structural remodeling in a heartbeat. You've got the vision for it."

Swallowing her doubt, she forced a smile. Forced herself to say, "Thank you." Then, she asked, "Why are you so afraid to enter the dome?"

He recoiled. "I don't think I'm afraid. Everything about it just—I don't know."

"Well, why do you keep it locked away if you hate it? Why not let others enjoy it?"

"I don't hate it." He peered up at the lights, thinking quietly for a minute, and then said, "I feel half blind when I look at it. Half mad. It's like I'm waiting for the day when I can walk inside and see it for the first time."

Clio looked up, too. The observatory was the most beautiful part of the manor—the part that would have led her here eventually, even if Nyah were still alive and well. She leaned against the door frame next to Nikolai, trying not to think about the way his breathing displaced the hair on top of her head.

"All you have to do is open your eyes, you know," she murmured. "You don't need to make things so complicated. If you want to love something, then love it."

"Is it that easy for you?" She could have sworn he spoke those words in her ear, they were so soft, but she refused to turn around to find out for sure. "Is that how you love dear fiancé number one?"

"Yes," she said tightly.

Nikolai sighed. They watched the lights fluctuate and Clio decided she would be happy to do this all day. She shouldn't, of course. Wouldn't. But she might have in a different world, if she lived a different life than the one she had now.

He cleared his throat. "You should go get some rest in a proper bed."

She turned, frowning. "My thoughts are too loud to sleep any longer. How about another round of chess?"

"Still coasting on your absurd case of beginner's luck?" Nikolai's eyes darkened with something like annoyance, but then a dimple appeared. He was more amused than he let on.

She brushed past him and sneered, "Beginner's luck, my ass. If I remember correctly, I'm firmly in the lead by about three games." She wanted to squeal with delight remembering the shock on his face when she won the first time—and his subsequent disbelief when she continued to hand him his own ass through the rest of the afternoon.

Nikolai fell into step beside her. The staircase pressed them close enough that their arms grazed every few steps. Clio told herself that the warmth in her gut was a response to his companionship, the same kind she had with Enzo. *Entirely innocent.*

"Be prepared to lose that lead," he grunted. "I went easy on you yesterday."

"Oh, really? Then why did you look like you were sucking on a lemon every time I took your queen? I think *you* are the sore loser, Nik."

He stuffed his hands into his slacks. Chin to chest, he resembled a pouty teenager. "Just wait. I'll make a sore loser out of you yet, and then we can join a lemon-face support group together."

Clio burst into laughter.

Nikolai's head whipped up. He studied her face as she turned toward him more fully. She was all too comfortable in this confined space with him. All too intoxicated by the faint ripples of cedar wood and clean linen.

His brow furrowed. "Wait. What did you call me?"

She blinked. *Oh.* She'd called him *Nik.* "I'm sorry. If you didn't like—"

"Don't be sorry. I like it." He smiled. "I can't remember the last time I've been called anything other than Mr. Trousseau around here. Even Nikolai is a stretch most days. No one bothers getting that familiar with me."

"That's because you're the boss. But you're not the boss of me, and we've sort of bypassed the whole acquaintance thing. We're sort of friends now, don't you think?"

His dimples made a grand entrance. "I wouldn't mind that."

Somewhere along the way, in the midst of the stories and their chess competition, Clio genuinely started to like Nikolai. She still had every intention to use this new connection between them in whatever way would give Nyah justice, but—he was so open, so unapologetically real. The complete opposite of what she saw in herself.

If she was being entirely honest, Clio wasn't sure who she was anymore. There were so many layers lately, these veils that hid her ugly from the world. And underneath it all, she was still angry and burning, like a fresh wound crusted in salt.

She was still... messed up. A rumbling in her head wanted her to show Nikolai, to tell him everything. And every time he looked at her like this, she came a little closer to giving in. But no. She had to focus.

Clio steeled herself, opening her mouth to finally ask about Nyah, when Nikolai staggered to a stop on the stairs.

"They glow," he murmured, staring intently at her face, at her *eyes*.

Clio's stomach dropped. He was referring to the mutation. She faced forward, her lips twitching as the conviction behind her smile disappeared. Maybe she would return to her suite after all—but before she could storm off, a cool bracelet wrapped around her wrist.

Clio marked Nikolai's hand, his thumb brushing against the

back of her palm. He was staring at her, an apology simmering in his blue eyes.

For a split second, she considered slapping him. She considered ripping away or shoving him down the stairs for the way his gaze traveled over her face, her lips, her neck—but she didn't. This was sin by omission, wasn't it? Letting him touch her. Liking it. Hoping he wouldn't stop at her wrist. *Wrong. Wrong. Wrong.*

"I didn't mean to offend you by commenting on it. I think they're—"

"*Fascinating?*" she hissed, and his thumb went still.

He released her, leaning back as if he suddenly realized he'd crossed a line. Tenderness filled his expression as he said, "Lovely. They're lovely, Ms. Farren."

"Please don't do that."

"What?"

"Lie to make me feel better."

"I would never." The look of confusion on his face nearly convinced her, but then he scoffed, as if to expel the unspoken truth from his head and nodded toward the foot of the stairs. "Come on, let's go grab your coat and I'll take you for a walk in the courtyard. You could benefit from some fresh air."

"And freeze half to death? The snow would bury me in minutes, I'm sure of it."

She tried to brush past him, but Nikolai lazily braced his forearm on the wall of the staircase, blocking her escape. "Ms. Farren, do you really think I would lead you outside if I thought it could compromise your well-being?"

Clio shrugged.

"For your information, most beloved guest," her skin prickled at those words—the carefully disguised affection behind his professional tone, "we've hit a brief respite from the storm. It happens every year. The world grows quiet and still and almost *warm*, just before the real brutality of the Freeze kicks in. The skies are clear right now and twilight is dawning over the garden. Don't you want to see it?"

A new smile spread over her lips, tentative. Forgiving. "Okay."

Clio couldn't recall the last time anyone made her feel as completely disoriented as Nikolai did. She told herself it was a first, just like she told herself a myriad of other, not-quite-believable things since discovering this manor shrouded in darkness.

Even while a voice in the back of her head whispered otherwise.

16

"Are you zipped?" Nikolai stood in front of Clio, looking her over for the third time in as many minutes as they paused at the back doors leading to the courtyard. "Pull your hood up. Do you have your gloves?"

Clio fought against the laughter bubbling in her chest. "You're being bossy. Quit it."

He gave her a frustrated smile. "I'm being a good host, Ms. Farren. If you got sick, that would reflect badly on the manor."

The mirth died in her throat. Of course. He was just doing his job. Entertaining her. Making sure she stayed healthy for the event she'd paid for. "Right."

When Clio bundled up to Nikolai's liking, he unlocked the back door and shoved it open, the door groaning against the sheet of snow that blew in under the patio cover. If the door was difficult to strong-arm, Nikolai didn't show it. He gestured for her to squeeze through first, then followed her. The snow was thick, the soft layers compacting under Clio's feet so that she waded through the knee-deep powder. At least her hefty snow boots had finally come in handy.

Nikolai was right. It wasn't snowing anymore. Looking up, all she saw was a dark sky lit with millions of stars. Not clear exactly—there were clouds fast approaching from the East—but calm... for now. The aurora had faded while she retrieved her winter clothes and on the horizon, a faint lilac hue shimmered, glowing across the untouched blanket of white. She gaped until Nikolai trudged past her, nodding to beckon her alongside him.

He led her around meticulously shaped hedges, onto a path that weaved between shrubs and statues, all covered in snow so thick there was no way to admire or identify any of it.

Nikolai said, "It's a challenge to keep a garden going around here. We have to transport new plants in every spring, but you should see this place once everything is warm and tended to. I've actually partnered with a nursery nearby that specializes in breeding arctic-hardy flowers. In the spring, we get these annual blooms that bring the garden to life at night."

"Really?" Clio huffed, focusing on her feet so she didn't nosedive. "That's incredible. I wouldn't have figured anything could grow here."

"We're right on the cusp of the Arctic Circle, so luckily, we get a sense of seasons. Spring and fall aren't nearly long enough though, in my opinion. I pretty much live out here during those two months."

"What about summer? I bet the garden thrives then."

Nikolai blinked, his lips parting as he seemed to search for the right words. "Summers here can be rough on the garden. On everyone, really. Where we get a couple months of polar night, we also get polar day. All sun and no rest. Much fewer guests. I don't remain on this continent for it."

"Why not?"

Nikolai chuckled, a low rumble that raked down her spine like a finger. "Have you ever tried to sleep eight consecutive hours while the sun was still shining? The light levels during the summer mess with circadian rhythms. Insomniacs love it, coincidentally. They're basically the only kind of people that come for the season." There was a humor in his voice, enough to make her smile, but she also got the feeling he'd purposefully skirted her question.

After another minute of walking between walls of lumpy snow, Clio broached a subject she'd spent one too many minutes wondering about since he'd wrapped up the story. "You seem to know quite a lot about the Church."

Nikolai nodded slowly. "Yes. I keep track of their movements, and teachings as they evolve."

Her brow pinched. She wasn't aware they evolved at all. The teachings had been the same her whole life. She wanted to ask what he meant, but instead she said, "Out of curiosity?"

He scoffed. "No. Out of self-preservation."

They walked in silence for a moment before she admitted, "I'm confused."

"I don't believe a Church of Divine Light would benefit the Arctic," he replied coldly, "or any of the communities that live here, myself included. I keep track of the Church to ensure they never encroach on our home."

Oh. "Why?"

"Because I don't trust them."

She paused, swallowed his words, then asked, "Who is 'them'?"

"The apostolates. The congregation." The words hit her like a brick to the stomach.

Clio tried not to let the offense seep into her voice, but she wasn't quite successful. "You don't trust me, then?"

"That depends." Nikolai smirked, and she hated what it did to his lips, the way it revealed a sliver of his teeth. His canines were so white and perfectly crooked. She couldn't see the tips of them, but the sudden desire to struck her. She suddenly wanted to see all of him, every hidden bit.

His voice brought her back to the crunching snow beneath her feet and the biting breeze against her cheeks. He stared expectantly at her.

Shit. He'd asked a question. "I'm sorry, say that again?"

"How much of the Church's teachings do you believe?" He repeated.

"All of it."

He snorted. "That's a lie."

Clio's spine bristled. "I'm not ly—"

"If you were one of their mindless sheep, you wouldn't laugh at the thought of marriage. You wouldn't sneak around at night to trespass on my privacy, and you certainly wouldn't lie about it. You wouldn't delight so much in winning the games we played yesterday," he paused, exhaling sharply, then added, "And you certainly wouldn't feel so much compassion for monsters with bloodied hands, folklore or otherwise."

She chewed on her lip. "Perhaps my beliefs are *slightly* different."

"A lot different," he amended, that stupid smirk growing wider by the second.

She glared at him. "Maybe I'm just a bad person."

"Or maybe *they are wrong*," he shot back, enunciating every word.

Dangerous... this is dangerous territory. "So what if they are? What's so wrong with believing in something you don't have proof of? What's wrong with possibly being wrong? No one can be right one hundred percent of the time." Her cheeks warmed, the chill of the breeze biting them more savagely. She didn't care. "Are you telling me you don't believe in anything at all?"

"I believe in myself, and this." He gestured to the yard

around them. "The physical world around us is reliable. It's real."

"And after this life," she retaliated. "What will you rely on then?"

Nikolai laughed roughly before he said, "I rely on the fact that I won't exist at all. I'll fade into nothing, and the world will go on without me."

She could understand his reasoning. If there was nothing, it would be awfully foolish to look up at the sky, at the darkness between the stars, and pray to a Light that can't be seen. If it was all a lie, then she'd have rejected so many pleasures for nothing.

The possibility terrified her, so much so that she rarely let herself consider the thought. In the moments she did consider it, in moments like this, she remembered that piece of her, down in her deepest parts, that felt a call to the stars. That piece that wanted to sing to the darkness beyond.

There had to be *something*.

And Nyah's final words—they told her to search for the Light. To trust it. So she did and she would, always. All while Nikolai didn't seem to trust anything and wasn't in the least bit tempted to try.

Clio finally murmured, "That seems so empty."

"There isn't always meaning to life." He smiled weakly, shrugging. "Sometimes, we're just unhappy accidents. A conglomeration of stardust and brain matter, and nothing more."

She frowned, her eyes stinging. "You're making me worry I'm going to wake up tomorrow and find you hanging from your neck on one of the chandeliers."

He laughed again. "Trust me, that's the last thing you need to worry about."

Clio stopped walking, crossing her arms over her thick coat.

"Are you sure?" Nikolai paused a few steps ahead and stared at her over his shoulder. "I've been wondering about you, you know. About what kind of man sits alone in a mansion for two weeks out of the year. What kind of man hides in his room for days at a time?"

Nikolai cleared his throat, stuffing his bare hands into his pockets as he walked on. "Do you have a theory?"

"A sad man," she replied as she followed him. "That's why you love stories, right? They make you forget how lonely it is to be by yourself. They take up your time and distract you from the present, so you don't feel the need to look for someone who might fill the loneliness but end up hurting you anyway."

Nikolai looked her fiercely in the eye and said, "You should be aware, Ms. Farren, that I'm never the one who winds up hurt."

She felt the truth in his response, the attempt to deflect her accusations. So she crooned, "No wonder you're so sad."

He chuckled softly. "I will admit, I'm very curious about you, Ms. Farren. What was it about my home that reeled you in? You made it clear on the first day you couldn't care less about the luxurious rooms, though you clearly appreciate the base architecture."

Clio rolled her eyes. "There's no need to get up in arms about your pretty rooms again. They're too flashy for my taste."

"I know. So, what was it? The auroral lights? The quiet? The snow?"

No. "It was the darkness," she confessed. She didn't meet Nikolai's gaze, though she felt it locked on her face. "The unending night and the way this manor seemed to be some light gleaming in the center of it all." A light on the other side of her grief—a hope shining. But he didn't need to know all that. It barely made any sense in her own head, so she pivoted the conversation and added, "And I suppose it was the snow, too. I've never seen so much of it before, not like this, not in person."

A few heartbeats later, Nikolai said quietly, more to the path in front of him than her, "Snow is a treasure many people never learn to appreciate. It's cleansing, in a way. A resurrection."

She nodded. And maybe she was silly for admitting it, but she said, "This is going to sound ridiculous, but I've dreamt of a place like this my whole life." She waved at the twilight around them. "Storms. Snow. When I was little, my dad and I used to crumple up paper and have snowball fights in the apartment," she smiled at the memory, a bitterness resting on her tongue, "because I wanted it so badly—as if it was this vital piece of the world I'd been cheated out of."

Nikolai pursed his lips, drawing a little closer to her side. "If it makes you feel better, I've never had the pleasure of hurling snowballs at anyone either, though I've met plenty of guests who deserved it."

"Did you think *I* deserved it the day we met?"

He was silent for a moment, before saying with a grin, "Maybe."

"Do it now."

"What?"

Clio crouched, gathering snow between her palms and forming a ball. Her gloves made the task more difficult than she'd expected it to be. She wiggled her eyebrows at him, slowly backing away toward a space between the white topiaries. "Fight me, Nik."

Nikolai's eyes were wide, looking her over as if she'd just asked him to—well, okay, she did just ask him to fight her. He shook his head. "No way. You're crazy."

Crazy? A small, dangerous titter left her mouth. "Oh, I'm definitely going to hit you now."

His head rocked back to send his own laughter into the dark sky. "I'd like to see you—"

The taunt caught off as a snowball hit him right in the face.

Nikolai shook his head sharply, rubbing the snow out of his eyes. When his gaze landed on her, he loosed a feral grin. "Okay, then," he growled. "I'll play."

Clio squealed, turning on her heel. A snowball hit her shoulder before she could throw herself behind the hedge. Snow scattered on impact, kissing her hair and neck. Her squeal dissolved into laughter as she gathered more snow, careful to avoid any hardened, icy patches. She didn't want to hurt him.

Circling the hedge, Clio watched Nikolai approach with an armful of glittering ammunition, crouching to scoop up more. As he stood, she made her next shot. It shouldn't have surprised her, how easily she hit her mark—she'd played softball every summer for years and switched to archery once she realized sports were better enjoyed alone.

But her stomach still fluttered as snow exploded in Nikolai's face.

He hissed, choking out a laugh, and she ran. For long minutes after that, there were no words at all. Nikolai followed her through the maze of white. The clouds looming on the edge of the sky drifted in. A fresh wave of weather fell, light and bright and soft. Despite the chill caressing her face and the snowballs colliding with her legs and coat, Clio felt warm.

But even though Nikolai was playing along, she couldn't help but feel like he was holding back. And that annoyed her to all hell.

Clio removed her gloves.

She threw harder, ran faster. The flurry around them fell in a wilder pattern. She stopped worrying about what the snowballs were packed with, how soft the powder was, as she slipped between the aisles of topiary, following paths they'd already stamped down.

There was only the burning of her fingers, brief glimpses of Nikolai's face, his blue eyes dancing as the game became something more, her laughter as she hit him again and again.

His hair became utterly soaked, clinging to his temples and both of those dimples marked his cheeks. His crooked canines were bared, pressing into his lower lip as he smiled, though she hardly had time to admire them the way she wanted to. He stopped stooping for snow and Clio realized this had become a chase, the pace leisurely and his focus a hedonistic, hazy thing.

No one had ever looked at her like that. Ever.

Clio didn't have the bandwidth to lie to herself. She liked that look. She lost precious moments continuing her assault, but she couldn't help herself. It was so satisfying—flinging snow at his face, hearing his low curses and rumbling praise.

Yes, that was his deep voice and not her imagination, praising her aim as he stalked after her. His eyes glowed in the pursuit, through the shadows of the garden, like spheres of stormy, crystalline ocean. A thrill ran through her spine as she spun around another hedge. She paused, thinking maybe... maybe she *wanted* him to catch her.

And the world went eerily quiet.

Nikolai's footsteps halted. There was no crunching snow or panting breaths on the other side of the white wall hiding her, no sweet voice teasing her from afar. It was so sudden and thick, that silence, that Clio didn't run.

She peered around the edge, into the aisle where she'd last seen him. He was gone. Her heart jumped into her throat. She craned her neck, leaning back to peek between the hedges up ahead, but there was only snow and stillness.

It didn't make sense. How could he have disappeared?

Clio scanned the ground, trying to trace the footprints, but they'd made so many tracks it was impossible to detect what was new. She backed up a step, then another.

The air shifted over her head and she got the frightening thought that maybe something had plucked him up into the sky. She ducked instinctively, twisting to return to the path behind her, when the hedge beside her shuddered.

She screamed, staggering back as a figure slid from the tall bush and landed in front of her. Black on black on pale skin. A force smacked into her, seizing her wrists and lifting them over her head as the world spun.

Clio landed in a soft patch of snow, but then a hard body covered hers. She blinked against the whirling of her vision and the water splattering her face.

Nikolai hovered over her, his mouth caught in a breath-taking battle between a smile and a snarl. He'd jumped a *whole topiary*.

His eyes were bright as he surveyed her. Those sensual lips curved with an unsettling wickedness, and then he buried his crown in the crook of Clio's neck. She cried out as his drenched brow connected with her collar, as his icy, sopping hair covered her neck.

"*Nik*," she screamed, her voice quickly overcome by a fit of laughter. She pulled against his hold on her wrists, but gained no quarter.

"What? You don't like this?" He shook his head against her neck, his breath puffing against her wet skin as he laughed with her. "But you were so ruthless with your attacks. You can deal it out, but you can't take it?"

She surrendered, her strength rendered useless as giggles racked her body. "I—I'm sorry," she gasped. "You're ri—right. I can't take it."

He lifted his head from her neck, remaining close enough that his face was all she could see. His fingers slid from her wrists, brushing over the skin of her palms and loosely interlocking with her own.

Those blue eyes snapped to the steam billowing from her mouth.

Nikolai's breath didn't steam like hers and Clio found herself studying his lips, parted and chapped and pale. His chest heaved against hers. Maybe she'd made him colder than she thought was possible. Maybe she should help warm him up.

Clio felt as though she could do so easily—warm him. Her body was pulsing with heat, her vision filling with so much light that his handsome face blurred a little. She squeezed her eyes shut against the burning.

"You have a beautiful laugh, Ms. Farren," he whispered.

Her primal focus snapped. *What the fuck am I doing?* "Shut up," she grumbled, trying to buck him off.

Nikolai didn't budge. He shifted slightly, off-loading his weight to one knee, but then his other leg slipped between hers, burrowing in the snow. He wasn't going anywhere.

Clio opened her eyes to glare at him.

"Why do you struggle to accept my compliments?" He demanded. "I meant what I said just now and what I said earlier. You're a lovely individual, and you're very beautiful."

Her mind went silent as they glowered at each other. Eventually she remembered that he'd asked a question, that he expected a response. "I struggle because I don't understand why you're saying those things to me." How could she say it was because it felt like a game, a joke like the ones played on her as a young child? Children could be cruel, little girls especially.

Nikolai only said, "I voice these things because I'm thinking them." His throat bobbed. He leaned in, his blue eyes flitting over every inch of her face. "In fact, I can't stop thinking them."

"You shouldn't..." Clio whispered. She felt his breath catch through the several layers separating them.

He brought his face closer, his lips curving into a sweet, angular smile. The tip of his nose brushed her own, cold and smooth, hesitant but—*oh no*. He'd misunderstood.

She clarified, "You shouldn't think those things, Nik."

And he certainly shouldn't say them, not when they did such staggering things to her head, to her body, to her soul. But she couldn't voice that second demand which would silence him. She was unwilling to let go of his words, the ones that she'd heard and the ones she secretly hoped might be said in the future. She loved listening to his voice, his thoughts, his stories, even if they weren't hers to keep.

Nikolai's brow drew tight, his eyes darkening. "Right. I'm sorry, you're right." His hands slipped from Clio's, bracing in the snow as he peeled off of her. He shook his head gently, looking away as he rumbled, "The lucky bastard."

Her brain was too scrambled to reply. She wasn't even sure what she could say other than, *Yes, the bastard.* And she'd hate herself later for that one.

Nikolai made to stand, but his foot slipped and he barely caught himself before crushing her a second time. He cursed, frowning at the snow around them. "Be careful, the snow turned slick beneath you." He knelt up. His hands wrapped around her arms as she rose.

The ground had melted and solidified again into a thick, glassy sheen only where their bodies had pressed into the snow. Around them, the flurry intensified, new flakes clinging to that pristine sheet of ice.

Nikolai released her and crouched beside the shiny bevel. His fingers pinched something in the snow, lifting to examine it, rolling the substance between two fingers.

"Strange," he murmured, seeming to forget Clio was still

present, shuddering behind him. The cold had finally seeped through her clothes. "The staff must have salted the courtyard before they left. What a waste."

Clio opened her mouth to get his attention, but her chattering teeth did the job for her. He dropped the rock salt and leapt to his feet.

"You're freezing. Let's get back inside." Nikolai guided her to the path, his hand a light pressure on her back. She was shivering too much to fight him.

He scanned her body and gasped, "Wait. Where are your gloves?" Before she could reply, he plucked them from where they were sticking out of her coat pocket and tugged them over her fingers. "You shouldn't have taken these off, Ms. Farren. I really don't want you to catch your death."

Clio couldn't help it. She laughed tremulously. "Where are we, medieval Europe? That's not how colds work."

His eyes narrowed. "Says who?"

"Says science—" She paused as his hand found her back again, rubbing up and down as if to warm her with friction. "Sure, the immune response can suffer in cold temperatures, but I'd still have to come into contact with actual germs to get sick."

"Didn't you just travel halfway across the world," his brow lifted smugly, "coming into contact with hundreds if not thousands of people?"

"And I'm fine. That was days ago."

He hummed, pulling open the back door and ushering her through. She sighed as dry, hot air blasted her body. Nikolai reappeared at her side. She was tempted to retreat to her room, to where she could curl up in bed and take a nap, but Nikolai herded her the opposite direction.

"Well," he said, "forgive me for being irrational, but I'm

going to insist you drink something hot to warm up. I can brew some tea for you."

Clio scrunched her nose. "Does it have to be tea?"

Nikolai chuckled softly. "Hot cocoa?"

"Much better," she breathed, allowing him to lead her into the kitchen.

17

Nikolai decided he must be more fucked in the head than he originally thought, tackling his guest the way he did. Nearly kissing her. And he had to be an idiot for sitting with her in the library again, playing chess, when her scent burned through his nostrils and self-control. She could hardly keep her eyes open, much less defend herself should she need to.

It wasn't that he *wanted* to push his limits, but he simply couldn't say no to her. She asked for a rematch, and after what he'd said and done in the garden, what was he supposed to do? Challenge her. Tease her. *Adore her.*

Idiot.

He hadn't scared her outside, not really. After years of hunting, he knew what the tang of fear smelled like. She'd been concerned for a moment, uncertain. But when she saw it was him holding her down in the snow, she'd *laughed.* The brief bitterness in the air had dissolved into something close to crackling embers—excitement, tinged with the floral notes of her blood.

His teeth ached. *Her blood.*

Despite the temptation, there was no place Nikolai would rather be right now. No *one* he'd rather be with. So he clenched his jaw and ground his instincts to dust.

"What's wrong with it?" Clio asked.

Nikolai blinked. "With what?"

"The cocoa. Why aren't you drinking it?"

His mug sat untouched beside the chessboard. She'd emptied hers a while ago, and discarded it on the floor next to her chair. Nikolai shrugged, his face pinching. "Sweets aren't really my thing."

Clio huffed a laugh. "Of course they aren't."

"Excuse me?"

Her head tilted to the side. "You try really hard not to enjoy your life. That's why you run a hotel in the most secluded place on Earth. You pretend to be painfully serious all the time, but I know you have to be bored out of your mind."

"What makes you say that?"

The dreaminess in her eyes sharpened as they locked with his. "The way you smiled today. You didn't think about it. Usually you hesitate, like you aren't sure if you're doing it right."

Nikolai's head rocked back against the chair as her words hit him. She was clever—dangerously clever. "Well," he picked at a seam on the chair, "aren't you turning out to be a perceptive little spook?"

Clio's mouth popped open. "Did you seriously—"

"Oh, calm down," he crooned. "I mean it in the most endearing sense."

Her eyes narrowed. "You didn't learn your lesson after all those snowballs to the face, did you? Calling me *crazy*, telling me to *calm down*. Maybe I should have packed them with rocks."

Her temper was adorable.

Nikolai leaned over the chess board, gripping either side of the table between them. She scowled, and he wondered how long her ire would last if he took her in his arms and bit that puckering lip. If he laid her out on this table and played a new sort of game. "What about *you*, Ms. Farren?"

She blinked. "Me?"

He nodded, holding her gaze. "Why do you flinch at sudden movements and avoid prolonged eye-contact? Who hurt you?"

Clio's body tensed. Her eyes widened, a glassy sheen sweeping over them. "We're not discussing that," she whispered. "Ever."

Nikolai's mind raced, devising a plan for what he'd do if he ever learned who it was. Which bones he'd break first. Where he'd begin when he filleted the skin off their body—the more sensitive parts, probably. But he said, "All right."

He knew not to push matters like this. Marie, his dear sister, wherever she was now, acted the same way when he asked about her mortal life. She'd gotten her sweet vengeance, of course, but after what she endured, the pain followed her like echoed footsteps in a long corridor, lingering with every stride she took forward. Nikolai imagined Clio might feel the same.

He shut his mouth and focused on the game. To his relief, Clio eventually relaxed. The softness returned to her eyes. Her body uncoiled until she was barely sitting upright, and her chess strategy suffered.

An hour and a few victories later, Nikolai frowned at the board. She'd left her queen wide open for the third time in a row. Instead of exposing the mistake, he said, "You look exhausted. Maybe you should retire while you're ahead."

"M'not tired," she said through a yawn. But even as her

mouth closed again and she propped her jaw on one hand, her eyes were drooping. Every blink stretched a little too long. Her upper torso swayed.

Clio's hand slipped from under her head and her face careened for the table. Before she collided with the sharp edge of the chessboard, Nikolai scooped her out of the chair. She yelped, jolting awake. When Clio saw Nikolai's arms around her waist and under her knees, she asked a bit breathlessly, "What are you doing?"

He crossed the room, crouched to twist the doorknob, and carried her into the hallway. "Saving you from a concussion, apparently. You should be in your room right now, where you can pass out on a bed rather than a table."

She lifted a brow as they passed through an arch into the lobby. "And you thought you would carry me there? Talk about room service." Her lips twitched.

"Only the best for you, beloved guest." He winked at her.

Her heart thundered against his breast. If he didn't know any better, he would have thought she was blushing, but her face suddenly hardened. She pushed away from him. "Put me down. I happen to have two functional legs."

Oh, he knew. Her legs were torture.

Nikolai let her down instantly, frowning as she swayed on her feet. She found her balance and ambled the last few feet to the elevator. He crossed his arms, trying to cling to the warmth her body had offered him.

She pressed the call button and instead of the immediate ding of the opening elevator doors, the lit button and arrows started flickering. In fact, the chandeliers and wall sconces and the steady hum of the furnace stuttered. Clio glanced around the room as the electricity surged back to life. The elevator pinged and the doors slid open, but she didn't step into the box. Her face was pale.

"It's alright," Nikolai assured her. "The power shorts out sometimes in severe weather, but a full outage hasn't happened in a long time. We have a generator, just in case."

She grimaced, warily eyeing that golden box. "I think I should still take the stairs, just in case."

Nikolai chuckled, nodding his farewell. But as Clio walked to the double doors leading into the stairwell, he saw her legs tremble. The stubborn girl was going to fall and hurt herself. He bit down on a growl and swept her into his arms for a second time. She gasped, gripping the front of his shirt as he shouldered the door open and began the ascent.

Clio's eyes fluttered. "This again?"

"Do you really think you could make it up several flights of stairs without collapsing on a landing first?" He smirked. "I'm doing you a favor, friend to friend."

Her gaze was unfocused, distant. She didn't argue, but stuck her tongue out at him. It was an effort not to wrap his lips around it and suck.

Fuck. His thoughts were losing all common decency, all sense—she was stealing what little he had left as her arms wrapped around his neck, as she rested her head against his shoulder and her bleary eyes drifted shut. "That's what I thought," he said softly, victoriously.

"Next time," she murmured. "I'm foregoing the snow entirely and it'll be a large rock hitting your face."

Nikolai chortled, and a small smile bloomed on her lips. "Promises, promises."

By the time they rounded the fourth-floor landing, Clio's breathing grew deep and even. He gazed at her sleeping face, memorizing the soft peak of her cupid's bow, her button nose, that small beauty mark under her left eye. He'd called her beautiful, but she was beyond that. There were no words for her appeal—nothing did it justice.

When he reached the threshold of her suite, Nikolai stopped short. "Shit." He squeezed Clio until her eyes cracked open. "Where's your key?"

She turned her face into his chest, rumbling in a slightly annoyed tone, "I left the door unlocked."

He scoffed. "Of course you did." *So little sense of privacy. So little desire for it.*

Nikolai carried her inside and placed her on the bed, slipping his arms out from under her a little slower than he probably should have, and her eyes flashed open.

"Wait," she said. "My coat and boots are downstairs."

He smiled, nodding. "I'll bring them up for you. Get some rest, Ms. Farren."

And just like that, she fell asleep again.

Her brow was glistening with sweat. She would overheat in that wool sweater and knit socks, but he knew this was where a line rested. He wouldn't touch her like that without her sentience and permission, wouldn't even entertain the idea.

When he returned to her room a few minutes later with her coat and boots in hand, he laid them at the edge of the bed and approached her side table. He placed the cup of ice water he'd filled in the kitchen there, ready to cool her off whenever she woke.

In her sleep, Clio tugged a pillow to her chest and curled herself around it. She was a vision of loneliness and effortless beauty. He didn't linger, though he wanted to. Watching her sleep would cross other, less certain, lines. Creepy lines.

But Nikolai saw her sleeping face in his mind as he left her room, as he took the staircase two steps at a time, as he entered his quarters and walked straight into his bathroom. Gray tile swallowed him, doing nothing to help him snap out of his daze. The spiraling thoughts of dark hair and silver eyes, and all the parts of Clio he wanted to feel and taste and see.

He turned on the shower, letting the water grow scalding as he stripped.

Nikolai's skin gleamed under the fluorescents, but his gaze slid over the reflection on the wall with little more than faint recognition. Sometimes, he truly regretted remodeling this room with an aluminum-backed mirror. With older mirrors, at least he didn't have to look at himself, didn't have to face the man or the monster as he bared himself so fully.

Turning away, Nikolai slipped into the shower and groaned, bracing his hands on the cool tile wall. He let the water burn his back, let it anchor him in the present when all he wanted was to be in her suite again. To be near her.

Clio Farren was going to ruin him.

With her long legs and piercing eyes, with her wit and laughter and that fucking *scent*. Every inch of her was hell and revival. He wanted her—that was the simple truth of it. He wanted her in his bed and on his tongue. He wanted her any way he could have her, any way she allowed. And after what she said in the courtyard, while he laid on top of her like a help-less lap dog, he knew that she would allow very, very little. Practically nothing, except her company.

Speaking of which, he couldn't comprehend how her mere company had made him this hard, made him ache this unbear-ably. How just the sight of her smile...

Nikolai groaned again, a hand drifting to his cock. The spray pummeled his back, scorching it red and raw. He didn't care. That was exactly how he felt on the inside.

Desire thrummed through his veins like a war drum and he answered the call with his fist. If he closed his eyes, he could imagine it was her hand wrapped around him. Her pink, taunting tongue. Her body. Her salty floral fragrance enveloping him rather than his own soap. And when he thought of the way she'd cried his name as he buried his face in her neck, Nikolai lost it.

He was glad to be so far removed from the rest of the suites, and even gladder still that Clio was fast asleep on the top floor of them. Because when he moaned her name, it echoed off the walls of the shower and through his quarters. He wouldn't have been surprised if it even reverberated into the crystal dome.

The truth lingered, punctuated by every pulse of his release—it shocked him, really, how much he'd come to care for this fierce, unpredictable woman. And it shocked him more, how little everything else mattered in comparison. The fragility of her existence. The unbreachable chasm between them. The evil that haunted his every thought. None of that meant anything.

Because Nikolai finally cared... for this lovely mortal whose heart belonged to someone else.

18

Clio stood in the center of the golden ballroom, her arms raised stiffly in the air. She looked up at the mirrored ceiling as the song she selected for her first dance resounded through the ballroom.

A woman's voice crooned sweet nothings over the sweeping melody and staccato drums. Swaying in small squares, she fell back on her decade of dance lessons—lessons that made her no more graceful than the gangly child who started them. She reminded herself how to move, forced her limbs to obey. At least the ceiling hovered far enough away to obscure her eyes. At least she knew the steps.

She'd been taught to give the illusion of ease even when every step warred like a battle close to being lost.

Clio spun faster, her peripherals streaked with gold and ivory. The floor became a chilly springboard beneath the balls of her feet. Eventually, she let her head loll to the side, eyes fluttering as she submitted to the melody. She really did love to dance, even if she was terrible at it.

Her mind wandered to hours before, to what Nikolai had

done for her. He could be so fussy, and not in the way Duncan usually fussed, with scolding and frustration and demands to do better.

Nikolai *worried*.

By the time she woke from her nap, her clothes and bed were drenched in sweat, so she took a shower to cool off. Her stomach had clenched under the shower spray, sending shocks through the rest of her body. Clio blamed it on her disrupted sleep schedule.

She hadn't seen a hint or sound of Nikolai since waking up, but didn't expect to. That morning, he'd mentioned hiking into the tundra tonight to watch the auroral zenith and encouraged her to camp out in the observatory in his absence. "Prepare to be dazzled," he'd said.

She wondered now, how the aurora could possibly get more beautiful. And as her head raced with possibilities, a frost coated her right palm. In the same moment, ice pinched her other hand and drew it higher, setting it on silk.

Her eyes snapped open and she found Nikolai smiling at her. Clio leapt back, letting her hand slip from his shoulder. "Glory," she gasped. "You scared me."

Nikolai caught her retreating hands and squeezed them. He stood at attention, his shoulders back and chest open. A ballroom posture. "Did I?" The words prickled across her neck, lazy and amused. His head tilted at an unnerving angle as he scrutinized her face and neck. "I've always been of the opinion that no woman should dance alone. Unless you prefer it, of course."

"No, I just," she sputtered, "I was—"

Clio nearly asked him to leave, her cheeks hot from the realization that he'd been watching her, but... *Amicable relationship. Nyah. Those stars in his eyes.*

She swallowed. "All right. Thank you."

"My pleasure," he said, returning her hand to his shoulder. His touch brushed over her waist, sliding to her middle back, and she battled the urge to shiver. *His pleasure.* The thought triggered in her head like a minefield, and she scrambled to cover it with a blanket of ice—freezing the explosion in its tracks.

Nikolai smiled. Every inch of her skin tingled. The song paused on its loop, and Clio didn't dare speak until the woman was crooning again. "I thought you were leaving the manor?"

"I still have some time before the show starts," he replied, swaying side-to-side, allowing her to synchronize to his rhythm. "Besides, you've finally shown interest in one of my ballrooms. How could I miss that?"

"I just needed a place to dance. This ceiling is convenient."

He glared and laughter bubbled in her chest. *So sensitive about his pretty rooms.* He stepped forward, leading them in an easy waltz. For a few rotations she roared the directions in her head, scared of stepping on his toes, but then his hand pressed more firmly on her back and their eyes met. All coherent thought flew out of her head, but her feet didn't falter. They continued gliding across the floor, her tempo a perfect match to his.

"You must have fiancé number one wrapped around your finger," he observed, his eyes flicking toward the speaker in the corner.

"Why do you say that?"

"This song." He grimaced. "Talk about a soppy train wreck."

"Hey," she balked.

He chuckled. "It's sweet, don't get me wrong. But not exactly what a man would expect to dance to at his wedding."

"Stow the toxic masculinity, please."

He gave her a disapproving look. "I have no issue

expressing or appreciating emotion, Ms. Farren. I'm simply pointing out that modern music doesn't do love justice."

Clio assessed the confidence in his voice, biting her lip. "You say that like you've been in love before."

He hesitated. "I've come close enough to imagine what it must be like."

"Sounds like something diverted the relationship you're thinking about."

Nikolai chuckled again, roughly. "Yes. A surplus of differences and mutual resentment for the world. Volatile passion has balanced on far less."

Her brow furrowed. "So, there was passion."

"Sure."

"That seems like a fine enough reason to fall in love with someone."

"If you desire that sort of thing." He shrugged. "I found passion rather lonely."

Clio raised an eyebrow at him. "Lonelier than an empty mansion in the middle of nowhere?"

His lips pressed together, but she saw the answer in his eyes. *Yes.*

She asked softly, "What happened?"

"Nothing I wasn't ready for." Nikolai's eyes were bright, as open as she'd ever seen them. "She hated the idea of putting down roots anywhere and I got to the point in my life where I needed to ground myself. We were better off as friends."

"I'm sorry."

"Don't be." He smiled. "Like I said, it wasn't love beyond the platonic."

"Still," she murmured. "It left you alone."

He took a deep breath and asked, "What about you? When did you realize your groom was *the one*?"

"The day I met him," she said instantly, mechanically.

He gaped. "Love at first sight? Ms. Farren, your self-diagnosed cynicism is looking less and less credible."

"I'm not cynical about beginnings," she clarified, rubbing the material of his button-up between her fingers. "It's the survival of them I don't trust."

"Well, now I have to hear about the day you two met."

"No way."

"Come on." His fingers squeezed hers. "You can tell me."

Her nose wrinkled. "It's not much of a story. You'd be wasting your time."

After a beat, Nikolai leaned in, his pupils dilating and his lips curving in an irresistible smile as he murmured, "I don't think it would be. Please?"

She nearly melted against his chest, almost lost herself in the abyss of his eyes. Only her own self-consciousness kept her from throwing her arms around his neck the way she did when he carried her to bed. Only pure willpower prevented her from stumbling over her own feet. He could be so persuasive and frustrating, and charming as hell. She doubted any woman would be able to resist him if he put his mind to it.

She also sort of wished she knew what that felt like—being seduced by Nikolai Trousseau. It was the gentleness in his voice that *really* affected her. She could almost imagine it being whispered in her ear, murmured against her skin.

Clio looked around the room, trying to shield the heat in her face from him, and dredged up the awful memory he'd asked for—because what else could she do? She willed her voice to flatten. Willed the emotions of that day to remain underground like the rotting corpses they were.

"It was the day of my friend's funeral," she said. "They'd just finished the final anointing and rites, and I ran out of the building before they could call friends and family up to say goodbye. I sat under a tree in the courtyard, drinking a flask of tequila I lifted from my mom's purse. I hoped the winter breeze and drunkenness would freeze me to death."

Nikolai's hand shifted at her back, his thumb sweeping back and forth.

"That's when Duncan showed up, peeking around the side of the tree in his golden robes. I tried to hide the flask, but he saw it—I couldn't even speak a full coherent sentence, much less make up an excuse for myself. He should have reported me to the Holy Abbott for it; drinking on church property is a fine-able offense. And if my mother found out," she shivered, "I would have never heard the end of it."

His fingers tightened. She let him pull her closer.

"But he just sat down next to me and asked me what was wrong. Took my hand when I started crying and listened to me blather for over an hour. When I was done, he promised me that I would see her again, but only if I cleaned myself up. He told me he would help me get my soul aligned with The Divine Light."

The story processed behind his eyes. He glared over her shoulder as he finally asked, "Your friend was devout, too?" The words were clipped.

"No," she admitted, but quickly added, "But Duncan says I can appeal to the Light on her behalf if I'm good in this life, if I can be good enough for the both of us." That's what Nyah had told her to do in her message: to find the Light and let it fill her emptiness. That's what Duncan had been.

Nikolai met her eyes. "And you fell in love with him after that?"

She blinked, unsettled by the outrage in his voice. "Of course I did. He was there for me when no one else was. When I needed someone."

"But does he make you happy?" The gaze he focused on her searched and searched, trying to pick the lock to her inner chamber, as if she was someone worth opening. As if happiness meant anything at all.

"He makes me a better person," she said simply.

Nikolai's eyes darkened, as cold and savage as the tundra outside. "Is that why he doesn't answer your phone calls? Because he's too busy making the world a better place?"

The sharpness of his words sparked in her blood and her careful numbness snapped.

"Look," she snarled, gripping his hand so tightly she was shocked he didn't react. "Did I wish for more passion with the person I plan on marrying? Sure. Do I wish I had a love bordering madness, love that feels like plummeting several stories? Yes—who doesn't? Anyone who says otherwise is lying to themselves. But the last thing I desire is to hit the concrete afterwards. And that's what happens. That's what always happens."

Clio didn't know how she expected him to respond, but she was surprised to find stars flickering to life in his eyes. "What if," he whispered, "it's not concrete at the bottom? What if it's just powdery snow?"

The only thing she could think to say was, "That's not how physics works. It doesn't matter what's at the bottom if you fall from high enough."

He smiled sadly, "You say that as if you've fallen before."

She had, and the body that splattered wasn't her own. It should have been her own. "What's the matter with wanting the easiest thing?"

"Nothing." He smirked. "If you're content to love someone who won't take your calls, that's your decision to make."

"Stop spying on me."

"Your voice is impossible to shut out," he leaned in. "You're very loud, you know."

Duncan's voice drifted into her head, reminding her that a

light-blessed woman was meek and quiet. Clio scoffed. "I am not."

"You are." A sly smile spread across his face. "You're completely inescapable, actually."

The thought formed immediately—that anyone unfortunate enough to love her would regret it. She wondered if that was how her father felt when he left. How he still felt to this day.

"I'm no prison," she muttered, her steps slowing.

Nikolai followed her lead, but held tight. "No." His eyes softened. "You're the moon." He reached up behind her and twirled a lock of hair in his fingers. Her spine trembled. "You cling to your place in the sky even when the sun emerges to outshine you."

The shock must have been evident on her face. She made no attempt to mask it.

How had he done it—seen her standing in the shadows? Shadows, all her life. That's how it had been with Nyah, with her mother, with Duncan. Hell, even the mutation dwarfed her. How many times had she glimpsed the outline of the moon during the day and wished for night?

And here he stood, this stranger, who saw all of it.

19

Clio didn't know what to do, what to say—except that she felt exposed. And she certainly wouldn't admit that.

Nikolai's throat bobbed as they stilled, his arms still wrapped around her, his fingers in her hair. His eyes were so dark as he gathered her hair in front of her shoulder, his fingertips grazing her neck.

She forced herself to say, "We've only barely met. You can't keep saying things like that. I don't know you."

He frowned, shaking his head slightly. His fingers continued twining in her hair. "You know me better than you realize. Better than anyone." Nikolai kissed the end of a lock of hair. He held her gaze the entire time, and the intent she saw there made her skin crawl.

"That can't be true," she said, but her voice wavered. Clio tried to disentangle herself.

Nikolai captured her chin and made her look at him. And yes, she let him hold her a little longer. "It is true," he insisted.

Their breath mingled. He didn't blink. "I have not lied to you yet, Ms. Farren. Not once."

This had gone too far.

Clio pushed his hands off of her and aimed for the speaker to shut off the music. It was giving her a headache. Or maybe that was the glaring chandeliers above them.

"Wait. Just one more dance?" She glanced back. Nikolai had stuffed his hands into his slacks and took a shy step toward her. "Please. I haven't had the opportunity to dance like this in ages, and I likely won't again for several more."

One more dance. It sounded so innocent. Her heart repeated the request in a way that bled the innocence dry. But maybe she could work the opportunity to her advantage.

"So dramatic," she teased, shoving her frazzled nerves beneath the surface. She could analyze them later.

"We don't have to talk about anything you don't want to," he swore.

"Do me one better and let me ask *you* a few questions. I feel like I've been on the wrong side of an interrogation table the last few minutes."

He walked around her, his woodsy scent enveloping her like a blanket. "Deal." Pulling his phone from his blazer, he synced the device and replaced her song with an instrumental piece.

When he took Clio in his arms this time, she felt friction in every inch of skin they shared. The tempo of the music bordered on dissonant, so she surrendered wholly to Nikolai's lead. They drew together, his arms tightening with each step. When he pivoted and his knee slipped between hers, she bit back a gasp.

Clio had never listened to music like this before. It bound her, held her on a precipice. A single piano played, the soft notes resembling tin bells ringing at the end of each stanza. They curled through the room, bouncing off the walls and vaulted ceiling—it was the sort of music designed for spaces like this.

She focused on the room past Nikolai's shoulder and, though she couldn't be sure, she thought he might be gazing at the profile of her face. "What is this?"

"A minuet. Do you like it?"

"It's very beautiful," she admitted. "But difficult to anticipate."

His breath warmed her ear. "That's why it's such a wonderful piece to dance to. It's meant to woo you."

Clio's cheeks burned. She listened closer, grasping at the spirit of the composition, trying to compare her own experience with it. She came up empty. Swallowing her disappointment, she asked, "Why do you never sit down for interviews with magazines, or release pictures of yourself to the public?"

"Why would I?"

"People like to see the face behind a business, especially when it's nice to look at."

He huffed a laugh. "Is that a compliment?"

"Don't let it go to your head."

"Of course not. I wouldn't want to jinx the beauty."

"Heaven help me," she grumbled. He wasn't wrong, but the return of his smug mask did strange things to her stomach. Fluttery, churning, heart-clenching things.

"I'd rather the manor speak for itself. This place is the real beauty." He paused, and then continued in a gentler voice, "It's everything."

What could she say to that? Everything crossing her mind seemed insensitive, or stupid. She'd never had anything like that before—something she loved more than herself. Which said a lot, since she could barely look in the mirror.

"What about earth conservation? Is that something you feel passionately about?"

Nikolai pulled back slightly. "What?"

"The gathering here a couple years ago." She kept a tight rein on her voice, looking past the rising tides in his gaze. "It must have meant a lot to you if you volunteered to play host over an arctic freeze."

Those tides froze, hardening into fortress walls. "Is that what you were looking at on the computer? My manor's extracurricular activities?"

"I may have stumbled upon it."

His eyes narrowed. She'd ever known a man who so blatantly refused to balk from close eye contact with her. *Other than Duncan*, that indignant voice in her head amended.

That was true. Duncan had never been afraid of her, and if he could see what she was doing now...

"I wouldn't say earth conservation is a passion, exactly. It is a concern I share with a few close friends—it's something I have a vested interest in. The particular gathering you're referring to was hosted here as a favor for an old friend of mine."

"Was it a large event?"

"Not really," he muttered. "It was more of a family reunion than anything else. A small group."

"I see." *Small group. Small pool of suspects.* "Maybe you could give me your friend's contact information. I'd love to hear more about his ecological efforts. My mother has been looking for a new cause to rally behind."

"I don't think so."

"Why not? If you have a vested interest, wouldn't my help benefit you?"

Suspicion screwed the corners of his mouth. "First of all, Ms. Farren, the sort of help you're offering is not what our cause needs or wants. We keep our dealings private. I would appreciate your discretion on the matter."

"Why does it sound like you're trying to hide something?"

"My entire life is not subject to your scrutiny," he said, his lips pressing in a flat line.

Her chest caved in. "No, of course it's not." If she could only work up the courage to tell him about Nyah, to explain why she came here, maybe he would understand. Maybe he could be trusted.

The words rose. "I just—" And they promptly died in her throat when her eyes met his.

Nikolai had no reason to trust her. How could she explain the truth now, after all this time? She hid her intentions, nurturing conversation and companionship for the sole purpose of extracting information from him. The truth sat in the pit of her stomach and made her sick.

'I haven't lied to you—not once.' But she had lied to him, so much that she didn't know where to begin to make it right.

"You what?" Nikolai urged.

She shoved the words down, swallowing them to join the ache in her gut. "I just wanted to help, if I could. You've been very accommodating, and I appreciate it."

"That's my job." His wariness ebbed. "You realize I would never give out information about my guests, even if I wanted to." Then he smiled, as if suspecting her questions had been a test and he aced it. "Any other questions?"

Clio managed a slight shake of her chin.

He guided her into a spin, nudging her under his arm with the hand on her back. When he tugged her into the circle of his arms, the negligible space between them disappeared. His body lined up with hers. And even though she knew she shouldn't, she melted.

His hand loosened on her back, waiting for that step backward. She didn't take it. Nikolai's breath caught. He wrapped his arm around her back, his fingers curling on the other side of her waist. She nestled her head against his shoulder.

Her body no longer warred. The steps came easily, easier than they ever had before. She let her eyes flutter shut, relishing in the relief of it. And Nikolai started humming.

The rush of air from his nose kissed at her bare neck. His deep, torrid tone vibrated against her heart—above and all around her. Though his suit carried a chill, warmth bloomed in her cheeks as she lost herself in his voice. He kept perfect pitch and time with the melody, as if this was his favorite song.

Clio didn't know Duncan's favorite song. She didn't know if he enjoyed music at all. Why didn't she know that?

The music crescendoed, enveloping her like a heavy curtain. Her mind slipped away. The manor bridged another gap in time, between what was and what had once been. For someone else. For another world.

She stood in the same ballroom, but the chandeliers evaporated. The room gleamed with candlelight. Women in vibrant, ruffled gowns surrounded her, alongside men in fine suits. The air thickened with the scent of liquor and felicity.

It felt like a dream, the scene and faces blurred at the edges, as she meandered through the crowd. Her breath labored, the corset around her ribs drawn tight. Eyes caught on her as she passed by. She held her chin high and met the glances without hesitation.

The crowd broke and she paused at the edge of it. In the center of the room, couples danced exuberantly—but that wasn't what she looked for.

Across the dance floor, she saw him. Nikolai.

Dark curls sprawled across his forehead as he sipped at a glass of amber wine. His free hand rested lightly on a young blonde's shoulder. She laughed up at him, her long shiny hair tumbling down her back. Another blonde woman smiled beside them, her hair a shade darker and braided in a crown across her head.

As if a string pulled taut between them, Nikolai spotted her across the room. A slow smile sprouted as he passed his glass to the laughing blonde and skirted the dance in her direction.

She let the crowd swallow her again, giggles tightening her chest as she squeezed between the bodies. Retreating from his approach as if it were a game. She only made it a few feet before a hand grasped her and turned her around.

Nikolai chuckled soundlessly and led her to the center of the room, throwing them into the dance. The room blurred as they flew across the floor, his face the only clarity—his smile the only anchor. She threw her head back, laughing with him, and glimpsed the mirror above them.

In the ceiling, the glass reflected a vacant room. Nothing danced but the flames. Nothing existed.

Not even her.

Clio eyes shot open. She lifted her head from Nikolai's shoulder and looked at the ceiling. There they were, the two of them, reflected in the glass. Swirling across the marble like ink in milk. She lowered her face and rested her chin on his blazer —still warm from her cheek.

Her thoughts reeled as Nikolai turned his head into the crook of her shoulder, as his nose brushed her collarbone. She tensed, gasping as his nose traced a line up her bare neck. "Nik, what are you—"

A rumble reverberated from his chest, cutting off the hum in his throat, and his fingers dug into her back. Their dancing fell off rhythm as his nose brushed her collarbone again, and lingered. Maybe it was because no one had ever touched her so possessively, so earnestly—but her neck arched. Goosebumps spread across her shoulder.

He rasped onto her skin, "You smell perfectly divine."

"Please—" Her head spun, and she didn't know what she was asking for. She was aware only of the embrace, the scent of cedarwood, and the tickle of his curls against her ear. The collar of his shirt gathered in her fingers as she drew him closer rather than away. There was only them and this one transcendent moment, burned into the parchment of history.

A click echoed through the ballroom and everything went dark. The music cut off cold.

It snapped Clio out of her—*was that a trance?* She pulled away from Nikolai and glanced around. Her eyes slowly adjusted, spots pulsing and fading across her vision, as she felt a hand touch her upper arm.

Nikolai whispered at her ear, "The breaker must have tripped. Stay here. I'll be right back."

The hand fell away. She stood motionless as her vision returned and she wrapped her arms around herself. A chill crept over her bare feet, teasing her legs as hot air ceased to billow from the vents. The manor creaked, the distant howling of the storm outside nearly drowning out the domestic whine.

What might have been moments or minutes later, Nikolai returned, a tall, thin candle illuminating his path. He'd changed into denim pants and a burgundy knit sweater. The hiking boots on his feet clunked loudly as he crossed the room to her. She had a hard time willing herself to focus on anything else.

He handed her the flickering candle. "It's not the breaker. I'm going to check the lines outside and start the generator. It won't power the whole manor, but it'll keep you from freezing to death before we can get the electric company out here."

Before she could process his words or assess the solemn look on his face, he turned on his heel. Her voice returned in a rush. "You're going out like that? Aren't you going to wear a coat or something?"

He paused at the threshold to the hall and looked over his shoulder, the profile of his face barely lit by the flame. A smirk tugged at his mouth. "Yes, of course. I'll be back in a little while, all right? Go watch the lights in the observatory. You don't want to miss them."

Nikolai slipped into the darkness and his footfalls grew softer and softer, until she couldn't hear him at all. She heard the rushing of her thoughts, though, and the rushing of blood in her veins.

The next step formed before her eyes, nipping at her toes like the frigid marble. Clio finally had the chance to search for her own answers.

And by the Light, she was going to.

20

Nikolai left the manor behind, letting it disappear behind a thick screen of snow.

The sky burned a brilliant red—*the blood aurora*, trickling through the blizzard, bathing the world in scarlet. The storm whistled in his ears, fluctuating as the wind changed direction again and again. He glanced up, waiting for the flurry to let up enough to see those ribbons of life. This was the closest he ever got to day, when the night detonated like an emergency flare.

Nikolai's teeth ached, and his tongue stung from the place he'd bit through it.

A coat...

Clio had been concerned with his well-being, with his warmth. And he'd nearly sucked her dry. If the power hadn't gone out, he would have tasted her. With his lips and tongue or his teeth, he wasn't sure how it would have begun. He only knew how it would have ended.

Nikolai didn't believe in a god, not one that would have cared enough to spare him existential agony. But perhaps Clio's god had saved her. Perhaps a divine patron out there saw her pure soul and protected it.

Good. Something should shield her from him.

He was in deep shit, deeper than the seven feet of snow beneath his boots.

Hazy memories flooded his lungs and stole away the luxury of air. The beast slammed against his chest again and again. So he did what he could.

First—space. The farther he walked into the tundra, the more her scent faded from his nostrils. He could finally think. He could breathe.

The power lines emerged in the distance, and it didn't take long to trace the cause of the outage. A section of line had been cleaved—line that should have been immune to the brutality of this weather. The electric smoke filled his nostrils, the molten plastic combining with a wilder smell—the scent of a rainstorm.

If he didn't know any better, he'd think a bolt of lightning struck the line. He surveyed the sky but found no sign of atmospheric charge other than the aurora.

Strange. Very strange.

Nikolai leapt over the smoking cables and continued on, the tundra as endless as his worries. His brow furrowed and the skin of his face cracked, his human skin brittling like ice would beneath warm water. Winter settled in his hair and stuck in an extra pearly layer over his clothes.

Still, he walked on.

The heat he absorbed from Clio's body became a distant memory, but he would crawl through hell to feel it again. He would drown for her, in his head or otherwise, because the girl was brilliant.

The last time someone bested him at chess had been over a century ago.

Reuben blitzed him on liquor and opium-laced cough

syrup, and when the pawn pieces started talking to Nikolai, convincing him to throw the game, he knew he'd made a mistake. In the presence of a being like Reuben, drugs altered reality in a way Nikolai did not care for.

Reuben had enlisted the help of a few of his "friends" to clinch the victory. *Underhanded asshole.*

But Clio.

In the library, her silver eyes sliced into him across the table, calculating and watchful. He thought at first she was learning the game when, in actuality, she'd been learning him— what strategies he favored, how he played his pieces. She assessed his weaknesses and then lunged for his throat with a trill of laughter. The most beautiful laughter.

Her scream, on the other hand, in the early hours of the morning, had turned his skin inside out. Her terror weighed on him.

Then there were the sketches, the smiles, the fury. *The compassion for monsters.*

Nikolai wanted to swallow the emotion stuck in his throat, but his organs had finally frozen. He wouldn't ever be rid of her from his head.

Clio was unexpected, hot-blooded and radiant like the sun, and he was fizzling out in proximity to her, like a wayward comet. He couldn't have her, couldn't even wish or hope for it.

Because in the end, she would destroy him, and if he managed to drag her down with him, the world would grow dark in her absence. There would be no aurora bright enough to replace her. He shouldn't even try.

Yet, his dead heart twisted so mightily that he thought he could hear it thump. Just once.

Nikolai shook his head, the vertebrae at the nape of his neck clicking with the motion. He assembled a list of responsibilities to distract himself.

The generator was first. It would maintain a livable temperature, but not much else. Clio would need warm meals, extra blankets, firewood for the hearth in her room. He'd call for assistance over the radio when he got back to the manor. Hopefully, the weather cleared up in time for expedited service. Before any of that though—

His beast needed to feed.

Once Nikolai hiked far enough away from the manor to extinguish every trace of Clio's essence, he halted. The blizzard hugged him like a ribcage, spooling around him as if he were an organ.

His next meal lumbered nearby—with black-padded paws and yellow teeth—blending into the snow like another drift. He wrangled the disgust in his throat, *his* beast growling in protest. What choice did they have? This was better than making the one mistake that would send him running toward the sun.

He raised a hand to his teeth and ripped his palm open. The gash welled with crimson ichor, his dark blood swirling with opaline dust. Magic and plague. It trickled between his fingers and dripped onto the snow.

Nikolai found a measure of clarity there, beneath the bloody aurora.

His entire existence he believed blood was the enemy, a necessary evil and a reminder that he could never escape the darkness. But now, as he stared at the stained snow, he thought it looked a lot like the mark Clio sparked in his shredded humanity. Permanent and undeniable.

As he dropped his arm, Nikolai's blood arced across the snow like paint on a blank canvas. He let his life spill into the earth, and waited for the prey to come to him.

21

Wax dribbled over the edge of the candleholder's bronze base as Clio slipped into the library. She'd made a brief detour to her room to pull on a few additional layers, and by the time she made it back to the lobby, the warmth of the manor had completely evaporated.

There was definitely a fault in the windows.

Her breath curled in a misty cloud before her face. The fur coat tickled at her neck. Her feet fell in echoing thunks despite her best efforts to walk lightly. She wasn't used to the weight of winter boots—never had a need for a pair before coming here.

Maybe if Nikolai was serious about hiring her, she could help him refurbish the manor. They could better keep the cold at bay, if Duncan let her come back.

A red glow radiated through the room down the staircase.

Clio paused in awe. That was what Nikolai had been hinting at: the fiery color. The aurora beckoned to her like a lullaby, its delicate fingers crooked in invitation.

Don't you miss me, it seemed to sing.

She shook herself out of the stupor, shivering. There would be time to admire the sky once she'd found more information about Nikolai's friend. A name and phone number, even an email address would do.

Clio set the candelabra on the chess table, wary of leaving behind a trail of wax. There couldn't be any trace of her transgression beyond the next door.

A phantom flame burned white in the corner of her vision as she grappled at the latch for Nikolai's quarters. The shelf swung open with a click, and she squeezed through.

She shut the passage behind her and, as her sight remedied the darkness, she noted the outline of a massive bed to her left. Thick curved posts formed a rounded peak above the mattress. Something dangled from the beams, but she didn't look long enough to determine what.

There were two doors, one ajar directly across from her that led into a deeper darkness, and one shut on the far side of the room. Between the doors, a desk was tucked into a portico. A few candles dotted the surface, all snuffed but one flickering softly in the center. *Thank heavens for his pyromaniac tendencies.*

As the flame drew her out of the darkness, a mass brushed against her shin. She squinted down at the cat sniffing her shoes. Clio bent to run a hand through her soft fur, whispering, "No cuddles right now, Poppet. Rain check."

On the desk, she spotted Nikolai's journal, positioned neatly directly in front of the candle. Long, deep scratches marked the surface of the wood, wayward splinters poking up in every direction.

What the hell happened there?

Grimacing at the cat sitting at her feet, Poppet blinked back, bushy tail flicking. Maybe she really could lash out—

could be vicious if she wanted to. Truth be told, Clio had the same fault.

She began with the small drawers stacked on the back of the desk, the warmth of the flame kissing her bare hand as she reached over it. They were empty save for a few paperclips, some black thread, and a broken quill. Each drawer emptier than the one before. Clio couldn't understand how someone could be so organized, so unattached to any degree of physical clutter. The assumption of his greed and selfishness had never felt so misplaced.

When she tugged the last drawer, it uttered a low groan as the contents were revealed.

A sea of journals, identical to the one on the desk, glared up at her. She took a quick peek of a few interiors, brief enough to determine they were all complete. There had to be close to a hundred of them, maybe more.

Clio muttered to the cat beside her, "Who fills up this many journals? Is he neurotic or what?"

The cat blinked and licked her whiskers. Clio could have sworn the creature nodded slightly. *Right*—she had to be losing it. She sighed and slid the drawer shut. "Okay, well, if I were Mr. Neat Freak, where would I put a key?"

Poppet leapt onto the desk, her fur dangerously close to catching flame. Clio shot up to grab her, but the cat met her gaze and sat back on her haunches. One of her front paws rested on the journal—her tail weaving like a serpent.

Clio managed her bewilderment, holding that gaze long enough to determine that it wasn't a coincidence. It was a response.

She let her fingertips graze the leather cover—decadent to the touch, smooth and giving. Dragging the book out from Poppet's paw, Clio curved over the dwindling candlelight. The journal split open to the most recently inked page, and there, tucked into the crease, a bronze key connected to a wind of thin red ribbon. He used the key to his office as a bookmark.

Clio's face cracked into a broad grin, and she careened forward to kiss Poppet's nose. "Such a clever girl. Thank you."

As Clio worked to unknot the ribbon and free the key, she glimpsed the page beneath.

She saw the numbers, *11-10*. Their chess scores. The cocky bastard was still ahead. Then, a few lines down a list began: *Call Mrs. Itzli back early. Notify snow service of the date change. Contact Reuben for blood.*

Her fingers faltered and she nearly dropped the key as the ribbon unfurled, slipping back to the open book.

Blood. What an odd thing to write.

Was he involved with a blood bank? Did he need regular transfusions? Was he sick? The last thought laid heavy in her heart. *Reuben.* The name stood out to her next to the very formal address of Mrs. Itzli. She was willing to bet Reuben was a friend. Maybe even *the* friend.

Clio shut the journal and scratched Poppet under the chin before retreating to the library.

The corridors were pitch black, a trial for even Clio's eyes to sort out, but she couldn't carry that leaking candle along with her even if the wax *did* blend seamlessly into the marble flooring. Nikolai would notice.

She saw enough to feel her way to his office, to unlock the door and stumble to the window on the other side of the room. As she pulled back the curtain, the force of the aurora flooded her eyes. She would have blinked back the luster if it had not immediately rooted in her gut.

Through the storm—the gray sheets of snow and hail—the world bled out.

The sky displayed wounds, as if begging someone to notice and stitch them back together. Clio's eyes throbbed, a million floating lights swarming her vision.

For a moment, she detached from her body, and it was only color and brilliance absorbing her every thought. Somewhere in the nothingness, a part of herself tingled. *I'm still here.*

She blinked, turning from the window, and observed the room smoldering under a valentine hue. Every surface reflected the light and the slight ache in her head intensified to a raging migraine.

A futile tug on one of the filing cabinets at her hip told her she would need to search for another key. She staggered forward, her legs spasming with the movement. Clio blew a puff of air towards her forehead—towards the sweat gathering on her temples. *How am I sweating right now?* Her entire body ached.

Clio looked through the endless stacks of folders and compartments of the desk, looking for a key ring. She nearly gave up, ready to admit that the whole investigation had been a waste of time and lay in the crystal dome for the rest of the night, when she yanked on the next drawer on the right side of his desk.

A set of keys were there, and so was something else.

The crystal vessel flashed. She went still. There was something about it... its very existence in Nikolai's desk an enigma. He had stored no other trinkets, nothing that lacked practicality except for this.

A hidden bit of liquor, perhaps? She'd found her mother's stashes before. Clarissa had a reason to keep it a secret, though. Who cared if a hotel owner partook now and again? Certainly no one of importance.

Clio licked her lips. What sort of liquor might a man like Nikolai drink?

She could imagine what cinnamon whiskey would smell like rolling off his tongue. Dusty barrels mixed with his woodsy scent, hot to the taste. Or perhaps gin. Juniper berries developing in the back of her throat as she sucked on his teeth—those bright, white teeth that stunned her every time he smiled.

The direction of her thoughts made her choke. She flushed the ideas out of her mind.

Beside the vessel, a stack of business cards stood against the wooden panel of the drawer. As Clio removed the container, she saw which one sat on top. Nyah's business card, for her interior design services, winked up at her.

Next to Nyah's business number, familiar writing scrawled her private number on the card—a gesture her best friend rarely did. Nyah knew Nikolai. He knew her. The card was proof, and it was on top, as if he'd called recently.

In a daze, her thoughts racing, she took the bulbous container and the business card in her hands. The glass was heavier than she expected. Several engravings massaged the skin of her fingers, but the room was too dim to see them clearly.

With shaking fingers, she pried the stopper off the vessel and brought it to her nose.

The scent burned up her nostrils, of iron and rust and death. She gagged. In the midst of swallowing back vomit, raising an arm to cover her nose, the crystal slipped from her hands. It collided with the floor and shattered, a spatter of black-rouge hitting her boots as the meager contents spilled across the pristine marble.

The card slipped through her fingers and landed in the center of it all, soaking up the—the—

She couldn't breathe, couldn't move as she took in the

bloody floor. Because that's what it was. *Blood.* And that was an eye dropper sitting next to the keys in the drawer.

It all struck her at once. His stories.

"Fuck," she whimpered. "Fuck, fuck, fuck."

Divine Light, spare me. He's a cannibal.

The monster hadn't checked into a room. No—it owned the whole damn mansion. She'd been right all along not to trust him. He killed a man on his own property two years ago and got away with it.

Maybe Nyah had known or seen too much while here, and he tracked her down to ensure she wouldn't expose the truth. Other thoughts—theories—rushed through her head, but they didn't make sense. They weren't *possible.*

Cannibal. That made sense, even through her fever and scattered thoughts. She braced her body weight on the desk, struggling to remain upright.

Was it Nyah's blood speckling her clothes? Seeping across the floor like rainwater, with no destination?

She would be Nikolai's next victim if she didn't do something. If she didn't run. There would be no hiding the fact she knew everything. All he had to do was open the door to his office or see the utter hatred in her eyes when he returned to the manor.

Moments ago she imagined kissing him, and she loathed herself all the more for it. She didn't know if she would ever forgive herself. Didn't know if The Divine Light would, either.

Her boots slid on the wet floor, leaving narrow red streaks as she rushed down the hall. She veered into the kitchen. It took longer than expected to feel for the knife block, but she sighed in relief when she found the steel teeth and withdrew one.

The edge of the closest town, the one with the airport, couldn't be more than a few hours away by foot, even through the flurry. She'd never traveled through such conditions—but what choice did she have? It couldn't be so difficult. Keeping her sense of direction would be the real challenge.

Emerging from the manor, Clio watched the oscillating red bolts in the sky and memorized their arrangement. It shone as the only constant to direct her path.

Her North Star.

22

There was only death in his mouth, in his hands, in his mind.

The beast raised his head from a shriveled artery, tipping back to look at the red sky, relishing in the surge of strength pumping through his veins. Demon blood too often trapped him, pulled him down below the surface. The animal blood sincerely pissed him off, but nourished in a way that was just sufficient.

He felt that other part of him—the human part—clutching tightly to the reins of their body. Only given enough lead to drop the massive creatures of the Arctic, the beast poked and prodded that control, looking for a weakness. A way to take the power back.

They looked at the bear laid out before them, the hulk of ivory carcass touching their knees, a drop or two of rouge the only evidence of a struggle. Behind them, a few yards back, another carcass sat. And a few yards more, a third.

They'd finally had enough. Their belly sloshed as they

stood and walked on, spurred by the human's desire to resurface.

The human tried to fight back the beast, to stay wholly present. *I'm here,* he thought. *Almost.*

The wind shifted and an achingly familiar scent filled their senses. Roses and sea. New and ancient and bold and undeniable.

The human stumbled, losing a mile or so of rein in the shock, and the beast went wild. Within seconds, they had tracked the scent to her, huddled and braving the blizzard one step at a time. They crouched, readying to pounce.

The beast thought of her blood in his mouth, in his hands, in his mind. *Blessed liberation.* But at the last second, the line pulled tight and Nikolai came to the surface.

Partially.

Nikolai was there in the tundra, but he was also floating above the ground in the lane in his head. All the crystal boxes, filled with foam and cyclones and memories, drifted all around him, sending vibrations every direction, into every corner.

He paused. *Every corner.* He'd never noticed the corners before. Nikolai suddenly came to the conclusion that this place of memories wasn't a street at all. It was a box. A cage that held him and his memories in.

Or was it keeping something else out?

He squinted past the glass walls of the moonlit lane. If he focused, he could almost see the whites of his eyes reflecting back at him. Beyond that, he couldn't be sure. Was another beast slithering on the outside, waiting to be let in?

What if Genevieve's magic had really left something in him? What if it was exactly what he always feared?

Clio's scent invaded once more on a strong gust of wind, and sent a fissure running through the barrier. It threatened to shatter his defenses. The salt of her blood grated against the crack, screeching and whining.

He recoiled, clutching the beast in both hands and shoving down, down, down.

I'm here, Nikolai told himself. *I'm here—right here.*

And he was.

23

"Ms. Farren." The rumbling voice touched her through the storm.

Her body tensed, pausing long enough in the snow to feel the ground crunch and sink. She half-turned, every twist of her stomach excruciating.

Nikolai stood a yard or so away, his tall silhouette static in the shifting downfall. He seemed to vibrate, his fists clenched tightly at his sides, his expression fierce. "What are you doing out here? You could have gotten lost and froze to death."

He took a small step towards her.

Clio lifted the knife between them. "Stay the hell away from me."

His eyes narrowed in on the blade, something predatory twisting beneath the surface. "And might I ask why?"

"I know," she whispered.

Nikolai's expression hardened, his mouth setting in a grim line. "Which part of my home did you encroach upon tonight, beloved?"

She ignored the question. The affection. "You're a monster."

"Yes." The response was instantaneous, and something flickered in his face. Something like *sadness*. He wanted to get her guard down. Wanted to distract her. Then he'd attack.

"I'm leaving. If you let me go now, I'll keep your secret."

He shook his head. "No, you won't. No sane person would." Nikolai took another step and the blade in her hand trembled. She saw how it would play out: he'd tear her apart and she'd become another carcass lying in the dark.

Her voice cracked as she asked the only question that mattered, "Why did it have to be her?"

Nikolai froze mid-step. "What are you talking about?"

"Nyah," she shouted, her tears blurring his figure before they brimmed over. "Why did it have to be my best friend—my only friend?"

"Nyah? Nyah Gazini?" Perplexity filled his face, but one kernel of shock and recognition held firm. "Are you telling me Nyah Gazini is dead?"

"Cut the bullshit. I found the container of blood in your desk." A senseless laugh erupted from her chest. She felt ill—veritably ill. Her head rushed, thumping so loudly she could hardly think. "You're real fucked up, you know that? Who did that blood belong to?"

His throat bobbed and he stepped forward again, holding his hands toward her in a facade of surrender. "Hold on. You don't understand."

"Oh, I understand plenty. Enough to know that if I let you near me, you're going to cut me open and boil my organs in a stew."

He grimaced. "Trust me, that's the last thing I would do."

"No. You'd bleed me dry first," she snarled. His eyes shuttered. "Like Nyah, like the dead man on your property two years ago, and however many others before them."

"All right, let's just calm down and talk about this. I don't want to bleed you dry. I don't want to hurt you at all."

"But you would, wouldn't you?" She snarled. "You just can't help it, right?"

Nikolai chuckled, actually smiled at that. And took another step.

She shuddered, straight down to her bones. "I'm not going anywhere with you without a fight and this knife is sharp, so I'd think twice before you touch me."

"I'm not going to hurt you," he repeated, closing in.

"Leave me alone." She stumbled backward and turned to flee.

His hand caught her elbow, tugging her back to face him, his voice softly pleading, "Please, give me a chance to explain."

So she drove the knife into his stomach.

Nikolai recoiled with a groan, his shoulders curving in until the two of them were nearly nose to nose. She gaped at her hand still wrapped around the steel handle, at the blade embedded in the fabric of his sweater.

A chill more furious than the weather prickled her scalp. Blood gushed, spilling over her fingers. Lukewarm and sticky. She ripped away, holding her hand stiffly away from her.

Heavens. She'd really just done that.

Gritting his teeth, Nikolai grasped the knife's handle and straightened. And as his eyes latched onto hers, she saw the wilderness. Frustration. Determination. Without breaking her gaze, he slowly withdrew the blade, inch-by-bloody-inch.

The wound gushed anew, and Clio couldn't look away. A low hiss of air radiated through his clenched teeth until the blade was at last raised beside him. She didn't understand how, but the blood stopped flowing.

Nikolai's head tilted, a cruel smile playing on his lips. He mouthed the words, "So dramatic." And dropped the knife. It sunk into the snow like butter.

Oh. Fuck. Me.

Adrenaline deafened her, blinded her—set her aching body into motion. She spun and smacked into a wall of coarse warmth and muscle. The abrupt stop almost flattened her, but she grasped at the bulk in front of her to stay upright.

Then, the bulk shifted under her hands.

Her eyes focused long enough to register black eyes and white fur before the bear rose, and her hands fell away. She backed up in a daze, but not nearly quickly enough. The moment settled like an exhale. Clio accepted her fate: that perhaps she was never meant to live. Maybe she was just an unhappy accident.

The animal became a mountain of predatory focus—every sharp, yellow tooth bared for her. It roared, the stench of rot and death filling her senses. She closed her eyes and waited for The Light, waited to see Nyah again.

But she heard him.

Nikolai said her name for what felt like the first time, screamed it over the roaring of the world and the beast. *Clio.* It rang in her ears like a call to revival.

She opened her eyes to the sensation of gravity pulling on her stomach and saw the world whirling around her. She landed back-first in the snow. The powder was soft, but not quite soft enough to prevent the air from getting knocked out of her lungs.

Through the gray and crimson veil of the storm, Clio saw Nikolai's red sweater. Then, a mass of white engulfed him as he tumbled across the tundra.

Clio forced herself upright, gasping as she dug her fingers into the snow.

The struggle came into focus. Nikolai wrestled with the bear, grasping for its neck as the animal tore at him with teeth and claws. He was bleeding again, his clothing ripped to shreds across his torso, the snow turning into a carpet as red as the hallway to the honeymoon suite.

Growls radiated through the storm and, at once, Clio couldn't determine what made which sound. Her fingers didn't register the sting of the ice. She was frozen, half crouching, lost in the madness of what unraveled before her eyes.

Somehow, Nikolai's gaze found her through the storm. With a vice grip around the polar bear's neck and his chin tucked to keep the creature from biting his head off, he screamed, "Get back to the manor."

She blinked, chest tightening at the desperation in his voice. Not a demand, but a *plea*. As if he cared about her. And what use was it to pretend right now?

The bear reared, but Nikolai held fast, dragged forward through the snow. He cried, "Go." Clio didn't know how or why, but she believed the look on his face—the concern in his voice. She believed in him, for just this one moment.

Scrambling to her feet, she lurched in the direction of the manor, but halted a few feet back. At the edge of a murky, red-stained hole in the snow.

The knife.

Nikolai would die out here. Cannibal or not—and a part of her was starting to doubt that assumption—he didn't deserve to become a mangled corpse like Nyah. No one did. It wasn't fair that the two people in her life who peered into her chambers, who saw her as more than an asset or inconvenience, would meet the same ravaged end.

Nikolai was protecting her, but who was protecting *him*?

She dropped, thrusting her fingers into the crevice. The bloody ice tore at her hand as she forced her arm deeper. Her other hand braced the surface, turning a frightening blue color teetering on the edge of black.

Clio's fingers brushed against something colder than the snow—a caress of steel. Before she could withdraw the handle, she heard a chuffing and squelching. The growling died.

Something about the silence made her turn to look.

The bear laid on the snow, sinking as its body pressed into the fresh powder. Above it, Nikolai crouched, his head buried in the bear's neck. It took a moment to realize that the bear's spine was severed, its head twisted at an unusual angle, and Nikolai was *biting*.

Feeding. Blood splattered his forehead and streaked messily over his chin. He lifted his face and met her eyes with his own. And they were black.

He stood, but Clio was already running.

She sprinted back to the manor, flying across the snow so quickly she might have been hovering. The lights intensified above her, beating erratically to the tune of her heart. She didn't look around or behind her, though she knew he was there.

He was with her, somehow. Could probably catch her easily. So why wasn't he?

That's all she thought of, his proximity and the delight she knew he must feel in chasing her, until she reached the manor. She tripped up the grand stairs and lurched into the lobby, flipping the lock of the main doors.

The storm had softened slightly, but she didn't see Nikolai. Her heart raced, as if she expected him to emerge from the red night at any moment, those black eyes reflecting the sky. She thought she might very well faint if he did, if she had to watch his bloody face approach the glass windows.

Clio rushed across the lobby, her gaze catching on the painting above the reception desk. They weren't folk tales.

They weren't nymphs. Those women were Nosophoros. *They're real. It's all real.* She dashed up the stairwell, her thoughts spiraling.

Cannibal—she hadn't been so far off. Half of her wanted to laugh at the absurdity of it and the other wanted to cry.

She tried to think up a plan. Anything that might save her. She could initiate an emergency signal with her phone, buzzing a radio frequency for as long as the device retained battery—it might eventually make it through the storm. If she barricaded her door, she might have a chance.

But when she reached the threshold of her room, the door was ajar.

Clio paused, trying to remember if she closed it after retrieving her winter clothes. Her memories swam, muddled from adrenaline and tainted by her fever. She simply didn't know.

She nudged the door open.

No noise echoed from within. The darkness didn't stir. She entered slowly, one hand lingering on the knob, her eyes scanning the room. It was how she remembered leaving it. Cold and dim. She exhaled and stepped the rest of the way inside, aiming for the double doors to the bedroom.

The suite's door slammed shut. Clio whirled.

Nikolai stood beside the closed door. Huskily, he said, "We need to talk."

She darted into the bathroom, managing to fumble in the windowless darkness and flip the lock milliseconds before the knob started rattling. A heavy thud reverberated through the door.

Nikolai growled on the other side and another thud followed. She stumbled back, grasping blindly at the counter. This was too dark, even for her. He roared, smacking the door again, a crack echoing as the wood splintered.

Shit. He was going to break in. Her stomach turned and turned, clenching as it had earlier that evening. She couldn't hold it back anymore.

Clio felt frantically for the toilet, puking before she fully found the porcelain lid. The bile soaked her front and she hung her head, letting it all pour out. Between her heaves, she realized everything went silent on the other side of the door.

24

Nikolai hated himself. Truly hated himself as he listened to Clio get sick beyond the door. It brought the world back into focus.

The bear blood made him aggressive, impulsive—it triggered that predatory instinct in him to hunt her down and lay in wait. He'd held back long enough to make sure she got back to the manor, not wanting the confrontation to happen out in the tundra where she would freeze to death first or summon another bloodthirsty animal.

The only bloodthirsty animal he wanted close to her was *himself*.

He studied the door and the hole he'd left in the panels. It would be easy to crash through, to put himself in her space and force her to hear him. But she was frightened.

A sourness permeated the air and he could taste it, even though the feeding should have dulled his senses. It was that potent—she was *that scared*. And he was to blame. Nikolai could use all the force and persuasion in the universe to get close to her, and she still might not believe him. Who in their right mind would trust a beast?

Clio continued to puke as he backed away from the bathroom. He drifted toward the dead hearth in the parlor. The staff kept a starter bundle of wood and kindling in each room for times such as this. He took the matchbook above the mantle and bent over the fireplace. In a couple minutes, he had a fire going.

The warmth anchored him—made him feel more human. And more miserable.

He wandered back to the bathroom, frowning at the rancid stench and her loud retches. In one of her pauses to breathe, he said, "I'm sorry."

She emptied her stomach, again and again.

"I'm so sorry," he repeated, raising a hand to touch the door. He wished it could be her face, her heart, her nerves. "I didn't want to scare you—that's the last thing I ever want to do."

A tense silence stretched, but eventually her vomiting stopped.

"I started the hearth. You must be freezing. Come out, and I'll explain everything."

Clio emitted a low, gruff sound that likely meant he could go fuck himself.

"Okay," he slumped against the door and slid to the floor. "I'll explain it from here, then. Just listen for five minutes, that's all I ask. Afterwards, if you don't believe me—and trust me, I wouldn't blame you if you didn't—I'll leave you alone, I swear." He stared at the crackling fire, then at the red glow filtering through the suite's curtains.

Nikolai cleared his throat. "You clearly know now that I'm not... a normal person. I'm—"

He paused, looking for the right words, the words that

would comfort her and not push her away. He didn't find them quickly enough.

Her voice came on a breathless whisper. *"Nosophoros."*

Nikolai nodded, even though he knew she couldn't see him. "I'm Earth's attempt at self-preservation—a human turned other. A plague carrier. A demon-eater."

Clio retched, dryly, and he clamped his mouth shut.

That was the last thing he should be explaining right now. She didn't care about him, not really. She'd clearly come here looking for answers about Nyah, and telling her about his purpose, his bloodlust, wouldn't help anything.

Nikolai would give anything to take her sickness away. His hands shook with the effort it took not to smash the door in and wrap her in his arms.

He said, "Nyah Gazini came to the manor two years ago, at my friend, Reuben's, request. Clio, your friend—she wasn't normal, either. You probably suspected as much if you spent long periods of time with her."

Clio sniffled and a different sort of sound echoed through the door. A sob. "I know," she moaned.

Nikolai's dead heart ached. He didn't know it could do that anymore. "She wasn't like me. Both Nyah and Reuben belong to a long line of druids. They call themselves Guardians, because they're descended from beings who were born of the mantle and magma of Earth's core."

Clio groaned into the toilet bowl. *How*, she seemed to ask.

"They carry a special kind of magic," he explained, "inherited from their ancestors. And those ancestors guide them— they linger in the afterlife as faint, whispering spirits. The more powerful the Guardian, the more they see of alternate realities, all the millions of dimensions that there apparently are. But the more powerful they are, the easier it is for them to be hunted for their magic by spirits not of this world. By demons, in particular."

Clio was weeping now, her gentle sobs reverberating off the porcelain toilet bowl. "I don't understand," she rasped.

"I know." Nikolai placed his trembling fists on the floor, letting the wooden slats shake beneath his knuckles. Anything to keep himself contained. "I—I'm sorry. You have no reason to trust me, no reason to believe me. This is more information than I ever wanted to overwhelm you with, but I need you to understand something about what happened two years ago, with Nyah and that dead body."

Clio didn't respond, only kept crying, so he took that as the only permission he would ever get to keep going.

"There was an evocation." Nikolai said evenly, clearly. "Guardians gathered here to summon a demon, and they succeeded."

A shudder interrupted Clio's sobs. For a moment, she stopped breathing. But then she raked in a desperate breath and spit into the toilet water.

Nikolai closed his eyes and quickly recounted the events of that night aloud. How Reuben had been anointed to slay the demon by the Guardians gathered here for the evocation, how the summoning brought forth a monster stronger than any of them anticipated, how Reuben nearly died in that sacred circle and how Nikolai was rendered useless by the spell protecting that sphere of tundra, how he was forced to watch his oldest friend teeter on the edge of death.

"And then," he whispered. "Nyah intervened. She slipped into the summoning ring and killed the demon herself. She took back the magic it had stolen to come into this dimension.

"Nyah absorbed a lot of magic that day, Clio. More magic than is usual for a Guardian her age. That whole night, while she and the other Guardians celebrated here in the manor,

Nyah acted strangely. Something was wrong, I could tell, but I kept my concerns to myself despite the friendship we'd formed during her visit."

A sharp inhale. "What?" Clio's voice was bewildered, but gentle. More like the compassionate mortal he'd gotten to know.

This was the crux of it—whether she believed he'd harmed Nyah or not.

"Nyah pinpointed me the instant she first entered my lobby," Nikolai explained. "She ambushed me about my outdated interior design, of all things."

He chuckled bitterly, remembering the way she'd towered over him even though they stood at the same height. *A tragedy,* she'd called it—that the manor's interior didn't match the magnificent exterior.

"If you were Nyah's best friend, I'm sure you know how forceful she could be. She imposed her interior design services on me and refused any payment beyond advertising her name should anyone ask. She steamrolled over all of my protests, so I told her she was welcome back any time, that she would always have a place to stay here. She never took me up on the offer, though I suspect now that she might have wanted to. That she should have.

"By the time twilight dawned after the evocation, Nyah was gone. She slipped out of the manor and left a note on my office door thanking me for my hospitality. She left me her card in case I had any problems with deliveries, but that was the last time I saw her."

A torrent of guilt surged within him, washing over his soul in broken bursts.

"Last year," he admitted quietly, "she called the manor a few times, trying to get in touch with me. I was never available at the right time, and whenever I called back, she didn't answer either. Eventually, the calls stopped. I didn't think anything of it, but clearly I—I should have."

What if she had been calling for help? That remnant of humanity, the outraged young boy who read books to both experience and hide from the world, pounded on his ribs.

"Whatever happened to her," Nikolai swore, "whatever or whomever is to blame, I will help you rectify it. I will hunt it down for her. For *you*. If you can trust me, I promise to make this right. And I know, right now, it feels like nothing can make it right, but please, I'm begging you to let me try."

Nikolai feared the silence that followed his promise. He worried it would tear him apart, her rejection, that it would blow his entire manor away—but then clothing rustled on the other side of the door. The metal knob shifted above his head.

He slid back, a smile blooming on his face as the door swung open. But his relief instantly snuffed out.

Clio's temples were matted with sweat. Her eyes were glazed, squinting in pain, her limbs shaking as she tried to hold herself up on hands and knees.

"Help me," she whispered. And collapsed forward into his arms.

25

Nikolai hefted Clio in his arms and carried her to the fireplace. Her head lolled, heavy and hot against his chest as she struggled to keep her eyes open.

The scent of acid burned his nostrils, stronger than her natural salty fragrance. He laid her in front of the fire, cradling the back of her neck as he rested her head against the hardwood floor.

"I'm too warm," she whimpered, pulling at the collar of her coat.

He grabbed her hands, blue and icy, and stretched them towards the fire. "I doubt that's true. You're in shock."

One of her hands pulled free and flew back to her coat. "I mean it," she said, grabbing at the fabric. Her body trembled so badly she couldn't grip the zipper. "I feel like I can't breathe."

He surveyed her body, sprawled out before him the way he'd imagined in his darkest moments. Her heart pounded, her gasps for air quick and strained. That sweet little furrow etched itself into her forehead. She was hyperventilating or would be soon.

This is more than shock.

Nikolai swallowed his fears—those fears of himself and fears for her—and leaned over to catch her gaze with his own. "Your clothes are filthy. Can I take them off for you?"

Clio went still. Her chin wrinkled, giving away the battle of her thoughts.

"I'll be a perfect gentleman about it," he added, offering a reassuring smile. "I promise."

She hesitated for a moment longer, then nodded.

He might have reached for her zipper with a little more enthusiasm than appropriate, but soon her thick winter coat and her sheer blouse were discarded. When he fingered the hem of her camisole, she covered his hands with her own and whispered, "That stays."

Acid had managed to dribble down her front, not a lot but enough to stain the white fabric—but he moved on to her jeans. As he unbuttoned her pants, she twisted her upper body and reached back to grapple with the bra strap beneath her shirt, her face screwed as if the motion brought blinding agony. His fingers faltered on the zipper of her jeans as the bra strap released, and he had to remind himself why he shouldn't be watching.

She's sick and she isn't mine.

He could think of about a million things he'd like to do to her if she wasn't sick and was his. A million scenarios that started exactly this way—pulling her tight, little pants down.

Nikolai gritted his teeth and shook the thoughts away, even as the jeans dipped low enough to reveal red satin panties. *Holy shit.* He averted his eyes and sloughed the pants the rest of the way off, its material soaked with a mix of bile and melted snow.

When he stood to gather the clothes, he kicked her matching bra under the bed. It was too tempting to have within eyesight. He deposited the clothes into the laundry bag in the bathroom, nearly slipping on a scattering of sandy debris on the floor.

On the way back to the fireplace, he pulled a pillow and the weighted duvet off the bed. Clio groaned in protest as he wrapped her in the blanket.

"Oh, hush," he muttered, tucking the pillow under her head. "You may have a fever, but you're also dangerously close to hypothermia. Let me take care of you."

He placed the back of his hand on her forehead. Clio could have been a furnace or the fire itself with how she burned.

"Your fingers feel good on my skin," she breathed. Then she groaned a second time, curling beneath the blanket, her hand pressing against her stomach. "Oh, no. It's going to happen again."

Nikolai retrieved the ice bucket from the other side of the room and positioned it beneath her in time to catch the vomit. He kneeled there for a moment, lost for what to do. Clio braced herself on unsteady arms. Tremors rippled through her torso.

Without second-guessing the instinct, Nikolai swept her hair back and fisted it at the nape of her neck. His other arm wrapped around her waist, offering support and what little comfort he thought she might accept. Her face relaxed fractionally as she spilled her stomach into the bucket.

She leaned into him and he welcomed it, tightening his arm around her. He wanted to turn his face into the crook of her neck and breathe her in, but didn't. *She isn't mine.* And he wouldn't fool himself into thinking it was possible—not like when they were dancing earlier.

That had been a mistake. Clearly.

Finally finished, Clio pushed the bucket away, but she didn't push him away like he expected. Then again, she hadn't pushed him away in the ballroom either. She looked up—ears pink from the cold, but perhaps from something else, too.

"I think it's safe to assume you don't want to eat me after all that."

He chuckled. "Well, want and plan to are two very different things. I won't, if that's what you're worried about."

"That's not funny," she grumbled.

"It's a little funny." He squeezed her and she whimpered, her hands flying to his arm around her stomach. "Oops, sorry."

Clio's fingers drifted to his abdomen. They brushed against the exposed and blood-crusted skin there. She frowned at the spot she'd stabbed him—at the lack of evidence it ever happened. "You're okay?"

"Yes," he choked out. "I mean, I had to stuff my guts back into my stomach after the bear ripped me open, but it's healed now."

"Good." She removed her hand. "I'm sorry I stabbed you."

He winked, hoping to dispel the guilt on her face. "You can stab me anytime, as long as I get to undress you afterward."

Her lips perked up a bit. "Shut up."

Nikolai mimed zipping his mouth closed and her smile deepened—but her eyes drooped, barely cracked. Her stare unfocused. Sleep was going to take her.

She swayed, her body going limp in his arms as she slurred, "I still would have fought for you."

For me?

～

The newest plague.

He realized it in the morning, when Clio didn't improve. A strange chemical scent twined with her blood, marring the floral rose garden of her body with poisonous thorns.

The virus of this century had found her. She likely picked it up on her travel to the manor. Whether it had lurked in her bloodstream the past week, waiting for a vulnerability in her immunity, or whether something in his own manor had infected her, he didn't know.

Right now, the how didn't really matter.

Nikolai paced in front of the hearth, watching his shadow move across her unconscious body. She'd been sleeping for hours. In her rest, he slipped away to gather wood for the fire, started the generator, and retrieved fever reducers from Mrs. Itzli's first aid kit in the kitchen. He'd even managed to get a radio signal out to the ranger station. They told him what he already suspected: no help would come until the storm had passed.

Nikolai tried to coax Clio to take pills, but it only triggered another vomiting spell. She couldn't even keep down a glass of water.

He did what he could. Boiled water in the hearth and kept her as clean as possible without running water. Added wood to the fire. Kept watch. None of that would save her. He'd seen humans die from a lot less.

His steps marked every tick of the grandfather clock in the corner as he considered how long this could go on.

Her lungs wheezed, whining beneath her sternum with every breath. How long would it be before her heart gave out from the duress? It already slugged along, though he couldn't remember what a normal heart rate was for sleep.

How long could she be without water, when she was already dehydrated? He tried not to mark the constriction of her veins, but who was he kidding—

"You're going to wear a hole through your pretty floor," Clio's voice rumbled.

He came to a halt, his shadow covering her face as she smiled at him. So weak. If he had a live heart, it would have burst. "How are you feeling?"

Her grin faded. "Fine."

"Liar."

Her eyes fluttered. "Horrible." she croaked. "I—"

The next word caught in her throat and she tried to dislodge it, brow stitching tightly. Throat-clearing turned to coughing and she lurched for the bucket again. She heaved and gasped for air. Nothing came up this time. Her gut was hollow.

He heard her lungs straining—she might as well be hacking one up. Then, a spatter of blood dispersed into the bucket. The time for intervention had come.

Nikolai snatched the steel letter opener off of the mantle, the rose-handled one he'd retrieved from his office, and knelt before Clio. As her coughing fit ended, she stared at the blood in the bucket. Tears welled in her eyes. She went paler than the moon, and he guessed it meant she was close to fainting.

"Clio," he whispered, gathering her in his arms. She didn't object, didn't even ask why he positioned her in a straddle over his lap. He lifted the letter opener to his neck and pressed it against his skin.

As he opened an artery to the air, Clio seemed to wake a little more. Nikolai didn't give her a chance to be disgusted. He tangled his hand in her hair and guided her face toward his neck—toward the only sure remedy for the virus in her body. "Drink," he demanded.

Clio gasped, her lips flush with the cut and already slick with his essence. A hot strip of velvet caressed the area. She licked him. *Oh, fuck.*

His fingers tightened in her hair as he forced himself to focus. Pressing her face more forcefully against his neck, he repeated, "Drink."

Her tongue slid into the wound, wetting and deepening the cut, and then her mouth closed over his artery. She drew him in.

Both of his hands found her hair, cradling her, relishing in the connection. His kind so often fed, but did not indulge in the ecstasy of being fed on. It was a small, rare pleasure—one he cherished. He couldn't remember ever enjoying it this much, though.

Clio moaned, the sound rattling through the artery and into his cock. He burned from the inside out. She shifted, wrapping her legs around his waist, looping her arms around his neck. He knew it was instinct—pure animal instinct and the effects of his blood—that had her grinding against him. But damn it if he didn't let her do it for a moment, didn't savor it, before he dropped his hands to her hips to still them. She let out a little mewl, fighting against his grip. The satin slipped under his fingertips. It tested every ounce of his self-control. *She's not mine.*

He couldn't take advantage of the moment, of the circumstance, of her. She was sick, and drunk on him, and he—he...

Nikolai wrapped a hand around her neck and brought her face-to-face with him. Her heart thumped wildly under his palm, but it was strong. Healing. Blood dripped from her chin. She sucked her bottom lip into her mouth, tasting the remnants there.

Without a thought in his head, he leaned in and licked the excess off her face, cleaning her cheeks and chin, halting only at the edges of her mouth. Her breath smelled of iron and heat and *him*. And maybe she wasn't his, but right now, it certainly felt like it.

She whispered his name.

The inch between their mouths charged as powerfully as the sky outside. She leaned forward, but his hand on her throat kept her at bay. He hoped she saw the words in his eyes. *Not like this.* "Bed," he rasped, turning his cheek. "To bed with you."

She stood, but when it became apparent that she would more than likely trip and fall into the fire, he carried her to the bed. He arranged the pillows beneath her, tucking her between the sheets and blankets.

"My blood needs time to fight back the viral pathogens in your body," he told her. "The effect isn't instantaneous, but you should feel better soon."

"My head isn't hurting anymore," she murmured.

"Good, get some rest. I'll come back to check on you in a little while."

As he backed away, her hand whipped out of the covers and grabbed his, the movement lightning fast—evidence of his blood at work.

Clio's eyes pleaded with him, glassy and swimming with emotion. "Will you stay until I fall asleep?"

Nikolai managed his surprise. He nodded and turned to retrieve one of the sitting chairs, but she tugged on his hand again.

"Here," she whispered. And he knew she meant the bed. He couldn't summon the wherewithal to argue. *Sleeping with guests was nasty business*—but right then, he didn't give a fuck.

Nikolai crawled up behind her and pulled her against him, his front to her back. Her hair, sweaty and matted, brushed against his cheek, but her scent was returning to normal, so he loved it.

After a minute, when he suspected she'd fallen asleep, she turned in his arms. Her wide eyes searched his face. "You're the little boy Genevieve stole, aren't you?"

He swallowed the venom and grief filling his mouth. "Yes, I am."

She nodded, frowning as her gaze distanced from him. "I know this isn't the same. I know it—it can't compare, but my dad left home when I was nine. He just disappeared. He never said goodbye. It felt like he'd died, or he'd killed a part of me—like neither of us ever existed to each other. Nyah convinced me to look him up, but I didn't muster the courage to reach out until she—until she wasn't here to pester me about it anymore. I called him when I got engaged and I've called him every day for months since. He doesn't pick up."

He combed a hand through her hair and tried to smile. Tried and failed. "Sleep now."

When he ran his fingers through her hair again, her eyes fluttered shut. Her hand reached out blindly and found his cheek, her thumb brushing against his stubble. "You're so much more than your beast," she said. The statement landed like an anvil in his gut.

Her hand fell to the mattress and she drifted off. He watched, smothering the daggers in his throat and the red film in his eyes. If they spilled over, he would only stain her further.

He'd been right—she was a light. He would even dare to say a guiding light, a true uncorrupted angel, if he could believe in such things.

For the first time, he wanted to.

26

Clio woke refreshed and warm between silken sheets. The fire crackled nearby—her nerves and the soreness from the night before nonexistent. She was blissfully content.

It took her a moment to remember why.

She bolted upright, reaching for the space behind her. Nikolai was gone and a small piece of her happiness dissolved as she looked around the room. The shutter doors to the sitting room were open, giving her a clear view of the fire. The light outside the window was pitch black, suggesting she'd slept an entire day away.

On her beside table sat a plate of crusty bread and cheese, a glass of water, and a note that said: *eat me, drink me.*

Clio's face broke into a tender smile.

Not funny, she'd said to him. But he was. And he knew it. *Bastard.*

As she ate, she tasted him. His blood between her teeth, layered like a film under her tongue and the back of her throat.

He tasted like earth and honey, like a dream coming to life and hell freezing over. Too good to be true.

Nikolai knew Nyah. They were friends of a sort, if his story could be believed.

Clio didn't know why that resonated so deeply with her—touching the fissures in her heart with molten gold, filling them and hardening to forge a new shield against the grief. But it did. She hadn't felt this okay in a long time.

As she chugged the glass of water and slipped out of bed, the reason occurred to her. She'd always wondered, as she laid awake at night avoiding her nightmares, what Nyah would have thought about Duncan. She faced the truth now.

Nyah would have hated him.

Her friend hadn't been there to intervene over the last year. She wasn't here now—the world moved on without her. *Clio* was forced to move on without her. And maybe she'd been a little too desperate, too lonely, a little too broken when Duncan stepped into her life. Maybe she'd latched onto him like someone might hold onto a life preserver in the middle of an ocean, in the middle of a deadly storm. Maybe it had been a mistake.

Clio's eyes drifted to the ring on her finger. Her throat swelled.

No, she couldn't think like this. Nyah was dead. She'd been a victim of the lies and secrets between them. The victim of a demon, apparently. What did it matter, what she would have thought of Duncan? What she thought of Nikolai? Why should any of that matter at all?

Nyah wasn't who Clio thought she was.

Clio didn't know where her bra went and didn't feel like digging through her bags, so she tugged on a pair of jeans, the darkest blouse she could easily find—a maroon frilly thing—and left the suite.

The door to Nikolai's quarters sat open, as if he expected her to come looking for him. She stood on the threshold and watched him hunch over a journal. He had changed, too—into those gray sweatpants and a slate blue tee.

Nikolai looked especially handsome in blue, with his jaw shadowed and his hair disheveled like that. His room was better lit tonight, warmed by the weak rush of air coming through the vents and tall bronze candelabras scattered around the space. A rich red duvet with golden stitches covered the bed, the headboard and curved posts gleamed with cherry oak.

Dangling beneath the posts, glittering in the candlelight, were what looked like strings of gold—

Nikolai cleared his throat, stealing her attention. He had turned in his seat to grin at her. "Morning, sunshine."

She entered the room, pausing just beyond the threshold. "Are you calling me that because I tried to kill you?"

"No," his eyes twinkled with delight, "but that would have been awful clever of me. I'll accept the praise for it."

"Thank you for the food," she said. She walked carefully, afraid any creak of the floor might change her mind—might remind her to be afraid. "And for everything else."

Nikolai went utterly still as she approached, tracking her with apprehensive eyes. As she paused beside his chair, she wondered how it was possible, how he could look just as nervous as she felt.

He said softly, "Was it enough?"

She heard the words left unspoken there. Did she believe him? Did she trust him? Clio had known the answer from the instant she opened that bathroom door.

"Yes."

A weight seemed to lift from Nikolai's shoulders. He exhaled, low and slow, and his hands reached out, as if by instinct, to pull her in. Clio landed sideways on his lap. His arms embraced her, loose enough that she could easily break free—but she chose not to.

The last thing she wanted was to resist, to put space between them, so she let him hold her tighter, closer. It felt so good to be in his arms. She needed this touch, this comfort, as badly as he did.

His fingers roamed up her back, lazily running through her hair as he rested his forehead against her shoulder. She looped her arms around his neck, fisting the material of his shirt between her fingers. Her cheek rested on top of his head, his soft curls tickling her skin. He filled her senses so completely that there was little room for second guessing this moment. His warm breath caressed her breast through the thin shirt, but she still didn't push him away.

Clio didn't allow herself to think about why she should. Not for a while, at least. They couldn't hold each other like this forever, though, as much as she wished for it.

"Nik," she finally whispered. He hummed in acknowledgment, that broad chest vibrating so close to her own. It took her a moment to gather her thoughts. "I have a lot of questions."

Nikolai sighed, his arms loosening around her. "I'd be shocked if you didn't, beloved."

She should have been appalled. But she smiled. "Look at you, indulging in pet names when you're so inexperienced with them."

"For my favorite guest," he swore through a chuckle, "anything."

Nikolai stood, gently setting Clio on her feet, and walked to the bronze liquor cart behind his bed. He plucked two short glasses and a bottle of liquor from the cart and met her back at the desk. He set the glasses down, filled each with a few inches of the amber liquid, and extended a glass to her.

His pupils were slightly dilated. Not in that scary black way, but—

"Have a drink with me."

"I shouldn't," she said slowly, though her gaze was already locked on the glass. It had been a long time. Since a flask of tequila under a bare-limbed tree.

Nikolai smirked. "You've had a rather distressing few days, Clio. We both have. A little inebriation might be needed for this conversation."

She didn't doubt that. Clio wanted a drink, wanted to have one with him.

The memory of his lap last night, hard and insistent beneath her, razed through her head. She shouldn't be thinking such things—but how could she forget?

Clio took the glass and lifted it to her lips, and choked on the first sip. Alcohol burned through her nose and throat—a cleanse that would give her mother a run for her money. She coughed, holding the glass up and away to prevent it from sloshing over her chest.

Nikolai laughed, dimples marking both of his cheeks. He reached over, as if he had the intention of transferring her liquor to his own glass. She swallowed and batted his hand away.

"I can finish it," she rasped. "Back off."

She took a smaller sip, letting the flavor develop on her tongue before sliding down her throat. It was strong, excessively sweet.

"Honey moonshine," he explained, reading the question on her face.

After the next sip, which he watched her take with unnerving focus, she nodded to let him know she liked it. He lifted his own drink and tapped his rim against hers before taking a hearty glug.

"I wouldn't have thought you could drink," she said.

He shrugged. "My body is still partially human, the brain especially. And I can abuse it with substances as easily as you can yours, it just takes more of an effort." He smirked. "I bounce back better."

She studied the carvings in the glass, sorting through her thoughts. "And you can bleed, too, but heal quicker."

"Yes." He hesitated, then added, "I could bleed out entirely and be fine as long as I have a source to replace that blood volume."

"Prey, you mean," Clio muttered.

He didn't so much as flinch. "Yes."

"You gave me your blood last night."

Nikolai leaned back, his eyes glazing. "What about it?"

"Well, did it hurt you?" She wondered. His lips twitched. "Do you have to replenish what I took from you?"

"Eventually, I suppose," he muttered.

Clio peeked up at him, fingering those carvings in the glass so hard she thought they might cut her. Maybe she wanted them to cut her. "I could help. Let you have some of my blood, I mean. It seems like the right thing to do, all things considered."

His eyes darkened. "I fed plenty out in the tundra. And besides, I don't feed on humans."

"At all?"

"Not unless I'm having sex with them." The bastard had the nerve to wink.

Her mouth flapped for a moment. "Oh."

"Yeah," he chuckled, draining half his glass, "'*oh*'."

The insinuation sank in slowly. Did he mean he had no intention of feeding off her because he wouldn't have sex with her? That he didn't want to? That couldn't be right—not after all his affection and long looks and the dancing and him caring for her while she was sick and the way he called her beloved and—

She asked another question to distract from her spiraling thoughts. "How old are you, exactly?"

"Three millennia."

Clio took a sip large enough to warm her heart in the swallow. Fuck, that was several centuries. "How?"

Nikolai bent to tug the drawer of journals open. After a couple minutes of digging, in which time her head started to fuzz, he produced an old book and threw it on the desk between them. Pointing at it, he said, "Genevieve had a better idea about the history than most of our kind. She spent her entire immortal life recording what she learned. I don't know how much of it is reliable, but you're welcome to read it if you wish. The only thing I ask of you is to keep the knowledge to yourself—what I am and what Nyah was. The human world is better off not knowing about us. I'd really prefer to avoid another witch hunt."

Clio wondered how many times he'd been outed in his existence. Considering the calm in his voice and the length of his life, she guessed a couple times at least.

She analyzed the cracked leather, the parchment sticking out in every direction, the binding falling apart. The cover was worn beneath her fingertips as she grazed the surface—the sort of wear that only comes from the constant touch of open air and oily skin.

Clio wondered how many times Nikolai had read it. "I want to know what you believe," she said, withdrawing her hand and meeting his stare.

His throat bobbed, but he said, "There was a war, amongst the first of our kind. Over the plant that turns us—apparently, it first grew as a tree with three twining stalks.

"One clan wanted to burn it, to keep any other humans from suffering the turn. The others had differing opinions on how to use it or hide it. The entire plant was eventually uprooted and dispersed into the farthest corners of the earth. It's said one was indeed burned, but the other two are still out there. That's what Genevieve was looking for all those years, one of the plants so she could turn me.

"Along with all the history she dug up, she wrote out a lot of the bullshit she heard from her spirits. They told her that beings like her—souls altered by the turn—belonged to the Earth. That when they die, they don't pass into the afterlife, but rather rest and are reborn. That's how she became so convinced that I was her son."

Nikolai smiled in a way that suggested he was closer to tears than joy.

"But her son never turned. She believed what she needed to, held onto what gave her hope." He drained the rest of his glass and poured himself another. "And she fucking ruined me for it."

Clio watched him—the man who saved her only hours ago. She watched the bitterness in his face, churning into something else beneath the surface. She guessed, "You don't believe that, do you? The idea of rebirth."

He scoffed. "No."

"Why not?"

"I just never have."

He really didn't believe in *anything*. It broke a piece of her, buried so deep she couldn't quite see it, buried so deep the light in her soul couldn't touch it. She knew in that moment, that she would do whatever it took to take that sadness from him—that hopelessness.

"So, let me guess." She raised an eyebrow and nodded

toward the closed door adjacent to them. "That's your skeleton closet?"

He shook his head. "That's the basement. And it's dangerous down there, so none of your snooping. I don't want you getting trapped in a place you can't escape from."

She laughed and his eyes lightened a fraction. "Keep your hair on, old man. I'll leave your basement full of polar bear hides alone."

His mouth quirked. "I appreciate it."

"If you don't mind me asking, why don't you want me to snoop? What's so dangerous?"

He glared at her over the lip of his glass. "Some things are just better off never seeing the light of day."

"Like you?"

He shrugged irreverently. "For now."

"Don't even joke about that," she snapped.

"I'm not joking about anything." He frowned. "If I wasn't such a coward, I would have done it centuries ago."

"Like Genevieve? Wasn't that enough of a tragedy?"

"Tragedy?" He chuckled. "That woman killed me."

"She loved you," Clio murmured, taking his hand, "and looked for that love in return in her own twisted way. Maybe it's selfish of me to say, but without her, I never would have met you."

Nikolai tilted his head and stared at Clio for a long moment as his lips pressed in a firm line.

Hesitantly, he lifted the hand that held his glass to her cheek and with one finger, brushed a strand of hair out of her face. "That's not fair. I should be able to hate her, but how can I when you say things like that?"

She felt friction in his touch again, in that finger lingering on her cheek. Shying back, she drained her own glass before setting it on the desk.

Clio turned back to face him, crossing her arms. Maybe it was the moonshine and the effects of his blood still flowing through her veins, but a special sort of warmth surged through her body. Bravery. Foolishness.

She asked, "Why won't you feed from me? I know you're attracted to me."

Nikolai's eyes simmered. "Oh?" He stepped closer. "What gave me away?"

"Last night." Her gaze dipped to his sweatpants. Clio felt fire burst in her cheeks as she quickly looked away. "I—I felt you."

"What about it?" His tone was so low, so baiting, she wanted to slap him.

Focus. She dug her nails into her forearms and said, "Your reticence to drink my blood isn't because you wouldn't have sex with me. Right?"

"No, it isn't." He gawked at her, but his eyes were alight with amusement. "Why? Are you offering something more than a meal? Some dessert, perhaps?"

Oh, holy lights, that look on his face. This had to be the stupidest thing she'd ever done, talking about this particular insecurity with him.

"No, I'm not offering. I just—" Clio shook her head. *Take it back, reel it in.* "Never mind. It's nothing." She looked behind her to watch the flames dance wildly in their holders, debated pouring herself another glass of moonshine even though her head was already soft and cloudy.

"Come on, Clio." Nikolai took a step toward her, mirroring her crossed arms, lifting one hand to sip at his glass. It hid a cocky grin—she just knew it. "You've learned an awful lot about me recently."

"This happens to be embarrassing,"

He gave her a disbelieving look. "And my diet isn't?"

Damn. There wouldn't be a way to talk herself out of this, would there? Her eyes drifted to the bed, looking more intently at the item dangling from the posts. It looked almost like a web. A golden web with delicate strings hanging from it. It looked like another riddle, something that didn't quite belong. Her hands fisted at her stomach as she said, "Well, my fiancé hasn't, I mean, he *doesn't* —"

Nikolai bit back a smile. "He can't get an erection?"

Her head whipped up to glare at him. "No. I don't know. He keeps me at arm's length." Once the words started, they rushed from her. "He never kisses me longer than a moment, never cuddles on the couch when we watch a movie. He says he wants to wait until—you know—"

"The wedding night," Nikolai finished.

She nodded. His eyebrows pulled together, frustration screwing his face. "And you think that's a reflection on you?"

Clio looked down, tangling her fingers. "I think it's because I'm not easy to admire," she admitted. "Maybe I'm more of an acquired taste, or maybe I've always just been barely tolerable. I'm trying to understand what *you* see, when you look at me."

Nikolai went quiet, but she couldn't bring herself to look, not as his feet padded across the floor to her. Not until he invaded her space so completely that she had to acknowledge him.

When she met his eyes, they were intense, smoldering. His breath filled her senses. Honey and cedar wood and tangy copper. His face was mockingly solemn as he said, "I see a woman who is very fas—"

"If you say fascinating," she hissed. "I'm going to scream."

He erupted in laughter and she shoved his shoulder. He caught her hand, drawing it flat against his chest. No heartbeat met her palm, but she kept her hand there as he twirled a lock of hair between his fingers.

"If what you are is an acquired taste," he said. "Then I am your connoisseur. From the moment you walked into my life, I've thirsted like a man stranded in the desert. I see visions of you from a distance, chase mirages hoping to reach you. All I can think of most days is holding you down and letting your richness fill my mouth."

A thrill ran up her spine and her hand flew to her neck. He gave her a lover's laugh—the sort that touched her in all the right places before he even raised a finger. "Oh, beloved," he said quietly. "I'm not talking about blood."

Nikolai's gaze dropped to her hand and the ticking vein in her neck. He caressed her wrist with his knuckles and every instinct in her body narrowed in on that lone contact. Clio trembled as his hand trailed between her breasts, over the planes of her stomach to her navel, and paused there in the hollow. Beneath, deep in her belly, a fire roared to life.

He looked her in the eye and whispered, "Not only blood."

There was a clink on wood as Nikolai set his glass down and took her chin in his fingers. He traced the line of her nose with the tip of his own, his forehead pressing against hers. His breath caressed her mouth, but he didn't close that last bit of space between their lips. For a moment, she thought it was a hesitation, but then he nudged her cheek with his nose. She sensed his smile. He was waiting for her, letting her make the final decision.

That was how he consistently treated her—with the freedom to decide, with openness and a faith in who she was. In whatever she wanted. Maybe he believed in something after all, even if he didn't realize it. Maybe he believed in love. Maybe he believed in her. And yes, he wasn't human anymore. Yes, he scared her, absolutely terrified her—but what she feared wasn't death.

Clio wrapped her arms around his neck and crushed herself to him. Their lips met.

Nikolai gasped, his hands gripping her arms as if he hadn't expected her to close the distance. The shock turned to fervor as he responded, his lips plush and slightly cold.

She tightened her hold on him, molding her body to his—melting entirely as he slipped his fingers into her hair. He fisted a handful and tugged, gaining better leverage to claim her. She opened for him, her mouth and chambers and whatever else he wanted. He could have it all as long as he didn't stop kissing her, didn't stop touching her.

He growled, a soft rumble in the back of his throat, as his tongue explored her mouth. She could have whimpered at the sensation, the fullness, the sound. Maybe she did.

A desperation seeped into the kiss—a force that had him gripping her hips and lifting her onto the desk. She hooked her legs around his waist, panting into his mouth. His hand cradled the back of her neck, tilting again for that access, but she bit his lip. Hard.

She wanted to be the one to taste him, the one to devour.

Nikolai only chuckled as her tongue swept in. His teeth were as sharp as she expected—smooth and menacing and sexy as hell. She sucked on them and her tongue came away with a tangy-sweet film. *Venom?* It tingled in her mouth and down her throat, heating the path to her core better than any liquor could.

Nikolai tore his mouth from hers and she nearly protested, but he shifted his attention to her neck. Kissing and licking and gently nipping, working his way to the space under her ear. She moaned at the tingle spreading through her skin at every brush of his teeth.

Clio squirmed, her bare heels pressing him closer.

"Such a beautiful, deprived little thing," he whispered,

scraping her earlobe with his teeth. Her scalp prickled, every hair on her body standing on end. "Don't worry. I'll take care of you." His knuckles brushed against her breasts, pulled at her poorly concealed nipples. She made another unintelligible sound and his mouth covered hers, devouring her noises like they were drops of blood he wanted to lap up. It was heaven.

Heaven. The word clanged in her head like a deep, jarring bell.

He thumbed the hem of her shirt, inched it upward, and the prickle spreading into her back turned into something far more nefarious. Through the haze of her libido, she thought of Nyah. She thought of heaven. And The Divine Light—what would it do to them both when her time came?

She might as well have poured ice water over her head.

"We can't do this." Clio shoved against his chest, violently, and slid off the desk. She elbowed past him into the open air of the rest of the room—into a space she could think—and reminded him, reminded *herself*, "I'm getting married in a few days."

She walked toward the passage to the library, her legs trembling at the thought of what she would do if he tried to stop her, if he touched her again. But he didn't.

In fact, the room went utterly still behind her. When she reached the threshold, she paused, glancing over her shoulder. Nikolai was exactly where she left him, his shoulders hunched, head bent, his hands hanging limply at his sides.

She didn't think he was breathing anymore, but of course he didn't need to.

His expression was hidden from view and she thanked the Light for that. She didn't want to know how badly she'd just hurt him, or, worse, have him see how badly she'd just hurt herself.

When she spoke, it grated her throat like sand. "For the

record, I hope Genevieve was right. I hope if you ever die, you come back and live a life surrounded by people that love you the way you deserve to be loved."

He folded, shriveling under the weight of her. *Some things never change.*

So Clio left.

27

Clio couldn't sleep.

She paced the suite, from the bedroom window to the fireplace. Too much filled her veins, her head —so much she could burst if she sat still.

She listened to Nyah's voicemail what felt like a million times, reanalyzing every word until her phone died. Her friend had never sounded so much like a stranger, nor had the goodbye ever seemed so empty. She revisited the books on her nightstand, but after a few hours her eyes skipped across the familiar text.

There wasn't a chance she would leave this room. Not tonight, maybe not even until her wedding day. She no longer trusted herself. The moonshine faded, even as the venom lingered on her neck. The aurora shifted to a warm salmon, its wounds closed and healing.

She didn't let herself think about it—what happened with Nikolai. Her lips were raw from chewing the skin away, her gums sore from violent brushing, and her palms stung from where her nails left new marks. Anything to distract her. Any pain to remind her of the reality.

Happiness doesn't mean anything. Not if it's temporary.

What future could she have with a man who wouldn't die, who wouldn't grow old with her? She could have a couple decades of passion before he got tired of her, and then what? At the end of it all, after life, when she pleaded her case in heaven, what Light would deign to shine on her? On Nyah?

How could she look at herself in the mirror, mutation aside, if she went back on her commitment to Duncan? It would make her as rotten as her father. Clio'd already betrayed the promise, the engagement, and a part of her knew she would never be able to tell her fiancé.

Didn't dare tell him.

Mid-morning the next day, her circuit past the bedroom window resulted in a view of something other than black tundra.

Headlights swept across the snow and as she drew close to the window, she heard the rumble of a large engine through the faulty seal of the window. The lights pivoted, revealing the silhouette of what looked like a snowplow. It worked the road beyond the lane, but Clio knew the service was here for the manor.

A knock came from the suite door. Her heart leapt into her throat, but she crossed the room and peered through the peephole. The hall was empty.

She cracked the door an inch and her eyes landed on a large silver platter, left on the other side of the threshold. On it sat a steaming plate of scrambled eggs and toasted bread, a few glass water bottles, and a stack of books.

Clio poked her head into the hallway, but it was vacant. Because Nikolai knew she didn't want to see him, but yet, he'd—

"Thank you," she whispered.

The note on the platter said, *The electricity will return shortly*. She didn't even realize she wanted it to say more until she read it for a fifth time. When she started undressing the curves of his handwriting in her head, she crumpled it up and threw it in the waste bin.

Nikolai must have cooked her breakfast in a fireplace. It smelled like char, and yes, tasted a little burnt in places. There were shells in the eggs. She didn't care.

The power flickered to life while she ate and a few minutes later, her phone buzzed for five minutes straight on the charging pad. Cell service returned. She glanced at the screen long enough to determine how many calls she'd missed from Duncan—seventeen—and promptly turned the phone off. She didn't want to see his name right now, or hear his voice. It would only make her sick.

A few hours later, Clio scowled at the stack of books spread in front of her.

Poetry. He'd brought her fucking poetry, and three absolutely filthy romance novels. Even Nyah would have blushed reading them. The book in her lap now, the one she'd spent the last thirty minutes getting into, had flipped on her mid-story. The villain of the story turned out to be a noble knight, and he'd just confessed his love for the heroine. Clio slammed the book shut as the characters kissed and threw it across the room in frustration.

Total. Complete. Ass.

Knees to her chest, she raked both hands through her hair. She could still taste him, even after all that teeth brushing. Smell him. Feel him, if she closed her eyes and let herself. She so badly wanted to. There was an ache in her stomach, a throb that wouldn't stop pulsing. The walking and reading and eating and hurting hadn't made it go away. It was unbearable.

Nyah warned her this day would come, when desire would flood in. Her friend had told her, in one of their drunken teenage giggle fests, what she could do to relieve it. She'd tried once before, out of curiosity, but nothing happened. She hadn't understood it. Not like this.

Nikolai had called her *deprived*. And maybe she was.

Clio grabbed the hem of the duvet and whipped the blanket so that the books slid away, then slipped under the covers. There wasn't enough space in her head for embarrassment, not with her body coiled into an unmanageable knot. She curled onto her side and slid a hand between her legs, exploring places that eased her tension.

It was his eyes she imagined, both the terrifying black and vibrant blue. His stubble and fitted jeans, his honeyed mouth and deep, joyful laugh. Clio came thinking of Nikolai touching her, kissing her, moving against her. She came with his name on her lips, moaning into a down-filled pillow. Then it was over, and she felt more alone than ever.

She laid there for minutes afterward and cried. It wasn't enough. She wanted him there, holding her through the aftershocks. She wanted *him*. The need caught in her throat and threatened to strangle her.

Maybe after all of the loneliness, the pain and fear and brokenness, she was meant to be here. To meet him. To want him. Maybe, after everything she'd been through and everything she'd lost, she deserved a little happiness. No matter how brief. Clio reached for her robe.

She wasn't married yet and, for fuck's sake, she could beg for forgiveness later.

The hall was a blur as she sprinted through it, but the elevator descended in slow motion—the operatic music sadder than she remembered. Music for a man that lost track of time itself; she wanted nothing more than to anchor him for an hour or two.

When the dingy bell rang out and the golden doors slid open, everything in her head went quiet. Nikolai stood on the other side, carrying another silver tray, stacked to the brim with food and books. "Hi," he murmured, mouth twitching with uncertain relief.

Her voice was huskier than usual—dark and warm and vibrating as she said, "Hey."

"I was just bringing you dinner." He glanced at the platter in his hands.

"And another cheesy, or otherwise disgusting, novel?"

He had the decency to look a little ashamed. "Can you blame me?"

No. She opened her mouth to reply, to say all the things rising in her head, but he shattered those plans as he said, "I'm leaving."

Her head went quiet again, but this time it was that ringing, empty, dead quiet. The quiet she felt when her father left.

"I planned to leave you a note to let you know that my hotel manager, Mrs. Itzli, will be here in the morning," he plucked the note from the platter and tucked it into his slacks, "but I suppose it's unnecessary now that you've left your room. She'll take care of you while I'm away."

She managed to ask, "Where are you going?"

He avoided her gaze, looking behind her—through her. "Out of the country. I have some responsibilities to tend to."

Away from polar night. *Away from me.* "Is that safe for you to do?"

"I have my methods. I'll be fine." Of course. He'd be fine. And she'd be stuck in this moment, this longing and utter rage. Silent, damning, brilliant rage. Nikolai would haunt her every thought like the phantom he was, and she'd simply fade from his memory.

For an immortal existence, that was the only way forward, wasn't it?

She stepped back, shoulder hitting the wall of the elevator, and prayed for the doors to hide her away.

Nikolai kept talking, as if he hadn't a clue that she'd just broken—that those golden seams in her heart were melting away. "The kitchen is running again, so I warmed some chicken."

She smashed the close doors button with her thumb. It lit up and the doors surged, but Nikolai threw out a hand to stop them. "Wait, I can get you something else if that doesn't sound good. There should be another poultry dish in there, I think."

"I don't want any fucking chicken right now, Nik," she snapped.

He blinked, recoiling, but kept his hand on the door. She lurched forward and tried to dislodge it, but he just caught her hand and tugged her to look at him.

When she looked, he wasn't searching her face. He stared at her hand, nose flaring. The hot foam in his eyes told her he scented what she'd done to herself in bed.

"What were you doing in your room just now?"

Clio ripped away from him and withdrew into the belly of the elevator. "What do you think, blood hound?" Her voice wasn't nearly as vicious as she wanted it to be.

His throat bobbed and he demanded quietly, "Say it."

She bit her lip, but he only waited. Stopped the surge of the elevator doors again and leaned in. Stars flickered to life, beckoning her toward him. Always toward him. Her rage splintered like an exploding constellation—her own sparkling galaxy.

She said thickly, "Thinking of you."

His lips parted, a huff of air seething out. And she could almost see it.

The tray clattering against the marble, the food spattering, his body and lips crushing her, his hands finding the hem of her pajama shorts. She could see surrendering completely to him, against the golden wall or floor—never making it back to her suite. It didn't really matter where. Only who.

The tray trembled. She took a step toward him.

Nikolai's head whipped toward the front doors, and he cursed under his breath. She felt the entrance first—heard it—as the manor opened to the blistering cold outside. Wind whistled through the lobby as she peeked past the threshold of the elevator.

There, standing in the foyer, pushing back the hood of his coat and shaking the snow from his blonde hair, glancing around at the extravagance with distaste twisting his thin mouth, was Duncan.

Clio echoed the curse, everything warm and lovely seeping out of her skin.

He pinpointed her across the room and smiled that sleepy, summoning grin of his. She obeyed, slipping past Nikolai. As she did, she felt the whisper of a caress on her arm, both a plea and comfort. She ignored it, didn't acknowledge the stare or touch, and met Duncan in the middle of the lobby.

"Hello, dove, surprised to see me?"

That didn't even begin to cover how she felt about his appearance.

Duncan wrapped her in his arms, the fabric of his coat irritating her cheek. His hot hands gripped her and pushed her an arm's length away so he could survey her body—taking inventory as if she were an item on a shelf.

He frowned. "This is hardly appropriate attire for a lobby."

Pulling the robe tighter around her torso, Clio said, "You're right. I'm sorry. I've been sick."

His midnight blue eyes narrowed. "I see. I'm assuming that's why you haven't returned my calls."

She gulped. "Yes, and the power went out for a couple days. My phone died. Service was spotty before that." All true. *True enough.*

He grunted. "Do you feel better now?"

"Yes. The host has taken good care of me."

Duncan smiled politely, his hands rubbing up and down her arms. "Then I should thank him. Introduce us."

But when she turned to face the elevator, Nikolai wasn't there. "He was just here."

"Was that the man talking to you?" Duncan's hands squeezed her slightly.

She hummed her confirmation, neck craning to scan the room, and spotted the food tray abandoned on the front desk, whirls of steam curling in front of the painting of his family.

The book was gone. He was gone. *It's over.*

Clio approached the desk. The book had been replaced by a room key and a torn piece of the original note he'd written for her. It said: *Room 201 for Fiancé #1.*

Duncan peered over her shoulder. "Fiancé number one? What does that mean?"

"Nothing," she said quickly. "It's just a joke."

His eye twitched. "I don't get it."

She crumpled the note and dropped it in her robe pocket. "Don't worry. It was a stupid joke anyway. Let's get you settled in your room."

"That's more like it, dove." He kissed her forehead and she wanted to rip her skin off. It didn't feel like her own anymore.

28

Mrs. Itzli arrived the next morning, just as Nikolai promised.

What Clio hadn't been prepared for was how much she instantly adored the woman. By way of introduction, the chef breezed into the honeymoon suite at the crack of dawn —well, whatever dawn could be called here. It was an ungodly hour.

Clio barely had a chance to rub the sleep from her eyes before the woman investigated the reeking bathroom and spouted a string of incomprehensible words as she scrutinized the damaged door.

Mrs. Itzli pulled Clio's missing bra out from under the bed and flung it at her.

Get dressed, she'd demanded in a thick, liquid accent.

Then, Mrs. Itzli dragged her to the kitchen, directing a cleaning crew in the lobby up after them along the way. She gathered her silvery black hair into a secure bun and cooked a breakfast that put Clarissa's private chef to shame. This one didn't shy from butter, thank the Light.

Clio finished her plate, too aware that the woman had been staring at her as she whipped up an egg and flour concoction—glaring actually, when she thought Clio wasn't looking.

Her bushy black brows stitched together. Whatever thoughts she was mulling over in her head, Clio wasn't sure she wanted to hear them.

"Thank you," Clio said, the steeping tea in her hands curling up to warm her nose.

"You are very welcome, sweet girl," she replied, setting down the bowl to dig through a cupboard. She produced a muffin pan and set to buttering each tin.

Mrs. Itzli snuck another look, but this time Clio returned it. The moment their eyes met, the pretension cracked. The old woman set the butter aside, wiped her leathery nimble fingers in a towel, and asked, "What happened here, between you two, while the manor was snowed in?"

Clio glanced behind her at the hallway, listening for any trace of footsteps. She was safe, *for now.* "I don't know what you mean."

Mrs. Itzli's voice dropped to a whisper. "Anyone with half a brain and a heart would know that's not true. Are you so untrusting of the hand that feeds you? What would I have to gain from disclosing your secrets? Only the loss of my job. Why are you frightened?"

"I'm not frightened," Clio hissed. "Why would I be frightened?"

She grimaced. "You must forgive me. Mr. Trousseau tells me I can be too frank for my own good."

Clio was muttering, "It's fine," when Mrs. Itzli bulldozed over her.

"But since I've lived this way six decades, I see no reason to change now. So, I'm going to say this: If you knew him like I did, saw the way he stared into nothing for weeks at a time, returned to this manor every year more tired than the last, and how he immersed himself in this work despite the fact that he hates the crowds, you could understand why I asked. When he called me yesterday, I hardly recognized his voice. The barrenness was gone. I believe that's because of you."

She swallowed her shock. "Please, I—"

"Do you know the last time my boss called me up and asked me for anything beyond my prescribed duties? Do you know the last time he worried about anyone, himself included?"

Clio stared through her.

"Never," Mrs. Itzli stated fiercely, fisting the towel in her hand. "Never before you. He asked me to look after you. Tell me why he would do that other than because he cared deeply for you?"

She could think of one reason. *Because I know his bloody little secret.* Even as it spread through her head, she knew it wasn't true, but she certainly tried to convince herself. "I don't think I affect him as much as you believe."

Mrs. Itzli shook her head, eyes gleaming with pity and understanding. "Sweet girl, I think something's blinded you to what you are capable of. And don't take this the wrong way, but you may want to take care of that before dedicating your life to another person. Love like this is forever," she grasped at a set of rings hanging on a chain around her neck, "even after they are gone."

The first pad of what Clio knew was scuffed loafers sounded in the hall and she cleared her throat, rising from her seat to rinse her plate in the sink. "Thank you for your totally unwarranted advice," she said sharply. "But I don't need it."

Mrs. Itzli didn't have a comment for that, not as Duncan appeared in the kitchen and she prepared a plate of food for him too.

Clio wished—truly wished—that what Mrs. Itzli told her could be true.

The next day, vendor deliveries started. The budding flowers, the ribbons, the chairs, the wedding arch. All the decorations sat in the dome, the flowers were organized by color and sat in several pots of water in one of the ballrooms, and she had officially forgotten what it meant to sit down for a meal. But at least she didn't have time to think of *him*.

Clio's mother swept into the lobby another day later, large sunglasses hiding her hangover and a plush white fur drowning her thin neck. Duncan had surprised Clio by convincing her mom to fly in a day early.

She wasn't sure whether to be appreciative or simply impressed that her fiancé managed to coax Clarissa into cutting her vacation short. Then again, he'd always had a certain sway with her. All Light-blessed seemed to have that effect on Clarissa, as if her mere interactions with them, whether good or bad, obedient or distasteful, would determine her worth.

Maybe, in a small way, it did.

Clarissa greeted her daughter with a dramatic embrace and gave Duncan a hug twice as long. As always, her mother looked lovely, even with dark circles beneath her eyes and snow-dampened hair. Clio dragged Clarissa to the dome without a moment to spare, eager to share her joy in the crystal haven she'd discovered. Duncan tagged along, finally showing a speck of interest in the preparations. But she should have known. Really, she should have.

Her mother took one look at the dome and laughed. When Clio fell silent, Clarissa quieted too, seeming to realize that it wasn't a joke.

"You can't be serious about this, sweetie," she murmured, gesturing to the dome as if the insult was obvious. "You can't get married in the dark."

"The aurora lights the dome at night," Clio said, reaching for her sketchbook resting on the edge of a box. "I planned to string some soft lighting down the aisle and over the arch."

She flipped to the sketches she drew of the ceremony and offered it to her mother.

Clarissa took a long look, her upper lip curling in disgust, but refused to take the work in her hands. "It's very unusual, dear. Have you even asked Duncan what he wants? He knows what the Divine will bless."

A heat stirred in Clio's stomach. *What he wants?* It seemed like everything about their relationship, about her, was altered to fit what he wanted. And it was suffocating. She looked to her fiancé and found him frowning.

"Your mother is right, dove. I agreed to get married in the Arctic, but I didn't agree to get married in shadows."

Clio let the sketchbook slam shut. He hadn't even glanced at them. He didn't even care. "Why can't I have this? This is all I want," she demanded.

His mouth formed a thin line, eyes narrowing, and she already wished to take back the words.

"Clio, don't be unreasonable," Clarissa scolded her, standing between them. Clio felt a very small measure of gratitude for it. "Duncan has compromised and now you must, too. I'm sure there's a room in this place that will appease you both."

Clio was sure there wasn't. A part of her knew she would never be appeased, but what did it matter? What did any of it matter? Why should she fight back, when it would only end in defeat and pain?

Her mother investigated the manor and Clio followed,

battling the prickle of her back when Duncan set a light hand on her. He was angry. *Glory.* She hated it when he was angry.

I shouldn't have argued.

They wound up in the ballroom with all the flowers—the golden one—a sea of pink and red dotting the landscape. Like blood dotting snow, the roses marked the marble and reminded her of the wounds that would never close. The wounds that would never heal.

She held the sketchbook behind her and crushed the binding at the small of her back. The room was wrong—but then, maybe so was she. There wasn't a point to getting hung up on minute details. Not when she couldn't have exactly what she wanted anyway.

Who she wanted.

Her head fell back, and she stared at her speck in the mirrored ceiling. Looking out at the vastness of the world from the dome hadn't made her feel like this. She acknowledged up there, watching the aurora, that she was small. In the dome, she didn't see or think of herself, but she felt her own worth.

Looking at her reflection here, she felt inconsequential. Meaningless. She felt like nothing at all.

29

O n the morning of the rehearsal dinner, a package
arrived at the same time the three-tiered cake did.
It was a nondescript, tall and flat white box, post-
marked as an overnight delivery. No sender.

Just Clio's name and a warning had been stamped across
the top that said, *Fragile.*

Clio dragged the heavy packaging to one of the columns in
the lobby and unwrapped it. Her mother hovered so close that
she could smell the expensive peppery perfume on her wrists.
"What is it?"

The last anchoring of tape gave and the structured card-
board front swung open. A painting stared back at her. A
familiar one.

The canvas gleamed shades of green and earth. A tree,
carved into the figure of a woman's body, curved under a
violent wind, back bent, surrendered in an expression of
rapture. Her bark crusted chest raised toward the sky, the line
of her neck continuing in a bow to the chin, her feet rooted to
the ground.

The earthly woman screamed, teeth bared in the thick of the leaves. Her eyes were closed, though. *Peaceful.*

This painting used to hang in the foyer of the Gazini house. It was one of the main focal points that never changed—that Greg, Nyah's father, never replaced or sold. Clio would stare at it for minutes at a time when she visited, and he caught her a handful of times.

She had been so sure he hated her, blamed her as thoroughly as she did herself. They hardly glanced at each other at the funeral, barely said more than a word or two since the morning she barged into his house and truth came knocking at the front door. His wedding invite, her attempt to surrogate Nyah's presence somehow, had gone unanswered.

Clio had been so *sure*—but this painting proved otherwise.

Every time Clio looked at the painting as a teenager, she thought of Nyah. It had just felt like her, and now she knew why. *Earth's Guardian.* She understood. The scene was more beautiful for it.

"It's a wedding present," Clio announced tightly.

Her mother leaned in, close enough to get a full look. "Who is it from?" Disapproval layered every word.

She swallowed the knot in her throat. "No name."

"Good. That'll make it easier to dispose of."

Her head whipped to look at her mother. "What?"

Clarissa gave her a level stare. "Look at it, Clio. You can't take something like that into a church."

That gave Clio pause. But when she looked back at the painting, she only saw the worship—the reverence—the joy in it. "Why not? It's beautiful."

Her mother spluttered, "For glory's sake, it's positively vulgar. Where would you hang it? Above your marital bed? Do you like the idea of a nude painting competing for your husband's attention?"

As if Clio couldn't compete with the beauty in a piece of art like this. As if she had to adjust her life, her tastes, her dreams to please Duncan. To please the Divine Light.

Maybe that was what she needed—what it meant to be blessed. Maybe that was the only way to be good enough: to be less.

Clio was in Nikolai's room again, but this time no candles were lit. Nothing burned, not even the embers of unrest in her heart.

The rest of the staff arrived that morning. Her family members checked in by the dozens. Tonight, she'd have to face them all for the rehearsal dinner, but right now, she let herself savor the quiet a little longer. She approached the bed, the painting braced against her chest as if the meaning could seep into her body and stay with her forever, even if the physical painting could not.

Nikolai would find a place for it. She hoped he would put it somewhere he could see it every day—a constant presence, so he might not forget her.

What power, what strength, did she have in the unknown world of Guardians? What chance did she stand against a demon? Justice wouldn't be possible, for either of them. Laying the painting on the duvet, she allowed herself another look, absorbing the last piece of Nyah. *It's time to let go.*

Clio's gaze lifted to the item hanging above the bed. Gold glittered against cherry-red wood. A thick, spherical wooden rod hung below the posts, and gold strands twined around and across it like a spider web. Around the circumference of the rod, thin strings of gold dangled down. At the ends were small golden pendants of suns and feathers, and occasionally a chain of three pearls.

So curious. Her fingers itched to feel it. As she reached out, Clio heard a rustle behind her. Felt a small displacement of air. She glanced back, not daring to imagine what she wished to see.

All she found was emptiness. Nikolai left. He said he would help her and then he left her to plummet by herself. A soft landing wasn't waiting for her at the bottom, it was only more nothingness. Her heart couldn't bear it.

Clio headed back through the gaping exit, but stopped short when she saw Mrs. Itzli standing in the threshold to the library. The woman catalogued the situation, her eyes wide and cautious—likely determining how to deal with it, with her.

Clio shut the door to his room and mumbled, "I was only saying goodbye."

Mrs. Itzli pressed her lips together.

All the unspoken words invaded Clio's head, filling her up so completely that she couldn't hide from them. Couldn't deny them. "If Nik cares so deeply," she whispered. "Then where is he? Why isn't he here?"

Mrs. Itzli's face pinched. "I can't answer that, but I do believe he has his reasons. He always does."

Clio's tears brimmed over.

"Come with me." Mrs. Itzli waved her closer. "You can help me knead the dough for cinnamon rolls. Tears will add a little extra flavor to the mix."

"Ew." Clio rubbed her nose with her jacket sleeve.

"Oh, yes, bring the snot, too. We use all blood, snot, and tears around here."

She laughed, allowing Mrs. Itzli to wrap an arm around her waist and pull her into the hall. *The old woman knows more than she realizes.*

~

The rehearsal went without incident—except for the fact that the officiant was a total creep. Every time his eyes grazed over her during the practice ceremony, a gross film layered itself over Clio's spine. She almost regretted the dress, but not quite.

It was everything she wished for in a wedding dress, dialed back into a cocktail gown. Vibrant red silk swathed her back, ending in cuff sleeves, closing in the front like a backwards corset. It did wonders for her chest, the cinched ribbons tied together in a bow and drawing attention to the center of her cleavage. The thin skirt fluttered around her legs in two layers, a slinky red slip underneath and a shimmering tulle cover falling in cascades to the ground.

Luckily, the material shifted easily with every kick of her legs, away from the thin heels of her shoes, since the two sides of the dress were held together only by the lacing of the corset. No tripping tonight.

Duncan winked at her while the officiant tied the marital knot around their hands, a rare affection that normally triggered a flutter in her stomach, but this time she forced the smile in return.

What's the matter with me? He's the same person.

It confirmed that she'd changed in the last two weeks, and maybe she was too different now to go through with this. Too different from the Light and all of its rules.

She had come up with a plan, a test, while baking with Mrs. Itzli. She would see if there could be a spark with Duncan, she owed it to the both of them to try. And if it failed, she'd choose herself. She'd take the next flight out of the Arctic and find a place of her own.

She doubted she would ever find a place that felt quite as right as this, though.

So far, the experiment was going well enough to stave off that plan. Duncan wore his finely pressed suit tonight, the plaid blue tie bringing out the muddled blue of his eyes. He looked handsome... perfectly handsome with his blonde hair combed back and smile lines crinkling his cheeks.

She didn't miss the dimples at all.

Duncan kept wrapping an arm around her back, rubbing her arms, fiddling with her curled hair. It was more touching than she was used to from him. Feather light, but purposeful.

Clio told herself to like it, repeating the mantra in her head, until she learned to lean into the caresses. It felt good to be touched, so she reciprocated. She showered him with kisses on his face and hands, even lingering ones on his mouth, which he graciously allowed.

The rehearsal party moved to Nikolai's favorite ballroom, waiting there for dinner to be catered. Clattering and cursing from the kitchen could be detected beneath the chatter if Clio listened close enough.

She'd been distracted greeting a couple distant cousins and their screaming infant when Duncan slipped away. He struck up a conversation with the officiant in the corner of the room, their heads bent close together in what Clio knew was a discussion she shouldn't interrupt. But now she was stuck between that and her mother's boisterous laughter a few feet away.

Relatives swarmed Clarissa as they always did, avoided her daughter's mutated gaze as they always did.

Rolling a smile over her face, she braced herself for her fiancé's potential wrath and approached. To her surprise, Duncan smiled and took her outstretched hand. The other apostolate watched them with his piercing brown-black eyes—stared like he wanted to peel all her layers off. Like he might not stop at the skin.

Clio shook the thought away and curled into Duncan's side. "Do you think we could spend some time together after dinner? We could watch a movie in your room."

Duncan's smile faded. "Divine tradition encourages separation on the eve of the wedding."

"I know," she said quietly, feeling the full weight of the other apostolate's glare. "I just need to talk to you. I've barely seen you all day."

"You see me now."

"Alone," she clarified.

His mouth pressed into a firm line and he glanced at his peer. A message passed between them, so swift and subtle she couldn't determine what it meant.

Clio pressed, "It's important to me. Please."

Duncan shifted on his feet, then sighed. "Alright, we can spend some time together after the party."

When she sprung up to plant a kiss on his lips, his response was stiff. Robotic. So completely passionless. That would be first on the list of things to address in his room. The hired apostolate cleared his throat when the kiss went on a fraction longer than was appropriate, and Duncan pushed her away.

"Go spend time with your family," he ordered, the skin around his eyes tight. "After tomorrow, you'll be feeling very far away from them."

I feel that way now. But she nodded and weaved her way through the crowd back to her mother. As she did, her eye caught on movement in the hall.

A short, muscular man walked backwards, down the hall past the ballroom, a green fedora perched on the back of his skull, drawing out the rich tone of his skin. His black trench coat hung open, giving a glimpse of the jewel green suit beneath. He gestured, as if in conversation, as he sauntered past the room.

Then, the object of his attention appeared in the doorway and everything paused. *Everything.* Because it was Nikolai.

Seeing him, Clio's lungs expanded with what felt like the

first deep breath in days. Her memories didn't do him justice. It hit her gut like a demolition ball—the wanting. He stepped to the side, allowing another body to slip into the ballroom.

And the air in Clio's chest evaporated.

The man who entered the room walked with a limp, his frame worn and hunched. His auburn hairline receding. He wore a rumpled cream suit, with a stained white button-up underneath. Nikolai bent to whisper in his ear, and those warm brown eyes flicked across the crowd and found hers.

Dad.

30

Clio pinched herself, because she had to be dreaming. But no. Her nails left a mark on her forearm, red and infuriated. When she looked up, her father was crossing the ballroom, his eyes locked on her. She couldn't break the stare, couldn't keep her feet from sweeping toward him.

Behind her, Clio heard her mother stop laughing.

The room fell silent and tense all at once, but she barely cared. The only person in her sight, the only thing in her head, was the man who halted a foot or so in front of her.

He rubbed his fingers together, his arms flailing as if they desperately wanted to fold behind his back.

Clio had to restrain herself from wrapping her arms around his waist, like she did as a girl, from nestling her head against his chest and breathing in his cologne. She didn't know why she still wanted to. He probably didn't even wear that cologne anymore.

Clarissa's voice cut through the silence. "Marcus?"

Marcus blinked, reluctantly dragging his eyes from Clio to

acknowledge the woman at her side. "Hello, dear. Looking as expensive and beautiful as ever."

Her mother gave him a once-over and sneered, "And you, like a piece of trash." *Heaven save me... and this entire room.* Clarissa was not a force to be reckoned with.

Clio glanced around for Nikolai, with every intention of strangling him.

What a floor show that would be. He'd probably laugh, and when everyone realized he was immune to suffocation, he'd do something stupid like undress her as reparation. A part of her knew she would let him.

Marcus turned back to Clio, his eyes soft. "Congratulations on your engagement. I'm sorry I didn't answer your calls. I wish you would have left a message so I knew it was you."

Clarissa gasped, whirling on her. "*You* did this? Why would you bring him here—invite him without telling me?" Her face twisted, filling with a thick, visceral hurt Clio had never been able to determine was real or forced.

It felt real enough now to turn her stomach. Clio couldn't find her voice—the words to defend herself. But she didn't need to.

Marcus waved a hand. "Let up on the girl, Clare. I came here on my own. I'm a certified party crasher, remember?"

"Don't call me Clare," she hissed, her chin quivering.

"Why not?" He asked. "That's the woman I knew."

"I have no desire to remember who I was with you or your horrible influence on my youth."

Marcus's eyes narrowed. "Our youth ended over a decade ago. You'll have to come up with a better excuse for your daily migraines than my teenage influence. Still battling them I bet, judging from your balance and breath."

Her eyes widened. "Real classy, Marc."

"The ultimate class act, I'm told." He shrugged. "Regardless, I'm not here to exchange venom with you. I'm here for my daughter."

Clarissa looped an arm through Clio's. "What daughter? That term implies some sort of relationship."

Duncan appeared on Clio's other side. He wrapped an arm around her back and asked, "Is there a problem here?"

Her mother laughed bitterly, a few fat tears finally trailing down her cheeks. How did she look so beautiful when she cried? It wasn't fair. "Yes. My ex-husband seems to think he has a right to interfere with your happy day." Duncan's hand tightened on Clio's waist. "Perhaps you could inform him what The Divine Light thinks of fathers that abandon their children."

A fierceness crept into Duncan's gaze. Clio felt positively sick seeing it aimed at her father. "I'm going to need you to leave," he told Marcus. "Immediately."

"Duncan," Clio whispered, cradling that sliver of hope burrowing its way out of her heart, that blade that started slicing through her hard shell the instant her father appeared in the doorway.

Duncan shifted his ferocity to Clio, and the weight of it silenced her. "He has no right to be here. He's an abomination, a dissenter of faith and family. He's worse than an adulterer." She forced herself to remain stoic as his spit spattered her face. "I don't want him around you."

Marcus interrupted, his hands raising in surrender. "Look, I didn't know I was walking into a church service. I don't want any trouble. All I wanted was to see you, Clio, and tell you that I'm happy you're happy. I just wanted to see you one last time."

"Too little, too late," Clarissa snapped, clutching Clio's arm like a pillar. Clio knew she was seconds from spiraling into hysterics.

After her father left, Clio became strong, cold, unfeeling. She had to. And she hated it—being depended on like that.

Marcus smiled sadly, as if he read Clio's thoughts and empathized with them, and backed away. He spun on his heel and disappeared into the hall.

It took Clio a moment to pry Clarissa's clammy hands off her arm. Her mother flung herself, bawling openly now, into Duncan's arms. He flushed, his eyes bewildered as she wailed in his ear.

As the rest of the family closed in to comfort the beautiful damsel in distress, Clio slipped out of the room. She found her father leaning against one of the stone alcoves in front of the manor, hunched slightly to light a cigarette between his teeth.

The lighter's flame snuffed out as she burst through the front entrance, the brilliant red embers flaring as he pulled in a lung-full of smoke. An Arctic chill slammed into her and, though the snow inched into her heels, she stood her ground.

Marcus's hand trembled as he pinned the butt between two fingers and held the cylinder away from her. He blew the smoke over his shoulder.

"Why are you here?" she demanded. "Do you need money? Is that it?"

He slumped against the stone. "I'm glad to see your mother's brainwashing took. That's good, it's probably better that you hate me."

The fury in Clio's stomach flared enough for her to spit, "Go fuck yourself."

A cloud of smoke wafted over her as he lurched forward, bracing the door to keep her from retreating inside. His eyes were panicked. "I'm sorry. You *should* hate me after everything that happened, I know that. I only meant that she always hoped you would hate me in the end, even while I was still around."

"You gave her plenty of reasons to," Clio retorted. "The gambling debts. The other women."

Clio backed away to avoid the smoke as Marcus took

another drag. He said in the exhale, "We were both fatally-flawed creatures, Clio. We didn't know how to take care of each other."

"You gave up."

He grimaced. "It felt like surrender at the time." Marcus glanced out at the snow falling over the staircase and then at Clio's dress, his gaze lingering on her shoes. "You should probably go back inside."

And even though that had been exactly what Clio just tried to do, she replied, "Don't tell me what to do." She crossed her arms, standing ramrod straight as she glared at him.

Marcus gave her a half-smile that confirmed what she suspected: that she was acting like a stubborn teenager. But she wouldn't give in. He perched the cigarette in his mouth as he stripped off his jacket and handed it to her. "Fine, but here. Wear this if you're going to keep me company."

She hesitated, only because his scent enveloped her as he placed the jacket in her hands. It smelled like his old cologne.

As Marcus leaned against the stone wall again, Clio slid the coat on. It was warm and the seams were frayed. The corduroy material had lost a lot of its fuzziness, but it felt *good*—rivaling the comfort of even Nikolai's embrace.

"I'm sorry for showing up unannounced." Marcus glanced at the manor behind them and frowned. "Truly. If I'd known your fiancé was a priest, I would have brought along a whip to castigate myself with, and saved him and your mom the trouble."

And there it was, his venomous sarcasm, ripping away what little goodness she found in his presence.

"That's really rude, you know," she spat.

Marcus scoffed. And maybe she should have thrown his jacket at him and gone back inside, but Clio remained there, scrutinizing the pain that flickered in his honey eyes.

"That's religious trauma, honey." His throat bobbed as he glanced at the aurora stirring to life above them. She vaguely wondered if he saw it the same way she did—as a stabilizer. "I don't believe in that shit anymore."

"Why not?"

Marcus studied her and took a long drag before responding. "Don't look at me like that, like I'm lost. I'm not a faithless man, Clio."

Her thundering heartbeat filled his pause.

He shook his head, staring out at the tundra as he continued, "I believe there's something out there, whether it's The Divine Light or another deity, but I don't believe it expects us to suffer. I believe that whatever is out there wants us to be the best and truest versions of ourselves, and when we've fallen too far from goodness, it extends a hand to help us up. I won't be a prisoner to guilt or shame. I won't be a prisoner ever again."

Prisoner. So she was a prison after all.

"I guess it's a good thing you hightailed it out of my life then," she said grimly.

He blinked. "That's not what I'm talking about. You were a joy to me."

"Until I wasn't."

Marcus's eyes darkened, the dark crescents drooping further as he said, "What happened that day never made me love you any less."

Clio's memory surged with a flash of blinding light, anger, and a living room carpet covered in blood. He still had a limp. Even several years later.

She remembered how his voice sounded that day: shaken to the core. *Our daughter is a demon, Clarissa.* His solution had been to leave. Her mother's solution had been to submerge her in religious practice.

"No." Clio's voice strained, her throat aching. "It only made you abandon me."

Pain screwed his face, a hand rising to clutch at his chest. "I left because I was a coward. I was scared of *ruining* you, and that fear drove me to make the greatest mistake of my life. I never should have left you to your mother's bad habits, to her insecurities and that fucking church, but I also had to fight a war of my own. I regret what I didn't do for you, and I'm sorry."

Clio leaned against the wall next to him, her legs weak and numb. After a moment, she asked, "Why didn't you come back?"

He shrugged helplessly, emptily. "It was easier to let broken pieces lie."

Easier.

"Don't misunderstand," he said quickly. "I did *try* a few times, when you were younger. But your mother has excellent attorneys. It took a long time to put myself together enough to have a fighting chance in the courtroom, to grow up and heal those parts of myself that hurt the people around me. By the time I was in a better place, I felt like it was too late to pursue a relationship with you. You were a teenager and I was just a piece of shit dad you hadn't spoken to in years. I wanted you to reach out first, to know for sure that you wanted to see me before I disrupted whatever life you created in my absence."

There was nothing for her to say... not as that shrapnel of hope cut through the final layers of her heart and emerged like a bloody dagger ready to strike.

Silence fell, and the whistle of the Arctic wind sang to her. Enough time passed that cigarette butts piled up next to the front doors. She didn't have the courage to scold him for it, even though she knew he wouldn't bother to pick them up.

She whispered, so softly she almost hoped he would miss it, "I don't know how to forgive you. Or if I even want to."

His expression told her he understood. "It's okay. Thank you for seeing me anyway. For following me out here and talking with me, and letting me memorize your face the way it looks now."

Clio rolled her eyes, but some pit in her stomach shallowed. "I didn't have much of a choice."

He chuckled and flicked a cigarette into the snow off the side of the staircase. "Yeah. Not when it comes to that Nicholas guy. He's a force of nature. I half expected him to announce *himself* as the fiancé when he beat my door down in the middle of the night and told me you were getting married."

"He's a meddling bastard," she murmured, though her heart was burning. Soaring. She slid her arms out of his jacket and returned it. He donned it without a word, a sadness filling his eyes as she turned toward the entrance.

Clio paused and said, "I loved you with all of my heart back then. Nothing would have changed that. Not Mom, not the church—*nothing*."

Marcus's hands stilled against the lapels of his jacket as he slowly lifted his gaze to meet hers. Before she could comprehend the movement, he was hugging her, squeezing her so tightly she couldn't breathe. And that was okay.

"And I love you still, with all of mine," he whispered in her ear.

When he pulled back, his arms a firm presence around her, he stared into her eyes and said, "Whatever it was you showed me that day, I hope you embraced it. I think, now, it might be a gift."

Clio averted her gaze, staring at the snow. She tried with all her might to be cold and unfeeling. "It's nothing. I lost it a long time ago." She killed that piece of herself. Let it wither away in a locked chamber, where it couldn't do harm or scare anyone away.

"That's a shame." Marcus let her go, grimacing as he opened the door. "I'll get out of your hair here within the hour. I just need to retrieve my bag from the room and call a cab."

He followed her inside, bowing his head as he limped toward the elevator. She was frozen in the entryway, watching him walk away.

"Dad," she called. It echoed through the lobby.

Marcus stilled. When he twisted to face her, his eyes swam with tears.

She shouldn't, but she wanted to keep him for a little longer, regardless of how tonight and tomorrow played out. Maybe he was an abomination, a dissenter, or worse—but he was her dad. She saw the man beneath her mother's distortion, the man who threw crumpled paper and pretended it was snow. The first person to ever face the monstrosity of her inner chamber. And he didn't hate her.

She didn't hate him.

In the dim of Raðljóst Manor, with the aurora peeking through the windows in an eerie glow, they were safe from the Light's blistering gaze. There was just enough light to see everything clearly. And she wondered if he was right... about all of it.

She whispered, "Will you—do you want to stay?"

31

No one missed her. Clio slipped back into the party, edging the crowd to reach the refreshment table. Her mother had stopped crying, but Clio could hear her voice neck-deep in a rant about Marcus. She tried to tune it out.

She retreated to the shadows of the room, wishing the glass of sparkling cider in her hand was moonshine as she sipped it. She sat in one of the alcoves, watched the life, the joy of family around her, and couldn't feel any of it.

Her father's words repeated in her head. *If you're happy, I'm happy.*

She asked him not to return to the party, but he chose to stay. And Clio couldn't stop those words from haunting her every breath. He found joy, pride even, in her happiness. She didn't know what to do anymore, what to cherish, what to think —but every second it was getting a little clearer.

A warm voice rumbled, "I'm assuming I have you to thank for the lovely painting on my bed."

Clio leapt out of the seat, turning to face the alcove behind her. The cider splashed on her dress and she seethed, wiping the dribble away. Her eyes lifted to the vent, where the familiar voice drifted from. Glancing over her shoulder, she couldn't see to the other side of the room, but she knew Nikolai stood before the opposite alcove. He hadn't bothered to approach her face-to-face. Maybe he sensed the danger in it.

She burned—not with desire, but her temper. She tried to control it, but her body betrayed her, welcoming the spark and stoking it into a fire. Nikolai always made her feel this way. Made her want to feel everything when she knew she shouldn't.

She growled into the alcove, "A regrettable decision."

A chuckle rattled through. Clio felt their intimacy, that softness from the day he'd told her his story, resurrected. It was these damn alcoves. A romantic secret, indeed.

He said, "Considering you trespassed and let my pet out, I'm inclined to agree with you."

Shit. That was what she felt in his room—Poppet, bolting out the door. She crossed her arms and said, "Wave some catnip through the halls. I'm sure she'll show up."

"Oh, sure. I'll just carry a dish of blood through the manor."

Clio's spine stiffened. "What?"

"Haven't you guessed it, yet? Poppet's not exactly a normal cat. She's almost as old as I am, and you just let her loose in beast-nip paradise."

Her family. The flame in her stomach flared. She poured every ounce of rage into her voice, willing it to lash and bite the way she knew her mutated eyes could. "I wouldn't have felt the need to trespass if you didn't vanish into thin air."

A beat. "I told you, I had things to do." His voice took an amused turn. "Men to meet."

She hissed, "Trust me, you don't want to bring that up right now."

Silence. Clio waited for him to say anything. He didn't. She leaned into the alcove and said his name, quiet enough that she knew only his strange hyper-hearing would hear it—vents aside. Nothing. Only the distant echoing laughter and chatter of the room. Did he leave?

Air swirled at her back and an all-too-wonderful scent wrapped around her. *His* scent. She wanted to turn—maybe to spit in his face, but every muscle tensed up as long, cool fingers swept the curls away from her left shoulder.

She'd missed him. Missed him so badly that as the realization hit her of exactly how much, her gut hollowed out. It had only been a couple days. How could she bear eternity without him? An entire life?

He stood so close, the lapels of his jacket brushing against her back. She wanted to melt into him. Wanted to let him have her in every way, in any way, he could bear to. Nikolai murmured her name, a caress of warm breath over her bare collar.

Terror roared up her spine. He couldn't—they couldn't. Not here. *He left.* Clio whirled, chest heaving. "What the fuck."

Nikolai's blue eyes seared through her, wide as they raked over her face. His black suit gleamed in the low light. "You're angry."

"Caught on, have you?"

His mouth parted, that dark gaze catching on the red bow of her dress.

"What?" She snapped.

Nikolai leaned in, his voice husky and soothing. "Has anyone told you how utterly ravishing you look right now?"

It made her realize that no one had. No one had told her she looked even marginally pretty, and she hadn't noticed. Hadn't cared until he pointed it out. Clarissa was always the star, the beauty, the one to admire. But Nikolai only had eyes for her. He wouldn't look away.

"Stop," she demanded.

He raised a hand to her arm, lightly grazing her skin with his knuckles, and stared at her with palpable despair. "Tell me how."

A moment too late, she noticed herself leaning into him. Surrounded by family. In the same room as her fiancé. She stepped back.

Glancing around, she spotted a glimpse of Duncan's hair through the crowd. He was distracted, as was most of the room, thank the Light. But a few feet away, watching from the shadow of a column, her old bodyguard, Enzo, caught her gaze. His brow furrowed, and she knew he saw the affection.

The room closed in, the air evaporating in her lungs. Her corset tightened like a vice. She averted her eyes to the marble floor, but it spun. Shiny, leather loafers stepped toward her, and she bolted. Clio lumbered through the hallway, numb to reality and the aching of her feet. She ran into library and stumbled up to the dome.

The aurora was bright purple—radiating through the crystal like a lavender sunburst. She let herself sink into it. She let the night consume her. The lights drew out her panic like a hand pulling string out of a knot.

She didn't know how the Divine could expect her to be content when she was so tremendously unhappy, when she felt trapped and suffocated and oppressed. She fisted her hair, disheveling the pins there.

Clio knew what she had to do, but she didn't know how. She wasn't sure how she would endure it—being alone. Because that was the only ending in sight. She was falling into space, into that void of darkness between the stars, and she couldn't find the courage to open her eyes. To see if anything was beside her.

Nikolai's voice startled her. "Aren't you the slightest bit relieved he showed up? It's an answer."

Clio wiped her tears, shying from his presence. Her back hit the wall of the crystal dome. "It's more questions," she croaked. "I'm more confused now than I've ever been." He waited for her to continue. The silence was too much to bear, so she asked, "Why did you do that? Why did you bring him here?"

"You *wanted* him here. You told me—"

"I told you I called him. But I never left a voicemail. Didn't that tell you anything, tell you that maybe I didn't want him to answer?"

Nikolai hesitated, mulling the question over in his head. "It told me you were scared. It told me that you needed a little push."

Clio's gut roared at the pure nerve and entitlement she heard in those words. She blinked back the blurring of her sight. She dug nails into her palms so hard that she knew he would smell it—smell her. It reminded her of the last time he smelled something on her hand. "That wasn't your decision to make."

His eyes glazed over. "You're right. It was *yours*, but you've been a coward." Nikolai was angry too, she suddenly realized. She'd never seen him angry before.

"A coward?"

"Yes. Running scared from anything you can't control, watering yourself down to appeal to the masses."

Clio skirted the circumference of the dome and he pivoted to follow her movement. "What do you want from me?"

Nikolai scoffed, running a hand through his hair. "From

you? Not a damn thing. I just want to understand. I want the real you, without compromise."

"No one should have me like that." She tried to avoid his stare, tried to reach the other side of the dome, but he closed in on her, forcing her back.

He approached slowly. "Why not?"

Clio made the mistake of looking up and saw the desperation in his eyes. That need she wholly understood. "Because I'm weak and wrong that way."

"I don't agree, nor would I care."

"You should. I'm human and someday I'm going to die. There's no happy ending for you and I."

"So, you'd rather never live at all?" His tension grew, filling the space between them. She wasn't frightened of that—his temper. She was scared of much more volatile things. Other things he might do to her, for different reasons. "You would rather walk around with a heart as dead as mine for the rest of your mortal life?"

"I need to do what's right."

"No," he exploded, a vein pulsing in his temple. "You want to sacrifice yourself to a god of your own making. You're a masochist."

She whispered, "Maybe pain is all I'm capable of." The frustration in his eyes faded. She dropped his gaze, slipping past him, and at the last moment his hand whipped out and caught her wrist.

"Clio." He said it like a prayer. She paused, like a god might, to listen with no intention of answering. "Don't marry him."

Stars were dying in his eyes. She couldn't let herself care. She needed time to think, time and space to make this next decision for herself. Still, she couldn't help but ask, "Why shouldn't I?"

"You don't love him."

She brushed his hand away. "What do you care?"

He blocked her way to the exit, scowling. "Because if you marry him tomorrow, you'll break *my* heart, as dead as it might be." There was only him in that moment, his eyes red-rimmed and bluer than ever. More human than ever. His hands hovered inches away, twitching—itching to touch her. He said, "I love you, and we both know he doesn't deserve you."

"And what," she breathed, "you think you do?"

He shook his head. "I know for a fact that I don't, but I want you to be happy, whether that's with me or... or not."

She looked past him, to the staircase, and it struck her—"You followed me into the dome."

His eyes softened. "I would follow you anywhere. I would do anything." A spark flickered in his gaze. "I'd like to peel you out of that dress and lay you out on this crystal right now."

Breathing became impossible. He looked at her like he never wanted to let her go, like if she said yes, he would hold her captive in this heaven forever. And she wanted that to be true, but a part of her knew it wasn't. "Would you scour the earth for a plant to turn me?"

Nikolai balked. "Don't ask me to do that."

Tears sprung to Clio's eyes, and she laughed bitterly to keep them at bay. "That's what I thought. Don't make promises you can't keep."

"This has nothing to do with what I want." He stepped forward but paused when she flinched back. His hands remained outstretched between them. "Of course I want you with me, *always*. But if you turned, you would hate me. You would regret it eventually. So, no, I won't subject you to an agony I'm familiar with."

"Even if that's what I want?" She pressed. "You and me— this place, forever?"

"You can't know what you want forever, not before you're in it," he stated, his eyes flicking around the dome. He sighed and it was the sound of surrender, but not to her. "It doesn't matter anyway. The last trace of those plants faded centuries ago."

The shard of hope in her heart retracted, hiding away in the open, festering wound Marcus created. Sometimes hope could be a dangerous thing. A weight pulling victims down to the ocean floor. "Then our decision has been made for us." Her voice broke. "I can't be with you if we don't have a future. I can't live without faith and hope, and you refuse to give that to me."

Clio saw the hurt in his eyes. And she wished it didn't have to be that way—but he wouldn't let her go any other way. *She* wouldn't let go any other way.

"Bianca?"

Clio jumped, finding the source of that voice standing on the threshold of the dome. The green-suited man she'd seen in the hallway stared at her, *expectant*, like—like he thought her name was *Bianca*.

The name clanged around in her head like echoing bells. "Excuse me?"

"You two know each other?" Nikolai asked.

The stranger said "Yes" at the same time she said, "No". Nikolai's gaze shifted between the two of them, his brows high.

"I've never seen you before in my life," Clio said.

The man blinked a few times, managing the look of shock on his face. His beautiful dark skin seemed to gray a little as he swallowed. "My mistake. You look like an old friend of mine. But I haven't seen her in a long time, and I guess my memory is a little fuzzy. I'm sorry for the misunderstanding."

Nikolai interjected, "Clio, this is Reuben. He's a friend. He can help us track down whatever was responsible for Nyah's death."

Clio blocked out the grief. She kept her voice and heart perfectly detached as she said, "Thank you for doing this, for trying to help, but it's time for me to let go. I can't pretend the truth will bring her back. It's over."

"What?" Nikolai scoffed.

"It's over," she repeated. "I have to get back to my party now."

Clio didn't bother saying goodbye before she descended the stairs.

32

The dome settled in Clio's absence. Nikolai let the emptiness steep the atmosphere before lifting his eyes to Reuben's. It felt different, standing in here by her side. But once she left, that half-blindness gripped him once again.

Reuben chuckled, removing his fedora to rub at his bald skull.

"Why the fuck are you laughing right now?" Nikolai demanded. He wasn't in the mood.

"I'm laughing at the utter humor of the universe."

Nikolai was going to punch him. The life debt could go fuck itself.

Before he could follow through on the impulse, Reuben replaced his hat and snapped his fingers. A burst of purple lightning and mist erupted. The familiar thud and slap of books filled the air and as the fog dissipated, it revealed a mountain of journals.

Nikolai looked between them and his friend, his forehead prickling. "What is that?"

"Seven hundred years of your life I helped you forget. I guess it's time to come clean."

"I don't understand."

Reuben shook his head. "I wasn't the one who saved you during the revolution."

"Of course you were."

"I hadn't even been born yet, mate."

Nikolai felt it again—his dead heart trying to beat.

"Think about it," Reuben continued. "Am I in any memories beyond that night? In that entire century? Do you even remember how you got here to the Arctic? Who designed this place?" Reuben glanced around at the purple-tinted crystal with a small smile. "You can't recall any of that—because it was *her*. And we were both wrong to believe she wouldn't come back and find you, just like she promised."

33

Clio paused on the threshold of Duncan's suite, wringing her hands in front of her stomach, the small gem of her ring digging into her palm. The door smacked into her back, nudging her the rest of the way inside, but she froze there as Duncan walked across the room.

His suite lacked a wall separating the bedroom from the parlor, so she got a clear view of him loosening his tie and discarding it on the mattress. She'd never seen him undress in any capacity before; he moved with slow, deliberate motions, removing his blazer to lay it next to his tie before reclining on the couch.

As he lifted the remote for the television and scrolled through the available titles, he folded the sleeves of his button-up to reveal bronze forearms. Duncan was exceptionally pretty, in a sun-kissed, boy-next-door sort of way.

And yet, she felt nothing staring at him. Nothing, as he glanced over and smiled.

"What are you doing over there?" His tone straddled the

line between exasperation and amusement. Always a dangerous line to tread. "Come sit down. We're watching one episode, then straight to bed."

She didn't comply. Her heart was pounding so hard, she surprised herself when the words came out steady. "We need to talk."

Duncan blinked, his face cold and indecipherable. He set the remote down. The screen settled on a romantic comedy with poor resolution, the faint dramatic music spilling into the room around them. "About what?" His flat tone sent a chill through her spine.

Clio swallowed her pulse. "Us."

He leaned back, studying her intently enough that her skin crawled. "Okay. Come sit down like a proper person, instead of barking at me from across the room."

She wasn't aware she'd been barking, or even speaking loudly, but she was practically delirious from nerves. Her head wouldn't stop spinning. Tremors radiated through her hands.

After another moment of hesitation, Clio approached the couch and perched on the edge, as far away from Duncan as possible. Not that it mattered. The instant she sat down, Duncan moved in. He sidled up next to her, close enough that their knees touched, and slung an arm across the couch behind her.

His eyes were threateningly soft as he leaned in; his smile a lazy, possessive thing. "Hi, there."

"Hey," Clio breathed, shying back even though there was no room. She looked away, but ignoring him wasn't easy. He captured her gaze even as it tried to roam.

"You know what," he drawled. His arm drew her in, wrapping around her shoulders as his other hand rose to caress her cheek. "I think this 'night in' might be a good idea after all. I've missed you."

She'd come to his room prepared to break things off, but the sudden sweetness disoriented her. Usually he was so hands-off, so distant. For months, she begged him for moments like this, breaking herself into little pieces so he would look at her this way. And now here he was, admiring her the way she'd always expected him to.

The affection gave her a bitter, icky sort of satisfaction, but her broken pieces latched onto it all the same. Duncan's face drifted toward hers, his gaze consuming and dark.

'You'll break my heart, as dead as it might be.'

Clio's sense snapped back into place. She braced a hand on her fiancé's chest, pushing him away as she shook her head. "Duncan."

His eyes narrowed. "This is about *him,* isn't it?" The arm on her shoulders grew heavier. Her heart skipped a beat. He couldn't know. How?

"Who?" she squeaked.

"The scum that calls himself your father."

Oh. She exhaled slowly. "Sort of. I asked him to stay."

Duncan's upper lip curled. "I'm not going to let him poison our wedding day, and I certainly won't allow him to walk you down the aisle if that's the sort of idea you came up here to discuss. Here I was, thinking you wanted to spend quality time with me—but no, you want to argue. I'm disappointed, Clio."

Every seething word reminded Clio of just how unhappy she was. How small she would remain if she went through with their wedding. Nikolai and her father's voice mingled in her head, making her strong, making her brave. "No, that wasn't what I wanted to talk about," she said. "But, about the wedding."

Clio took her ring off. Duncan's gaze narrowed in on that, his expression spinning through a dozen emotions. She caught the fury and disbelief and—yes, that was fear there, too.

"I've been thinking a lot the last couple weeks." She continued, swallowing her nerves, focusing on the ring rather than the glare Duncan aimed at her. "And I don't think we're right for each other. I think it would be better for both of us if we called off our engagement."

"Where is this coming from?" His voice was a low snarl. Clio did her best not to let it derail the words she needed to voice.

She tentatively touched his knee to soften the blow, to keep him from becoming angrier as she said, "You have to see that we don't make each other happy. I can't be what you want—an innocent dove. That's not me."

"Stop," he commanded, his voice slicing. "You don't mean this, you're just nervous about tomorrow. That's normal."

Clio withdrew her hand. He was trying to disregard her thoughts, her feelings, her instincts, and she was so fucking sick of it. She knew what she wanted, or at least what she *didn't* want. "I'm not nervous, Duncan." She placed the ring on the coffee table in front of them. "I'm done."

Duncan went still, his gaze searing like a brand. Suddenly, his arm around her shoulders shifted and his hand gripped the back of her neck.

"You're done when I say you're done," he growled, and hauled her face to his.

His kiss was fierce and punishing, his lips pressing hard enough to bruise. He took and took, invading her mouth with his tongue. It was all fire and brimstone—frightening and rough and insistent. She told him to stop and, when he didn't listen, bit his lip hard enough to make him jerk back.

His hand came down across her temple.

Clio hit the floor, her cheek prickling. The pain came a moment later, pumping through her veins like acid. She shut her eyes, pressing her forehead to the ground to prevent the room from blurring. She heard the couch shift as Duncan stood, heard the tell-tale clink of his belt opening, the slither of leather unfurling from his hips.

"What have you been doing here? Who's been whispering lies into your ear while I've been away?" His voice was throaty, hot, formidable. "Have you been traipsing around with that owner? Letting him defile you?"

"No," she whispered to the floor.

"You're *mine*, Clio. Put my ring back on your finger. *Now*."

The lick of leather was moments away, she could almost taste it in her mouth. She refused to endure worse than she needed to, so she rose on shaky arms and grappled for the gold band on the table. When she slipped the ring on her finger, her stomach turned.

Her father's words cycled through her head, shading the night in a grim auburn char.

When had Duncan ever helped her stand taller—told her he loved her for all that she was? In the past year, how many times had she looked up at him from the ground, wishing for him to extend a hand?

Clio fought against the bile creeping up her throat, the pain searching for a way out.

She knew it intimately—this ache that resulted from people ripping pieces of her away. Bit by bloody bit.

Duncan hovered. "You better not have ruined yourself. Believe me, Clio, I'll know on our wedding night, and there will be no blood-letting in the world that will fix that deception."

Life is in the blood, the church always said. *And so is forgiveness*.

"I haven't," she swore.

"How will you prove it to me?" He said, his tone mocking.

Her back prickled as she braced for impact. Every lashing she took here on earth, at his hand, meant a sin forgiven by the Light. But it didn't feel like repentance anymore. It felt like sickness, and hatred, and brokenness—with no hand to help her up. Maybe, at one point when this started, she'd appreciated him. The way he released a part of her. The way he allowed her a moment or two of liberation from her own cages. It was a revival, though a flawed one.

When Duncan first saw the light seeping out of her bleeding lashes, he'd been shocked, but elated. He took it as a sign that the Divine approved of him, of his "righteous" anger, of his punishment. And when he looked down at her with admiration, even if he didn't know it was really a curse, she wanted it to happen again. She *allowed* it to happen again. And again.

Not anymore. She'd rather join Nyah in the abyss and burn. These scars and his sense of entitlement were her own fault for letting it go on so long. But now she wasn't sure how to stop it, or what would happen if she truly tried.

A thud and the clink of metal sounded near her feet and Clio slowly peeked under her arm. Duncan had let the belt drop.

He didn't kneel to embrace her though, as he usually did when the fury was over. "I don't want to give you the belt tonight—not when we have such a happy day ahead of us. Tell me you're sorry and I'll forgive you, and we can start fresh in the morning."

"I'm sorry," she said flatly.

Duncan growled, as if sensing that hint of rebellion in her tone. But he said, "Good girl. Now, go back to your room and repent to the Light in prayer."

When the bathroom door slammed shut, she let herself shatter. Her tears splattered the floor as she pulled on her shoes, but she knew at that moment it could have been blood.

The end credits were rolling as Clio left the suite.

She walked right into Poppet, whose little pink nose was sniffing at the crack under the door. *Thank fuck.*

Clio bent with a sob and gathered the cat to her chest. Poppet's claws dug into her shoulder, spreading an odd tingle under her skin. The cat's fur raised, a growl rumbling through her small body as it stared at Duncan's closing door.

Soothing the tiny blood-drinker was more difficult surrounded by other human scents—but Poppet allowed Clio to hug her tightly and the growls shifted to purring as they walked down the hall to the elevator.

Clio didn't realize the elevator was occupied until the doors slid open to reveal Clarissa and the officiant. Her mother was clinging to the man, but she straightened when they saw Clio in the doorway.

"Clio, sweetie," she slurred. "You should be in bed." Clarissa was drunk, exceptionally so—but then again, when wasn't she?

"So should you," Clio retorted.

Clarissa's mouth flapped, searching for coherent words. "Of course. Ezekiel was just walking me to my room."

Right. The officiant led her mother into the hall as Clio entered the box.

Poppet hissed, baring her long, ivory fangs.

Clio dug her fingers into the cat's milky fur to keep her contained. She lurched for the buttons, desperate for isolation from what could have been Poppet's next meal if she hadn't intervened, if she hadn't been here in this hall to prevent it.

As the doors slid shut, Clio marked the wine and glasses in the apostolate's hands, the giggle her mother made as she slipped into her suite. Before Ezekiel followed Clarissa into the room, as if sensing the weight of Clio's eyes, he paused and smirked at her over his shoulder.

The golden doors of the elevator met and the box plummeted. And Clio began to doubt that servants of the Light could be trusted.

34

Clio hesitated with her hand on the latch to Nikolai's room. *It's okay*, she'd been whispering to Poppet. Even though it wasn't okay. *She* wasn't okay.

She should slip the cat through the door and leave. Return to a room too large and romantic for what happened to her tonight, slip away in the early hours of the morning and catch the next red eye just like Nyah did.

But she didn't want to leave.

Nikolai's room was lit by the candles on his desk. Old books were stacked around his desk chair, several volumes with yellowed pages splayed under the candle glow. The bindings seemed strangely familiar—the simple binding of his journals, she suddenly realized, though these seemed even older than the ones she'd discovered in the drawer.

As the door shut behind her, Clio realized that the small room directly across from the entrance was shut. A shower ran beyond it. She failed not to imagine Nikolai under the torrent. His ivory skin gleaming, that dark hair dripping—

Her imagination didn't have to roam for long.

The shower cut off, the slap of feet against tile and the creak of metal hinges prickling across her skin. And suddenly, he was there, wrenching the bathroom door open. She caught a blur of skin and a red towel before she averted her eyes from the light streaming past his silhouette.

"Ah," she turned her head, letting her curtain of hair fall to shield her.

"What is it?" he asked, concern layered in his voice.

"The light."

"Oh, sorry." Nikolai flipped off the fluorescents and the room fell back into a mild glow.

She hesitated to face him.

Nikolai took a step toward her. "There's something else. What's wrong?"

He stood like a phantom against the shadows of the bathroom. A glorious, broad-shouldered, forgotten god. Steam from the room billowed around him, touching her in a wave of heat. The water from his body pooled beneath his feet. He grasped at the towel slung around his hips, tucking it closed. Every muscle danced across her vision, the rigid build of his torso and lower stealing every coherent thought from her. For a moment, it was all she could do not to throw herself at him.

After what she said to him, after she swore it was over, how could she? She didn't know what to believe in. Who would want her, dead or alive? Light or faithless?

And finally, Clio asked herself the questions she never dared to consider.

Who did *she* want to want her? Was it the Light she desired in the end—the being that demanded pain for deliverance? Did eternity make up for a lifetime of suffering? She wasn't sure.

Was the world grayer than she ever imagined? Ill-defined, like the night?

Nikolai's eyes pierced through her, pulling her back to this moment, tinged with a sadness she knew well. *What's wrong?*

"Everything," she admitted. "Can I stay here for a while?"

His lips parted as he scanned her body, shrouded in the shadows of the room, but he nodded. He retrieved a bundle of cloth from the bathroom and turned away.

"Where did you find her?" he asked as he tugged on his gray sweatpants under the towel. She didn't fool herself into thinking she couldn't watch.

Nikolai's muscles rippled, a build perfected over three millennia of hunting, the tendons of his upper back so ridged she imagined letting her tongue sweep over them like rain across a mountain range. He ambled towards the bed, but kept an infuriating distance from her.

Clio crouched to let Poppet out of her arms and the cat hurtled through the cracked door to the basement. "She found *me*, actually." *Right when I needed her. When I needed you.*

"Good. I'll let Reuben know he can stop scouring the halls." Nikolai hung the towel over his shoulders and rustled his hair until it became a fluff of dark curls.

When he discarded the towel on the nightstand, he crossed his arms and contemplated the space between them. His jaw ticked, his mouth parting as if to crush her entirely.

"Don't ask me to leave," she whispered.

Nikolai's brow furrowed, his head shaking slightly. "I wasn't going to. I don't want you to go." This was it—the point of no return. But she'd already decided how she wanted to spend the rest of her night.

Clio peeled herself off the door. Their eyes locked as she approached him. When they were finally toe-to-toe, she spread her hands over his chest, savoring the softness of his skin.

Nikolai's entire body trembled beneath her touch.

It felt right—this *thing* between them, no matter how or

when it ended. It was all she wanted. She was done telling herself no.

"It doesn't seem fair that I have a heartbeat and you don't," she murmured, sliding her hands across his collarbone. His skin was slick, those lovely dark curls dripping water onto his neck. "You make me want to live more than anyone I've ever met."

His face crumpled and she had to look away. Her gaze dropped to the planes of his stomach. *Lower.*

Nikolai cradled her chin and made her look up. "Whatever the matter is, whatever you need, I'm here for you."

Clio believed in him, in what they had. She saw faith in his eyes, hesitant and small but ever-growing, and that was more than enough. When she needed a hand to help her, he was there. When she was sick and hurt, and yes, even a coward, he was there. When she was lost...

"Can I have my deposit back?"

Nikolai blinked. And then his head tilted back in a roar of laughter. When he looked at her again, his eyes were crinkled and bright. His crooked canines flashed as he threaded his fingers into her hair. Gently, so delicately, he cradled her skull in both hands and drew her in. He said, "I might let you persuade me." And he brought his mouth to hers.

The kiss was what she imagined the moon must feel like. Soft and luminous. Ever-present, like a blue tattoo on her lips. She felt it go on into either end of eternity, as if she could have always been here, embraced by him. As if she might remain until the end of time. Her heart unraveled. A key slipped into the lock of her chambers. She only needed him to open the door.

He pressed in, filling her mouth with his venom. It was a balm for her throbbing temple, her frayed nerves, and tumultuous thoughts. It was such a blessed relief that her throat swelled and her eyes seeped with tears. After a moment,

Nikolai seemed to realize her face wasn't wet from his hair. He broke off the kiss and sighed, brushing the tracks from her cheeks.

"Beloved, don't cry. We won't do anything you don't want to."

"Don't stop," she gasped, wrapping her arms around his neck and kissing him urgently. "Don't you dare."

He said around her lips, "You're upset."

She pulled back, only far enough for him to see the gravity in her eyes. "I'm happy. I want you, despite the future or lack of one, despite the past and the beasts." Nikolai gazed at her with wide eyes. New tears warmed the air-chilled tracks on Clio's cheeks. "Please, don't stop loving me."

Panic filled his face.

One moment she stood before him, and the next he had his arms around her waist and under her ass as he swung her around. She landed in the center of the mattress, beneath the strange golden web. The tendrils reached down to touch her, like bottled sunlight stretching through the darkness.

Nikolai appeared a moment later, crawling up after her, his knees digging into the mattress on either side of her thighs. He leaned down, and their noses brushed as he said, "I will never stop loving you. Never."

He kissed her once again, deep and slow. Her heart thundered like mad.

"This dress has tortured me all night," he growled, leaning back to admire her. He reached for the ribbons between her breasts and fiddled with them like a cat might play with yarn, letting them twirl around his fingers.

Nikolai smirked. He tugged the bow free and, with nimble fingers, unthreaded the corset. When the ribbon pulled through the last anchors, Nikolai unfolded the panels from her torso and released a shaky breath.

She'd never felt so naked and beautiful as she did when he looked at her then. It had her shrugging out of the sleeves. He gently helped lift her body to slide the dress onto the floor. As he laid down beside her, he let a hand trail from the base of her neck to her navel. She turned to embrace him, but he stilled her with a firm pressure on her stomach, smiling wickedly.

Nikolai kissed the space beneath her ear and whispered, "When you were thinking of me the other day, did I do this?" His hand slipped beneath the band of her panties.

The first touch of his fingers scattered her thoughts, as he brushed tenderly on that one *particular* spot. Her back arched and she caught a glimpse of twinkling gold above her before surrendering wholly to sensation.

He kissed her neck, nipping the skin over a pounding artery. "Tell me, Clio."

"Yes," she whispered.

He withdrew his hand and she whimpered at the sudden loss. The mattress shuddered and she opened her eyes to see him crouching like a lion at her hip. She didn't have time to process the heat in his eyes before he said roughly, "Did I do this?" And lowered his mouth to her breast.

Clio gasped as he rolled the nipple between his teeth and tongue, leaving behind a prickle of venom. He hesitated before taking her other breast in his mouth, that wicked grin of his deepening. She knew what he wanted and forced herself to shake her head.

No. She didn't imagine this. Satisfied, Nikolai bit her other breast. The venom triggered a wave of goosebumps across her chest. He raised his head for a moment, scanning her face. It was in his eyes: *Tell me to stop and I will.*

Clio only ran her hands through his damp hair and smiled.

His pupils dilated enough to consume her. Those cool

fingers found her panties and guided them down. "What about this?"

Her breath caught, and she didn't bother trying to replace it as he slid off the bed and pulled her body to the edge along after him. Her head spun. Her body pulsed. Unbuckling her heels, he let them fall to the floor, dragging a nail up the center of each sole. She squirmed. He spread her legs and knelt, winking on the way down.

Embarrassment set fire to her cheeks, though she wasn't sure why—but she understood in the next breath, when he hooked her legs over his shoulders and started kissing her. *There.*

At first, they were gentle, grazing kisses. His lips and stubble skimmed her folds, nuzzled the creases of her thighs. He trailed light kisses along the sensitive skin on one side, then the other. Her hip bucked without her permission.

And then suddenly, the kisses became... something else.

His nose nuzzled her folds, spreading her, and his tongue slipped in, traveling down and back up, exploring every inch of her most intimate place. He scraped his teeth against the mound at the apex of her thighs, and that *fucking tingle* seeped in. Gently, he sucked.

She cried out.

Nikolai smiled, but kept kissing, kept nipping. It was going to drive her insane. She was going to—going to—

Her thighs began to shake. "Nik, please, I feel like I'm going to explode." She sat up.

Nikolai met her with clashing teeth and tongue.

"Sounds beautiful," he murmured, wrapping an arm around her waist and pulling her against his chest. "Let's see it."

Clio let him hoist her back onto the bed, let him lay her against the pillows.

When Nikolai enveloped her again, he'd discarded his pants. His hips nestled against hers. He spoke into her ear, his voice the exact opposite of his body, all honey and warmth and tenderness. "Can I have you?"

She could feel him lined up against her. All a tangle of limbs and need, but not nearly close enough. "Please," she begged.

"Hmm," the rumble of his amused voice tickled her ear drum and she shivered, "how can I argue with such manners? But, unfortunately, you didn't answer my question."

"Don't make me stab you again," she groaned.

Nikolai chuckled, the eternal stars swirling in his gaze. "Just say 'yes,' beloved."

"You're a bastard."

"I think you mean gentleman."

Clio scrambled for a retort, but his hand once again slid between her legs. "Yes," she moaned.

He kissed her deeply. And when he sank into her with gentle rolling thrusts, she only felt the fullness of their joining. Only *surrender*. By the time he'd seated himself fully, her head was oscillating against the mattress. Her back arched for a measure of friction.

Nikolai chuckled, nipping at her jaw as he withdrew and started the slow, glorious torture over. He reached places in her no one ever touched before. Kissed wounds that had never known healing. It was magic.

Wild, blinding, life-giving magic.

35

Nikolai's hands fisted in the sheets, his arms trembling with restraint. He knew he couldn't drive into her the way he wanted, as hard and frenzied as he wanted. Not her first time. So he kissed her slowly, drawing out the sensation of their bodies fitting together just perfectly.

"*Fuck*," he growled. "You feel so good, I'm going to lose my mind."

Her hands scratched his back, nails piercing skin. She drew blood. Clio tilted her hips to meet his steady, deep thrusts. "More. Give me all of you."

He gulped, meeting the need in her eyes with his own. "I don't want to hurt you."

"You won't," she whispered, framing his face in her hands. Her eyes were glassy, but completely open. Alive. "You would never hurt me." She meant it. And something sick stirred in his chest. He wanted to believe she was right, but—

He thrust forward harder and she made a soft airy whimper. Her eyes fluttered. Her muscles clamped around him, and he nearly lost his grip on reality right then.

Nikolai gripped her thighs, lifting and pressing them down on either side of his chest. Curling her tighter. When he slammed home the next time, she emitted a guttural moan from the back of her throat and dug her nails into his shoulders. He did it again.

Clio cried out, nodding fervently, and he unleashed himself.

There was only her, writhing beneath him in pleasure, and he could only watch, *only worship*, as something broke within her. Light sparked beneath her skin, as though her soul were radiating star-fire and the veil that usually shielded it from view had at last ripped away. Her veins shimmered, illuminating her from the inside out.

"Look at me," he whispered, needing to see her eyes.

She met his gaze as she unraveled, her mouth forming a perfect little oval, her legs trembling as he lifted her ass to thrust deeper. Spheres of molten gold seared into him—her silver irises filled with rays of sun. It shone on him like the dawn of a new day, and he knew he would burn in it if that was his fate. Burn in her.

She continued to smolder as her head fell back, her eyes glassy and distant, her luminescence washing his skin in golden warmth. The scent of her blood drifted up from where it stained the sheets, marking him permanently—too heady to ignore.

Nikolai groaned, baring his teeth above her. Venom dripped on her neck. She arced. Her hands drifted to his hair and tugged him closer.

"Clio," he rasped warily.

She smiled groggily and locked her legs around his back. "Do it. I want you to."

One more, almost painful, tug on his hair had him careening for her. He sank his teeth into her neck. Her blood hit his senses, his beast, his cock all at once.

She tasted like the sea and dewy blooms, an early morning rain—like magic more ancient than the earth. And it brought him *back*.

His physical body continued driving into her. She climaxed again, moaning his name. But his mind was far away, in that lane of memories, and he watched it shatter. The glass box erupted, exposing him to the elements. He rose like air finally set free. Looking up, he saw the light. *The surface*. He barreled directly for it.

As he ascended, saltwater invaded his lungs and the unknown became known. The mysterious deep told him everything, and the ocean rippled, brightening, as he burst through the surface. He looked out at the ocean that surrounded him, the truth that had frightened him.

The unknown waters were *her*. Bianca. The parts of his life, of himself, that she'd touched, and all the parts he'd chosen to forget. They were never truly gone.

A light-damned fool, indeed.

Nikolai opened his eyes and found Clio waiting for him, smiling and sated beneath him. Her dark hair sprawled across the ivory pillows, her cheeks deliciously pink. Her neck bled, the two pinpricks oozing red. Beneath her shoulders and scattered over the mattress, coarse salt peppered the sheets. The element sifted between his fingers where they were braced on either side of her.

Clio didn't seem to notice one bit.

He had so much to say, but he only stared at her for what felt like the first time... the first after a damn-near eternity apart. His eyes welled and he didn't bother holding the emotion back. The linens were already fucked.

Clio's gaze softened into something close to awe, framing his face in her hands as his crimson tears fell. They marked the pale skin of her neck and chin.

He leaned in and kissed her. Once, twice, a third time—savoring her warm lips.

"Beloved," he rasped, letting her precious eyes pierce his heart like white-agate daggers. "I'm so sorry."

She giggled. "What could you possibly be sorry for right now?"

I should have protected you. I should have saved you.

"I'm bleeding on you." He couldn't tell her the whole truth, not while he was still buried in her. And she needed to know. Nikolai went to pull out, but she clenched her legs around him, keeping him on top of her, inside her.

"Never apologize for that. It's a part of you." She leaned up and licked his cheeks—licking the blood away. "And I want every part of you."

Clio brought her lips to his, her tongue sweeping in to mix their blood together, and he lost himself in the kiss. He hardened under that coaxing and she moaned into his mouth.

The first time, he'd made love to her in desperation, as though she were the sun and he could finally feel her after centuries of ice and darkness. But the second time, with every shred of his humanity, he immortalized her.

She'd crossed the barriers of death and destiny to find him, and he could never let himself forget.

36

Nikolai couldn't stop looking at her, touching her, staring into those sleepy silver-core eyes. Lying face-to-face under the covers—Clio's breathing still labored, her heart rate settling—he carefully combed through the knots in her hair.

He'd tucked her in earlier, when he noticed the prolonged blinks, the way she kept nodding off. She slept for a couple hours, his head racing too much to join her, before he needed to kiss her again. *Only an innocent peck*, he'd told himself—but then she woke more than ready to reciprocate.

"You can't get into my head, can you?" she asked breathlessly. "When your eyes turn black like that?"

He chuckled. "No. Why?"

"Well," she bit her lip and nuzzled his chest, her cheeks flushing, "I thought you might have for a minute there."

Not quite. He just knew her body like it was his own. A few centuries fucking like rabbits tended to do that. Even with this brand new vessel, he knew every muscle, every vulnerable spot she liked him to nip. She hadn't let him flip her over and take her from behind, which was different, but other than that her responses were just as instantaneous.

And she was also just as vocal as he remembered, which was a delight to discover.

She'd looked like a goddess riding him, the candlelight and golden strings of the dream net curving around her like a halo. Her body had shone on him as she moaned at the ceiling. She still didn't notice the light or salt that rained down, and he didn't comment on it.

I'll tell her everything soon. He just wanted to stay in this ignorant bliss a little while longer.

The contentment in her face ebbed, a little v forming between her brows. "Why *can't* you get into my head?"

He kissed the tension between her eyes. "You're special. Strong. Your mind puts up too much of a fight."

"But how? In the story you told me, you made it sound like your kind can bend human will."

"That's true," he admitted. "Though, there's more to humanity than meets the eye. Veins of gold can be found in abiding stone. You're a surprise—the metamorphic."

Clio blinked a few times. "Mutated, you mean."

"Lovely." He brushed a thumb over her lips, smiling softly.

She grimaced. "Speaking of gold," she said, looking pointedly at the net, "what is that thing?"

"It's a dream net—a talisman created here in the Far North from a few millennia ago. The natives on this continent string them. They believe that gold is a holy material, so when hung above a bed, any message in the universe intended to harm or scare will pass through the web and wilt. Only what's good and purified travels down the rest of the talisman to the dreamer."

Clio's face grew solemn, slightly hopeful. She let her hand brush through a few dangling strands. Was her inherent nature still chasing her, like his beast chased him?

"Does it work?" She wondered quietly.

"So I've been told."

She let her hand drop to the mattress and turned her full attention on him, cuddling into his side. An impish smile tugged at her lips. "I thought you weren't a superstitious person."

"I'm not."

She quirked a brow. "Do talismans not fall under that ilk? It's an item of faith. Why do you sleep beneath one?"

Because it was a piece of you. He grimaced. "I need to tell you something, but I'm not sure how well you're going to take it."

Her face fell, the arm across his stomach retracting to curl over her bare chest. "Was I—was this not— " He could finish the thought in his head. *Good.* Somehow, she was still worried about being good. What an ironic anxiety *that* was, considering who and what she was.

"Fuck, Clio. That's not it." He wrapped both hands around her neck, bracing his thumbs under her chin so she would listen. "Listen to me. Nothing compares to what we have; no one compares to you."

Tears welled in her eyes. "What if you're making a mistake loving me like this? What if you regret us, regret me, when my time is up and you're left alone again? What will we do when I'm too old to be with you?"

Her concern for him filled the cracks in his confidence—at least, temporarily. He brushed away the first spill of her tears. "First of all, I will always be much older than you. So, no worries there."

"I'm being serious." She sniffled, her lower lip quivering. He wanted to bite it, bite her all over, but restrained himself.

"As am I," he said softly. "I—I lied to you earlier tonight, about the plants."

Clio visibly reeled. "What do you mean?"

"I have the one that turned me. It's in the basement."

Her eyes bulged and her heart sped to a thrumming rhythm. "You changed your mind? You want me to turn?"

He clutched at his last thread of common sense, of sanity. "No, we shouldn't rush into a decision like that. It just didn't feel right keeping that secret from you. I told you once that I don't wish to lie to you and I broke your trust tonight, even if I thought it was to protect you. And I'm sorry."

Regardless of their past, the turn needed to be her decision. No coercion. No obligation. No unfair influence based on the life they'd once shared.

Clio should want it, not the ghost of the woman she once was. Nikolai needed to tell her everything, and then insist on some time for her to process her feelings, to formulate a plan to ensure she made it out on the other side of the turn in one piece.

His mind kept flashing back to that night so many centuries ago, when Bianca turned behind his back. He remembered how terrifying it had been, how she'd faced it alone, how close she'd come to death. All because she didn't want to wait. He didn't want to risk that again, not so soon after finding her, after finding himself.

Clio couldn't understand any of that, and so her eyes steamed. "Why bother telling me the truth if you're just going to hurt me with it?"

"Hey," he stopped her from pulling away, pressing her body flush against his, "I'm not saying no. I'm just saying not right now. Give yourself a little time. You might change your mind tomorrow or next week or next year." She might change her mind the instant he told her the truth, might run from the manor, might run from him. He had to prepare himself for that. None of her was guaranteed to him.

Nikolai ran his hands up her curves, threading them into her hair, and tangled his legs with hers. "Please," he pleaded, brushing kisses over her nose. "Let's not discuss this tonight. I just want to love you. We can fight about it tomorrow if you want."

She tilted her face and kissed him, a whimper of surrender in her throat, but when he shifted to cover her body with his, she broke away.

"I'm never changing my mind," Clio declared, searching his eyes with that predator's stare, "and I'm going to convince you of that one way or another."

Nikolai smiled. "I don't doubt you could. I'd love to see how you try."

Her gaze softened and a hand glided over his stomach, triggering a shiver up his spine and through his cock. "I know where I'd like to start," she crooned.

Clio threw herself at him, showering his face with kisses, teasing him with her fingers. She kept kissing, so sweetly, so eagerly, her lips curved in a delicious grin. Her enthusiasm seeped into him and his cheeks began to ache as he returned it. She shifted over him, resting her breast against his as their mouths met, and he slid his hands around her back, tracing the line of her spine until she shuddered in anticipation.

And then his fingers grazed something else.

He leaned back. "What's on your back?"

All the color drained from her face—all the rosy, warm goodness stripped in an instant. "Nothing."

She tried to push his hands away.

"It's certainly not nothing." He sat up, pulling her with him, and fought against her arms until he pinned them together in one hand. Turning her, he got a full view of her back—of what she hid.

Welts lashed her skin, a collection of scars in varying stages of healing. Some were a faint blush, near ready to fade to white, while others remained vibrant pink—raised and irritated, hardly more than a month old.

Frozen in utter shock, he released her hands and she ripped away from him. Sobs hooked in her chest. The shock slipped away from him and he careened for her, despising the way she flinched at the movement. He gripped her upper arms and scanned the rest of her, cataloguing every shadow and wrinkle, until his eyes caught on a mark.

Taking her chin, Nikolai tilted her face toward the light and growled at the beginnings of a bruise on her temple.

In a voice quiet but unyielding as death, he demanded, "Who did this to you?"

She hesitated. "I let him do it, Nik. I'll be fine. I'm fine."

"There is nothing fine about this," he hissed.

Clio closed her eyes, as if she could keep her true emotion from spilling over. As if she could keep herself contained. He wished she would let go, wished she would burn the whole world down for what had been done to her.

But she only whispered, "I agreed to the punishments."

At that moment, he knew.

"I don't care if you begged on your knees for it," he swore, leaping off the bed. He wrenched his pants on. "He's a dead man."

Clio scrambled after him, grabbing his arm as he shot toward the door. "Let it go, Nik. I'm leaving him. Just calm down before you do something you can't take back."

His stomach dropped. He whirled to face her. "Hold on. You haven't dumped the stupid fucker yet?"

She stuttered, "Last night he—he wouldn't—I tried."

His gaze flicked to her bruised cheek and a visceral instinct churned in his stomach. A deadly calm settled in his bones. *I'm going to rip him apart, limb from limb.*

Clio raised her hands in supplication. "Please. By tomorrow, he'll be gone, and it won't matter anymore."

"This will always matter," he argued, pushing past her.

She flung her naked body in front of him, blocking his exit. He knew he could easily remove her, but her expression stilled him. "Why?" Her voice cracked. "Because the scars ruin me for you?"

"Fuck no," he spat. "It matters because he hurt you. He made you feel small and scared—like someone you aren't. Those scars will stand as a reminder of what *I've* done. I'm not going to stop until everyone who's ever hurt you is a splatter of blood on the walls of our manor."

The words registered slowly. She murmured, "What are you talking about?"

"I'm talking about *this*. About us." He took her hands and held them to his chest. "I need to tell you the rest of my story now. Then, after you've heard, we'll discuss the piece of shit upstairs and decide which of us gets to rip him to shreds first: my beast or your divine temper."

Clio pressed her lips together, her eyes fluttering in apprehension. But beneath the confusion, there might have been a small spark of hope. "I'm listening."

His eyes flicked to the dream net. He gathered his scattered memories and told one last story.

37

"After I turned, I spent a millennium killing. Feeding and fucking, desperate for meaning. The loss of my real family broke me, in ways I couldn't face for a long time. At that time, I felt incredibly alone, violence serving as a temporary relief for me. I wore a stolen military uniform to disguise the blood on my hands. I targeted enemies of the civil war raging throughout the country. My excuses for death were easy to believe in.

"One night, as I passed a chapel in the center of the city, I caught a scent my beast couldn't shake and, though I had never blindly hunted before, I did then. I followed it into the church. The candles flickered along the ends of each pew and across the front of the altar, and that scent led me past the few that lingered in late hours to pray, directly to a dark box in the far corner. I kneeled in the booth, face turned to the lattice screen, toward the source of that incredible smell I couldn't resist as much as a human can't resist the instinct to breathe.

"The silhouette was there, of a petite form shrouded in cloaks. I saw a chin, a thin nose, but nothing more as the priest nodded to encourage me to speak. I didn't know what to say at first, only that I was there without knowing why and that I couldn't leave. So I began to speak. And I told the truth.

"I told the figure about the blood on my hands and how I didn't know what it meant to live anymore. I kept talking, telling the booth and that human everything I couldn't even admit to myself. I spoke of the death swarming me at every turn and of the emptiness, so much emptiness in my existence. I spoke of the hatred, towards myself mostly. And even as I spoke, I thought of those veins pumping so near, taunting me with their scent. I was going to kill for it, there was no denying myself, and so I spoke more than I should have. I said too much.

"When I spoke of drinking it—the blood—the human turned its eyes on me. And they were silver."

Clio took a small step back, but Nikolai held her fast to him. The real story was only just beginning.

"The instant they landed on me, they seemed to anchor me to the booth, they seemed to pierce me through to my very soul. Before I knew what was happening, the booth shuddered and that dark figure was gone. The human fled from me, with nothing more than a compulsory whisper. And when I heard her voice, I knew it was a woman I'd bared my soul to.

"I followed her into the alleys of the city, chasing glimpses of her black cloak and those silver eyes. I herded her towards places I knew would trap her and, eventually, she made a fatal turn—or so I thought it was at the time. When I flipped her around and bit her, she laughed.

"I thought I was hunting her, but she was the one hunting *me*. Her blood burned me from the inside out—like liquid sunlight. I collapsed, clawing at the poison trickling down my throat, and I knew my mistake had killed me. I was done.

"All I thought of in that moment was Genevieve, of

whether I'd met the better end those spirits told her about. I called out for her, hoping for an answer before the abyss consumed me. And through the burning agony, I glimpsed the mouth of the alley—the retreating figure cloaked in ebony and gold.

"She hesitated at the crumbling corner. She heard my screams and turned back to look at me, the same way Genevieve's magic did. Like—like she'd changed her mind."

Nikolai remembered. The way her eyes cut through every stain and shadow and found him in that mud-addled alley. His salvation.

"The last thing I saw before I passed out was her bare, bleeding feet sauntering towards me. Her cloak descending on me. I woke the next morning in her home, healed, and she introduced herself as Bianca, a divine saint of The Light.

"After threatening to blast me to bits if I so much as glanced at her wrong, she told me that my screams the night before had made her turn back, made her look a little closer. They reminded her of the grief she felt in her father's death, and when she saw the sliver of magic hovering above my body, she decided to save me."

Clio's brow furrowed, her eyes darting across his face like lightning.

"I knew in that moment," Nikolai breathed. "I knew it would be so easy to fall in love with her."

Her expression crumbled. "I thought you'd never loved anyone before."

"No one but you." He smiled weakly.

Anger pierced through her eyes. "You can see how confusing this story is, then—"

"Shhh." Nikolai pressed a soft kiss on the corner of her mouth, but Clio jerked away. Her face twisted as she shoved him. "Clio."

Catching her wrists, he pinned them on either side of her head as they fell against the door. He leaned into her soft body. She gasped and he buried his face in her hair, breathing her in, nuzzling the mark he'd left on her.

Clio trembled against him, responding to every slight tilt of his hips. She huffed a curse.

Kissing her collar, he whispered, "Give me a chance to explain before you tear me to shreds. I know you can, beloved, just—hold on. Please."

Clio's eyes were wary when he leaned back, but she nodded. His fingers released her wrists and trailed to her shoulders. She shivered as he brushed his thumbs down her ribs, pausing at her waist to trace feather-light circles.

So soft. How could he have forgotten how soft and sweet she was?

"Bianca told me her origins as a divine saint—that the Light spoke to her in dreams from childhood, preparing her for a life of hunting monsters like me. Ancient power marked her blood, and her eyes served as a lantern to guide her through the darkness. For nearly a decade, she fulfilled her duty without blinking. Until me.

"The Light hadn't told her beasts were separate from demons, that at our core we were still human. My ability to enter the church, to regret the death I'd caused, finally made her doubt what she'd been taught. From then on, we were partners, sorting our way through the confusion of what we believed and the truth, turning our hunt on the true evil—the demonic—with the help of Guardians we found along the way. She gave me purpose and, I think, in a way, I gave her hope.

"The Light wasn't prepared for her to turn, to become the very thing it intended for her to destroy. Neither was I—but things changed for us, during that time of discovery. We fell in love, and when she made up her mind about us, that was it. It was us, forever, in spite of her prescribed destiny."

Nikolai's throat swelled, his voice dropping to a thick whisper. "She believed life to be more than a constant balancing of the scales. She believed we could find goodness, even in the dark. Especially in the dark."

Clio's eyes fluttered, her lips parting as if she might interrupt. After a moment, when he was sure she wasn't going to, he continued, "After the turn, she managed to keep her divine gifts, her purifying elements, but at a cost. The light and salt she carried could harm her if she wasn't careful, so she mitigated her magic through special cuffs called siphons. One slip of her temper to the wrong organs—to her beast—would kill her, so she was careful... and we endured. We found eternal night together. We built a home. We taught any beast who crossed our path about our true prey, and we created a family of our own to cherish."

He smiled bitterly, even while dread loomed closer. "You asked me if I ever found my way back home. I did, because she was my home."

Clio tentatively placed a hand on his chest, over his dead heart. He wondered if it might start beating just to kiss her touch.

Nikolai squeezed his eyes shut as he whispered, "But then those we welcomed into our life betrayed us. They conspired to create an army to dominate Earth—they believed we were superior to humans—and so, one night, they snuck into our bedroom and pulled us out of bed, searching for the plant they knew we protected."

He opened his eyes. Blood flowed down his cheeks.

Clio shook her head, but it had to be said. All these words, building under his skin. All the memories he'd buried for so long.

"We fought back, but they wrestled me to the floor to decapitate me—and Bianca caught my gaze across the room. With crimson tears streaming down her cheeks, she said she would find me again... and I saw the rest written on her face."

Tears ran down Clio's cheeks, too. "No—"

"She exploded, projecting her elements out of every pore of her skin without siphons to protect her. The drop of magic in my soul whipped out somehow, creating a shield strong enough to weather her waves of purifying heat. When I opened my eyes, every beast in the room had been turned to ash.

"She sacrificed herself for the world she spent her whole life protecting. Sacrificed herself for *me*, even though I didn't deserve it. Fury followed me for a decade as I tracked down every traitor that hadn't been in the room—all the cowards who had fled or waited elsewhere. And when it was over, I showed up on Reuben's doorstep. There was nothing more to be done. All that death hadn't done anything to bring her back.

"Her words were my only hope. '*I'll find you again.*' She believed in the afterlife, in resurrection—believed that though Genevieve had been misled by some of the voices in her life, there had to be truth at the core of that journal. I tried to believe, too, for a long time. But eventually, my loneliness became too much for me to bear. The day came when I asked Reuben for a permanent solution."

Nikolai frantically raked a hand through his curls, his fingers trembling. "Every moment of her absence was agony. Every moment, I considered walking into the dawn. I knew, if she could see the way I lived without her, her heart would be broken. The empty centuries convinced me she wasn't coming back and a part of me figured the Light had taken her. She was a divine daughter after all—*golden*—and what was I but a beast? If she had to choose between peace and another life here in the darkness, how could I expect her to return to me?

"I submitted to the relief I saw on the horizon, the only option that wouldn't have made Bianca weep from her place in heaven—I decided to forget."

A spark of discernment flickered in Clio's eyes. Her head tilted slightly in disbelief. "Nik."

"I thought it was the right choice, but then—then you came along and showed me how wrong I was. I didn't—" His throat bobbed, brows slanting. "I shouldn't have given up. Bianca embraced me in the woods and the darkness. She brought me to life. Clio, she was everything."

Nikolai cupped Clio's face, kissing her tears and that delicate Cupid's bow. Looking into her light blessed eyes, he confessed, "And she was you."

38

Clio's head was spinning... or maybe that was the room. The tears wouldn't stop. Every word he spoke struck like flint against her heart. Sparking.

Bianca. Reuben called me Bianca.

Nikolai said, "I know you don't remember, but it's in you. I know it is. Your blood, the ancient light flowing through you, broke the spell Reuben bound me with. He stored my memories in a pocket of altered reality within my mind. You shattered the barrier keeping me from them."

Clio's entire body tingled as she lifted her hands to cover his. He said she couldn't remember, but in a strange, roaring place deeper than her chamber, down a staircase she'd never noticed before, she heard singing drift up to touch her.

Nikolai continued to fill the silence, to fill her thoughts as she sorted through them, "Reuben tried to explain, but I couldn't trust it at first. It was too good to be true. And then, I saw the truth in my own handwriting, and I became terrified. How could I explain the history or love we shared when I could not remember it? Who was I to place that on you, when you were getting married—when you seemed so sure? How could I expect you to forgive me? How could I forgive *myself* for what I did? You said it was over and I didn't deserve you and—" He took a shaky breath. "But, I *know*—I have *always* known you, Clio, and I have never stopped loving you. I'm never going to stop, not for one second."

The words radiated through her heart, along those golden fissures. *He loves me. All of me.* Somehow, she'd always suspected that there was more.

"I don't know how it's possible," she murmured, "but I feel you."

His chest heaved in a stifled sob. "You believe me?"

"I do." Before she could finish the words, he was kissing her. He clutched her to his chest, with a strength almost painful, and guided her away from the door. His hands traveled to her back, caressing the scars there.

Her lips muffled his voice. "You trust me?"

"I do," she panted.

The back of her legs hit the bed and he spun her around, bending her over the edge. His hands slid up, and pressed her upper body into the mattress. She couldn't breathe fast enough, deep enough, as her body responded to him. She rose up on the balls of her feet, lifted her ass, waiting for him to take her the way he wanted to earlier. He brushed featherlight kisses across her back, across the pink welts counting her sins. He growled loud enough to send vibrations through her torso as he kissed them, his hands trembling.

She gasped for him, ground herself against him through his pants. *Why are they still on?*

Nikolai kissed the length of her spine. He let his weight rest on her, nuzzling her ear as he whispered, "Then you'll have to forgive me."

Breathlessly, she asked, "For what?"

His tone shifted suddenly—to a promise of pure savagery. "Killing one more worthless human prick."

In an instant, his weight disappeared from her back, and she flipped over to find the room empty, the door to the library slamming shut behind him.

39

Clio scrambled for her clothes. She haphazardly tied the central anchors on her dress closed and shot up the staircase. She followed the faint scent of copper and cedar, turning around the landings as the marble bit at her feet.

I recognized his scent the very first day.

The moments returned to her. The ones from the ballroom when she saw a different time; the ones in the dome, when she'd felt more at home than ever; the moment he'd filled her mouth and her body responded instinctually... needing him, knowing him.

Her head rang with a song—the same song he'd hummed in her ear—and she knew it was the song Genevieve hummed to him so long ago. The one that brought him peace in impossible circumstances.

The memories were fragile, but they were there. *He* was there, always.

She started to understand her nightmares. All that fire and

heat and shadows. Clio wondered if the millennia she'd been gone was spent fighting to return.

Had the Light tried to keep her, as Nikolai assumed?

She felt an obligation to that buried piece of herself, to save Nikolai from the violence, the revenge. He'd crawled out of bloodshed on his hands and knees after she was taken from him, empty and broken and hopeless, and she wouldn't let him return to it. Not for anything.

Approaching Duncan's suite, she found the door open and feathering against the edge of the jamb. Mere paces away, Clio heard a crash. The door wrenched inward and a powerful chill blew into the hallway. She staggered to a stop on the threshold, her eyes watering in the frigid air, her lungs catching.

The suite's bay window had been shattered.

Clio lurched for the jagged pane. Snow drifted in, coating the floor in a slick sheen. She was careful not to slip, sidestepping the twisted sheets strewn on the ground and the overturned furniture, bracing her hand on the wall next to the window.

A new storm had begun, veiling the tundra—but lucky for Clio, she saw more than the average mortal. Directly below the window, the snow had been compressed, bloodied. And that blood continued in a long streak into the wild. If she squinted, she could barely see the figures in the distance.

They were moving too swiftly, the speed of a predator securing his prey.

Clio spun on her heel, scanning the room, looking for an answer when it felt like there wasn't one. When it felt like every answer was locked away, deep within her, kept from her by the constraints of her humanity. Her eyes caught on the shoes sitting beside the door.

There was only one solution. She had to go after them.

She slipped Duncan's shoes on and returned to the hallway, closing the door firmly behind her—hoping that would be enough to prevent anyone from feeling the chill of the Arctic seeping into the manor, prevent them from seeing more than they should.

She should have known better than to assume no one would notice the disturbance.

As Clio turned down the hall, she came face-to-face with Enzo. He stood outside his suite, his robe partially tied around the waist, his brown eyes bleary but alarmed. His gaze traveled down her body and back up, noting every oddity of her appearance.

He frowned and took a step toward her. "What was that noise? Are you okay?"

She didn't have time for this. She shook her head and bounded past him. "Nothing. I just dropped a glass. You can go back to sleep."

"Clio, why are you—"

Clio didn't linger to see if Enzo returned to his room. She was slipping into the stairwell again, tugging the laces on Duncan's shoes as tight as possible, even though they slid around with every step.

When she hit the lobby, Mrs. Itzli was pacing the entryway, scanning the tundra as if—as if she'd seen who disappeared into it. She clutched at the shawl around her shoulders, her face unusually pallid and eyes wide. She turned at the first clunk of Duncan's shoes.

Mrs. Itzli lifted her hands, waving them as she said, "Ms. Farren, now is not the time to be roaming the halls. It's late."

"I know," Clio growled, her sights set on the tundra beyond.

Mrs. Itzli stepped in front of her. "What are you doing?" The old woman's eyes burned, half driven to madness and half to worry. She *did* see. *She knows more than she ever let on.*

"I *know*." Clio gripped Mrs. Itzli's arms, the threads of the shawl worn and thick beneath her fingers, and turned so that nothing stood between her back and the doors. "I have to find him and you need to find Reuben. Send him after us as quickly as you can."

Mrs. Itzli grew even paler, but nodded. Her eyes gleamed with the auroral lights.

Footsteps echoed from the stairway and the double doors slammed open. Enzo entered the lobby, his eyes locking on Clio across the room. He stalked toward them, unyielding will in his stance. He knew something was wrong—of course he did.

"And I'm sorry," Clio breathed, unable to break her body-guard's stare. "But you'll need to somehow keep Enzo from following me."

Mrs. Itzli slipped her shawl off and threw it over Clio's shoulders, nodding brusquely. She pushed Clio toward the door. "I'll manage this. Go."

Clio didn't need to be told twice. She shoved through the entrance, even as Enzo's voice shouted for her to stop. As she descended the stairs into the flat, white expanse, she could have sworn she heard Mrs. Itzli's voice rising above the wind.

Duncan's blood led the way, staining the snow in what felt like an endless trail. Her feet stumbled in the snow and the wind bit her fingertips, but Clio only pulled the shawl tighter around her arms and continued on.

The blood grew darker, the trail heavier. She began to worry that she was going to find them too late. She thought of Nikolai, of his last words to her. Not the words of the man, but the beast. She didn't blame either of them, for whatever they'd decided to do to Duncan.

He deserved it.

After last night, after what Nikolai confessed, she was freed from the belief that Duncan had any clue what the Light was. If Clio was a saint, if she was blessed, what did that say about those who thought it right to oppress her, abuse her?

Duncan was a special kind of monster. But if anyone was going to give him what he deserved, it should be her. Hell, she *wanted* it to be her. There was nothing left to stave off her anger. Her temper.

As quickly as she'd been chilled by the Arctic, her blood heated. Her breath wasn't the only thing steaming. Clio ran across the packed earth, leaving crystallized ice in her wake. The trail brought her to a grouping of snow-coated rocks.

She slipped between the sharp aisles and, once shielded from the brunt of the storm, she heard Duncan's cries. Past the next curve, she discovered them.

Red soaked the snow.

Nikolai crouched above Duncan's body. The beast's eyes were wholly black. His crooked canines were on display, dripping with a pearly substance. Clio knew Nikolai hadn't bitten Duncan, knew pleasure was the last thing he would impart on the man before him.

Duncan convulsed, his hands pressing against a gushing wound on his side. Both of his legs were broken. The left side of his face sliced up and swelling.

Nikolai didn't acknowledge Clio, didn't even glance her direction as he placed his hand on Duncan's chest, and pressed down until a snap sounded. Duncan screamed. The beast grinned, the curve feral, and stepped to Duncan's opposite side, kicking him in the wound that bled. He was going to break him apart, piece by piece. Slowly. *Cruelly.*

"Nik, stop—" Clio surged forward, seizing his arm. His skin was cold, utterly freezing. He shook her off. Nikolai had no idea she was here, had no idea who she was or what they were or why he should stop. The beast was too focused on the torture, on the game.

Clio wrenched on his shoulder, reaching out to touch his face. He needed to *see* her. She'd *make* him see her. "Wake up, Nik. I'm right here."

The beast snarled, its rumble echoing off stone and snow as it turned on her. His eyes pierced into Clio, void of love and emotion and joy, void of *life*. Against her best efforts, Clio stumbled back and tripped.

Her hands flew out to stop her fall, but she collided with a rock wall. Her palm sank through the powder and slashed open on a jagged edge.

Clio shoved away from the wall and collapsed, cradling the gaping wound to her chest as she kneeled in the snow. The blood dribbled onto her dress, darkening the material. Her vision swam with golden sparks. Her pain radiated into the air.

When she looked up, Nikolai had gone still... terrifyingly still. The air between them swirled with glittering particles of light. *Salt*, vibrating in the atmosphere around her like a small, golden globe.

She slowly got to her feet.

Nikolai's eyes were still black, detached. His nostrils flared. He'd scented it—her divine blood, her irresistible lure. And now his beast had refocused.

"There you are," Clio whispered, and took off between the rocks. She'd brought him to his senses through a chase once before. She could do it again.

Nikolai was good. Kind and gentle and desperate for love. Human. He couldn't be whittled down to his base existence— his beast and the darkness inside him that he never asked for. She wouldn't let him feel that way again: lost.

Clio kept the elements radiating from her blood, let the ground melt and solidify into sheets of glass beneath her. Slick enough to make the beast lose his footing. She heard him slam into the rocks behind her, heard the sediment crumble and his growls of frustration as he pursued her.

The further from Duncan she could get Nikolai, the better. She didn't let herself think beyond the next step, the next corner. *Run, run, run.*

By the time Clio emerged into the flat tundra, she dropped the dome from around her. She spun to face the opening between the rocks, but Nikolai didn't appear. The wind whistled in her ears. Her hand continued to bleed, but the trickle wasn't nearly as heavy as it had been a minute ago.

Maybe Nikolai had come to his senses. Or maybe he'd returned to Duncan. Clio waited another agonizing moment. She took one step forward, swaying with the breeze. *No.* There was no way he stopped following her.

A fresh wave of ice encroached on her from behind and before she could turn, her body was being pinned in the snow. She blinked, her eyes meeting those onyx chasms of Nikolai's beast. His strong body trembled above her. The shadows in his eyes shifted.

Nikolai was trying to breach the surface; she could feel him there, so close. He lowered his face, drawing his nose along the column of Clio's neck. The sounds coming from his chest were pure animal, pure desire. Yes, this was what he needed.

"That's right," Clio murmured. "You remember this, don't you? Just like old times."

Then, she did the only thing she knew would bring Nikolai back to her. She arched, offering herself up to the beast, and let those crooked canines sink deep into her neck.

40

The venom permeated Clio's veins. It fizzled through the valves of her heart and seeped into her muscles— she felt like the foam at the brim of a champagne glass.

Ecstasy wasn't a strong enough word for what she experienced when Nikolai bit her, when he held her so tightly she couldn't tell where his body ended and she began. When everything beyond them faded to the background, and the world was a distant star, and life became a concept instead of reality.

Nikolai drank deeply, his teeth the conduit fusing them together. The feeding was rougher this time, but Clio didn't care. His hips arced into the cradle of her thighs. She moaned, holding him as best she could, twining her fingers in his hair, wrapping her legs around his waist while he swept her body into a driving rhythm of lust and need.

She wanted to get rid of the clothes, to feel him inside her, but there wasn't enough room to slip even a hand between them. So she met every dry thrust, echoing the guttural sounds

Nikolai made against her neck as the venom lifted her higher—so high she forgot her name.

The friction. The roll of his hips. The sound of his muffled voice against her artery. She was helpless to the feel of him.

She came hard, stars swirling behind her eyes. The climax went on and on, fueled by the sharp sensation of Nikolai's teeth buried in her skin and the venom that continued filling her limbs. Heavy. She felt so heavy. When the lightheadedness didn't fade, she opened her eyes.

The aurora blazed above her. *Wake up*, it said.

Nikolai kept drinking. Her head began to pound. Wait, no. That was a pulse. *Her* pulse, thudding along far too slowly. The grate of nails scraping through layers of ice sounded around her head. The beast was still here, in full control, and it wasn't going to stop.

Nikolai wasn't coming back in time to save her.

"Nik." Her voice was weak, frail. She braced her hands on his shoulders, pushing with all the strength she had left. It was a laughable attempt, really.

The beast burrowed his teeth deeper, snarling as if to order her to remain still. A sob cleaved through her chest. She couldn't let this happen. Nikolai would never forgive himself. He would never believe in love or happy endings. He would never believe in his inherent goodness and the humanity that still clung to his soul.

And, well, Clio decided she didn't want to die. She wanted to live.

Finally, she had something to fight for. Her future, where for so long she saw nothing. Her purpose, when for a majority of her youth she saw only dust. Her life.

Clio was going to fight for herself.

She choked out, "I'm sorry, Nik." Because she knew this

was going to hurt. She sank down into her chambers. Into the blinding light, and radiant heat, and the singing of her soul.

She'd never tried to summon the light on purpose before, but it wasn't difficult. It always came to her when she wasn't thinking, when she wasn't in control of her emotions. It came when she most needed it.

Standing in that chamber, the light curled around her, welcoming her like a long-lost friend. The song radiating from the stairwell to her deepest core grew louder.

She heard a voice. *Bianca's* voice.

Salt crystallized and clung to her, forming a thick layer like armor over her skin. As Clio ascended, she brought that protection with her into the world, into her blood.

The first thing she heard as she came back to awareness was screaming. Clio blinked, trying to clear her eyes of the sediment and light that blinded her. Her body remained weighted, but the sharp sensation on her neck was gone.

She rolled over, bracing her body so she could lift her heavy skull. And she saw him.

Nikolai thrashed in the snow a few feet away, clawing at his throat. His eyes were bloodshot, but bright blue. Blood streamed over his temples and cheeks.

He'd realized what he did just now, what almost happened, or he was in so much pain that it brought him to tears. Probably both.

With a jolt, Clio realized he was straining for air. He... he shouldn't need air, but he was gasping for it. She suddenly remembered that when she'd done this the last time, it had nearly killed him. And Clio didn't have an instruction manual for this.

She snuffed out the light swathing her body and the salt fell from her skin, from her soul. The world went dark, but Nikolai continued writhing.

Clio scrambled across the snow, her head spinning from blood loss, and grabbed Nikolai's shoulders, shaking them to bring his gaze to hers. When he saw her, he bit down on his bottom lip, containing the cries to his brutalized throat. The skin on his neck turned a purplish-red color—his tissues burning from the inside out.

Beneath that bruising, faint webs of gold spidered their way across his skin, spreading over his collar and up over his jaw. Her divine temper, spreading internally.

"Tell me how to stop it," Clio demanded. He only stared at her, choking on another scream. Blood bubbled up and seeped between his lips. She shook his shoulders again, watching as those golden webs traveled down over his chest. Her voice became as frantic as her heart. "Nik, I don't know what to do. Please."

Nikolai let his head rock in the snow. He didn't know how to stop it. Only Bianca did.

Bianca saved him that night in the alley, because she knew everything he hadn't, everything Clio currently didn't. Bianca had herself and her magic and the True Light, and Clio had... nothing.

If she couldn't save the man she loved from herself, then she was no better a monster than Duncan or Nikolai's beast or the demon that killed Nyah. What was the point of this life, this *light* in her, if it couldn't be good?

The webs and purpling of Nikolai's skin had reached his temples when he mustered the strength to speak. He took her face in his hands, smearing her skin with blood as he rasped, "I'll find you again."

Her heart constricted. *Stay,* she wanted to scream. *Stay with me.*

Tears coursed down her cheeks and dripped onto his face,

mingling with the blood splattered on him. His eyes fluttered, eternal sleep looming in. She raked in a breath to say goodbye.

"I love you."

Nikolai's fingers trembled in her hair. He gasped, a sob ripping from his throat, but his lungs caught. His blue eyes welled with a red veil and finally slid shut. His hands slipped from her hair and into the snow beside her.

Clio clutched at his chest, but he didn't stir. She called his name, but he didn't answer.

She understood why Nikolai decided to forget. Though she had the faith to believe he would return to her, she wished she could go with him somehow, wished she could sleep beneath the dream net for a few centuries, letting cobwebs and dust seal her into a mausoleum until the day he found her under their auroral sky.

The future she fought for— she thought it would include him.

Don't go.

Don't leave.

I want you to stay.

Through her tears, Clio saw the aurora dip to caress her cheek, the purple wisps kissing her skin and leaving behind a warm tingle. *Look up,* it whispered.

That wasn't possible.

She shook her head, squeezing the tears from her eyes. And when her vision cleared, her gaze landed on a shimmering form crouched in the snow. Shadows danced around the transparent figure, stretching out over Nikolai's prone body.

But the silhouette directly in front of Clio—it was a woman.

If Clio really focused, which proved difficult in her current state, she saw features that reminded her of the man she loved in a million minute ways. The glowing blue irises. The tender sadness hidden behind a smile.

Genevieve was here, her body flickering in the wind like a flame. Real, but not completely. Solid for milliseconds at a time.

Clio wondered if she was hallucinating. *Can blood loss do that?* Maybe she'd died after all. Maybe she'd passed into the spirit world and was caught forever in this moment, this horror, with Nikolai slipping through her fingers.

But Genevieve took her hands, the sensation like running her hands under a high-powered fan. She guided Clio's palms to Nikolai's chest.

When the woman spoke, her voice was barely audible. And yet, Clio heard every word distinctly, as if they'd been whispered in her ear. "Don't be afraid. Call it back to you."

Clio fought the fog in her head. She was so tired.

Genevieve's hands pressed down on her own. The purple shadows above them pulsed, and she solidified for a moment, unmistakably real as she leaned in with that piercing gaze and said, *"Feel* what's inside you."

Bowing over Nikolai's silent chest, Clio shut the world out. She breathed him in. *Her home.* The magic in her body roared to life, and she felt those pieces of her running through Nikolai's veins, felt them like the bloody bits of herself she'd been trying to restore all her life. They were hers.

Clio, her entire life, had always hesitated to look at herself. The inside seemed so vast, so dark, and she shied from it in fear, hoping the light would save her from *herself,* as ridiculous as that was. But it was only so scary, so unknowable, because her existence went on past this life, past mortality.

Ever since she'd arrived here, she treaded this line, teetering on the cusp of an incomprehensible depth. And in that darkness, she saw glimpses, just as she saw one now.

The smoke billowed in front of her, white and thick and

utterly ordinary, crossing the dark room with lazy tendrils. Poppet purred in her lap, kneading the thin underdress she'd stripped down to once she was back in the privacy of her own home.

Through the haze, she watched the sleeping form stretched out on her father's old bed. The entire room was coated with dust and she found it funny, that this man had nearly been more of the same... but she'd dragged him back here instead, into this room that had been vacant for years. A room she thought would be vacant forever.

Chuckling around the pipe in her mouth—the pipe sitting in Nikolai's library, her pipe, Clio suddenly realized—more smoke clouded her vision.

She didn't know why she did it, exactly. Why she saved this stranger, this monster who had been ready to devour her. She only knew that his cries had called to her, called to something deep within, and once she saw that magic hovering above his body, she couldn't let him die. She'd remembered her father's words to her, his gentle guidance through adolescence, through this world of death and hunting and brutal light. This lonely world.

"The Light may have given you this gift," he'd said before passing, "but it is yours to do with as you deem right. This is your burden, your responsibility, and in the end you will always answer to yourself. That is the price, and your greatest freedom."

So she took it all back. And she wasn't sure what that meant, what any of this meant, but she wanted to find out.

We're all capable of terrible things, Clio had once told Nikolai. *Some of us simply forget that we're capable of just as much good.* She remembered that truth, even if she hadn't remembered the rest.

Clio chose to believe that one more time. She willed her blood to listen.

She imagined her magic, that gleam of light behind her eyes, calling to the darkness between the stars, calling for the likeness she knew was out there. Her palms grew hot, absorbing the heat from Nikolai's skin. She kept that light alive in her head, in her chest, radiating like a beacon... pulling, pulling, pulling.

They would endure this. Together.

Clio let the warmth surge through her body, again and again, on and on—until eventually, the pull ran out and her hands went cold. The magic evaporated, leaving her exhausted and empty. She raised her head, even though she wanted nothing more than to nod off.

Genevieve's ethereal figure faded. The purple flames above them twisted towards the sky, as if to join the aurora.

Nikolai's eyes were closed, though every sign of her divine temper, the bruising and golden webs on his skin, were gone. Clearly, she'd succeeded in drawing her magic back. So why wasn't he awake?

That feminine voice sounded in her mind again. "He will wake."

Glancing up, Clio saw one last flicker of blue eyes blaze through the darkness. And maybe she was simply curious, or had been repossessed by this hope that came so close to going out, but Clio said, "You were there for Nikolai the day I died, weren't you? You protected him."

"I'm always here." An airy laugh echoed, filled with a quiet joy Clio imagined Genevieve never felt in her immortal life. The wind distorted her last words. "We all are."

Before Clio could process that statement, or even remember how to breathe beyond a shallow gasp, snow shifted behind her. She turned on her knees and found Reuben approaching, his body layered with fur and wool.

He drawled, "I see I'm late to the party."

"You're right on time," Clio's voice broke. Tremors racked her body.

Reuben's smile fell as he surged forward, stripping his coat and draping it over her back. He'd come out here prepared for the weather, with leather gloves and multiple scarves and earmuffs, so she didn't resist the offer. "Will you carry Nik back to the manor for me?"

Reuben nodded and knelt beside her, folding Nikolai's arms over his chest. A gentle laugh drifted toward her. "You beat him up again, didn't you? Good work."

Clio frowned, digging her fingers into the snow. She needed to get on her feet, but she wasn't sure she could. The gravity of what she'd done to Nikolai hit her in the gut.

It scared her—that power.

A warm, dark hand squeezed her arm and Clio jumped. Reuben smiled and said, "Don't feel bad, Bebe. He was overdue for a fair fight. In fact, he'll probably thank you for the thrill once he wakes up."

"My name is Clio," she murmured.

Reuben's hand fell away and he gathered Nikolai in his arms, standing in one fluid motion. He grimaced down at her. "Sorry, I know there's a difference, but it's easy to forget."

She nodded, and Reuben headed back toward the manor, walking beside the trail of ice she'd created on her way out here.

Slowly, she stood.

Her knees buckled a couple times and her vision swam with dark spots, but she managed it. She focused on her breathing, keeping it deep and even, absorbing strength from the aurora... enough for what she had to do next.

Reuben turned a few yards away and shouted, "You coming?"

"I have something I need to do," she replied. "I'll be right behind you."

Once Reuben continued on, Clio slipped between the rocks. She walked carefully, avoiding the slick remnants of her salt and heat. When she turned the last corner, she halted. Duncan had crawled a few inches, but no more. He looked up at her from his bed of blood, clawing the red slush in her direction.

He wasn't making it out of the tundra alive. His body was too broken, he'd lost too much, and for all that he had done to her, she wasn't going to carry him. Clio stood there, still as the death hovering over them, trying to detect any measure of guilt within her. She did not find it.

"Clio. Help me." Even as he laid there dying, Duncan had the nerve to issue commands. Had the nerve to sound angry.

Clio heard a faint crunching of snow beyond the rocks. White fur shifted amid the flurry. She swept forward and knelt beside her fiancé, taking his outstretched hand in her own. His eyes were as dark, as cold and empty, as ever.

Leaning in, she whispered, "No, dove. I don't think I will."

She slipped back before Duncan processed the words. His eyes widened as he looked in his hand and found the engagement ring there, *his* ring. If it meant so much to him, he could die holding what he believed to be his property.

As Clio turned to leave, something wet hooked around her ankle and nearly tripped her. Duncan's bloody fingers dug into her leg. She tried to shake him off, but it only made him grip her tighter. His nails and the sharp edges of her engagement ring pressed into her skin.

"You belong to me," he growled. "You *promised*."

"I belong to no one but myself." Before Clio could reach down and pry him off, he smiled. His bared teeth parted. From his throat, an inhumane rumble echoed, carrying a clump of black goo with it. She watched in shock as that clump unraveled, whipping out with thin tendrils to pull itself from his mouth. It crawled down his jaw and across his chest to his arm, hurtling toward the hand around her ankle.

She started fighting again, crying out as Duncan's nails broke skin.

The black sludge sizzled as it speckled the snow, sinking down like rocks dropped in water, eating up the blood and skin on Duncan's face as if it were acid, destroying everything in its path.

Corruption—that's what it is. Within an inch of touching her.

Clio swallowed her disgust as a familiar warmth sparked under her skin and in her eyes. Her temper, a faint glimmer of its full glory from minutes ago, flared. Every muscle roared in protest, but this was instinct, this was survival.

This was her destiny, and her body, her *light*, would always rise to the call of it.

Salt spewed from her palm, the one with an open wound, curling in the air as she reached down and tore at Duncan's hand. The world brightened from the light radiating out of her skin. Duncan flinched, recoiling as the salt coated him. He let her go and she scrambled back across the ice.

The black sludge shuddered.

Her salt ate away at the corruption. The darkness shrank. Her magic was purification, a threat and consequence. That piece of knowledge returned to her all at once, settling in her bones like a beautifully carved piece of marble holding up her heart.

This is what she was: a weapon of wrath. *Powerful.*

Clio sent all that still hung in the air, all the glittering salt twisting around her body and light weaving through her hair, toward Duncan. It pummeled his body, sinking into the raw parts of his face and throat. He screamed, scratching at the salt as if he might rip himself apart to get it out. She siphoned everything into that tar-like substance. Her body begged for rest as she crawled away, leaving behind the battle of light and darkness.

The chill of the Arctic sobered her enough to stand. She clawed at one of the bloody walls to support her rise.

Her light and salt were fading as the polar bear appeared, as it leapt on Duncan's writhing body and began to feast. He screamed as she turned away, holding on to enough anger and hatred to curse her name.

Clio didn't hesitate, didn't glance back as she walked home. And she smiled, a mile back, tears of freedom streaming down her face, when his screams cut off cold.

41

Through sheer willpower, Clio made it back to the manor before twilight dawned. She barely made it through the front entrance before she heard her name being called.

"Clio, thank goodness." Enzo leapt up from his seat on one of the emerald couches and stalked toward her, but stumbled when his gaze registered her bloody neck. "What the fuck happened to you?"

Clio lifted a hand to keep him from drawing too close. She pulled her hair over her shoulder, to cover the bite marks. "I'm fine now. Really. I just need to rest. Can we discuss this in a few hours?"

She inched toward the corridor that would lead her to Nikolai, to the dome, to her home.

"Absolutely not." Enzo closed in, blocking her path. "What is going on? Duncan is missing. His suite's window was shattered. You come back inside from a storm—not the best decision in those clothes, by the way—bleeding and roughed up like you are. And this woman," he jerked a thumb towards Mrs.

Itzli, who rolled her eyes, "smashed my phone against a column when I called your mother to inform her of the current predicament."

"I already apologized. I thought you were calling the police," Mrs. Itzli interjected.

Enzo turned to her, his eyes blazing. "Considering your reaction, perhaps I should have."

"Wait, you called my mom?" Clio's breath hitched. She couldn't deal with that right now. Clarissa was the last person she wanted to see or talk to, not until she could gather her thoughts.

Enzo frowned, folding his arms. "Yes, not that she bothered answering—I'm sure she's dead to the world at this hour, as usual. Anytime I get close to the elevator or beyond the immediate grounds, this crazy lady threatens me with a meat hammer. She won't leave me the hell alone."

Mrs. Itzli smiled then, tucking said meat hammer under her arm. Clio smiled too. When Enzo saw the matching grins, he shook his head and ran a hand through his graying hair.

He said softly, so only Clio could hear him, "I feel like this should go without asking, but is this some sort of a hostage situation?"

Clio sighed, waving her hands weakly between them. She gazed up at her companion and the smile dissolved into something a little more tender. "No," she murmured. "This is where I want to be, Enzo. I'm not leaving."

He scanned her body, his scrutiny lingering on her face as he drew a few steps nearer. "Where's Duncan?"

Clio wrapped her arms around her torso, rubbing the threads of Mrs. Itzli's shawl between her fingers. "He left."

Enzo's eyes dropped to the floor. And when she followed his gaze, she realized—

She was still wearing Duncan's shoes.

Her bodyguard wasn't treasured for his strength alone. From the very first day he'd been assigned to their family, Clio sensed the sharpness in him. The first words nine-year-old Clio ever said to him was, "How many people have you killed?"

Enzo spared her from the answer, but she heard the truth in his silence. The medal that hung from his visor told her the rest, once she was old enough to decipher the ribbon's colors.

Clio knew if he'd walked the perimeter of the grounds, he would have seen the blood as well as the shattered glass. There was no doubt about it. Enzo knew she was lying. Yet, when he looked up from the ground and met her gaze, his eyes were warm. They shone in the dim light of the chandeliers as he reached out to hold her chin in his dry, callused hand.

Tilting her face up, Enzo's focus narrowed in on her temple —on the bruise Duncan left. "Good riddance."

If she wasn't so spent, she might have told Enzo how much that meant to her. How much he'd always meant to her. How his mere presence in her life had held her together when she might have otherwise fallen apart. And the way he wanted to protect her, even now, after lying to him about arguably the grayest thing she'd ever done.

Clio hugged him.

Enzo stiffened, but after a moment his arms wrapped around her and patted her back. "Alright," he said tightly, "get outta here before your family wakes up. I'll send them away for you, if that's what you need."

She nodded, choking back tears. He let her continue hugging him as long as she needed, too—until her exhausted tears fell back beneath the surface. When Clio finally released him, she said, "Everyone except my parents."

Mrs. Itzli stepped forward. "Not to worry, dear. I've already thought up the perfect story to send the crowd away with," she said with a smirk.

"Of course you have," Enzo grumbled, eyeing the meat hammer swinging at Mrs. Itzli's side as she turned on her heel. He gave Clio a terrified, if not slightly awed, look before following the chef into her kitchen.

Clio slipped into the corridor leading to the library. The key was still sticking out of the tumbler, the door barely ajar. She put the key away before letting the door clasp shut behind her.

Without the aurora, the library was a sea of shadows and muted specks of colors. Clio didn't bother turning on the light. She saw the figure there—Reuben, lounging on the bottom step of the stairs, spinning a pocketknife between his fingers.

Clio watched him tilt his head in her direction. His brow furrowed as she crossed the room and twisted one of the sitting chairs to face him. As soon as she sat, a groan fell from her lips. It felt so good to get off her feet.

"Nikolai's in bed." Reuben said, the hint of a smile in his voice. "Tucked him in and everything." Clio's thoughts were too scattered to appreciate the humor.

"When do you think he'll wake up?"

"I don't have much experience with the recovery from your sort of magic," Reuben said carefully, shifting in his perch on the stairs. "But I did look him over with my own, helped ground his spirit in this dimension. Hopefully, that means he'll wake sooner rather than later."

Clio nodded, letting her eyes drift shut. Her head rolled against the chair and she thought for a moment that sleep might take her too quickly, against her will.

Reuben's voice anchored her. "How was your detour? Did you finish the job he'd started?" A faint earthiness filled the air, and Clio guessed that meant he was wielding his magic once more, to keep her here, awake, to keep her talking.

She cracked an eye and saw wisps of purple snaking over

the floor, kissing Duncan's shoes on her feet. Clio cried out in disgust and bent to rip them off, sending them skittering over the floor toward Reuben.

The guardian chuckled. "Not your favorite pair, I'm assuming."

"They aren't mine," she snapped back. "I don't want anything to do with that ma—" Her chest tightened and tears stung her eyes. She didn't know if he was a man. So many questions, more and more with every new revelation, and she had no answers.

Reuben's voice softened. "I'll take care of them—of the body, too. Don't feel guilty for what happened out there. It's not your fault."

"You're wrong." Her eyes met his. "It is my fault that *thing* out in the snow is bleeding corruption into the Earth right now. I believed he carried light within him. I let him rule me as a superior when he was the opposite. I should have seen. *As a fucking saint,* I should have known."

"Rewind," Reuben said, the knife stilling between his fingers before he pointed it at her. "What do you mean 'bleeding corruption'?"

As succinctly as possible, Clio informed him of what she'd seen Duncan do. What she'd felt. Reuben's lips curled, the dark skin of his face crinkling in the shadows.

"I know what it must mean," she murmured afterwards.

"Do you?" Sarcasm dripped from his voice.

"Nik told me—"

Reuben cut her off, his tone brusque and cold. "Nikolai has not even *begun* to fill you in on this new world. You may remember what it was like in your last life, might recall even easier once you turn, *if* you concentrate well enough. But things have changed too much, even since you were Bianca." He scoffed, spinning the knife. "All the blood on Nikolai was human, Clio. Trust me, if you encountered demon blood, you'd know the difference."

The whiplash sent her head spinning. Duncan was human. Clio wasn't sure whether to be relieved or mortified. She'd really let him die. Maybe he'd deserved it, maybe there was nothing she could have done. But if he had a soul, then she'd let it wink out, wanted and encouraged it to.

Yet, Clio still couldn't reconcile his humanity with the darkness she saw, the inky snow, his year of cruelty. "How?"

Without looking at her, Reuben replied, "Demons and their children feed on suffering as much as they feed on magic. They prey on the human instincts they most identify with. Anger. Greed. Jealousy. It isn't difficult for demons to sympathize with mortals, nor is it difficult to seduce a few thousand of them at any given moment. Just look at what happened to your precious church."

Clio's breath caught. "What do you mean? What happened to my church?"

He gave her a chastising look. "You're a clever girl, Clio. Connect the dots. Demons have been running the Light's pretty little show for a long time now. The true believers out there have nothing to do with the congregation."

She'd heard of them—those the church called defectors. Maybe, if she hadn't been so scared all her life, she would have seen the truth. "You said the demons have children? Do you mean that the way I assume you do?"

"No." Reuben rolled his eyes. "I mean it as literally as one might call you a daughter of the Light. Your deceased fiancé was a willing host." She flinched.

The guardian frowned, regret flitting over his face. "What I'm trying to say," he said more gently. "Is that he may have been human, but he was not good. He wasn't alive anymore. When a body is given up like that, surrendered to demonic whims and filled with their temporary magic, the mortal soul dies. The soul is replaced by demonic power, by that rot you saw. He'd been decaying since the day he became a host, and I promise you, there's no coming back from that. What died tonight was an echo of who he'd once been. Don't blame yourself—do not even think of it long enough to care."

Slowly, Clio nodded. The earthiness in the atmosphere ebbed; Reuben was finished with the conversation and was finally willing to let her consciousness drift. But she held tightly to the train of thought she'd ridden on her walk home.

Before she went to sleep, before Nikolai woke up, before Reuben left, before she did *anything* beyond sitting in this chair, she needed more answers.

She asked, "You know about Genevieve, right? The woman who turned Nikolai?"

Reuben blinked, the whites of his eyes burning through the dark. "I've read her journal once or twice. Why?"

"Was she a Guardian?"

He turned his attention back to the pocketknife. The blade spun faster between his dark fingers. "I assume so. All the signs were there." Reuben paused. "She was bastard-born, separated from her father. Genevieve didn't understand why she felt and heard the things she did because no one was around to teach her. I'd bet she came from a very powerful, especially pure bloodline—but when you fear yourself like she did, fear gifts without acknowledging that they are a part of you, they control you instead of the other way around." He glanced up. "So yes, she was probably a Guardian, but I doubt she ever learned what that meant before passing on."

Clio propped her chin up on one hand as her head started drooping. "What happens to Guardians when they die?"

"They linger. Hover really, like overbearing parents." Reuben rolled his eyes and the pocketknife slowed in its dance.

"They spend the afterlife guiding descendants wherever they wish for them to go, wherever they think is best." He didn't seem proud of that, or happy.

All families has their issues, Clio guessed.

She admitted, "I saw her tonight—Genevieve. She saved Nikolai. She helped me."

Reuben's head whipped up. "She actually appeared to you?" A muscle ticked in his jaw.

"And spoke to me. Is that even possible?"

His throat bobbed, but he said, "Rarely, ancestors can slip into this dimension. It's rarer still for a mortal to see them when they do—but you *are* unusual. Your eyes must pierce through more than darkness."

"I was just wondering if..." Clio paused, organizing her words. "Genevieve told me she's always close by. That they all are. Does that mean Nyah might—"

"Be hanging around you?" Reuben interrupted. His tone took on a sharpness, a firmness. "Maybe. But I'm going to be blunt, Clio. Even if Nyah had enough magic in the afterlife to appear to you, which I doubt considering her heart was ripped out, she couldn't speak with you as Genevieve did."

Clio blinked away the stinging in her eyes. "Why?"

"Her throat," he whispered. His jaw worked for a moment, stuck on the next words. "Nyah's larynx was ripped out for a reason, too. The demon likely charmed and burnt it, to prevent her from voicing what happened to her in the afterlife. That's common practice for Guardians when we summon demons, to stop them from seducing our people in the next dimension. Whatever caught up with Nyah returned the favor."

Nyah, the girl who couldn't be held down, who didn't shrink back, had been silenced. Clio's tears dribbled over. She rasped, "But you can see into other dimensions, can't you? You could look for her."

"No." Reuben snapped his pocketknife shut, glaring at the wall in front of him. "That's not something I'm able to do. Relations with my ancestors are strained right now."

Clio's heart sank. "Oh," she muttered. "I'm sorry to hear that."

He chuckled, the tone derisive. "Don't be. They're a load of invasive assholes." His family had to be just as impossible to deal with as her own.

When Reuben stood, Clio remained in the chair. She debated lingering in the library, surrounded by the smell of parchment and dust and a history she hadn't been given a moment yet to think about. But as Reuben passed by, he rested a hand on Clio's shoulder.

He chewed on his lip for a moment before he said, "If you think you sense Nyah nearby, she probably is. Lost Guardians make themselves known in strange ways sometimes, but it's not uncommon. I'm—you have my deepest sympathies, for your loss."

She slid her hand over his, the grip warm and gentle, comforting. And every hope she had for sleep winked out. "Reuben, can I ask one more favor?"

42

There was earth in his mouth. Gritty, acidic earth. That was the first sensation Nikolai registered in his rise out of the blackness. He tried to center himself, tried to grasp his last coherent moment, but the memories sifted through the sieve of his mind like sand.

He opened his eyes.

Nikolai saw the chess board first, lying directly in front of his face. String lights circled the square crystal platform and reflected off the curves of the chess pieces. Beneath the board, there was more crystal, clear and cold under his fingertips.

His eyes followed the lights, the coils that littered the crystal dome and stretched around his body, to where the glimmering strings eventually disappeared down the staircase. A blanket was wrapped around his torso, separating his bare skin from the crystal floor, and a pillow propped his head.

The faint film of gritty earth on the roof of Nikolai's mouth informed him that Reuben had been here recently. Judging from the familiar surroundings, he also assumed that meant he was alive. Nikolai wasn't sure how—but the how didn't matter as his eyes caught on the woman sitting across from him.

Clio held her head between her hands, rubbing her temples in slow circles. Her eyes were closed, her brow furrowed, and her elbows rested on her knees. She looked utterly fried, nerves and all. He'd done that to her.

Fuck.

Nikolai sat up, wincing. Hot spears of pain radiated through his body. It had been centuries since he'd been this sore, since he'd woken up in a strange, dim bedroom in the heart of France.

The same beautiful face turned to look at him now that looked at him then.

Clio's back straightened, her legs falling to one side as she twisted to face him. Her eyes were guarded—not that he blamed her for it.

"Clio." Nikolai turned to crawl around the chessboard, his every thought focused on getting her back in his arms and making her feel safe.

She shook her head sharply. "Stop. Stay there."

His stomach dropped, heavy and churning with her blood. "Of course," he whispered. What was he thinking? She'd never feel safe with him again. "Are you okay?"

Clio said evenly, "I'm going to be just fine." Once she left, that was. He saw the resolve in her eyes. It was over and he would never forgive himself.

"I'm so sorry, Clio." His throat was unbearably tight. He forgot the way her blood affected him so completely. How it pulled his humanity to the surface and polished it like a jewel. He felt so much. He'd never underestimate the gravity of human experience again. "After what I did tonight... I know I ruined everything. I know I don't deserve—"

"Stop it," Clio snapped. He looked up to find her eyes

burning. "Right now isn't about what you deserve, Nik. It's about what I want."

Nikolai swallowed hard. He tried to keep his hopes from running away from him. "And what is that?"

She smiled gently. "You." He couldn't believe it, not right away. But Clio kept smiling as she glanced around the dome. "Me. This."

When Clio returned her gaze to his, his hands were trembling. He whispered, "Then why don't you want me to hold you?"

"I have an idea." Her smile grew as she gestured at the chess board. "One more game, winner takes all."

How could she possibly be thinking about their competition right now?

"I don't understand."

Clio's head tilted, her stare piercing. "If I win, you're going to help me turn. Today."

Nikolai's jaw dropped. For a moment, he could only gape at her. He found words, sense, and said, "Do you understand what happened last night? I nearly killed you. I'm in love with you and I still couldn't stop myself. That's the kind of existence you'd be signing up for."

Her face settled like stone. She leaned over the chess pieces and snarled, "You nearly killed me because I'm *mortal*. The only reason we're both here, alive and breathing, is because we save each other. That's what we do, Nik."

"That's not the kind of life you deserve—saving me and needing to be saved. You need someone who won't hurt you at all."

"Everybody hurts the people around them, whether they intend to or not. Even with the best intentions, the purest love. Look at my dad. Nyah. Genevieve."

Nikolai flinched.

But Clio continued, her voice unwavering, "It's not a matter of loving enough that you don't make mistakes. Mistakes are inevitable. What I'm signing up for is an eternity of reminding you what it means to be good enough, what it means to never be alone. You're more than the bad parts you struggle to control and I want to be here, helping you when you lose your way."

Nikolai's resolve crumbled by the second. Her mind was such a beautiful, awe-inspiring, incomprehensible place. He doubted he would ever fully grasp her scope of empathy, her understanding of the world. But every word dared him to try.

He said weakly, "I don't know what I can offer you." Nothing would ever suffice.

"You'll do the same for me when I need it." Her lips trembled slightly in an attempt to smile. "We'll endure—*together*. That's the kind of love I want. That's the only future I see, and I'm happy in it. Wouldn't you be happy, too? Is that such a terrible wish?"

Nikolai fisted his hands, because there was a physical pain attached to the space between them. He wanted to close it. Fuck, he wanted this as badly as she did. There was no language out there that could describe what he felt for her. He had no argument, no strength to fight against her wishes when she looked at him like this.

The look of a woman on fire.

"I'm done searching. I have you right here, and you have me, and I'm not giving us up." After a moment, Clio's lips twitched and she added quietly, "And not to wound your ego or anything, but this is about more than you now. I have no intention of living my life as a fraction of myself. That person I was —she's mine. If I have to prove I'm wiser than you in order to win her back tonight, so be it."

A chuckle rustled in Nikolai's chest. "Beautiful, conniving little thing."

"I'm also fair." Clio shrugged, but her eyes twinkled with light and mischief. "If you win, I'll let you fuck me however and wherever you want, for as long as you wish. How is that for a wager?"

He braced a hand flat on the ground, leaning as if he might prowl around to her. "I could do that right now, game or not."

"But you won't," she said, looking pointedly away from him and down at the board. "Until one of us wins, you're going to stay right where you are and you're not going to touch me."

Nikolai exhaled forcefully. "You are exactly the same, even all these years later."

She lifted a brow.

"Meaning you're still a stubborn pain in my ass," he explained with a laugh.

She echoed his laughter. "I can't wait to remember all the times I've ticked you off."

"You're exceptionally good at it."

She nodded, biting her lower lip. And if he didn't know for a fact that Clio was born decades ago rather than centuries, he would have sworn Bianca was the one who smirked at him, the one who leaned in and moved a pawn. "Play with me, baby."

To Nikolai's credit, he made her work for it. Every move, down to the pawns, was made with confidence, with a swiftness that would have left champions reeling. And all the while, Clio held his attention. Her hands trailed over the slits in her dress, curled higher on her thighs. Her fingers grazed the softness between her legs, where he knew for a fact she was without panties.

At one point, her hand slipped lower, pressing against herself, and she moaned softly. The sound scattered his thoughts so completely that he had to close his eyes and center himself before making the next move.

"Are you alright, Nik? You seem frustrated."

He smelled her arousal, thick and musky and fragrant as a blooming rose bush. All Nikolai could think of was getting his mouth on her, tasting her as he had earlier in the night.

Perhaps this was her plan all along: to distract him.

Nikolai glared at her. If he looked too long at any part of her, he was going to pounce. He tried to bring his emotions under control, tried to hide his desire. "Do I? What gave you that impression, Beloved?"

She shrugged, her eyes falling to his lap. Right... there was no hiding *that*.

Clio held back before, when they played for fun, when he won those few measly games. Or maybe he'd just gotten lucky, because she showed no mercy this time, no hesitation to take piece after piece, to attack from unexpected angles, to risk a vulnerability to her queen for the victory.

Finally, he saw it—two moves that would let him take the game. He didn't particularly expect to win at this point, a small part of him didn't *want* to win. But the opening was so glaring, he couldn't ignore it.

His eyes slid to where Clio trailed her fingertips over her collarbone, her silver eyes sparkling in the dim light. She was practically pouting. But the instant he slid the first piece into position, taking her knight, she let out a trilling laugh. He blinked at her broad grin as she asked, "Are you going to be a sore loser, Nik?"

His gaze dropped back to the board, scanning the arrangement more closely.

She'd trapped him.

Nikolai chuckled. Of course she did. If he moved his king

to the right, her queen or rook would take him. If he moved to the left, her bishop would strike.

Clio hesitated, studying his smile as if to determine whether he meant it. He held her stare. He laid everything bare in that moment, his hope and joy and relief.

"You aren't losing," she whispered. "Not really. You get to keep me now."

"I know," he said with equal softness.

"And lucky for you," Clio plucked her queen from the board, "I want you to fuck me anyway." Nikolai smiled as she placed her queen in line with his king. Slowly, he started crawling toward her.

She glanced up from beneath her lashes, her fingers lingering on the crystal. "Check—" Clio's voice cut off in a yelp as Nikolai seized her ankle and dragged her across the floor to him. He pushed her skirt away and lowered his face to that incredible scent.

She gasped, collapsing back against the floor as his tongue slid against her flesh. Her warmth and salty taste enveloped him, carrying him the closest to heaven he would ever get. He would never have enough of her, not tonight or several centuries from now. If she wanted him to keep her, he would.

His mouth kissed every millimeter of her swollen skin, sucked and nipped at her sensitivity until she was moaning his name. He wished it was a song he could record, one he could dance with her to in the ballroom. Her pleasure. His growls of approval. Their happiness.

Clio's fingers sifted through his hair, twisting in his curls, holding on for dear life. She pleaded with him, but he wasn't going to stop this time, wasn't going to leave this paradise yet.

He pinned her with a hand on her stomach and drew his other down between her legs. For long moments, he traced featherlight circles along the inside of her thighs, drawing closer and closer to where her core pounded. He felt her heart thundering under his mouth, her muscles clenching around his tongue as he drove into her.

Nikolai chuckled as her hips bucked, as she fought against the pressure on her stomach, as her cries turned guttural. He circled her entrance, around and around with a finger. And when she finally resorted to begging, he slid that finger inside.

Clio groaned as he brushed her front wall. Whimpered as he withdrew, and gasped as he added a second. She tugged violently on his hair. He released her stomach and let her ride him, his free hand gripping her thigh. His fingertips dug into the sweet, tender skin there. He'd feed from the delicious, pulsing artery in her thigh someday, soon.

Nikolai rolled Clio's clit between his teeth and she arched off the ground, her muscles clenching around his fingers.

Her cry echoed off the dome as he continued feasting, wringing every moment of bliss from her that he could. He watched from between her legs, the way her body shuddered, how it glimmered with a faint light even though her temper was thoroughly depleted. Not a million years would make him sick of her brilliance. Even if it tore him apart, even if it killed him.

When she collapsed in a heap of trembling limbs, Nikolai knelt up with a snarl. He pulled her upright and ripped the bodice of her dress, leaving her bare and beautiful before him. "I'd say I'm sorry to ruin your dress, but I'm not."

"Burn it for all I care." Clio's eyes fluttered as she gripped his shoulders for balance, and he noticed again how pale she was.

He paused, pulling back slightly.

"Where are you going?" She demanded, digging her nails into his shoulders to keep him close.

"You look like you're going to faint," he growled. "I'm an

idiot for starting this right now. I took too much from you earlier—you need to be resting."

She huffed a laugh and straddled his lap. And for fuck's sake, he let her. His hands braced her hips as she settled close. Clio stared pointedly at his neck as she murmured, "The only thing I need is you." The meaning sank into his bones. A thrill ran up his spine.

"You have me," he replied.

Nikolai plucked a metal pin from Clio's hair and bent it open before bringing the sharp edge to his neck. He opened himself up, letting his blood call to hers. The pin clattered to the floor as they embraced each other, as Clio's mouth latched onto the wound.

She drew him in.

Their passion became a blur of hands and nails, of tongue and teeth. Clio fed on him as he fumbled with his pants, kicking them away before he knelt up on the blanket and slowly lowered her onto him. Her moans rippled through his artery as they began to move.

Nikolai bucked into the slick heat of her, gripping her hips as she took control of the rhythm, as she ground him deeper with every thrust. He was going to lose his fucking mind—

Clio released his artery and threw her head back. Blood dripped from her mouth, dribbling over her chin and down the column of her neck. He licked her skin, groaning as her grinding became rougher, more demanding.

He fisted Clio's hair at the nape of her neck and made her look at him. Her eyes were dazed and dreamy, but her smile was bright. "Tell me again," he demanded.

Her smile grew, his blood lining her teeth, healing her from the inside out. "I love you."

Nikolai nearly lost it, hearing her say those words for the second time tonight, but he lifted her off of his lap. She protested but he silenced her with a kiss before flipping her around onto her hands and knees.

Her right hand swept the chess board and scattered the pieces, sending them tumbling across the crystal floor with a beautiful tinkling.

"Checkmate," he rasped before knocking her legs open and slamming into her.

Their mingled groans filled the dome. He kept one hand on her hip, lifting her slightly and steadying her trembling limbs, but he threaded the other into her hair, pulling on her scalp until her neck was arched for him.

She met his punishing thrusts, urging him faster. He nibbled on her back, her shoulders with gentle bites. Kissing her scars, one by one. Not drawing blood, but leaving trails of his venom, marking her with pleasure and thin red scratches.

She was *his*.

"*I love you.*" He slid his hand on Clio's hip to between her legs, circling her swollen flesh with his thumb, and she shattered.

Nikolai followed in the next breath.

43

C lio held the ladder for Marcus as he straightened the painting of Nikolai's family in its new place. When he reached for Nyah's painting, Clio lifted it to him. He hung it on the wall, careful of the delicate canvas.

She waited for him to climb back down, his left leg shaking a little.

Clio told him she didn't need the help, but he insisted. She admitted to herself, as he closed the ladder and set it off to the side, as he returned to her side to admire his handiwork, that the gesture was sweet. Special, even.

The paintings fit together perfectly, taking up the entire wall behind the front desk. All the green and pastels meshed with emerald upholstery throughout the rest of the lobby, as if Nyah had always imagined this painting here.

Clio brushed a tear from her cheek, smiling faintly as she scanned the room for the thousandth time this morning. She felt Nyah here, in every inch of glamour and elegance. Always felt her, from the moment she arrived two weeks ago. And maybe her friend was here in spirit, maybe not. But Clio held onto the palpable presence. Cherished it.

Marcus said quietly, "I'm glad you had her."

She glanced at her father, whose own eyes swam with tears. He'd been up early, waiting for her in the lobby when she and Nikolai finally emerged from their room.

They'd had breakfast together, all three of them and Clio told him everything. Well, everything save for the fact that Nikolai was basically a walking corpse and Clio was a saint. A *saint*, of all things. She struggled to comprehend that label, even as her body hummed with the rightness of it.

It was therapeutic to speak of the past year to Marcus, to purge that brokenness and fear. Nikolai stood close by, pretending to sip at his tea, his knuckles clenching so tightly at moments that it was a relief he didn't manage to break the mug. There was no judgement in her father as she explained what Duncan had done, what she'd let herself be coerced into—he showed her nothing but relief that she came out on the other side.

After breakfast, Nikolai left them with a lingering kiss on Clio's cheek, and she and her father continued their reunion through the manor, exploring the endless halls, retrieving Marcus's luggage from his room and browsing the library.

Incidentally, Marcus loved the dome. He even asked if he could camp out there the next time he visited. Clio wasn't sure when that would be, but she agreed.

The summer was coming. Polar day. She and Nikolai would have to leave soon, chasing the night until winter returned, chasing whatever ripped Nyah out of her life. Clio would take justice into her own hands; she decided she was strong enough to fight after all.

She nodded. "I'm glad I had her, too. For as long as we were given, anyway. But I miss her, all the time. Sometimes, it feels like one big trick, a prank. Like she's going to call me at any moment and ask me to come pick her up. Like she's lost and I'm supposed to find her."

Marcus hesitated, then draped an arm around Clio's shoulders and squeezed her gently. "You didn't say goodbye. In your heart, she never left."

She rested her head on Marcus's shoulder, the corduroy of his blazer irritating her cheek. Clio couldn't shake that feeling though, the instinct in her gut telling her to keep searching, that Nyah was right around the next corner.

Maybe Clio would feel that way until the day time stopped.

She wondered aloud, "Do you really believe it's different than we think—the Light? You think it's *good?*"

Marcus's arm drew her closer. He mumbled gruffly, "That's where true faith lies, Clio. Hope for the good, especially when you can't see it."

His answer settled around her like an embrace, soothing the jagged pieces of her soul, because she still loved that voice calling to her from the darkness, the one beckoning her to fill it with brilliance. The light she found within. She loved her gift, what thrummed through her veins, whether it stemmed from some distant god or not.

"How long do you have?" Clio murmured.

Marcus glanced at his smartwatch and sighed. "The cab is on its way. Miraculously, it looks like I managed to avoid another run-in with your mother."

"That's probably for the best. She's not going to be happy about the wedding and she's not a morning person, anyway. These are fatal conditions for anyone on her shit list."

Dropping his arm from her shoulders, Marcus faced her with a tender smile. "I can linger if you want. I'll absorb her wrath for you."

"No. I can face her myself. I *need* to face her by myself."

Her father's mouth parted, only to be interrupted by the faint sound of breaking glass and wood. Clio's gaze traveled to the recently hung portraits, but they hadn't moved. Silence fell as she met her father's gaze, the same questions echoed in his eyes: where had that come from?

Footsteps thundered into the lobby.

Nikolai emerged from the corridor and ran across the room, headed straight for the stairwell with Reuben hot on his heels. Neither of them so much as glanced in Clio's direction as they disappeared through the French doors to the marble staircase.

Judging from the tension in the air and the tightness of their eyes, something was wrong. Very wrong. Something must be happening in the floors above them, too far for her mortal ears to hear.

"That can't be good," she muttered.

Clio started toward the stairwell. Marcus followed. In the same heartbeat, a horn blared outside. The cab. He glanced between the windows and the stairwell, then turned to her. "I can tell it to wait—make sure everything is okay here?"

A rock bobbed in her throat. Every time he offered to stay, it brought a bittersweet tang to her tongue. But depending on what was happening upstairs, it might be in their best interests to part. "You should go. As you can tell, the manor has a lot on its plate right now, and none of it concerns you." She urged him toward the sitting arrangement nearest the entrance, where his luggage waited—to safety.

Marcus frowned. "Right. I'm sorry. I completely understand." Clio tried to bury that twinge of guilt as he limped away, even as it burned up her throat. She didn't have time for a better farewell.

It was easy to determine where they'd gone, especially once the hysterical voices came into focus on the second landing.

There was a distant, unintelligible screaming and a closer, garbled voice, speaking so quickly Clio's head spun trying to decipher it.

She burst into the hallway of the second floor and paused, taking in the situation.

Halfway down the hall, Nikolai was holding Mrs. Itzli by her shoulders. She was so agitated, so frenzied, that she kept slipping between her mother tongue and common. Nikolai tried to interrupt her, but she was in no state to be silenced. Clio could barely understand more than a word here or there. *Blood. Body. Mess.*

Nikolai gave Clio a sweeping glance as she approached, worry swarming his eyes.

Mrs. Itzli's face flickered with frustration as she also acknowledged the arrival, but Nikolai twisted the woman back towards him and caught her gaze. Clio saw how quickly his eyes dilated, how black they became as he focused all three millennia's worth of experience in will-bending on the woman. Mrs. Itzli gasped slightly, but held the stare.

"Everything is fine," Nikolai said softly, persuasively. "You came up to check on the room and found it empty. Someone spilled black-current wine all over the rug and you're simply upset that you have to order a new one."

Her eyes widened, glossing over as he spoke. She swayed slightly, as if caught in a daze. But then suddenly, she blinked, shaking her head slightly as she pushed out of his grip.

"*Mr. Trousseau,*" she hissed. "Don't be messing around in my head after what I just witnessed. My poor, old heart can't bear it."

Nikolai balked. "Hold on a minute—"

Clio's gaze flicked between the two of them. She couldn't help the smile teasing her lips as Mrs. Itzli raised a brow and said, "What? You think I haven't sensed the *other* in you after three years of fussing? I've lived a lot of life, and you are not the first to surprise me by defying the laws of humanity. By the stars, after all I've done for you, I deserve an explanation. Not compulsion."

Nikolai floundered. His eyes flitted across her face, then glanced toward Clio long enough for her to catch the shame and shock there. Clio shrugged, cocking her head in quiet delight. A long, much anticipated conversation had come due.

Nikolai returned his attention to the chef and said, "You're right, Luisa. Forgive me."

Mrs. Itzli blinked rapidly, the tension in her shoulders dropping away. Clio was willing to bet that was the first time Nikolai ever addressed her by name.

She swallowed audibly, crossing her arms as she muttered, "I'll forgive you as soon as you tell me what's going on."

Nikolai nodded before turning to Clio. He framed her face in his hands and a spear of icy terror ran up her spine, because there was such tender concern and sadness in his eyes. Something was wrong beyond the chef. Gently, he said, "You may want to go help Reuben with your mother."

Her mother's suite was on this floor.

She pushed past Nikolai and spotted the open door several feet away. The screaming she heard on the stairwell landing had dissolved into whimpering, but she'd recognize that voice anywhere. Clio charged into the doorway.

The stench hit her first. Sulfur and rot. It was what she imagined the rust and mold coated basement of a serial killer's house might smell like. Clio slapped a hand over her nose and mouth, fighting a gag as her eyes watered.

In the center of the floor, twisted in the sheets from the bed, the body of the officiant lay face-down. Dead. The sheets and the rug beneath him were soaked in blood so dark and thick it looked like tar. Black.

The priest was naked, mostly. Other than the sheets clinging to his skin and a thick bandage wrapped around his chest and shoulders. The gauze over his shoulder blades bulged, as if he had broken bones protruding from his back—but that couldn't be right.

Clio didn't dwell on that detail very long. She stared at the cat crouching on top of Ezekiel—Poppet, chewing a hole through the man's neck. From the look of it, the cat had been feeding for a while.

The door to Nikolai's room—Clio couldn't remember shutting it behind her when she chased after him. Was this her fault?

Crying in the far corner of the room broke Clio from her distraction. Clarissa cowered there. She clutched at the sheer nightdress hanging off her arms, the hem blackened and pooling on the floor. In the other hand, her mother held a lamp. The lampshade was missing and the bulb was broken. It trembled in her grip.

"Don't touch me," she repeated. Over and over, she said those words, in varying volumes and inflection. Her eyes were trained on the corpse, on the cat. "Don't touch me."

When Clio saw the black ichor dripping from the jagged glass of the lightbulb, the truth hit her. Clarissa had been the first to draw blood, not Poppet.

The scent of blood likely drew the cat in.

A cursory glance around the room validated Clio's suspicion. One of the brass vents had been pushed out of place, the metal cover dented and the wood panels around the opening scratched up. Another glance at the priest revealed the thick bloom of blood on the sheet around his hips.

Clio wouldn't be surprised if the missing shards of glass from the light bulb fell from that portion of sheet once the corpse was turned. She didn't want to think about what led to this, why her mother felt the need to defend herself.

Reuben hovered a few feet from Clarissa, frowning at Clio as she entered the room. "She won't let me close enough to assist her. This isn't the sort of thing a mortal like her can handle. I can take the events from her memory, but I have to get close enough to touch her."

Clio grimaced. That was exactly what he did to Nikolai, storing all the painful memories away. As sour as she felt about that trick, it *had* worked properly for centuries. It would work for her mother, hopefully until the day she died.

In this situation, Clio saw the good of it. She skirted the priest's body, approaching her mother slowly, calmly. "Mom."

Clarissa's face swiveled toward Clio's voice, even as her eyes clung to the body on the floor. Finally, as if being torn forcefully away, Clarissa's gaze snapped to her daughter. The shift was instantaneous. Clarissa's face crumpled, a sob racking her chest as she dropped the lamp. The lingering glass of the bulb shattered against the wooden floor and Clio surged forward, catching her mother around the waist before she collapsed on the sharp pieces.

She huffed beneath her mother's full weight, even as wispy a figure as she had, and dragged Clarissa to a chair. She held tightly to Clio's torso, weeping into her stomach. These tears were the real deal. They were ugly and broken and loud. Clarissa had been exposed, not like a model on the cover of a magazine, but in a far more terrifying manner.

Clio crouched, pushing her mother far enough away to catch her stare. "You need to let Reuben help you. He's safe, I promise."

Clarissa gasped around her sobs, recoiling from the suited man steadily looming closer. "Is—is he a doctor?"

Reuben smiled, his face so gentle and devoid of sarcasm

that Clio had to double-take. "Of a sort. I can sedate you, if that sounds like a good plan."

Relief flooded Clarissa's face. "*Please.*"

And just like that, Clarissa released her daughter. Clio backed away, sorting through the emotions that flooded her. The initial love and pride that her mother clung to her, squashed by the rejection that rose whenever Clarissa chose substances over her, which was apparently a habit of a lifetime, and the inherent numbness that overwhelmed both.

She had grown accustomed to the pain that came with loving her mother.

Reuben bent over Clarissa, raising his dark hands to cradle her face. Clarissa gripped his wrists, at first seeming unsure of her decision, but then her nails dug into his skin as purple strands of energy unspooled from his fingertips. His magic circled Clarissa's head, as if assessing her state by osmosis, before dipping to infiltrate her ears.

Her eyes went glassy. Her grip on Reuben's wrists loosened. The panic Clarissa's body had been spilling into the room dissipated.

Groggily, Clarissa said, "Holy Lights. Give me a prescription for some of that."

Reuben chuckled politely, good-naturedly, as her eyes fluttered shut. Her body slumped against the cushions.

He asked over his shoulder, "How much do you want her to remember?"

Clio glanced at the man laid out on the floor again. There was no telling what happened before Poppet showed up, what would have happened if her pet didn't charge in when she did.

"Nothing," she muttered. "All she remembers is that she got black out drunk at the rehearsal party."

Reuben nodded. His magic pulsed, expanding into a fog that swarmed Clarissa's head, obscured her beautiful features for a moment. Then, all at once, Reuben dropped his hands and the magic faded into nothing.

"It's done," he said as he straightened. "You might want to guide her downstairs. She's going to be exceptionally confused for the next several minutes."

Mrs. Itzli's voice sounded at Clio's back. "I'll gather her personal items and bring them downstairs." The woman started doing exactly that, treading carefully to avoid the wet stains on the carpet. There was a heaviness in her eyes. Not from fear, exactly, but the gleam was troubled enough that Clio could guess Nikolai had been honest.

Good. If anyone could be trusted to defend this manor and all of its secrets, it was Luisa Itzli.

Clarissa's bleary eyes cracked open and Clio helped her up. Nikolai helped carry Clarissa to the elevator, but once they entered the box, he leaned her mother against the wall and braced a hand against the opening of the elevator, preventing it from closing them in.

"I'm going to take care of matters up here," he said, pressing a light kiss to the corner of Clio's mouth.

"The blood," she whispered, framing his face between her hands, keeping him from pulling away. "That wasn't—"

Nikolai silenced her by running his thumb over her mouth. His eyes flicked to Clarissa, who was moaning softly and rubbing her temples a couple feet away.

He said in the barest whisper, "Wasn't human. You're right. Once you send Clarissa home, we'll talk further." Clio's heart hammered in her ears. Not human. That thing wasn't human. And if Poppet was drawn to it like that, enough to crawl through the maze of vents to follow the scent of its blood.

She knew what it was.

Clio pulled Nikolai into the elevator. She slanted her lips against his, held him tightly, let the feel of him chase away her fear. He returned her affection, deepening the embrace until she was pressed flat against the wall, his hips pinning hers. His tongue filled her mouth, and it was as good as a spell, as good as magic—making her forget everything except for what they had together.

That was, until a sharp voice cut in. *"What the hell are you doing?"*

Clio broke off the kiss and looked at her mother, who glared at the two of them with the sort of vehemence that could damn even the kindest soul to hellfire. Apparently, Reuben's grounding touch had done nothing to rid Clarissa of judgement.

But that didn't scare Clio anymore. "Kissing the love of my life, obviously."

"Where's Duncan?"

"I got rid of him."

Clarissa's eyes bulged. Clio couldn't remember a time in her whole life when she'd managed to shock her mother into silence, but here she was, utterly stunned.

Nikolai nuzzled Clio's hair and murmured into her ear, "Someday I'm going to fuck you in here, against this very wall."

Clio inhaled sharply, her cheeks heating as he leaned down and kissed the side of her neck. Hopefully the elevator music had been loud enough to cover those words. Clarissa was a statue—a pale, ogling gargoyle.

Nikolai pulled back, his eyes hazy and soft. He didn't even glance at the woman beside them as he said, "Sorry, beloved. Looks like you'll be fighting this battle on your own."

"You can make it up to me later." Clio restrained an honest-to-Heaven *pout* as he pressed the lobby button and slipped out of the elevator with a wink.

As the doors slid shut, Clarissa found her voice. "I'm

appalled, absolutely *appalled* by you. What have you been *doing* around here?"

For once, Clio didn't feel the guilt and shame she so often associated with her mother's voice. Anger had always fueled Clarissa's lectures, but Clio finally heard the other emotion buried a little deeper—her fear. Clarissa was an exquisitely terrified person, the kind of someone who made fear look beautiful, admirable... sensible, even.

But fear wasn't any of those things.

Clio smiled and said, "I've been living."

44

Mrs. Itzli took the news well enough. She wasn't looking at Nikolai as she flitted around the suite. But at least she was still on her feet. Nikolai went over the basics with her, fully prepared to tell her everything, but she stopped him when he reached the topic of his diet. That had been more than enough for her—knowing that he wasn't technically alive. Apparently, she guessed as much. She'd met one of his kind before.

The cat, however, was new to her, hence the panic. Mrs. Itzli finished packing Clarissa's bag, giving the small creature a wide berth as she rushed out of the room. Once the door shut behind her, Reuben leapt from his perch on the desk.

Nikolai stepped forward and scooped Poppet off the dead body. She hissed, but didn't try to claw her way out of his arms. The demon blood was pumping through her veins, taming the feral.

Reuben grasped the bandage attached to the body and ripped it away, revealing the twin wounds seeping black ooze. From those rotting caverns dug into the demon's shoulder blades, nubs had formed. Gray bones twisted together and protruded slightly, the calcified cells scaled like reptilian skin.

Wings.

"I didn't think it was really possible," Nikolai mumbled.

Reuben flung the bandage to the side, barely acknowledging the strange appendages before he flipped the corpse over. "They're getting bolder. You should have known from the instant they infiltrated the Church that it would eventually come to this."

He had known, but desperately hoped otherwise. If this angel had been growing its wings back, there was no telling how many humans were sacrificed to make that possible, or what he'd planned to do with them once his glory was restored.

The world wasn't prepared for a winged god to roam the streets. Too many would die. And the rest would bow.

Reuben didn't hesitate. His magic manifested, curling around his right hand with wisps of purple lightning and smoke. He thrust that hand into the demon's chest and a sickening crack sounded through the room.

When Reuben jerked his hand back, a transparent turquoise diamond gleamed in his palm. The only sort of heart a demon carried. Reuben crushed the shard of life and a river of magic spewed from the gem, twisting around his arm before settling through his chest.

One wisp of purple light curled over Reuben's shoulder, as if to peek at Nikolai. It churned, as if in curiosity.

Before Nikolai could take the step back he'd intended to, the wisp catapulted forward and impaled the center of his chest. He bit back his gasp as dizziness overtook his head. The shadows all around the room began to buzz like static. He blinked, staggering a few more steps as a simmering spread through his veins.

And then it was all gone. Everything returned to normal.

Nikolai rubbed the point of impact on his chest as Reuben stood, but let his hand drop before he turned around. He knew how touchy his old friend could get about the magic.

Rarely, when they were hunting together, the magic Reuben harvested from the demons would turn toward Nikolai, the same way his mother's magic had. And Reuben was never pleasant about it.

It seemed, at least this time, that Reuben didn't notice the lone deserter. He gestured to the door behind Nikolai. "If you fetch your vessel for me, I'll fill it."

"Yes, about that..."

Reuben rolled his eyes. "You broke another one?"

Nikolai grimaced, but Reuben simply snapped his fingers and a purple rift tore open above his hand. A decanter fell through and landed in his palm.

"One day," he warned, "I'm going to run out of these crystal bottles. You need to be more careful."

"Noted." Nikolai watched as the rift in the air closed up and Reuben crouched with the container. Purple energy burrowed into the wound on the demon's neck, spiraling until it became something like a funnel, guiding the blood into the bottomless vessel.

As Reuben finished up, corking the container, Nikolai asked, "What if this one had friends?"

"The churchy ones rarely do," Reuben replied flatly, handing the blood to Nikolai.

Nikolai had to hold tighter to Poppet to prevent her from swatting it out of his hand. *Insatiable little creature.*

"But I'll do some digging once I get back home," Reuben said, buttoning his emerald blazer. "See what I can find out about this one."

"Good," Nikolai nodded. "Thank you, Ru."

Reuben smiled, patting his arm. "Of course, mate. Do you

want me to help with disposing of this body before I sod off? I already snuck out while you were waking and dropped the human waste into a chasm between dimensions."

He thought for a moment, and shook his head. "I appreciate the offer, but I think I'm going to have Clio take care of it. It's time she saw what she can do to them."

"Wish I could stick around." Reuben chuckled.

As the two of them descended the stairs into the lobby, Nikolai tucked the charmed vessel into the inner pocket of his blazer, where he usually stored his journal. He didn't need the reminders anymore, the constant insurance to track his thoughts.

For the first time in centuries, Nikolai felt wholly present.

When they hit the last landing, airy laughter caressed Nikolai's ears. Not joyful laughter, but rather bitter, anger huffs.

Reuben shot him a look that said, *good luck mate.* Then, he slipped through the French doors, heading left towards the back door. Nikolai emerged from the stairwell and turned the opposite direction, but lingered in the shadows of the room.

Marcus hadn't left, even though Nikolai heard Clio ask him to.

Clarissa paced in front of one of the emerald couches, where Clio sat with great stillness. She patiently tracked her mother's every movement. The woman shook her head, laughing breathily. "Well, I'm glad to hear you finally mustered some self-preservation *on the eve of your wedding.*"

Clio sighed. "Mom—"

"No, truly." She laughed louder, a bit hysterically. "As if it wasn't bad enough that you decided to keep secrets from me, lying about your reasons for coming here, there's the impropriety with the owner, whose head is so far up his own ass he looks like he hasn't seen the sun in years. And add on top of all of that, the fact that you spent a small fortune on an event you didn't bother cancelling in advance."

Clio jumped to her feet, walking around the glass table as she spat, "An event that you and Duncan shoved down my throat at every opportunity. Just admit that the instant he came into my life, the instant he showed one speck of interest in me, you were itching to pawn me off on him."

Clarissa's jaw dropped.

Nikolai bit back a chuckle as he leaned against a column, sliding his hands into his trouser pockets as he watched the slaughter. Whatever timid girl Clio had pretended to be, tried her best to be for her mother, was long forgotten. Her eyes were livid under the chandeliers, lined with the coolest silver.

Clio continued, "I deserved better. I wanted better—but I didn't think that was possible. You made me believe the worst about myself. And I'm done. I refuse to believe in a god that expects me to hate myself. If that makes me an abomination, so be it." She paused, taking a shaky breath. She was strong, powerful—this woman who owned his heart. "I don't believe the Light is so brutal that it would burn me for loving, that it would blind me for looking up in search of more."

Clarissa's eyes welled with tears as she processed those words. But then she spun towards Marcus. "What nonsense have you been filling her head with?"

Marcus gazed at Clio with tenderness, admiration, in his eyes. "Nothing nearly as enlightened as that."

"Why are you even here still?" She hissed. "You don't have a place in our lives anymore."

"No," Clio said quietly. The word echoed through the room so thoroughly, she might as well have shouted it. "*We* don't have a place for *you*. You are the one that is not welcome. From this point on, if you can't bring joy and love to my life, I don't want you in it."

Clarissa took a dazed step back. "I can't believe this. You're abandoning me, just like he did." That accusation hit hard— Nikolai saw it in Clio's face.

But she said, "I'm standing up for myself."

"You're acting like a child."

Clio scoffed. "Say whatever you want about me, but do it while you get the hell out of my home." *Home.* Nikolai's body tingled.

"*My* money rented this manor for the day," Clarissa sneered. "So I think I'll leave when *I* decide to."

"I haven't touched your accounts. Everything I used was from my personal trust."

"Trust or not, it came from me. All that you have is because of me. Don't forget that."

Clio blinked. Another impact straight to her heart. Thoughts spiraled behind those silver eyes.

Nikolai stepped forward, ready to intervene, but paused again when Enzo appeared at Clarissa's side. He must have been watching from the shadows, too.

"Ms. Clio told you to leave the premises."

Enzo took Clarissa's elbow in one hand, her luggage in the other, and started walking towards the entrance.

"What do you think you're doing?" Clarissa jerked her arm, but Enzo kept a firm grip on her.

"I'm escorting you out," he said flatly.

"Let go of me," she demanded. "I have half a mind to fire you here on the spot."

"That won't be necessary. I quit." Enzo let go of her arm to gesture toward the front doors. "Now, if you'd please."

Clarissa was seething as she ripped her suitcase out of his hand. "Good luck finding someone to hire you once I'm finished." She stalked away and Enzo followed her outside, ensuring she made it down the staircase.

"I'd better catch the cab before Clarissa runs away with it," Marcus mumbled, inching closer to Clio.

Clio exhaled shakily. Her hands fisted at her sides as she whispered, "I told you not to wait."

"I know. You told me this place doesn't concern me, but," he smiled sadly, "*you do*. I will always care about you, Clio." Marcus took one last step forward and nudged her chin up with a knuckle. "And I know this might not mean anything to you, but I wanted you to know how proud I am of the woman you are."

She took another slow, trembling breath, but didn't respond.

Marcus grabbed the handle of his suitcase and turned to leave, that smile chiseling into his cheeks. "Keep your light safe, honey."

Before he'd taken his first step outside, Clio bolted from the room. She ran into the corridor leading to his—*their* room. Nikolai made to chase after her, but the door to the manor opened a third time, letting Enzo back inside. He brushed the snow from his hair, glancing around the lobby until his gaze met Nikolai's.

One more business matter to attend to first.

"May I have a word?" Nikolai approached slowly, allowing Enzo to assess him before he extended a hand.

Enzo shook his hand, the grip warm and firm. "We'd better." His gaze flicked to the corridor Clio had disappeared into. He was still worried about her, understandably so. That was why he lingered.

Nikolai smiled kindly. "I wanted to discuss a concern with you. Raðljóst Manor is in need of better security. From what I overheard just now, it seems you might be available for the job."

"What?" Enzo stared back in disbelief, his jaw slack.

"I'm offering a job, if you want it. I don't know if I would be able to compensate you as richly as Clarissa did, but while you are on my staff, you'll always have room and board. And as you can see, we only entertain the best food and company around here."

Enzo studied Nikolai's face, speechless, waiting as if for a punchline to come. Then his gaze slid past Nikolai, to some point beyond his shoulder.

Glancing back, Nikolai glimpsed Mrs. Itzli's shadow slipping from the threshold of the kitchen corridor. It took every ounce of self-control not to smile as Enzo cleared his throat and jerked his head slightly.

Enzo said, "I accept, at least for now. Perhaps we could work together on a trial basis, to see if this is a good fit."

"Of course. Mrs. Itzli will get you all squared away."

Enzo's wariness faded as his eyes fell on Poppet, who was kneading Nikolai's blazer over where the vessel lay. Before Nikolai could step back, Enzo reached out and scratched the cat's neck. Poppet leapt to attention, but instead of nipping at the man's hand, she leaned into it. Her chest started rumbling, flopping like a doll in Nikolai's arms.

All right. So maybe the cat wasn't so vicious.

"Cutie," Enzo mumbled before ambling off in the direction of the kitchen.

Nikolai chuckled softly and carried Poppet back to the library. He released her there, where he knew there weren't any vents for her to slip away through, and continued on into the bedroom.

Clio sat on the bed, weeping. He'd expected as much. What he hadn't expected was what she held in her hands.

The dream net was removed from the bed. It laid next to her, the spherical rod pulled open, the strings splayed over the disheveled duvet. In her hands, she cradled thick golden chains attached to two amber stones. She'd found them—her siphons.

Nikolai quietly approached, admiring every sweet angle of her as she cried. She lifted her head, meeting his eyes as she clutched the bracelets to her chest. "You kept them."

He crawled up onto the mattress, kneeling next to her. "I couldn't get rid of them." *Couldn't get rid of that piece of you.* "How did you know they were there?"

Clio trembled, tears coursing down her cheeks. "I didn't. I came in here to take a shower and—" Her eyes glazed. "I looked at the net and this *memory*, I guess, hit me. It happened before, in the ballroom, when you danced with me. I think, this time, I remembered the day we arrived in the Arctic."

Nikolai rasped around his swelling throat, "You did?"

"Yeah. I remembered the igloo we stayed in. The natives. They had these nets hanging in the room, but those ones didn't have seams." Clio gazed down at the net, at the opening on the base—the opening Nikolai had created to store her siphons centuries ago. She looked up and repeated in a whisper, "You kept them."

He pulled her into his arms and she latched onto him in an instant, straddling his lap, burying her face in his neck. Between kisses he trailed along her jaw, he said, "I always believed in you, Clio. You are the only god I worship. The only hope I hold on to."

She sniffled. "My whole life, I've missed you. I missed you so much it hurt, and I couldn't figure out why."

Nikolai held her tighter, letting her scent cover and invade him. "I know."

They sat like that for an hour or more, just holding on. Eventually, though, reality seeped in. There would be time to rest in Clio's arms later, once they'd taken care of the corpse in their manor.

"Well, now that you've found your siphons," Nikolai murmured. "Would you like to use them?"

45

The stench had gotten worse.

Clio took shallow breaths as she re-entered the suite. Whatever tissues made up a demon's body—it deteriorated quickly, brutally. Already, maggots infested the hole in its neck.

"Fuck, do I really have to touch it?" Clio groaned through the sleeve of her sweater.

Nikolai huffed a laugh, but otherwise his chest remained deathly still. He was holding his breath. *Bastard.* "Yes," he replied tightly. "Hurry up, before the smell absorbs into the walls."

Clio elbowed him in the gut, hard enough to make him gasp.

The air invaded his lungs and he coughed around a breath. *Serves him right.* "You have some strange fetish for causing me pain, don't you?"

"Don't tease me right now." She glared at him, then down at the body. "I have no idea what I'm doing."

He simpered. "But that makes teasing you so much easier. What am I going to do once you know more than me again?"

Clio smiled. "Deal with it." *Incredible,* she thought—that she might know more than him in just a matter of hours. It shouldn't be possible.

Nikolai drew her close to him and withdrew her siphons from his pocket.

She presented her hands to him. He carefully clasped the bracelets, first around her wrists before sliding the anchor rings onto her two outer and middle fingers, kissing the tips of each of them. Once the golden chains were drawn taut, the amber-resin stones sat in the center of her palms.

Clio studied the way they molded to her skin, tilting her palms and watching the amber gleam in the light. "What do I do?"

He backed away, shoving his hands into his pockets. His eyes were trained on the siphons, a wariness filling his eyes as he side-stepped out of the range of her hands. "You know what to do. Trust your instincts."

She turned back to the corpse, walking until her shoes passed into the black circle of blood. It was dried, thankfully, but she was still going to throw away these slippers once she was done.

Crouching, Clio let herself sink into that ancient chamber. Most of the temper that had been there before, that had built up over the years, was depleted—but she managed to extract a faint thread of light. She coaxed it out, willing it into her veins. Salt crystallized in her hands, drawn toward the siphons like powdered metal to a magnet. The element coated the amber, and the stones started vibrating. Heat pulsed from the center of her palms into the siphons.

They began to emanate a warm, golden glow.

The heat didn't invade her entire body—with the siphons,

the light latched onto the conduit, followed the route from her chambers directly to her hands. She kept her fingers stretched and stiff, so that when she lowered her palms to the dead body only the siphons made contact with the demon's purpling skin.

When she released the final leash she held on her temper, a flash of brilliance erupted beneath her hands. The demon's body mutated from the point where she was pressing on it first. Skin and sinew gave way to black grit. Black *salt*. The change spread outward, crumbling the entire corpse into a sheet of dark matter.

Clio was lost for words. She just stared down at what was left of the demon, nothing more than dust.

Nikolai's arms wrapped around her waist and helped her stand. When he hissed, she realized she hadn't dropped the temper radiating from her hands before touching his arm. She let the siphons go dark, and they were still warm against her palms but harmless once again.

She looked at the mark she'd left on Nikolai's arm, the golden webbing that shrunk as his blood battled it back. Twisting in his arms, she met his gaze.

He didn't show her the pain he likely felt.

"It's okay," he said before she could voice an apology. "You've done worse, and I survived. Besides, maybe I like your particular brand of pain," he smiled wickedly, "as long as it doesn't go too far."

Clio glared at him. "And you accused *me* of the fetish."

Nikolai laughed, brushing his nose along hers. "Beloved."

The shower was on the verge of scalding, even to Clio's skin. If Nikolai suffered under its torrent, he didn't show it. He only sat on the gray tile floor and tugged her naked body to his.

The only thing that remained on Clio's body was the siphons attached to her hands.

Nikolai wrapped his arms around her waist, arranging her between his legs so her back rested against his hard chest. The shower sprayed their legs this way, but Nikolai told her what to expect in the turn.

All that blood and bile. The hot water would wash it away.

A teacup sat to their left, the liquid still steaming. Water from the shower ricocheted into the cup, sending ripples over the surface. One white flower swayed at the bottom. Clio stared at the cup for a moment too long.

"Hey," Nikolai grasped her chin and Clio craned her neck to meet his eyes. "We don't have to do this right away. There's no rush. You're already remembering—"

"Barely," she retorted. "And the things I see aren't clear. They aren't familiar like memories should be."

He frowned. "We can still wait if you're nervous. The plant downstairs isn't going anywhere."

"I'm not having second thoughts. I'm just—" Clio swallowed the lump forming in her throat. "I'm worried about the turn itself. You said that you pass through a dream, but you never said what kind of dream."

Nikolai's eyes shuttered. "It's different for each of us. Marie, my sister, told me she dreamt of flames. In Genevieve's journal, she mentioned a forest of gnashing teeth."

"What did you dream?"

After a quiet heartbeat, he said, "I dreamt of the dandelion field Genevieve stole me from. I dreamt of my family, my human one, sitting around a fire for a meal. I tried to run to them, but I couldn't reach them. And then a voice called to me from the edge of forest behind me. I followed it into the darkness, and then I woke up."

So, her worst fears, perhaps, were what she'd face. She could do that.

Clio kissed Nikolai's cheek. "I'm ready."

She seized the teacup and swallowed the contents. The tea coursed down her throat like liquid metal, but she weathered the taste with little more than a grimace. Letting the cup clatter to the tile, Clio offered her arms up and Nikolai gripped them tightly, turning her forearms so that the amber siphons were directed at the ceiling.

"Don't let go," she whispered.

Nikolai kissed the back of her head. "Never."

46

Nikolai held Clio tightly through the turn. Through the purging of her blood and the slowing of her heart. Her siphons gleamed faintly, but sputtered out by the time her breathing stopped. This turn was nothing like her last.

He still remembered that night so long ago, how her temper erupted behind closed doors. She almost died that night and he'd been helpless to intervene, to comfort her. He'd sat and held Poppet on the other side of the door for hours like he held Clio now, just listening to her screams.

She hadn't loved him at that point—Bianca.

Bianca had her own reasons for turning that time, behind his back because he refused to help. She'd shocked him with her decision, just as she'd spent her entire life shocking him. When it was done, when he opened the door, he saw her born again through the blood and loss. And he'd seen the instant regret in her eyes.

This time, the blood ran down the drain instead of pooling beneath her on a dusty wooden floor. Her body convulsed in the safety of his arms; she wasn't alone for one second of it. This time, she loved him before the turn. Any fear he felt was only towards the woman that would open her eyes in the end. He didn't know what to expect, only prayed that she would still love him.

That was one similarity. The praying.

When she turned as Bianca, he'd prayed. Prayed she wouldn't die, begged a god he didn't believe in for it—a god he was sure hated him. She'd come out of it, and so that was his first hint that maybe there was something real to the whole thing. He knew it was not on his side, but maybe it was on *hers*. And that was all that mattered.

Clio didn't scream this time, didn't seem to feel an ounce of pain once the heaves ebbed. That was his second hint in three millennia, a vow perhaps straight from the Light itself, that it saw him, that it heard him, because the silence gave him incomparable peace, to know she was not hurting. To know that she was safe. Nikolai buried his face in her damp hair and hummed to her. She wouldn't hear him, wherever she was, but he carried the melody anyway, letting it soothe his nerves, letting it echo through the bathroom.

After an eternity, Nikolai felt a muscle in Clio's arm twitch. He opened his eyes. Her pointer finger twitched again. Then, the rest of her fingers curled.

Before he could even sit up, Clio lurched forward through the hot spray. She gasped loudly, catching herself on her hands and knees, breathing deeply as the shower hammered the mutilated skin of her back. The scars were all white now, noticeable only because he knew where to look. Water saturated her hair, plastering it to her temples.

Nikolai reared up behind her, hesitating to pull her into his arms the way he wished to. He knew how delicate the balance was between humanity and beast in those first few minutes.

"Clio?"

Her muscles tensed. Slowly, she twisted to look at him. Her silver eyes were guarded, unfocused, unsure, as if she were staring at him through a thick screen. She opened her mouth to speak, but promptly shut it again, shaking her head as if to clear her mind.

He didn't know why he said what he did next—how he dared to believe strongly enough to say it.

"Bee?"

The haze in her eyes cleared. A heart-wrenching, toothy smile spread across her face. "Niky," she breathed.

She threw herself toward him and he met her under the spray. It drenched both of them, the weight of love between them. It felt like coming home, like dandelion fields and warmth in a dark forest. It tasted like an eternity of salt and roses.

Nikolai wasn't sure what he did to deserve this—deserve her. He wasn't sure what powers or stars or gods were at work to bring them together, what transcended the totality of death so they could find each other, against all odds and reason.

He only knew that he thanked it... whatever it was.

Epilogue

White walls, all around, above and beneath her.

Clio turned in place, absorbing the stark white room. It was definitely a nightmare she'd had once or twice in her life. The color used to haunt her—reminding her of her mutation before she understood the meaning of it. Usually, such light bouncing around a room like this made her eyes hurt. But not this time.

Green vines sprouted above her and spread over the ceiling. They twisted and curled down the surrounding walls. Flowers bloomed. Tree began to grow from the ceiling, reaching down around her with their wispy limbs. She ran a hand through their leaves, and they *felt* real. They twined between her fingers, an embrace of soft bark and leathery veins.

The vines touched down on the floor and criss-crossed, racing in to circle her feet. Air shifted at her back, a feather-light whoosh, and she whirled to face the source.

She choked on a sob.

Her eyes scanned the body—the strong legs, firm torso, and

dark green jumpsuit. When her gaze finally met another pair of brown eyes, she staggered forward a step. "Nyah?"

The woman smiled. Her lush, pink lips parted, as if she might have laughed, but no sound left her mouth.

Clio darted across the room and Nyah burst into motion, too. They collided in a tight embrace. Nyah lifted Clio and spun her around. Tears fell.

Nyah set her down, but they remained close together, fingers threaded in each other's hair. Her best friend was just as beautiful as she remembered. Clio had so badly wanted to see her one last time, to say goodbye, but now that Nyah was in front of her, she couldn't bear to utter that word...

Clio glanced around the room, which was now more green than white, and asked, "Where are we?"

Nyah's fingers drifted to cover Clio's ears. Purple energy teased her peripherals, and then she heard a familiar voice in her head. *In between.*

Clio covered Nyah's hands with her own. She never thought she'd hear that voice again, that lovely lilting tone. She spoke through a fresh wave of tears, "What do you mean?"

Nyah blinked a couple times, chewing her bottom lip. *You're not dead, but not alive either. I pulled your soul into this place to speak with you, a place in between what you were and what you're about to become.*

"Like a waiting room?"

Nyah laughed again—soundlessly. She nodded. The trees lengthened behind Nyah, kissing the ground. All the questions Clio had, all the words she thought she might say, faded away. And something entirely different escaped her lips.

"You figured it out when you met him, didn't you? Your guides told you or something." Clio swallowed hard, and forced the rest of it out—her suspicion. "What the manor, what *he* meant to me?"

Nyah pressed her lips together, her eyes large and guarded as she nodded.

"That's why you stopped answering my calls. That's why you stopped seeing me before you died."

Nyah recoiled, pulling her hands away, but Clio held on, not letting her budge an inch, not allowing her to distance herself. They had been best friends. That was true. But the last couple years of their friendship evolved into something else. The hugs stretched longer, the space between them during overnights smaller, and drunken teenage kisses turned into sober ones.

That summer two years ago, things changed. Nyah detached from her, and Clio hadn't understood. She did now, fully—but it didn't make the memory hurt any less.

"You should have told me everything," Clio said bitterly. "You should have given me a chance to protect you."

Nyah only shook her head, trying once again to pull away.

Clio snapped. "Say something, damn it. *Anything.*"

The earthy sap of Nyah's eyes hardened. She turned one of her hands to grip Clio's and wrenched it down to the dark hollow of her neck. The skin there was soft, sallow. Nyah said into her head, *I was protecting you. I was ensuring that what came after me never looked twice in your direction. I couldn't voice the truth to you then, just as I am incapable of doing so now.*

Reuben had explained this—that Nyah would not be able to speak. It seems, here in death together, she found a way around that handicap. But Clio only glared at the loss. Her heart shattered into a million pieces, seeing it first-hand. Nyah, the girl who couldn't be ignored, couldn't be held down, was silent... forever.

"Tell me how to fix it," Clio whispered.

There is no fixing this.

"There has to be something. I'll do anything."

Nyah's eyes shuttered. *You should not say things like that.*

"I mean it."

Stop, please. Nyah's chest rose and fell rapidly, teetering on the verge of hyperventilation. Her eyes glossed over. She staggered back, her legs buckling. Clio gripped Nyah's waist, softening her collapse to the floor.

"What's going on? What's wrong?"

The voice echoing through Clio's head changed. Duplicated. Several voices invaded her thoughts, clanging like dull bells. Clio winced, bowing over her knees as they grew louder. One voice sliced through them—a warbling, feminine, wise voice.

Nyah's eyes rolled back into her skull. *Did you mean that, girl? Do you wish to help us?* Something was wrong. Nyah... wasn't Nyah right now. *Well? Don't waste our time.*

Clio couldn't speak around the thundering fullness of her mind, so she thought back, *If it will help her, yes.*

The feminine laughed. *Would you like to see Nyah again, in the land of the living?*

Clio groaned through the chaos of her mind. *More than anything.*

Do you promise?

Yes.

We will send someone to you. The background voices roared in approval. *Do not let us down, or Nyah will become a dwindling whisper on the wind.* Nyah's hand, which had been fisted in Clio's hair, released.

The pressure in Clio's mind disappeared as she fell back. Her temple throbbed and that voice seemed to echo through the room around them. *Do not let us down.*

Clio sat up, swaying slightly, trying to trace that echo back to its source. But there was only Nyah, her chest heaving as she turned her wide eyes on Clio. Her lips quivered. Tears welled in her brown eyes.

Nyah closed the space between them and raised a hand to Clio's cheek. *What have you done?*

Black spots crowded Clio's vision, speckling the nature in the room with growing spots of rot. The life beyond death was calling to her. *I'm going to bring you back, Nyah. I swear it.*

The last thing Clio heard before the darkness took her was a guttural sob, and Nyah's voice in her head saying, *You do not understand.*

No, she didn't. But she would soon.

The End

If you enjoyed this story, please consider leaving a review on Amazon and Goodreads.

Acknowledgments

To my reader, thank you for taking a chance on me.

Jaron, you have been my biggest support, my kindest ear, and my most devoted reader. Thank you for giving me the time and space to write, and for being the best daddy in the world to our children.

Thank you, Mom, for teaching me the love of books and the value of imagination. You have always been my biggest fan. I love you.

To my writing friends and the best critique partners in the universe: I don't know where I would be without you. Skyler—you were my first true writing friend. Thank you introducing me to so many incredible writing buddies and for giving me the hope I never knew I needed to keep writing. Shannon—your gifs, humor, and honesty kept me going when the critique got tough (seriously, you're the best partner a girl could ask for). Kirsten—thank you for being the best cheerleader, the most encouraging friend, and the safe place to vent about the hard days (you are the best older literary sister). Ashley—thank you for being my last critique partner. You truly have an eye for those little, meaningful moments. Thank you for seeing the heart of my story and helping me tie a pretty bow on the final words.

There are so many incredible betas that also helped me along—particularly from our shared discord groups. Thank you all, from the bottom of my heart. You know who you are.

As for Lake Country Press—Brittany, Allie, and everyone else in our publishing family who played a part in making Beneath the Bloody Aurora what it is today—thank you for seeing the light shining through the darkness of my story.

About the Author

Beka Westrup lives in Boise, Idaho with her husband and two sons. Her love of storytelling can be traced back to a half-baked mermaid book written on a neon green, 90's iMac (*you know the ones*) in middle school. Nowadays, when not writing or reading, she can be found at home rewatching The Office for the millionth time or sitting in her favorite coffee shop drive-through, performing as a backup dancer to Taylor Swift's Reputation album.

www.bekawestrup.com

Also by Beka Westrup

Beneath the Bloody Aurora

Coming Soon...
Vengeance in the Moonlight
Song of Dark Tides

9 798986 074856